International acclaim for *Your Absence Is Darkness*

WINNER OF THE 2022 PRIX DU LIVRE ÉTRANGER

"Jón Kalman Stefánsson is a poet . . . *Your Absence Is Darkness* is poetic and beautiful and so full of love and grief that it leaves no-one untouched."
Morgunblaðið (Iceland)

"One of the great contemporary works of literature."
Stern Magazine (Germany)

"A wonderful family saga, pieced together through memories, myths, legends. Page after page, the characters emerge from the background, step closer, come alive. You just want to spend more time with them and never leave their world."
Corriere della Sera (Italy)

"Incontestably this winter's most beautiful title . . . Once again Stefánsson proves his exceptional talent."
Livres Hebdo (France)

"Stefánsson has created a masterpiece with this new novel. You don't want it to end."
NDR Kultur (Germany)

"In his deeply unique 'history of humanity', Stefánsson doesn't want to provide answers. His aim is to bring to the fore the pivotal, perhaps impossible questions each of us feels when confronted with the spectacle of life – the spectacle of dozens of human lives, all mysterious, miserable, and resplendent."
La Repubblica (Italy)

"Captivates with its complex questions about love, life and death, composed in a poetic and comical way. Stefánsson is unsurpassed in writing about death and oblivion."
Trouw (Netherlands)

"One doesn't write a novel like this without having been pricked by the heart's compass needle yourself . . . During a time when no-one can tell how things are going to turn out in this vast, dark world, Jón Kalman Stefánsson offers heart-wrenching wisdom, which purifies without placating."
Politiken (Denmark)

"Written in a language that hits you in the solar plexus, and a little above and below it too."
NRK (Norway)

"Stefánsson explores heartbreak, loneliness, and most of all hope . . . It is difficult to imagine how there could be a book published in 2024 that I will love more."
Lori Feathers, Interabang Books (Dallas, TX)

Jón Kalman Stefánsson

YOUR ABSENCE IS DARKNESS

Translated from the Icelandic by
Philip Roughton

BIBLIOASIS
Windsor, Ontario

First published as *Fjarvera þín er myrkur* by Benedikt Forlag, Reykjavik, in 2020
First published in North America in 2024 by Biblioasis

This book has been translated with financial support from

Icelandic
LITERATURE
CENTER
MIÐSTÖÐ ÍSLENSKRA BÓKMENNT

FIRST EDITION
10 9 8 7 6 5 4 3 2 1

Library and Archives Canada Cataloguing in Publication
Title: Your absence is darkness / Jón Kalman Stefánsson ;
translated from the Icelandic by Philip Roughton.
Other titles: Fjarvera þín er myrkur. English
Names: Jón Kalman Stefánsson, 1963- author. | Roughton, Philip, translator.
Series: Biblioasis international translation series ; 45.
Description: Series statement: Biblioasis international translation series ; 45
Translation of: Fjarvera þín er myrkur.
Identifiers: Canadiana (print) 2023057176X | Canadiana (ebook) 20230571786
ISBN 9781771965811 (softcover) | ISBN 9781771965828 (EPUB)
Classification: LCC PT7511.J53915 F5313 2024 | DDC 839/.694—dc23

Readied for the press by Daniel Wells
Cover designed by Jason Arias
Designed and typeset in Minion by Libanus Press, Marlborough

PRINTED AND BOUND IN CANADA

CONTENTS

CONSONANTS, VOWELS AND VOWEL COMBINATIONS

ð, like the voiced *th* in *mother*

þ, like the unvoiced *th* in *thin*

æ, like the *i* in *time*

á, like the *ow* in *town*

é, like the *ye* in *yes*

í, like the *ee* in *green*

ó, like the *o* in *tote*

ö, like the *u* in *but*

ú, like the *oo* in *loon*

ý, like the *ee* in *green*

ei and *ey*, like the *ay* in *fray*

au, no English equivalent; but a little like the *ay* sound in *sway*. Closer is the *œ* sound in the French *œil*

A list of characters may be found in the last pages of this volume

*Tell My Story and I'll Get My
Name Back, or in other words:
The First Opposition*

What matters and has a lasting effect on you, deep feelings, difficult experiences, trauma, intense happiness; hardship or violence that cuts into your community or world, can work its way so deeply into you that it's pressed into the genes, which then carry it from generation to generation – thus shaping those yet to be born. It's a law of nature. Impressions, memories, experiences and setbacks are passed on from life to life, and, in that sense, some of us exist long after we're gone, are even completely forgotten. So the past is always within us. It's the invisible, mysterious continent that you sometimes feel when you're half-awake. A continent with mountains and seas that constantly influence the weather and the shades of light within you.

SOME COMFORT CAN ALWAYS BE FOUND
Maybe I dream this:

That I'm sitting in the front pew in a cold church in the countryside;
the deep stillness outside broken by the occasional bleat of a sheep
and the distant screeching of arctic terns, windows frame the blue
sky, the sea, the edge of a green hayfield, a nearly barren mountain.

I hope that this is a dream because I don't remember myself, don't
even know who I am or how I got here, don't know . . .
 . . . but I'm not alone in the church.

Just now, I looked over my shoulder to see a man sitting at the far
end of the rear pew, close against a weathered flagpole lying across
the backs of the five pews. Slim, probably middle-aged, with a thin,
sharp-featured face, a receding hairline, and prominent lines on his
forehead. And staring mockingly at me.
    Maybe I'm just dead.
    To think, that this is how it happens: everything goes out, self-
consciousness is erased, and then you're restarted in a small church
and the devil is sitting a few pews behind you – come to claim
your soul.
    I glance behind me. No, it's hardly the Evil One himself. But
something in the man's demeanour suggests that he's no stranger
here. I turn to the side, look straight at him, clear my throat: Sorry –
but are you the priest at this church?

*

The man stares silently at me for a long time. Uncomfortably long. Priest, he repeats at last; does just my sitting here in a pew make me a priest? And would that make you the bishop, since you're closer to the altar? Would I be a coach driver if I were standing next to a coach, a doctor if this church were a hospital, a robber or a banker if we had met in a bank? And if I were all those things, how long is a person what he is, because isn't life supposedly always changing you, that is, if you're reasonably alive – when does one stop being a priest or a criminal and become something entirely different? If there are such things as questions, then shouldn't there be answers to them? When is a person's name Dingdong or Snoopy and which is better? But keep in mind that sometimes life is the questions, death the answer – so tread carefully, mortal!

His voice isn't exactly deep, but has a touch of darkness, and there's a kind of power in his expression. In the sharp features, the deeply lined forehead, the blue eyes. Such people can be dangerous, I think reflexively.

So you think I'm dangerous? the man asks.

This startles me. I didn't mean to, I begin saying, but then he waves his arm as if wanting to silence me, sweep me away or ask me to leave; I choose the latter. Get up, nod at him. The floor creaks as I walk down the aisle and . . .

. . . step out of this old country church standing near the mouth of a short fjord, surrounded by low mountains with an expansive, cold blue bay beyond – but the near-barren mountains appear to become both greener and slightly higher further up the fjord. The churchyard is clearly much older than the church, because the oldest graves have transformed into large, nameless tussocks, with all of those resting here having long been forgotten although the green grass captures the sunshine and sends it down to them in the darkness. Maybe some comfort can always be found.

The most recent graves are on the south side of the church, and the newest that I see on my way through the churchyard has been tended carefully. The name of the woman inscribed on the cross, however, is splotched with bird droppings, but the phrase below it, "Your memory is light, your absence darkness", indicates that she'd been loved. The same isn't as certain of her neighbour, Páll Skúlason of the farm Oddi, because the gravestone, a big, heavy rock from the seashore, offers nothing other than a quotation from the Danish philosopher Søren Kierkegaard: "If eternal oblivion were forever lying greedily in wait for its prey and no power were capable of snatching it away – how empty and hopeless would life then be?"

Your absence is darkness.
    Eternal oblivion besets your memory.
    So where do we find comfort?

EVEN THE DEAD SMILE, AND I AM ALIVE
Someone – maybe me – has parked a blue Volvo so close to the high churchyard wall that anyone standing among the headstones wouldn't see it. To my great relief, the car turns out to be unlocked, but just as I'm about to get into it I notice a woman approaching from the direction of a concrete house perched on a low hill a short distance above the church. Thin, with long, dark, tousled hair and a brown backpack hanging carelessly on one shoulder. She isn't alone; a russet sheep runs ahead of her straight up to me, sniffs my shoes, and then tries to fawn on me like a dog, so energetically that I nearly topple backward. Stop that, Hrefna! the woman cries sharply, and the sheep stops.

Oh, sorry about Hrefna, the woman says with a smile, having reached me, she can be a handful – but, it's so good to see you! Jesus, you wouldn't believe how happy I was when I looked out my window just now and saw you here in the churchyard. Happy, but surprised, of course; seeing you here was about the last thing I could have expected. When did you get here? I never saw you drive up to the church; I ought to have noticed – cars are hardly ever out and about so early on a Sunday morning. But you're probably on your way to the hotel, to see Sóley? She'll get a shock when I tell her who's on the way!

*

The woman knows me! So maybe she can help me with my amnesia, at least tell me my name; that alone could possibly open some doors.

But something stops me. Maybe the words of the priest in the church – who might be a coach driver or the devil himself: "Keep in mind that sometimes life is the questions, death the answer – so tread carefully, mortal!"

The woman looks at me with a smile in her big, dark eyes, probably waiting for me to say something, but then the sheep bleats and looks up at a black and white puppy that has come running down from the house, dangling its tongue enthusiastically, so full of frolicsome life that even the dead smile. I kneel down to it to avoid saying anything for the moment. Hrefna rubs against me so hard as I scratch the puppy that I have difficulty keeping my balance. That's enough, the woman says sharply to the sheep, before apologising to me again for this unusual creature – she actually believes she's a dog.

Constantly sniffing around, says the woman, and marking her territory instead of eating grass and being timid around people like normal sheep. But she can't help it; she was raised by a bitch that a Norwegian couple ran over last summer. I guess something had to give way to the flood of tourists. My poor Snotra; it's hard to imagine a better dog and companion. The Norwegians were devastated, that's for sure, they sent me a card last Christmas along with some goat's cheese, which was lovely of them, but of course did nothing to help me forget Snotra. As if I could forget lifting her, badly injured, from the side of the road where she'd been thrown by the collision, and taking her behind the house to put her out of her misery. Snotra looked straight at me the entire time with so much trust in her eyes, certain that I would help her. Instead, I shot her.

I'm sorry to hear this about your dog; it's very sad, I say without thinking, without trying to determine the most appropriate thing to say. Very sad, I repeat.

You were always so fond of dogs, says the woman, so warmly that I get a lump in my throat. But when it came down to it, she adds, I couldn't be without a dog and got this bundle of joy here from my dear Eiríkur. He's a pure-bred Border collie, named Cohen. Mum would have been happy with that! But Snotra adopted Hrefna here as a newborn. It was a beautiful relationship and Hrefna was just a year old when the couple drove over Snotra. Poor Hrefna stood outside the house bleating for weeks, having no idea what had happened to her mother. The bloody thing will have to be put down; I can't think with all that bleating, Dad sometimes said when she bleated loudest, but he didn't mean it. He . . . She falls silent again, or rather, her voice seems to fade away.

The sun rises higher in the sky, the morning grows warmer and the woman unzips her dark-blue fleece jacket. Underneath, she's wearing a thin green shirt, the top buttons unbuttoned. I catch a glimpse of her rounded breasts and look down when I see her nipples rub against the fabric as she shifts her weight from one leg to the other, and feel something deep inside my abdomen, unsure whether it's lust or reluctance – shouldn't I be able to tell the difference?

The woman laughs softly, almost deeply. Oh, I'm so ridiculously happy to see you! It was as if you'd literally vanished, evaporated. Can I give you a hug, would that be alright? she adds, seeming a bit hesitant, but then she puts down her backpack, steps up to me and hugs me. Squeezes me so tightly that I clearly feel her warm, soft body. Then she leans back, maybe to get a better look at me, and strokes my face with her right hand. Her palm is so small and delicate that it resembles a butterfly. A butterfly with calluses, that is, because her hands have been marked by physical labour. I guess that I stiffen at the unexpected intimacy; she senses it and is about to release me, but then I hug her in return. Hug her tightly, soak in her warmth and softness as I fight back tears.

And am most certainly alive.

DO THE DEAD LOSE THEIR NAMES IF WE DON'T TELL THEIR STORIES; IF YOU TELL MY STORY WILL I GET MY NAME BACK?
The Volvo threads the narrow, pitted dirt road lying about a hundred metres above the shore, fairly straight but with a few blind rises, and my surroundings become greener as I drive slowly up the

fjord – which turns out to be deeper than it appeared from the churchyard.

I'm on my way to the hotel where Sóley will "get a shock" when she sees me. Of course, I don't know where this hotel is or what this Sóley looks like. Still, the hotel could hardly be that hard to find; the fjord is sparsely populated and a large building would surely stand out. Only thirty-six people live here.

Of whom, six are children, the woman had said. Not a good percentage.

She said she didn't want to let me go right away. I have some snacks here in my backpack, she said, let's enjoy the weather and sit down with my mother.

But instead of going up to the house, she ambled into the church-yard and I followed – her mother turned out to be the woman with the splotched name and dark absence. Who died just over three years ago. The woman greeted her mother's neighbour, Páll of Oddi, as she walked past the large tombstone inscribed with Kierkegaard's words, said hello to him happily, as if he were an old friend, then took a few things from her backpack, various refreshments that she said she'd "stuffed in a hurry" into it, and finally a blanket that she spread out on the ground and arranged the snacks on. Plates of flatbread, butter, smoked lamb, four slices of rhubarb tart, two wine glasses and a bottle of red wine that she asked me to open. I sat down with my back to the churchyard wall, she opposite me, closer to the grave. Sat cross-legged, her dark, tousled hair full of sunshine, and her big, dark eyes with a delicate web of crow's feet extending from them, and looked at me so warmly that a lump rose again in my throat.

Red wine on a Sunday morning, in sunshine, with a badly missed friend, that's how a person should live, she said – did you know that Mum sometimes called this corner of the churchyard her and Dad's favourite café? It seems to be sheltered in every direction, and here they sat when their lives locked together. Or when life finally began, as Mum used to say. You know the story. I don't want to bore you with it. Even though it's beautiful.

I think that oblivion, I said cautiously, with a knot of anxiety in my stomach over saying something wrong, is the black hole lurking at the centre of all galaxies, destroying the light that can shine from memories. I might remember the story, but not entirely. Tell it to me. It's so nice to hear you tell stories.

She smiled, leaned forward, and wiped the bird droppings off her mother's cross, revealing the name – Aldís.

So her mother is called Aldís.

Or was called Aldís, because she's dead, of course, when you might not be called anything anymore. Death takes our names from us and leaves us nameless. But her father is called Haraldur, he's still alive, yet not.

Mum and Dad sat here almost half a century ago, the woman said.

Almost half a century ago. When more people were alive than now.

She looked at the cross for a moment, drained her glass, refilled it, looked at me.

AND NOW, THE FIRST STORY
The first opposition?

IT'S ALL OVER NOW, BABY BLUE – IS IT MATURITY OR TIMIDITY TO SETTLE FOR YOUR FATE?
Aldís came here to the north to make love with her fiancé in the Krossneslaug swimming pool. She was nineteen years old, had graduated from Reykjavík Junior College in the spring, and would be starting at the university that autumn. They hadn't planned on stopping in the fjord. They hadn't even bothered to find out its name. The Krossneslaug pool, which is located about a hundred kilometres to the north, "an outdoor, concrete pool near the shore, 12 × 6 metres in size", was the only reason they went. It was their engagement trip. Ólína, Aldís's mother, had held a party for them in their big house in the Laugarás neighbourhood, likely the last party she would hold

in that house; Aldís's father had died of cancer the previous autumn and the house was up for sale.

The young couple had heard that Krossneslaug, sometimes called the Swimming Pool at the End of the World, was not only isolated, standing off by itself at some distance from the nearest village and facing the open, churning Arctic Ocean, but was believed to have mysterious powers. So they drove all that way north, eight hours on very patchy gravel roads, for the sole purpose of making love opposite the roiling power of the Arctic Ocean, enwrapped in the warmth of the pool's water. It was meant to be a kind of consecration and then a supplication or votive prayer to destiny that their lives be saturated with the power of the ocean but bathed in the warmth of love.

But then their car blows a tyre. Two kilometres south of the farm Nes. A hundred kilometres from Krossneslaug. And the jack is broken.

On the other hand, it was a fine summer day: a gentle wind, fourteen degrees Celsius, the grass crackling dry, the noises of haymaking carried through the fjord, the air smelled of the sea.

But there was no-one home at Nes.

Haraldur's mother had driven one of the tractors to Oddi to get the hay loader that the two farms shared, as well as to borrow one of the sons there, Halldór or the giant Páll, so that she and her own son could finish gathering the hay from the big field before evening – the field that Haraldur was windrowing on the red Zetor, with the doors of its new cab open wide to the sunshine and Bob Dylan's *Greatest Hits* at full volume on the tape player, when the young couple from Reykjavík came walking down the mown field and heard a familiar song through the noise of the rotary rake.

The yokel's listening to Dylan! And I thought he never got any further north than Borgarnes, let alone all the way here to this backwater, Aldís's fiancé, Jóhannes, had said, surprised and with a touch of admiration in his voice as they stood there in the hayfield and watched the farmer windrow. The hay was so dry that when Haraldur drove towards the sun, he had a hard time making out the line

18

between the mown grass and the part he'd windrowed, but he enjoyed being alone, with the song "It's All Over Now, Baby Blue" having just started when he saw the two strangers in the field, with the curious farm dogs around them. It was obvious from their clothing and how the man behaved towards the dogs, rigid and half-frightened by their enthusiasm and curiosity, that they were southerners. Haraldur sighed and turned the Zetor in their direction as Dylan sang through the rattle of the rake and the hoarse sound of the tractor's engine: Forget the dead you've left, they will not follow you.

Good song, Jóhannes called out after Haraldur stopped the rake, shut off the tractor's engine and jumped down onto the field; slim, suntanned, wearing blue jeans and a wide-open chequered shirt, which he didn't bother to button up.

Good song.

He didn't answer, and looked down to hide his curiosity.

Far from an everyday occurrence for strangers, let alone from Reykjavík, to be standing in one of the hayfields at Nes. After drawing nearer to them, he looked up and pushed his hair back nonchalantly from his forehead. There were probably three things that won me over, Aldís would tell her daughters, more than once: how your father jumped down from the Zetor, brushed his hair back from his eyes, and then how he looked at me, quickly, firmly, and impertinently after he'd jacked our car up and poor Jóhannes started changing the tyre.

Haraldur had graduated from the Agricultural College at Hvanneyri that spring, and would take over the farm at Nes in due course. As his father Ari had taken it over from his father, who had taken it over from his, and so on continuously for six generations. Haraldur, his parents' only surviving child after his older brother drowned at sea a few years earlier, would be the seventh generation. It was so obvious that it was never discussed. But one spring evening, just over two months before Aldís and Jóhannes' tyre blew above the farm, Haraldur had been sitting with his parents at the kitchen table over coffee and refreshments; Ari hunched over his lambing records, which sheep had given birth, how many were left, which ones were due next, Agnes humming over her knitting, one of the dogs asleep under the table and a murmur from the radio, the evening reading from *Mother* by Maxim Gorky. A mundane moment in the Icelandic countryside, with all in the usual pattern. Inconstant, difficult, demanding yet generous nature and steadfast, solid human life in which everything was in its place. Haraldur had been sitting there with his cup of coffee cooling in his hands, observing his parents, their calmness, composure; people whose lives were secure. They're happy, he had thought. Yet it had never crossed his mind to associate that word, happiness, with his parents. But now it dawned on him that despite the blows that life had dealt them, the gruelling struggle, the long working days, they lived in a place that they loved. That they couldn't imagine another existence, and the certainty that Haraldur would take over the farm gave meaning to all their toil.

It was the sounding board to their existence.

He looked down at the sturdy kitchen table, built by his grandfather sixty years earlier from driftwood gathered down at the shore. His parents didn't suspect that in recent months he'd felt as if he were stuck in a crack and couldn't move. He'd half hoped that his studies in Hvanneyri would satiate his most intense hunger for education, help him accept his fate and his obligations to his parents, his deceased brother and their ancestors, an uninterrupted line of seven generations that rested in the churchyard and watched him silently. But his yearning for more knowledge, to get away, had, on the contrary, grown over the winter, and when he came home in the spring he made the decision to stand up for himself and his dreams; to enrol in the university and preferably live abroad for a few years.

But the thought of telling his parents about this was overwhelming. He knew that he would hurt his mother, sadden her. He knew that he would hurt his father, too, but he feared more that his dad would be so unhappy that their relationship would never recover from the blow and that that discord would poison all of their lives, not least his mother's, who would see herself torn between the two men she loved. She who always walked with her head lowered, as if continually deep in thought, unless she'd adopted that posture in order to appear no taller than her short-statured husband. Haraldur had inherited her cheery disposition and enthusiasm, which just over thirty years of farming on hard land, in the monotony of the country-side, had, however, dampened a little.

Haraldur stared down at the kitchen table, listening to his mother humming "Roads Lie in All Directions" by Ellý Vilhjálms, which had taken over from the radio's evening reading, and his father muttering something to himself over the lambing records; short-statured but so strong and tough that some of their neighbours called him the Iron Man between themselves.

Roads lie in all directions, no-one steers his course.

So, if the roads lie in all directions, is there always a possibility of getting away, no matter where you are? That all you need is to . . .

He looked up when he realised that his mother's knitting needles were no longer clicking and she had stopped humming. Looked up and met her eyes. Is everything alright, Halli? she asked so frankly and so obviously full of worry that it dawned on Haraldur that he'd failed to hide his growing unease and anxiety since coming home from Hvanneyri. He glanced at his father, who was still hunched over his records as if unaware of the other two, although he no longer muttered to himself. Then Haraldur began to speak. Began without thinking, for some time didn't even hear his own words due to the anxious throbbing in his head, despite having thought hard over the last few weeks about how he could deliver them the news in the gentlest way, because he wanted to explain everything, so that they would realise just how difficult it was for him, too. That he just knew that he . . .

. . . would simply be unhappy as a farmer. I love the land, but can't imagine taking over the farm. I can't imagine it. I want to get an education. I long to get an education. I can't imagine life without getting an education first. I want to be happy. Maybe in twenty years, I'll want to take over the farm. You two aren't that old. Yes, definitely.

I won't let you down. But I just want to be happy, and to get an education. I've got to go. Forgive me.

Following this declaration of his, there was a long silence; all that was heard was the murmur from the radio. Well, my boy, this was rather unexpected, his mother then said, laying her work-weary hands on the table, as if she needed to support herself. Haraldur's father continued sitting there silently, hunched over his records, but then began to fill his pipe unhurriedly, took a drag on it to stoke the embers and smoked with his eyes half-closed.

Happiness, Ari finally said, as if he wasn't quite sure of the word, had never said it before; he had taken the pipe out of his mouth, and watched the embers cool and fade. Then he tapped them into the ashtray, got to his feet, put the pipe, the pouch of tobacco and the box of matches into his pocket and said, without looking at his son, take over from me at three. And went out to see to the sheep.

Sixty of them had yet to give birth, the lambing had begun unusually late this year, the spring had been cold, wet, they'd had to keep the sheep inside and watch over them round the clock. Look after life. His mother began to clear the table, he saw that her hands were trembling. This will all work out, she said, as if trying to pluck them up, but her voice cracked. Then days passed.

And winter finally began to recede.

They started fertilising the fields in early June. Haraldur on the tractor, which had no cab at the time, while Ari handled emptying the fertiliser bags into the spreader. The matter hadn't been discussed further. As if his father were attempting to erase Haraldur's words with his silence. Pretend that they'd never been said. And some things are just so daft and irresponsible that one doesn't discuss them, lets the silence see to erasing them.

Haraldur knew that it was up to him to bring up the subject again. Unless he simply let it go and accepted his fate. It's good to have dreams, but a person does, however, have his responsibilities, his obligations.

There's the rub, then, or is it maturity or timidity to settle for your fate? Is it responsibility or cowardice?

Haraldur rattled around the fields, ring after ring, on the cableless Zetor, while his mind spun in its endless, uncertain, desperate circles. But his father had been unusually talkative that day – summer was here, after all. They saw the snowdrifts shrink, the earth appear from beneath the snow, life was returning after a long, hard winter and a treacherous spring. Haraldur backed the empty spreader up to the machinery shed, where his father was waiting by the fertiliser bags.

Now's your chance, Haraldur thought, before hopping down and going behind the tractor. Ari bent down for the first bag, then straightened up easily with it in his arms and emptied it into the spreader. Haraldur cleared his throat. His father gave him a quick look, almost smiling, then bent down for another sack. Dad, said Haraldur, surprised at how resolute, almost acerbic, his voice sounded, and he cleared his throat again and tried to soften his voice. Dad, what I spoke to you and Mum about the other night . . . it's weighing so heavily on me, Dad, and I feel terribly bad about it, terribly, I actually feel sick about it, I'm just afraid that I can't— He stopped when he saw his father bend double. Dad, he asked uncertainly, Dad, are you alright?

His father said nothing and slumped onto the bags, as if he'd suddenly decided to rest, maybe even take a nap – sleep off his son's nonsense.

But he never got up again, and was buried in the churchyard ten days later. The day after, Haraldur ordered a cab for the Zetor.

WHERE DO YOU GO WHEN YOU'VE STOPPED THINKING –
TWENTY POEMS ABOUT LOVE, AND ONE ABOUT THE
LIEUTENANT'S WOMAN
Jóhannes puts the spare tyre on the car and the blown one into the trunk, they say goodbye to the young farmer, continue their journey.

A good two-hour drive north to the swimming pool. Up heaths, around fjords where the road hangs in some places like an interloper onto the steep slopes. They make love in the swimming pool a stone's throw from the heavy, surging Arctic Ocean. Jóhannes moans when he comes inside Aldís, who is leaning back against the side of the pool and thinking the entire time about the farmer.

They drive south the next day. A few days later, she takes the coach to Hólmavík. It's the start of September, in the mid-1970s.

Ólína, Aldís's mother, knew of course what she had to do when her daughter returned, distracted and considerably upset, from her engagement trip; the girl locked herself in her bedroom, rarely answered Jóhannes' phone calls, barely ate, broke down on the fourth day in her mother's arms.

At first she just cried, but then it trickled out of her, for a long time disjointedly, but it all lined up in the end: that she couldn't stop thinking about that farmer, whom she still knew nothing about. Apart from the fact that his name was Haraldur, he listened to Dylan, had ridiculously blue eyes. Yet she'd believed that she was happy, that she was looking forward to life with Jóhannes, to having a beautiful house with him, three children, travelling together to distant lands. But in a single moment, it was as if everything had been snatched from her – and she was standing on the edge of a kind of precipice, desiring nothing more than to throw herself off it.

I must be insane, Mum. All I think about is how he looked at me, with those eyes of his. All I can think of is going back, and . . . which is of course stupid. Why should I do that? I would just make a complete fool of myself. And besides, he's a farmer. And fat chance that I would ever want to live there, as far from everything as you can get. Still, I can't think of anything else. I feel like I'm losing my mind. I've never felt so bad. Yet I've never felt so good!

Of course Ólína knew what she had to do – remind Aldís of her responsibility, how lucky she was to be engaged to such a promising man, a kind, reliable fellow, who was head over heels in love with her, would do anything for her; and then take her with her to New York,

24

where Aldís's brother was studying. Let the big city wipe away the effects of that backwater farmer.

But for the past few weeks, Ólína has been preparing to move to a smaller home and has had to go through everything that had accumulated around the couple's lives during their thirty years of marriage. She's sorted photos, letters, papers, clothing, books . . . Those who, for some reason, have to dismantle their home, simultaneously fumble through their memories, relive their existence, and put their lives on the scales. Ólína has clearly had a good life, even an enviable one. But she never loved her husband, Þorvaldur, the father of their children.

Dismantled their home, took apart the past, sometimes misses Þorvaldur's company. Has had a good life, yet feels she's been cheated of something. She's ashamed about looking forward to life without him; and then Aldís cries in her arms. Cries and talks almost deliriously about some farmer who looked at her with strange blue eyes and everything changed. That she and Jóhannes had continued their trip, he'd been so happy but she was as if paralysed, heard herself answer and then smile when she thought it was appropriate. They went to the swimming pool, they were together . . . and Mum, then I knew I didn't love him, that I've never loved him, that I will never love him. I'm terribly fond of Jóhannes, he's so wonderfully good and would do anything for me. But I can't love him. I'm so awful. Maybe I thought it was unnecessary to love passionately. Yes, I probably thought that too much love would make me vulnerable, confused, irresponsible. And look at me now, too, Mum! This is so stupid. This is so ridiculously stupid. Five days have passed and I can hardly breathe. Is this love, is it so stupid, then, blind and completely unrealistic – does it really think I want to love a farmer in some ugly fjord out at the end of the world? This is so stupid. I think I've got to go back.

Instead of trying to talk sense into Aldís, distraught, so upset that it's clearly impossible for her to think a reasonably clear thought to its end, and then buying tickets for the first flight to New York,

Ólína accompanies her daughter early in the morning two days later down to the long-distance bus terminal.

You should have the opportunity, she says, that some women never do, or don't have the strength or courage to pursue: namely, to shape their own destiny. Go north and see what awaits you. You can always come back. You may discover that this was all just a silly dream, but that's okay. People learn most from their mistakes. But you've got to go to have a chance to come back.

She gave Aldís money and two books that she'd recently read for her reading club. Books that had stirred her soul as she was preparing her move and had made her rethink her whole life. A poetry collection by Pablo Neruda, *Twenty Love Poems and a Song of Despair*, and a recent novel by a young English author, John Fowles, *The French Lieutenant's Woman*. It rained that morning, the wind blew, Ólína stood up against the wall of the terminal with her hands over her heart and blew her daughter a kiss as the coach pulled away. Towards uncertainty.

The trip was endless. Much longer than the trip that summer and it rained most of the time, so hard and densely that the countryside disappeared and the world along with it. The roads are crooked, narrow, and time and again the coach was on the verge of breathing its last from the exertion on the most difficult slopes. At one moment, Aldís wanted only for the coach to rush onward and deliver her quickly to her destination, and at the next she prayed fervently that the journey would never end, and that eternity would be this coach trip with Fowles's novel and Neruda's poetry collection at her side.

But all journeys end, and it was nearing five o'clock when she stood in the car park of the Co-op in Hólmavík, in a biting wind, eight degrees Celsius. It had stopped raining by the time they reached Hrútafjörður, but the clouds over the grey village were heavy lead slabs, the sea rough, bleak, the people glum, aloof, they ignored her.

Neruda could never have written a poem about love and despair in this place. Most likely, he would just have been filled with despair and not written anything, except maybe about fish, sheep, rheumatism, grey existence, liquor.

She sniffed, blew her nose, sought refuge in the Co-op's shop. Got a hot dog there but had no appetite, threw it in the dustbin after the first bite, and there lay the hot-dog bun upside down, appearing as it were about to burst into tears. Neruda never wrote about crying hot-dog buns.

Aldís had promised to call home as soon as she arrived in Hólmavík, but first she had to find the post office, the only place where it was possible to call south. If it wasn't already closed. And what should she say to her mother? Everything had seemed so easy when they were planning the trip here, her mother had been enthusiastic about it, in fact, had spoken as if Aldís were embarking on a wonderful adventure – said she was jealous of her.

An adventure?

She looked out at the cold blue sea, the grey buildings, the dust that the sharp wind whirled up. This is an ugly village. It looks as if nothing beautiful could happen here. How could she ever have thought of coming here? How could her mother ever have thought of allowing her to make this trip, take the coach here, into this wretchedness? Oh, if only Jóhannes would appear out of the blue in his Toyota here in the Co-op car park, come to pick her up. How could she ever have thought of leaving him; maybe she should call him instead?

She closed her eyes, took a deep breath, scolded herself in her mind, kept her eyes closed as she thought of the farmer, how he'd jumped down from the tractor, brushed the hair from his eyes, how he'd looked at her. Opened her eyes, prepared to go and find the post office, call home. Yet didn't know what she could say. Didn't want to worry or disappoint her mother.

And how was she supposed to get out to that damned farm, Ystanes?

Pff, just ask someone to take you there, her mother had said; no-one could refuse such a beautiful young woman that favour.

Aldís looked around but saw no-one who seemed interested in helping a "beautiful young woman". Two young men came out of the

Co-op with a few small items, got into a fiery red Willys Jeep, peeled out of the car park and disappeared. Then there was nothing left but the wind, the bleak sea, the sleepy houses, the hunched farmer pumping petrol into a blue Land Rover and the chubby salesgirl who had first looked at Aldís out of obvious curiosity, then hunched over a copy of the magazine *The Week*, sunk herself into its gossip about famous people, dressed in an overly narrow, brown shirt, her mouth stuffed with a big piece of caramel. Aldís went to the counter and had to clear her throat twice to draw the girl's attention away from *The Week* – could she tell her where the post office was?

The girl took her time answering, maybe unable to bring herself to stop chewing the caramel, trying to soften it up and enjoying the sweet taste. Finally heaved a sigh, almost ruefully, reached for the caramel's wrapper, took the half-chewed morsel out of her mouth and wrapped it carefully in the paper. Wiped her shirt, came out in front of the counter, said, that's a really nice coat. Took the newcomer by the elbow and added: and wow, how soft it is! But look there, she then said, pointing between the houses, there's the post office, and it's just about to close, so you've got to hurry. But I've never seen you here before. I suppose you're from Reykjavík? Do you have any relatives here in Hólmavík? Is anyone coming to pick you up? I mean, I hope you're not going to the countryside, you really can't, I mean, not in that coat, because then I'll just have to keep it for you, ha ha ha! Are you alright, by the way?

Aldís came very close to bursting into tears in the face of the unexpected warmth that flowed from the girl's stream of words, but she managed to compose herself and explain reasonably calmly that she just needed to make a phone call home, to Reykjavík . . . and, yes, then get out to the farm of Ystanes – maybe she knew how to get there?

To Nes? Are you going there? To Haraldur? Of course he would get himself a girl with such a fine coat! I would have nabbed him myself a long time ago if I weren't already spoken for! Are you sure I shouldn't keep your coat for you? Ha ha ha, I'm just teasing you! But look, you're in luck, because at the moment it'll be no problem whatsoever getting there. You see that fellow there at the petrol pump, filling his car and the two petrol cans – that's Skúli from Oddi. Oddi isn't far from Nes, she added when she saw Aldís's puzzled expression, and I'm absolutely sure you can get a ride from him. He's so brainy, you'd think he'd gone to university. But still, a really fine chap. Hafrún, his wife, is probably with him. They're always together and she's absolutely lovely.

Aldís walked hesitantly across the car park. The farmer saw her heading towards him, pulled the nozzle out of the petrol can it was in and straightened up. Tall, sinewy, with chiselled features. Strong, grey eyes that seemed to drill through Aldís and read her to her core. Aldís looked down at his big hands, the hands of a labourer, and anxiety trickled down her spine. She could hardly tell a man with such hands that she'd just endured a bouncy eight-hour coach ride for the sole purpose of seeing the eyes of the farmer at Nes once more. It seemed so utterly silly. People in the district would laugh at her about it for years. Which of course didn't matter to her, because she was going to take the next coach back, and never come here again.

Can I help you? the farmer asked, and she noticed that the space between his eyes was unusually wide. Does he see more of the world than others? she thought, before looking down; she'd been about to put down her small suitcase but discovered that she was standing in the middle of a puddle, in her fine leather boots. Damn, she thought, and then, straightening up, she noticed a woman with grey-flecked black hair coming from the post office with a package under one arm. The farmer followed Aldís's gaze. That would be Halldór's records, he said. Yes, here they are, said the woman; the boy will be happy to get them. But who do we have here? she added, looking at Aldís. Well, said the farmer, scratching the back of his neck, I'm just trying to figure that out, but it's not going very well. I think it's more of a project for you.

The woman opened the back of the Land Rover, put the package in it, then went over to Aldís, who was almost a head taller than her. Hello, friend, she said, holding out her hand, warm, strong and calloused, as Aldís felt when she took hold of it; my name is Hafrún and that fellow there is my husband, Skúli. How can we help such a young, beautiful, elegant woman?

How can we help . . . this utterance, the firm grip, the woman's stone-grey, warm eyes liberated something within Aldís, eased the constriction in her neck; she said she'd come by coach, that she didn't know anyone here, but needed to get to the farm of Ystanes.

But I guess it's named Nes, or is called that. The girl in the shop said Nes. If I'm not mistaken. But, yes, she needed to get out to Nes. Or do you say north to Ystanes? I don't know if you go out to the farm, down to it, or north to it . . . I don't know what people here say. I'm a complete stranger. I've only been here once before. Though not really. But first I need to go over to the post office to make a call to Reykjavík. Call home. My mother.

The couple listened in silence as she churned out these disjointed explanations. It's no problem for us to give you a ride, Hafrún then said, but you'll have to sit between us. The back's full of boxes, as usual after a trip to town.

They waited while Aldís went into the post office and placed a call home, which her mother answered immediately. Everything's going well, Mum, said Aldís hurriedly, I'm in Hólmavík, have found someone who'll drive me to the farm, I'll be in touch, she added, before saying a hasty goodbye to keep herself from bursting into tears.

Then they drove out of town.

Hafrún was quick to turn on the radio, which was playing Haukur Morthens singing "Eight Years Ago", a poem by Tómas Guðmundsson set to music by Einar Markan. A song about how your life can turn into mournful regret if you don't seize the opportunity when it appears to you.

Beautiful song, said Hafrún, though a bit sad, isn't it? But wouldn't you say that we need sadness sometimes, in one way or another? There are so many rooms in existence, and most of them we likely don't know. You don't have much luggage, dear. But I didn't know that Haraldur and Agnes decided to get a hired hand. Yet I'm really glad they did. They certainly can do with the help. It was such a heavy blow when Ari passed away in the spring, so unexpectedly, not even sixty and always in perfect health. To be honest, we've been worried about them, especially Haraldur, he's been so down, he isn't happy with – oh, what am I blathering about?! Don't tell him, he doesn't care for pity, that boy.

I have only this little suitcase because I'm not going to be stopping long. And I'm not a hired hand, said Aldís, I'm a student at Reykjavík Junior College. And I'm not sure I know how to work. At least not how to do farm work.

Then why do you want to see Haraldur at Nes, dear?

I don't know. I think I've stopped thinking.

So when a person stops thinking, is it best to go out to Nes?

I think I'm in love with the farmer, Haraldur, I mean. Forgive me, I'm not used to saying things like this.

I'd say that's a perfectly valid reason for a visit. Even if you've stopped thinking and don't know how to work. But I didn't know that Haraldur had a girlfriend. That's wonderful news.

Aldís: He hardly knows I exist. He's only looked at me once.

Hafrún: And maybe isn't expecting you at all?

Aldís: I took the coach here. My fiancé said he would die if I left. If I broke off our engagement. My mum encouraged me to come here. She said that you've got to go to have a chance to come back. I think she meant that people should take opportunities when they arise. As in the song earlier.

Hafrún: She seems to know a thing or two, your mother.

Aldís: But still, I don't know if there's any sense in doing this. I actually feel like I'm crazy and have no control over anything. Mum loaned me two books for the coach trip, an English novel and a collection of South American poetry about love and despair.

Hafrún: It's absolutely necessary to have something to read on those long, tiring coach trips. But then, you're engaged to someone else?

Aldís: Not anymore. My ex-fiancé, I should have said. I left the

31

ring with my mother, and a letter to him in which I tried to explain everything and ask him to forgive me.

Skúli: And you're not worried about the man dying?

Aldís: No, he can't tolerate chaos and the unexpected.

Hafrún: And Haraldur has only looked at you once?

Aldís: I know.

Hafrún: What do you know, dear?

Aldís: That this sounds as if I'm a hysterical idiot. And that's just probably what I am, after all. But he looked at me in a way that changed everything. Since then, I haven't been able to think of anything but him. Whom I know nothing about. He has blue eyes. But he's a farmer, of course, and I hardly know the difference between a sheep and a cow. I guess you would say I'm a person who has never had to get my hands dirty. You could also say that I've almost never dirtied my clothes. I've never been in a sheep shed and am afraid of passing out because of the smell. You can hardly have much respect for such a person. Forgive me, I'm not used to expressing myself so . . . so irrationally. You might think I was brought up badly.

Hafrún: Oh, I wouldn't worry too much about that now! Rationality and love have rarely got on. It would be strange if they did. Then we would really have cause for concern about people. And the young don't necessarily need to be rational. Leave it to us old folk to try to pretend to be rational. Life would simply die of boredom if you young people never did anything irrational.

Skúli: Last I knew, the school still needed a teacher for the winter. If you've misunderstood young Haraldur's look somehow, or you two need time to sort things out, because sometimes things need time to be sorted out, then let's just say you'll be the new teacher. Apparently, people here in the district sometimes listen to what we have to say, although why, I've never understood. But you're educated, and therefore you can teach. Besides, the fjord needs a person like you.

Aldís: What sort of person am I?

Skúli: One who dares to throw everything away because of a single look. And in doing so, keeps life from stiffening.

32

When Aldís and the older couple from Oddi arrive, Haraldur is
moving a load of driftwood from the shore on the hay wagon to dry
over the winter in the large machinery shed. The couple immediately
go in to have coffee with Haraldur's mother, and leave it to fate to
deal with the young people.

He drives up the headland in the Zetor, from whose open cab
door comes the voice of the Canadian musician Leonard Cohen,
singing from his first album, I showed my heart to the doctor, he
said I'd just have to quit. Haraldur swings the tractor into the farmyard, looks at Aldís standing next to the tall churchyard wall as he
backs the big wagon up to the machinery shed, shuts off the tractor's
engine, turns off Cohen, steps out.

Another blowout? he asks.

She's wearing a beautiful coat. Probably no-one has been seen in
such a beautiful coat here in the countryside, or in such black,
high-heeled leather boots.

Another blowout?

She bites her lip and her heart pounds so hard that it hurts.
Maybe it was all a stupid, humiliating misunderstanding; his look,
and what she thought she'd sensed in the farmer, his nonchalance
and sorrow. Maybe he'd simply looked at her distractedly, as one
does, without thinking. Maybe he'd looked at her lustfully, a country
bumpkin who isn't interested in anything but talking about haymaking, his animals' health, the price of lambs. Maybe he wasn't
interested in anything but taking her from behind against the
churchyard wall. Lifting her dress, ordering her to get down on all
fours and taking her like any other sheep. Maybe his eyes weren't as
blue as she remembered.

He's standing straight as an arrow about two metres from her,
arctic terns crying down on the headland; the two dogs accompanying him have sniffed their fill of Aldís and now stand between them
and look alternately at them, as if to ask – and what now?

Haraldur runs his hand through his hair, asks, another blowout,

33

but adds when she doesn't answer immediately: My name is Haraldur, by the way.

Then she bites her lower lip, completely unaware of the effect that it has on the farmer. Now be rational, young woman, she says to herself, before remembering the words of the farmer's wife, Hafrún, that life would simply die of boredom if young people acted rationally.

I know your name is Haraldur, she says, hoping that her voice isn't too trembly. I hadn't forgotten that. No, no blowout. I took the coach here. I've never taken the coach before. It was a terribly long trip and I had nothing to occupy me but the rain, an English novel, and a South American collection of poetry about love and despair. By Neruda. Have you read it? Or the novel, *The French Lieutenant's Woman*? Mum says she's hardly ever read a better novel, and she reads a lot. I'm sorry, but I simply had to come back. Mainly to ask you why you looked at me the way you did. I know it's silly to say such a thing. Do I shock you? The couple at Oddi have said I can stay with them, and then I'll take the first coach home. No need to worry about me. No need to show me consideration. Has anyone mentioned to you that you have incredibly blue eyes? My name is Aldís, by the way. Could we maybe sit down somewhere, we need to talk. The dear farmwife, Hafrún, gave me a bottle of aquavit. Do you say that, farmwife? I've never talked to people in the countryside before. Sometimes you've got to loosen these people's tongues, she said. But naturally, I don't know what kind of person you are. Maybe I'm allowing myself to talk to you like this because you were listening to Dylan and now to Cohen – even my favourite song by him. You didn't have to do that. But now I'm here and I've got to find out who you really are. Will we need to drink a whole bottle for that?

Haraldur brushes the hair back from his eyes and smiles in such a way that Aldís's heart abruptly skips a beat, then he nods towards the churchyard and says, I know a good place where we can open this bottle. But I don't know how much we'll need to drink. Are you pressed for time? I'm really glad to see you again.

*

34

I'm really glad to see you again.

And they are so young that time seemed not to exist.

THE NORTHERN LIGHTS ARE GOD'S POT SMOKE

They didn't need to finish the bottle. Aldís took one sip, shuddered, he laughed. Then they were silent, looked at each other until she said, I've never kissed a farmer before. Neither have I, he said. I'm going to university this autumn, she said. I was going to go to school, too, but Dad died, he said. My condolences; I'm so sorry. Thanks, but that's why I can't go. There are always solutions. Are there? Yes, and I think that if a person like me can kiss a farmer, then anything is possible. What kind of person are you? The kind that kisses you, she said, leaning forward.

They got married the following summer.

She went to university in the autumn, studied French for a year, but couldn't stand being away from Haraldur and moved for good to the north; accustomed herself just fine to the smell of the sheep shed, taught for many years at the school, which later became a hotel. Her mother, however, never got used to the smell of the sheep shed, despite the fact that she regularly came north, stayed for weeks and got on well with Haraldur's mother, who for some reason always broke into unstoppable laughter after her first glass of sherry, and Aldís made sure that there was always a bottle of sherry at Nes. Yet her dream of studying lived on and when Sóley, their eldest daughter, started junior college in Reykjavík, her parents rented the farm to Páll at Oddi, moved south, and enrolled in the university; they didn't return until seven years later, after living in both Reykjavík and Paris. There are always solutions.

But in March, just over forty years later, they're coming home from Hólmavík, along with their younger daughter – the one who sat barefoot opposite me in the churchyard and told me her stories. They'd treated themselves to dinner at a new restaurant in Hólmavík. It was a starry night, and the northern lights were awake in the sky as they headed over the heath on their way home; the lights surged and billowed so strongly and enchantingly that Aldís couldn't help but unbuckle her seatbelt to get good photos on her phone, and make foreign friends happy by posting them immediately on her Facebook page, under the title: The northern lights in Iceland are like God's pot smoke!

Mum was amusingly tipsy, her daughter said just over three years later, and she always became so uncontrollably enamoured of Dad when she was under the influence. She turned into the nineteen-year-old girl who had sat in the Land Rover between Hafrún and Skúli. I drove that night, and Mum was so terribly playful that after she'd finished putting the photos on Facebook, she tried to crawl to Dad in the back seat to mess around with him, but burst out laughing over something he said and got stuck in between the seats, helpless with laughter. She got little help from Dad, who'd also unbuckled his seatbelt, laughed no less than she did, and had sunk to the floor. You two are nuts, I said, looking at them.

Which I shouldn't have done, she said, looking at her mother's cross. The road was terribly icy and I was stressed about the two glasses of red wine that I'd had with dinner and whose effects I seemed to be feeling uncomfortably much on the heath with all its curves and hills. Mum shrieked like a girl, begging Dad to help her. Swim to me, he shouted from the floor in the back of the car. Then I turned and looked.

The road was terribly icy, she repeated, as if explaining the accident to her mother, apologising.

Because she turned and looked and the heel of Mum's leather boot hit her in the right eye, she lost control of the car, which ran off the road at the top of a high slope, rolled three or four times and stopped upside down six metres below the road. The next she knew, she was hanging upside down from her seatbelt, like a sluggish bat. When she regained consciousness, Aldís was bloody, broken, and dead in Haraldur's arms.

WHAT SORT OF PERSON AM I?

The sort that keeps life from stiffening.

But then we die; nothing can stop it. Death strikes so heavily that even the gods fear it.

My name is Aldís, by the way, and I'm dead.

And my name is Haraldur. I'm paralysed below the waist and her absence is darkness. But what's your name?

SOMEONE FIRES A SHOTGUN AT A LORRY, A MAN WITH A DEGREE IN LITERATURE SELLS JET ENGINES, REFUGEE WOMEN FROM SYRIA MAKE DANGEROUSLY GOOD FOOD

It's torturing me that I can't remember her name. Obviously a worldly person, with a long university education behind her. Had come here to the north three months before the accident – "battered by life", as she put it. I don't know the context, the story, but it appears to have been a shipwreck; someone cheated on her; she couldn't have a child. It was all woven together, turned into a tragedy so painful that she fled to her parents to recover. She had felt sheltered here behind the world, that the slopes of life weren't as steep and rugged. Enjoyed lying on the couch at night, reading and listening to Haraldur and Aldís banter affectionately but passionately about who was the better songwriter, Dylan or Cohen, who a better crime novelist, Arnaldur or Mankell, who a better cellist, Pablo Casals or Pierre Fournier, who a better footballer, Zidane or Thierry Henry. It was so good to listen to them . . . but then the car ran off the road.

She came here to recover, to let the most difficult wounds heal, grow over. Had no interest in taking over the farm. Hadn't earned a doctorate in historical philosophy to end up as a farmer on a tough, remote farm. But Haraldur couldn't think of leaving, and she could hardly leave him alone at Nes, paralysed below the waist.

We have around a hundred sheep, she says when I ask about the farm. A hundred and two, last winter. Of course, no-one can live on that, even if there were four times as many, but we just don't have the heart to get rid of the poor things. We like to have them around us, and for the last two years I've been involved in an interesting, innovative project using wool. It makes farming more diverse, you get a kind of strength from it, and we mow the fields so they don't go to seed. Dad got Eiríkur and Ási at Sámsstaðir to build a big platform with a wheelchair lift out in the sheep shed, where he likes to spend his winter days listening to music, reading, even writing a bit, receiving visitors, and . . . You know, it's not bad at all living here in the fjord. Granted, we're hardly what you'd call a proper farm anymore, but on the other hand all sorts of people have washed up here in recent years, some of them half-fleeing from life. Living in Vík, for example, is an old professor of history; a former lecturer in literary studies, who for some reason sells jet engines in distant lands; he was allowed to build a summer house at Sámsstaðir and stays there for long periods of time. Last year, Sóley hired two Syrian sisters, refugees; they live at the hotel and cook such criminally good food that people travel long distances just to eat lunch there. There's life here, in spite of everything, and you remember how beautiful the fjord can be, even in the winter when we seem so far from everything that it's as if we no longer belong to the world. "The silence here is so deep that you can hear the draught of the northern lights and eternity," says the hotel's website. Sóley managed remarkably well to attract foreign tourist groups here before the coronavirus paralysed everything. Though we saw quite a few tourists here last year and the year before, a lot of groups, but the last half year has been pretty dead, of course. We got a few Icelanders this summer, but the foreign groups disappeared, understandably. But we determinedly went on promoting ourselves on social media, even put in more of an effort, and Sóley is expecting the first big group today.

So you run the hotel together? I ask.

No, not directly. I just help my sister with promotions, take photos for the Facebook page, and am sometimes tempted to put photos from here on my page, mainly for the pleasure of friends abroad. Of the winter stillness or summer serenity; lambs in sunshine, seals sleeping on rocks at the shore. It's like living in a poem, said a friend in New York last winter. Maybe I do, to some extent, and am therefore enviable. My main source of income for the last two years, however, has been translating leaflets for various medications, which can be so boring that I sometimes take my shotgun out and shoot at fenceposts. Some of them are in pretty bad shape after the winter. But it can be fun to discharge a shotgun; it gives you an outlet. My Eiríkur, on the other hand, has been charged with firing a shotgun at a lorry and might be on his way to prison because of it. Life can be so unfair.

Again, this Eiríkur. Who seems to live at Oddi, as the philosopher buried in the churchyard did. Eiríkur gave her a puppy, then fired a shotgun at a lorry and, because of it, is on his way to prison. The woman says his name affectionately. Are they lovers? Why does a man shoot at a lorry, and is perhaps going to jail for it, when he has a woman like her in his life; obviously intelligent, with strong charisma, an almost unabashed gleam in her dark eyes, a vague but captivating melancholy at the corners of her mouth . . . anyone loved by her would hardly fire a shotgun at a lorry, but instead shoot off fireworks in celebration of his life.

Haraldur, however, doesn't celebrate with fireworks, he lies paralysed from the waist down in his bed, sits at the kitchen table that his grandfather made in his day from driftwood gathered at the shore, is out in the sheep shed or at the large living-room window that frames the fjord, that expansive bay, the farm Vík across the fjord, the old church, the churchyard, part of the big field that he raked with Dylan almost half a century ago. The days pass, the weeks, months become years. He reads biographies, books on history, listens to music, disappears into long-past times, immerses himself in the lives of others. If your life stops, he says, you just live through others. Some evenings, the father and daughter read to each other, watch movies together, educational programmes, news commentaries, post on social media, they live together, then he says good night, good night, dear daughter, goes into his bedroom, lifts himself into bed, falls asleep, and then Aldís comes to him, not bloody and broken but radiantly young, and says, my love, oh, I miss you so terribly much!

THE ONLY WORDS THAT MATTER

I don't know the details, and most of it seems to come to me in fragments. Maybe there is no complete picture. Maybe life is found nowhere but in the fragments.

Bury me, Aldís said to Haraldur as they lay there together, broken, bloody, and she dying in the wrecked car – bury me where we sat together for the first time. Remember when I had just arrived by coach, we drank a little from the bottle of aquavit that Hafrún slipped me as she said, we'll be inside with Agnes, dear, should you need a ride afterwards. But of course I didn't need a ride because I had come home, I had come to you. And I've never belonged anywhere but with you. You've always been my home. Hold me, love.

Hold me, love. Her last words.

And the only ones that matter.

WHAT WE LIVE, WHAT WE CREATE

No, I don't know the details well enough to see the big picture.

Details, big picture?

The former we live, the latter we create.

MY NAME IS ROBERT DESNOS AND I KNOW THAT IT TAKES A LOT TO ASK FOR HELP, BUT BE COMFORTED, I'M WEARING MISMATCHED SOCKS AND LIFE IS A SUNDIAL

How deep is this fjord?

The distance grows between me and Nes, the land turns greener the further inland I go, the mountains rise higher, have a verdant tinge, and relatively lush fields spread out at the fjord's head.

I said goodbye to the woman, she hugged me, we nearly finished the bottle. It's good to feel tipsy in the daylight, she said; one really shouldn't do anything else. Then I left. Then I drove off. In the Volvo in which I must have come here. Whenever that was. Maybe in another life. But it was difficult to see the farm and its surroundings, barren and green at once, growing more distant in the rear-view mirror, then disappear entirely behind the landscape's ridges and hills. What disappears from you seems not to exist any longer. And it's torturing me that I can't remember her name.

Incredible how you managed to get me to talk, she said in parting, while you're so silent; it's unlike you – what happened to you?

What happened to you; very good question.

I don't know the answer.

I drive slowly onward, listening to the song that began playing when I started the car. "No Introduction" by Nas. I recognised it right away. One of the big songs. I wrote this piece to get closure .

Strange.

I seem to have forgotten everything about myself. I don't know what I do, what talents I have, whether I'm loved, I don't even know if I have children – how can anyone forget that? My memories have disappeared without a trace, leaving nothing but a poignant sense of loss. I feel . . . as if my very self has been taken away and someone has filled the void left behind with the world, its history, its intolerance, its regret, its longing for balance . . . but to what purpose?

Maybe there is no purpose apart from the one we ourselves create.

When Nas disappears from the rear-view mirror, the Irishman Damien Rice takes over from the American musician: It takes a lot to give, to ask for help, to be yourself.

It takes a lot to ask for help.

Doesn't this apply perfectly to Haraldur?

Hasn't he shackled himself, even both of his daughters, to the fjord, the farm of his ancestors – trapping all three of them in the hesitation because he neither can nor will ask for help? Trapped in the hesitation of life. Married to death. Unable to part with his wife.

He who was once so young.

Of course, everyone has been young at some point – yet no-one precisely like Haraldur.

No-one jumped down like him from the Zetor, having just listened to Dylan – who was also young at the time. To think, even Bob Dylan himself was once young!

Jumped down from the Zetor, landed softly in the fragrant, mown grass, with his long, dark fringe that he had to brush back regularly from his eyes, although his boyish, radiant smile had darkened slightly two months before when his father died and, with his death, shackled his son to the farm.

Forget the dead . . . they will not follow you.

Unfortunately, Dylan doesn't quite have it right – the dead always follow us. Dark and bright, comforting and accusatory.

Before we got up from an almost empty bottle of red wine, the woman had told me about a French journalist who came here to the fjord in late August last year and attracted attention for wearing mismatched socks. A cultural journalist from Paris who was such a fan of Icelandic music and literature that he came here to write a major article for *GEO* magazine about the country, its culture and nature. Why did you choose to come to us, Sóley wanted to know. Because I knew nothing about this fjord; I found little information about it online, but from the map it appeared to be shaped like an open palm, and on top of that you've got a beautiful swimming pool and a hot spring where people can bathe.

Sóley had called her sister: There's a French journalist here, a rather fine specimen, he came here in mismatched socks to write an article about Iceland, one sock black, the other white, each with a poet's name printed on the fabric. I recognised the names; they're poets that you like. I'm sending him to you.

I was supposed to, the woman had said, setting her glass of red wine down on the grass, carefully in order to keep it balanced, then running her hand through her thick hair, lifting it as if it were dark wings; I was supposed to show him the church and the sunken graves, the terns' nesting ground and the old, dilapidated freezing plant down on the headland, the driftwood from Siberia and preferably tie it all in with Susan Sontag's theories, because the French seem to have a hard time understanding nature without tying it in with philosophy. The Frenchman came, and was fascinated by it all. Yet mainly by the church, the sunken gravestones and all the forgotten stories they contain. I got to have a look at his mismatched socks and sure enough – they sported the names of poets such as Robert Desnos, César Vallejo, Elizabeth Bishop, Sylvia Plath, Cavafy. You're a man of good taste, I told him. He stayed for five days here in the fjord, he and my dad got drunk on the platform in the sheep shed and hit it off quite well. When he left, he promised to send me a pair of socks from Paris, which he would select specially for me at a sock shop in Le Marais. He reiterated his promise in letters that he wrote to me this winter. Apologised for writing letters instead of sending emails, but said that he was certain that we put more of ourselves into handwritten letters, not to mention that it's fun finding them in our mailboxes – and what's more, they created jobs. His article appeared in the January issue of *GEO*; he sent us a copy. The man can write, Dad said. In the letter that he sent along with the magazine, he said he dreamed of visiting soon. How is your fjord in the spring? he asked. But not long afterwards, the virus hit the world and cut off most travel. In his last letter, he said that he'd bought the socks, and hinted that they were on their way here to this country. His wording is actually so vague that I honestly don't know whether he sent them by post or intends to bring me them himself. I must admit that I'm a bit excited to see which he's chosen, and of course whether he himself comes. I don't know exactly what I want; I could even think of loving him, but I'm not sure my heart is strong enough for it. He was wearing the Robert Desnos socks when he said goodbye to me, with lines from a famous poem that the poet wrote to his lover in the 1920s. "J'ai tant rêvé de toi" (I've Dreamed of You So Much). Of course, that damned bastard was wearing the socks with the most powerful lines printed on them:

J'ai tant rêvé de toi, tant marché, parlé, couché avec ton fantôme
qu'il ne me reste plus peut-être, et pourtant,
qu'à être fantôme parmi les fantômes et plus ombre cent fois
que l'ombre qui se promène et se promènera allègrement
sur le cadran solaire de ta vie.
(I've dreamed of you so much, walked, talked, slept with your
    ghost so much
that all that remains for me to do perhaps, and yet,
is to be a ghost among the ghosts and a hundred times
    more shadow
than the shadow which strolls and will stroll cheerfully
on the sundial of your life.)

To be honest, I don't know, she had said, looking at me with those dark eyes of hers, why I've told you this. Is it because I suspected that you would enjoy it, or that you would be less likely to think that my life was a failure, doomed to loneliness and monotony here so far away from everything, that it has become little more than a shadow? But what do you think, I mean, do you think it's possible for a good-looking man, a reasonably intelligent, interesting creature to come to a girl like me, wearing socks with those lines on them, is it acceptable, can it be justified, or is it just pure wickedness?

THE TRAIN PLATFORM CALLED LOSS AND THE TRAIN THAT
IS ETERNALLY TAKING AWAY THE OBJECT OF YOUR DESIRE
She hugged me goodbye. Pressed herself tightly against me. Slender, with dark, mesmerising eyes that lit up when she smiled – but there was melancholy at the corners of her mouth. Should I have desired her? Even got an erection when I felt her breasts, her warm body?

But no such thing happened. All I felt was a deep longing for touch. So deep and strong that I had a hard time hiding my emotions; maybe she sensed it, because she smiled that pained smile of hers as she gently stroked my cheek and said, God, how nice it is to be able to hug again.

*

I park the car at the side of the road and step out to pull myself together. I'm feeling the effect of the wine, but I was also so suddenly overwhelmed with emotion that my eyes filled with tears. I step out, lean against the car, close my eyes, breathe in the scent of grassland and sea, and the stillness seeps comfortingly in. I open my eyes, look up, and start in alarm when I see a woman and a man standing next to the fence just below the road, staring at me. There are barely five metres between us and the woman is armed with a rifle.

I'd been so distracted and half-blinded by tears when I parked the car that I didn't notice the fence or the farm and its unpainted outbuildings just above the river that runs along the bottom of the fjord and bleeds into the sea. It's as if the couple have positioned themselves between me and the farm, where I see three children playing with swords and shields. The farmer is tall and slim, the woman is somewhat shorter, quite plump, holding the rifle but pointing the muzzle down and to the side.

Nice weather, I say, trying to sound cheerful to hide how startled I am to see them, while having a hard time taking my eyes off the rifle. They don't answer; the woman looks quickly at her husband, then down at the rifle, as if weighing it and pondering whether she should shoot me, then she lays the weapon over her arms, resting the barrel like a child in one elbow, turns round and walks towards the farmhouse. The man clears his throat, spits, reaches into his back pocket, pulls out a flat plastic container, opens it, takes a pinch of tobacco in his fingers, tilts his head back a little and sprinkles the tobacco over his teeth. Or his gums, rather, as it looks to me as if he's missing half his teeth, the remaining ones reminiscent of crooked, weathered gravestones in an old churchyard. The farmer puts the container back in his pocket, nods curtly to me, turns round, follows his wife.

What was the woman doing with the rifle? Do I look dangerous, or is it customary to go around with firearms in this fjord, shooting at lorries, at fenceposts and people who are so tormented by amnesia that they become paralysed with sadness behind the wheel? Do people

45

here usually say, well, dear rifle, sweet shotgun, should we go for a walk, I need to take you out for a breath of fresh air, who knows, maybe you can shoot someone? – which would make their firearms quite happy.

But I'm back on the road. Distancing myself from the farm and rifle, heading for the hotel. I don't know what awaits me there; hopefully something other than firearms. I drive slowly, enjoy listening to "The Train Song" by Nick Cave, who followed Damien Rice. Nick Cave was born in Australia in 1957, meaning he's starting to get on a bit, because everything ages and eventually all who live will be gone. Even the children. Death is the great standstill, it says somewhere, yet it never stops. It goes through people, trees, empires, presidents, mountains, the most passionate confessions of love. Stops nowhere, except perhaps in a few songs, a few poems:

Tell me how long the train has been gone, and was she there?

The lyrics could hardly be simpler. A few exclamations repeated endlessly.

Anyone could have written this. Even a surly stockbroker, a square politician on the world's greyest day. But no matter where you look in human history someone's always harping on about love, loss and desire. A monotonous, repetitious refrain and, strictly speaking, so thoroughly overused that it has long since become a jaded cliché. And it's so terribly easy to deal with clichés. So easy to wrestle them down. You smile and shake your head, and rest secure in your world. But suddenly, and even on the most ordinary Tuesday, the humblest Monday, that monotone refrain hits you at full force, right between the eyes.

Rips open your chest.

Tears into your heart.

Chops apart your will.

And it's you who runs around the train station shouting, my God, has the train left, departed, is it gone – tell me, was she on board? Tell me, was he there, did you see how he was dressed?

Did you see how she'd combed her hair?

46

Running around desperately – a person hit by the world's oldest melody. The thickest castle walls can't protect you, the most sturdily built fallout shelter can't keep you safe – not even the happiness or warmth of everyday life can protect you. The ancient melody, that damned refrain, penetrates everything. Effortlessly penetrates knowledge, wisdom, muscles and experience. Flee to other countries, continents, hide in remote valleys, in the narrow streets of big cities, that damned melody, that blasted refrain, will seek out your heart, whether you're in Buckingham Palace, in the depths of the Pentagon, under the Pope's bed. It will seek you out, knock all weapons out of your hands, and start to sing:

And was she there?

And was he there?

I drive so slowly along the road that one might think I was on my way into an unmarked grave, where no-one will come to visit me, no-one will seek me out . . . except that song, that refrain, and then the sense of loss that brings even death itself to its knees.

But suddenly, a powerful car horn honks at me.

I'd been so distracted that I didn't notice I was on a steep blind rise, drove so slowly that the car was practically stationary in the middle of the road and now a giant lorry comes tearing down the slope, filling the narrow road and heading for me, at too high a speed for it to have any possibility of stopping in time. I step firmly on the accelerator and manage at the last moment to peel to the side of the road and then off it, where the Volvo turns, lurches, and comes to a halt with its front tyres on the loose gravel at the roadside, its rear tyres in the tussocks. The engine stalls, I'm thrown against the seat back and the song stops. The call for her who disappeared with the train.

So she's gone.

And will always be taking away the object of your desire. Gone, and the train leaves you behind on the platform called Loss – where her name will be called out until the end.

As the lorry passes by and the Volvo practically rocks from the air pressure, another identical lorry appears at the top of the slope, going no slower. Everything had happened so fast, so violently, that I wasn't able to see the driver of the first lorry, but it's a woman driving the second one. Young, with long blond hair, and she blows me a kiss as she rushes by, with only one hand on the steering wheel and all those tonnes on the narrow, potholed road. The same illustration adorns the trailers of both vehicles, a large, yellow power station in a beautiful heathland landscape, a foaming waterfall and a family of four, radiant with the joy of life. The two children, of around eight to twelve years old, look smilingly at their phones, the woman stands with her legs spread, focused but cheerful, holding a tablet computer, the man holds tightly to a sheep's horns as he looks brightly towards the power plant and arching like a smile over the family are the words:

WE PUT PEOPLE FIRST!

A LAND CRUISER FULL OF HAPPY DOGS

Yes, they tear through here twice a week, at life-threatening speed, as inconsiderate as the most fanatic liberals – they're always in a rush to reach their destination. Twice they've run over puppies belonging to Eiríkur of Oddi, pure-bred Border collies. Two the first time, one the second, flattened them. You wouldn't want to see what a lorry's twelve heavy wheels can do to a puppy. All that was left were splotches, pressed into the road, nothing reminiscent of life, let alone puppyish joy. They pass through and leave death behind, said Eiríkur, angry and sad, and the lorry operator claims that Eiríkur fired his shotgun at the lorries in retaliation. He who was so inebriated after half a bottle of Calvados that he was obviously more likely to hit the moon or himself than the lorries, and now has a charge of criminal recklessness hanging over him, if not a prison sentence. At the moment, I don't remember whether it was for shooting at the vehicles or for missing them . . . but don't pay much attention to what I say, and even less to Eiríkur, as far as this is concerned; he's such a great animal lover that the puppies were almost like his children, which explains his harsh reaction. But there's more to it . . . I also asked Eiríkur whether he'd been shooting at fate more than the lorries, and he just laughed. But, as I said, don't pay much attention to me; you remember how I can be. And unfortunately, I've got little better, even though a year has passed. It's often said that age brings maturity. I haven't noticed it, neither in me nor others. To be sure, age slows some people down, makes them even more sluggish. Snuffs out their enthusiasm. If that's what's meant by maturity, then I hope to God I never reach it . . . but drink down that beer, you're upset, naturally.

I've arrived at the hotel.

So here he is, she'd said, the woman I shouldn't pay too much attention to. Sóley. The woman who is both a sun and an island. The one who would supposedly get a shock when she heard I was on my way to her.

So here he is.

I had sat in the car for a good while, dazed by the adrenaline that had shot into my veins when I yanked the car to the roadside, spun around there, lurched sideways leaving the bonnet pointed straight up at the road and watched the two lorries speed away. Soon, however, they slowed down, turned left and crossed a narrow bridge – and it was then that I saw the hotel on the green mountainside across the fjord. Lost in the music, paralysed with sadness, I hadn't noticed the turn and had driven too deep into the fjord.

The lorries were gone when I finally made the turn, crossed over the bridge, and passed two farms shortly afterwards. The first farmhouse was unpainted, grey as the landslides and cliffs on the mountains. But care had been taken with the farm's sign, which was made of driftwood and sawed to look like a dog lying cosily with its front legs outstretched. The farm's name, Oddi, in red, beautifully painted letters.

So this is Oddi. Skúli and Hafrún lived here half a century ago, she who said that there could be no rationality in love. So Páll, the one lying in the churchyard next to Aldís, was their son – but now death has fetched them all and oblivion has begun to work on them. Judging by his gravestone, Páll had been interested in Kierkegaard. Is it common here for farmers and their families to read obscure philosophy and go to study in Paris? That's hardly good for farming?

I slowed down above Oddi, stopped at the sign, forgot to look at the farm itself. I was going to step out to breathe in the surroundings, the tranquil day, the birdsong and the murmur of the river that flowed to the sea about a hundred metres below the grey farmhouse, but stopped when a slender man with dark, nearly shoulder-length hair, in a red shirt, black leather vest and dark jeans, came out of the house, with an electric guitar on his back and a fairly large speaker in his arms, followed by three happy Border collies. Eiríkur himself – who is on his way to prison for shooting at a lorry, or for missing it. He walked across the farmyard to a red Toyota Land Cruiser standing there with its boot open and another identical speaker in it, put the one he was carrying in the trunk, fastened them both down, took off the guitar, looked at the dogs, smiled and apparently said something because they jumped almost immediately into the Land Cruiser, one after the other, then clambered over the seat back. Then he stroked his long hair again, glanced towards the road and caught sight of me. I raised my hand, unsure if I was greeting him or apologising for parking next to the farm sign, staring at the farm. Raised my hand, then started the car, drove off. Eiríkur stood in the farmyard holding the guitar and watching me; a slender string in existence. The dog lover, Eiríkur. On his way to jail for firing a shotgun at a lorry. A troublemaker in trouble.

The second farm is named Hof. It was clear that actual farming was being done there. A large number of white, round hay bales are stacked against the barn gable – the bales resemble a fortress wall, built to withstand the long winter. The farmhouse is two-storeyed, three if the basement is included, white with a green roof, and the front door is halfway open. Maybe a message to the world that the door is never closed here, that it's always welcome, we're all brothers

50

and sisters. There's still hope, I thought, and, soon after, I turned up the side road to the hotel, which stands quite high up the mountainside; four cars in its big car park, three flags hanging limply in the calm.

I stood for a good while next to the flagpoles, regarding the fjord as I gathered the courage to enter the hotel. Soon, Eiríkur drove past, his Toyota Land Cruiser full of happy dogs, three panting muzzles. I watched the car drive into the distance and felt a poignant loneliness as it disappeared with Eiríkur and the dogs over a hill nearer the mouth of the fjord. I looked to the right, towards the head of the fjord, where the narrow road wound like a giant, fossilised snake up from its grassy floor.

The way out. So it exists.

The big hotel building and the area immediately around it are tidy-looking, including the swimming pool located a little lower and further down the slope. At one end of the pool is an oblong building clad with corrugated iron, and steam rises from a warm, natural hot tub next to the pool. In the pool, three people float on inflatable mattresses. A tall man with a big belly that rises from him like an awkwardly shaped haystack, a thickset woman in a bright-red bikini, both so motionless that they could have been dead, and a slender younger woman who pushes herself lazily along with slow, almost dreamy hand movements, clad only in flimsy shorts. You have a beautiful back, I muttered, and the woman looked up as if she'd heard me. Raised herself languidly onto her elbows and revealed her naked, sleeping breasts, which seemed to waken at my gaze, became warm, sensual. I swallowed and felt a mild lust in my abdomen, but also shame; wasn't I actually staring at her breasts? But if I were caught looking away, couldn't that be interpreted as prudery, that I was a petty bourgeois who was offended by . . . her liberalism, her relaxed attitude . . . a few difficult seconds passed, I stared into uncertainty, and then the woman smiled, waved at me, lay back down, hid her breasts, and freed me from her spell.

So here he is.

Sóley had said when I stepped into the hotel foyer, my heart beating rapidly knowing that I was about to meet a woman who would "get a shock" at the sight of me. She was fussing with the printer behind the reception desk, but kept looking up because her sister Rúna had called from Nes and said, you'll never be able to guess who sat with me at Mum's grave out in the churchyard – and is now on his way to you!

So here you are, she said, looking up and smiling in a way that nearly frightened me. Smiled and asked, oh, can I give you a hug, would that be alright? But she didn't wait for an answer, just came out from behind the reception desk, walked lithely towards me, hugged me tightly, and it surprised me how well I felt in her arms. Even as if I belonged there. Instinctively, I closed my eyes, enjoying the moment as the young GDRN sang over the Bluetooth speaker on the reception desk: I need you, to remind me, of where I come from, and where I'm going.

I need you.

Don't let go, I thought, but then she let go, took a step back, smiled quickly and my heart skipped a beat. She's about ten centimetres shorter than me, slim yet strong-looking, with shoulder-length hair so white that it resembles angel wings. Her right hand continued to hold my elbow loosely, as if she feared that I would disappear, evaporate. Held my elbow as she regarded me, screwing up her amber eyes as if she were taking my measure. Her lower lip was a little wider than the upper one, which rested on its sister like a sleeping kiss.

Would it be alright if I hugged you? It took you so long to get here that I was starting to think you'd given up on coming, and you know, she added as she let go of my elbow, and you mustn't be upset, now, but I think I was a bit relieved. My first reaction was of course anger; damn it, I thought, so I have no more pull than that – but then I felt relieved. Or at least I tried to convince myself that I was, thinking, oh, it's probably for the best – what's done is done. Nor was

I sure I would survive having you back here. Think of the drama. A person of my age! Remember, you said you were leaving to save us both. Or maybe it was I who said it? But now you're here and it just makes me happy to see you. Everything will be fine between us, won't it?

My head was spinning – so there had been something between us. Something real. Still, I don't remember her. How is it possible to forget those peculiar eyes, that fair hair, that smile, what forces have tampered with me, what have they done to me?

Everything will be fine between us, won't it?

What does she mean?

And why did she have to be playing that beautiful, sad song when I came . . . need you, I need you, need you . . .

I scratched my head and gripped the first thing that came to mind; the mysterious couple who had looked at me so strangely, he with teeth that looked like old gravestones, and she armed with a rifle.

Sóley laughed at my description. That would have been Einar and Lóa, she said. They took over the farm Framnes about ten years ago. Einsi is the little brother of Ási, who took over Sámsstaðir a few years before. You'll really have to meet Ási; the man is an entire novel unto himself. Did the rifle frighten you? But Lóa is so harmless and kind-hearted that she becomes practically bedridden with sorrow and anxiety when it comes time to send the lambs to the slaughter-house. To everyone's surprise, though, she took part in a shooting competition at Sævangur during the National Day celebrations in June last summer; she'd hardly ever touched a rifle before then but beat a lot of renowned shooters and, since then, has taken every opportunity to practise shooting, determined to defend her title. So was it because of them that it took you so long to get here?

Well, yes, I said, or no, because there was that damned lorry. Or lorries, I added, telling her what had happened, that I'd almost been flattened. Death by blond.

You poor dear creature, Sóley then said, to have had to face that! We know them. They tear through here twice a week. Then said that

53

about maturity; that she would hopefully never mature. But it must have shaken you up. Come on, let's go and sit down in the lounge, I'll get you a beer, your favourite, a dark Leffe. We always have plenty of it, although other brands are more popular. You'd almost think that I've always been hoping you would show up. Incredible how we let life get in our way. But now you're here – so you're having a beer!

Then she led me into the cosy lounge off the foyer, sat down opposite me, smiled as she watched me sip my beer, and told me – after I'd mentioned the man with the dogs and speaker at Oddi – the story of how Eiríkur supposedly shot at the lorries, or perhaps fate, flattened puppies, half a bottle of Calvados, his imminent prison sentence.

You certainly are good at getting me to talk; I just can't seem to stop. But come on, drink your beer, that rifle startled you, naturally, those life-threatening lorries, and then to meet me after all these years, I who blather so much that you can't get a word in. I'll go and get you another beer – it'll do you good, won't it? And by gosh, I think I'll go ahead and have one, too, just to keep you company.

She smiled again. Smiled, and brushed the back of my hand gently with her palm. Then she was gone.

Went and left the warmth of her palm on the back of my hand. And her smile everywhere.

I reached for the Yahtzee score pad on the small side table, tore off the top sheet, wrote on its blank back:

"Some smiles can change worlds. Including those that mustn't be changed."

YOU'RE ALWAYS YOU, YET NEVER THE SAME – DESPITE THAT, THERE'S STILL REASON TO LAUGH, IN THIS UNIVERSE

The mild August light streams in through the large window, illuminating the spines of the books in two brown bookcases, and a neat stack of magazines on a small round table next to them. Out front, Sóley is laughing. The phone had rung in the foyer, I heard her answer, then laugh, and I immediately began to miss her. Her presence, her voice, to see her smile and to look into those peculiar eyes . . . still, I'm somewhat relieved to be alone. No need to answer for myself in the meantime. With a constant, mild knot of anxiety in my stomach about being found out.

"Remember, you said you were leaving to save us both. Or maybe it was I who said it?"

Why did I or she have to leave in order to "save us both"?

Out front, Sóley laughs again.

I get up, go to the two bookcases to scan the spines, but the cover of the top magazine catches my attention. A magazine on astronomy, the cover a dark night sky cloven by a bright headline in the form of a ray of light: *How Many Universes Are Out There?* I sit back down on the couch with the magazine and turn to the front-page article. I was only going to take a quick look, but I become so engrossed in the article that before I know it, I've read it to the end; then I put the magazine down, stand up, go to the window and look out over the quiet fjord at the mountainside opposite. I see Einar and Lóa's farm and a small, convex caravan about half a kilometre from it. The caravan is closer to the sea, with a few trees and clusters of shrubs between it and the farm. I sit back down on the couch, open the magazine again and stop and reread at random places in the article, thinking that I may have misread or misunderstood something. A long, well-written article meant for the general public, the wording not too theoretical and the main conclusions extracted here and there for simplicity's sake. Except that there are no conclusions, but rather questions on top of questions, uncertainty on top of uncertainty. According to the article, humanity isn't in much of a better position than I am.

The article's three authors, two women and one man, all professors of astronomy, assert, with uncomfortably convincing arguments, that mankind has from the beginning been shackled to erroneous world-views. That in all of human history, man has, in other words, never had a correct image of the world, and therefore has always lived with a completely skewed worldview. His views have of course changed and evolved, but what they all have in common is that they've been wrong: the world in which man has thought he lived has simply never existed.

Five centuries ago, it says in the article, the Earth was assumed to be the centre of everything, and the solar system to be the entire universe. That was the unshakable worldview, and the importance of man and the Earth were defined by it. However, man's knowledge grew slowly but surely and, about a century ago, the leading scientists were unanimous in their view that the solar system was a small part of a giant galaxy, which was the universe itself. Then decades passed, knowledge, technology advanced rapidly, and we discovered that our galaxy was only one among thousands of others – thus multiplying the size of the universe.

Our worldview has rested on that knowledge for decades.

But now, there are ever-increasing indications that the infinite universe is simply one of countless other universes. The universe that yesterday was incomprehensibly vast and considered to accommodate both God and eternity turns out to be only one of hundreds or thousands of other universes. What was infinitely expansive yesterday is today no more than a small piece in a giant and mysterious puzzle. To perfect the uncertainty, and underline our ignorance, what the other universes look like is completely hidden. No-one has the slightest idea where they are, whether the universes are subject to the laws that we know, whether they touch each other anywhere, have ever done so, or what such contact, closeness or even collision would entail – and finally whether it's possible to get from one universe to another:

When it comes to the biggest questions of existence, we are, despite all of our achievements and the tremendous speed of developments in science in recent decades, still little more than cavemen who warm themselves by the fire at night, look up at the starry sky and have no idea what all those glittering points of light represent. All logic now tenaciously suggests that there are infinitely many universes and, at the same time, that it is in all likelihood impossible for the human mind to understand

56

the fundamentals of existence. Thus, it is not unlikely that some universes reflect each other, yet possibly in some strange if not astonishing way. For example, you can exist simultaneously in many different universes, under different conditions, and possibly different laws of nature. You are you, everywhere, yet are nowhere the same. In other words, the ancient question, 'Who am I?' has taken on such vast dimensions that it's almost hopeless to try to answer it.

I close the magazine, stand up, put it back in its place, and then look out the window. Try to calm my mind in the tranquil August light, the serene fjord. I don't know if I'm relieved or terrified.

So there isn't a great difference between me and the world – both are shut up inside a world of ignorance. Yet while I'm suffering almost complete amnesia, as far as I can see, the world is afflicted by something much more difficult.

Sóley is still on the phone.

I catch a word or two. Now she laughs. So there's still reason for her to do so. In this universe.

Two ravens glide over the ruins of an old farmhouse not far from the grey, single-storey house at Oddi. Can life cross whole and unbroken from one universe to another? And what are the universes but futility itself if life cannot cross between them, what's the purpose if it's not life that connects them?

Or is death perhaps the space between them?

I AM DARKNESS AND FOG

I honestly don't know what weapons we have that are sufficient, that could have a real effect. Elías tried his best to get them to drop the charges, which were ridiculous, as they know, and my sister and I spoke to an old friend who is going to help us. But isn't it sometimes the case, Dísa, that you experience your own powerlessness when you're really put to the test? says Sóley, smiling at me and pointing at the phone handset, as if to explain, sorry about the delay in bringing the beer.

I've gone back into the big foyer, except that it's called reception. Everything has to be called something, have a name, otherwise it becomes much harder to describe it, embrace it. I'm not kissing you until you've told me your name.

Sóley gestures at the refrigerator holding the beer, then at me and back at the refrigerator, and I understand – I can get myself a beer. Which I do. I go and get another dark Leffe, open it with a bottle opener shaped like a seal that Sóley pushes towards me across the table.

Yes, she says on the phone, as she now paces the floor, you're absolutely right, intolerable, unacceptable. I don't know what forces . . . what . . . no, or yes, I know that Eiríkur said something similar, most recently this morning, strolled over here so early that not even the devil was awake, excited for the dinner party tonight, and then he said . . . I don't catch what she says next, what Eiríkur said so early this morning that the devil was still sleeping deep below the Earth's crust; what he'd talked about, what was right but unacceptable, whether Eiríkur had maybe thought of buying a rifle, since the shotgun hadn't sufficed for lorries tearing through; Sóley goes into the dining room and the rest is cut off. Unfortunately. It's so nice to watch her. See the soft curve of her spine, look at her slender back. See how she walks, straight-backed, proud, yet softly, yet reflectively. She disappeared into the dining room and the world grew duller. Life became poorer. A melody sparks inside me and Lennon's pained voice sings about how it's no fun doing what he does when his love isn't there.

Her laughter carries from the dining room. Worlds can doubtless be built on her laughter. Entire universes. The God who never laughs can't be almighty.

I step closer to the dining room, hear Sóley's voice again. Yes, she says, I'm standing here at the window, looking out, and understand what you mean, although it would certainly be more comfortable not to understand it. Most people, as you know, choose to understand little. Understanding tends to involve overly heavy things such as taking a position, responsibility, while prejudices and indifference make your life a lot easier. Life always becomes more complicated if you try to understand things. Eiríkur? Yes, I know, and God, I'm looking so forward to it, really! Besides . . . Sóley probably moves further in, at least her voice begins to fade, and then dies out completely. There is no fun . . .

Outside, the flags still hang motionless, as if they're in deep contemplation or are dead. The Icelandic flag, the Canadian one, and the European Union flag. I turn around and regard the row of clocks on the wall behind the reception desk. Twelve clocks that show the time in as many different parts of the Earth. The clock that measures the time in Iceland is approaching eleven. Again, I inch my way closer to the dining room in the hope of hearing Sóley's voice. Then it's as if something stops me – and everything starts rushing around inside of me.

As if I'd received a powerful electric shock that unleashed a flurry of vague thoughts and unfathomable feelings within me. I walk quickly to the reception desk, set eyes on a stack of A5-size memo sheets with the hotel's name at the top. I reach over and take a few of the sheets, find a pen and start writing. Without thinking, actually.

Unless I think by writing?

I write quickly in order to get down on paper what assails me, terrified that I'll forget it all, like my life. What flows into my head, fills my blood – and maybe comes from within the darkness or fog that I am?

"Eiríkur of Oddi. The man who has an electric guitar, dogs, three dead puppies, a shotgun to fire at lorries or perhaps fate. What more does he have?"

You're Dead, and Therefore Have
Come Further

IT'S IMPOSSIBLE TO TELL THE STORY OTHERWISE

Eiríkur of Oddi. The man who has an electric guitar, dogs, three dead puppies, a shotgun to fire at lorries or perhaps fate.

What more does he have?

He walked across the farmyard, from the unpainted concrete house to the car, an old Toyota Land Cruiser, big and powerful enough to handle the rigours of heavy winter weather, difficult driving conditions, and to accommodate three dogs and two large speakers. The vehicle was once red, but its colour has faded. Lucky is the person whose heart is an old Land Cruiser, full of happy dogs – the heart is red, does it always fade, too, and become winded in the snowdrifts that life piles around us? Eiríkur's dogs, on the other hand, know little more exciting than to get to sit in the Land Cruiser with the person they love and trust, not to mention that it's so strange to sit still while the land itself, that which never moves, is the stillest of all, rushes by. Shoots past. They never get tired of that wonder.

But Eiríkur carried the speakers to the Land Cruiser, put them in it, and backed away from his house.

That concrete house that has never been painted. Some people who drive past and don't know any better think that the unpainted house bears witness to slothfulness, that whoever lives there must be an afternoon farmer, which is one of the worst profanities and criticisms that we know, but what's right there in front of our eyes, what are we to believe?

The house was built almost a decade ago, but Eiríkur has only lived in it for three years, which is also the age of his oldest dog.

That three years is more than enough time to paint a house, almost two hundred square metres – is certainly true. But slow down a bit, there's a catch, there's a story here, there are destinies, which is why we need to go back a bit, into the past, to where we all come from, from where we're all descended, where most explanations are to be found, where it all begins. Let's go back in the hope of understanding better, and to get our bearings. So slow down a bit. Or rather, let's slow down time. It's impossible to tell the story otherwise.

MAYBE IT'S THE MISTAKES THAT SET LIFE STRAIGHT

Halldór and Páll Skúlason. Remember the names, but otherwise, don't stop at these two, not for now, we name them and almost immediately they retreat into the shadows, are backstage, watch from there but step forward when the call comes. It was the older, former one who bore the brunt of building the house, a dexterous man, got it from his parents. Hafrún, their mother, was born in the old turf house that stood near the river flowing slowly between grassy banks. A good-natured river, apart from its three or four tantrums a year when it bursts forth from its icy cloak or when the weather suddenly warms up and it rains vigorously onto the snow in the mountains, where all rivers are born; then it respects no banks, vandalistically inundating hayfields and meadows, submerging gravel banks and scrub. But is gentle and dreamy in the summers. So gentle that it's as if it watches over the salmon that spawn in it, as if it cares for them, doesn't want to harm the fish, disturb the eggs. Maybe it simply likes feeling the salmon in its belly. Maybe the salmon's movements are soft strokes that fill it with tranquillity. But because of the tantrums, the old farm stood about a hundred metres from the riverbank, a turf house built around 1900, its ruins still quite clear from the road, and there Hafrún was born. The name as rare as she is, one of the pearls of this district.

Born in the early 1930s, in a dwelling that had little in common with that restless century, made of turf, stone, and wood washed up by the sea. She often said that her name had two parts, Haf and

Rún, to emphasise that she was of two times, of an ancient past with deep roots in stagnation, hardships, but, at the same time, possessed of a certain closeness between people, and then the modern age, the twentieth century, which certainly presented its own difficulties, although stagnation would be the last word that would come to mind in describing it. Strictly speaking, the twentieth century hadn't yet found its way all the way north to Iceland, and not at all to this fjord, behind a hundred heaths and rugged mountains, when Hafrún was born in the clean but dimly lit turf house. Among both the pros and cons of living so far from others is that changes don't take effect immediately. The Industrial Revolution revolutionised Europe in the nineteenth century, railroads both cut the continent apart and connected it, cities swelled, factories sprang up faster than weeds and yielded unprecedented, dizzying profits, prosperity, pollution, employment, slavery and cruel injustice. But here in Iceland, time had hardly moved for a thousand years, it stood as still as a work of art and barely budged for almost the entire nineteenth century; it was as if we Icelanders lived on another planet. Down south in Europe and out west in America, factories and cities rose, trains became faster and faster, pistols more and more accurate, while here, birds could hardly be startled from their perches, we continued to be poorly shod, our feet forever wet, we kept going out into the same dark sheep sheds, the low cowsheds, mowed tussocky hayfields using thousand-year-old methods. Our immobility tied centuries and generations together into one unbroken whole while everything out in the world fell apart, everything lost its core, other than the uncertainty that has propelled the world for almost two centuries. Here, surrounded by restless, ever-changing, dynamic nature, stagnation connected all of us, at all times.

Bloody remarkable, I would say a miracle, said Skúli, that this nation didn't suffocate long ago from boredom, simply putrefy in that damned stagnant state.

Skúli was almost two years younger than his wife. Born in a wooden house out west in Rif, a tiny fishing village at the far end of the

Snæfellsnes peninsula, unless it was Hellissandur, no way we can remember everything, or tell apart two fishing villages lying so close to each other, when we're unfamiliar with the place. The only constant in his existence was the glacier, which on some days didn't appear against the sky but seemed literally to hold that roof up. He was seven or eight years old when he came here to the fjord, brought by the postman like any other parcel. He's a tough one, said the postman upon delivering Skúli to the farm Botn. Tough, yet with gentle eyes, replied the housewife who would take his mother's place. Skúli's father was the son . . . No, sorry. We've got ahead of ourselves. We haven't got to his father, nor to Hafrún and Skúli, actually; it's a mistake to let them in right away.

But maybe it's the mistakes that set life straight.

Let's turn to the earthworm.

IT'S HARDLY A GOOD EXAMPLE TO CONSOLE A FRIEND
WITH LONELINESS; AN EVENING IN FEBRUARY, MIDNIGHT
IN NOVEMBER

The earthworm is a humble creature, cold and blind, a modest poet in the dark soil, and of the family of hermaphroditic annelids. Its task is to overturn the soil, prevent it from losing oxygen and suffocating, mentioned here specifically and placed in the context of how fate unfolds because Skúli's grandmother, and Eiríkur's great-great-grandmother, published at the very end of the nineteenth century a very readable article about the behaviour and nature of earthworms in the journal *Nature and World – a Journal for the General Public*, published in Stykkishólmur, edited by four educated and influential men, three of them living in that village, but the fourth the priest of a parish a short distance from it, Reverend Pétur Jónsson. Maybe not as passionate about the journal as the others, although he lacked neither skills nor knowledge, and had received high marks in his studies at the University of Copenhagen. He came to Snæfellsnes with his wife and two young children, intending to stay for only a short time, maybe five years, his benefice conceived of as a step on a secure path up the administrative ladder. It's wonderful to be young, to have dreams, we have so many plans, and then life chastens us.

It rained terribly the day we arrived here, Pétur wrote in a letter to a friend; the old church resembled a large animal that the heavens intended to slaughter.

He took over from a priest who had been dismissed in his old age, after growing more and more confused and at last making no clear distinction between the living and the dead. At times, he would address churchgoers whom no-one saw but him, some having lain for years in the churchyard's dark soil, so disfigured that he couldn't refrain from remarking on it: nice to have you here with us, Ásgeir, you've been away for some time, but you're a poor sight to see, as if you've been rolled up from the ground; Engilríður, your right arm just fell off, remember to take it with you when you go, it's very untidy leaving body parts behind.

It would not surprise me, wrote Pétur to acquaintances of his soon after his arrival, if some people here were to find me rather dull, quite average, and hardly able to match up to my predecessor, a priest who was in direct contact with folk in the kingdom of death!

Yet Pétur and his wife were generally given a good welcome. They brought the power of youth, he with his learning, she a driving force, immediately becoming popular with the parishioners, helping women with childbirth and doing it so well that the women said she had healing hands. You have hands of light, Pétur often said to her, as he hugged her, kissed her neck, at the time when everything was good and the world a better place. My dear Halla has hands of light, he proudly wrote in letters to friends. There were many letters written during their first years on Snæfellsnes, lively and inspired, but they have decreased somewhat in number, and it seems as if life has slowed down somehow and perhaps darkened around them when Pétur sits down in his office, his cubbyhole, fifteen, sixteen years after the couple came to the parish, to read through an article on the earth-worm submitted by a common woman.

At the close of the nineteenth century.

Evening in November, midnight in February.

Pétur has so little interest in reading the article, however, that he immediately pushes it aside, forgets it and instead sinks himself, as the evening grows older and darkens, into the work of the English poet William Wordsworth. He reads and drinks just over half a bottle of red wine. He'd bought ten bottles on his last trip to the village; four weeks later there are only three left. Or rather, two and a half. Yet they were supposed to have lasted three months. It's painful, he writes in a letter to his friend, the German poet Hölderlin, to witness how quickly the best in this world runs short, but how slowly what is of lesser quality disappears.

He's down to half a bottle. And will probably have to wait a few weeks until he can afford a new supply. Jesus turned water into wine, Pétur writes to the poet, which tells us that he appreciated it. So I'm not doing wrong.

It's approaching midnight in November, or perhaps it's rather late in the evening in February. A dark month, the snow had recently melted away, making the darkness even heavier, it's so heavy that the Earth's crust bends under its weight, so dark that the mountains are lost. He has finished over half a bottle, had been reading Wordsworth's poems, everyone asleep at this church farm. The two children who are still at home; the third, an eighteen-year-old boy, is at the Learned School down south in Reykjavík. Halla is sleeping, the old farmhand with the beautiful singing voice is also asleep, as are the two maids, one in her fifties, strong as a man and short-tempered, no shortage of flare-ups from her, the other in her twenties, quite homely-looking, if not almost – God help us – ugly when you first see her, but that changes quickly, her joy of life, warmth and cheerfulness make her beautiful. Those who judge according to surface appearances don't understand much.

And it's so dark that anyone who ventured out would surely disappear without a trace and never be found again.

It's going on midnight. Earlier in the evening, Pétur had heard the bustle of life seep through the walls, the farmhand singing, Halla joining in, the younger maid clowning with the two children, their shrieks carried in to him like messages from joy itself. Little makes him happier than to hear them laugh. This is a good home, it's a balanced world. Yet Pétur has finished more than half a bottle and is writing a long-dead poet a letter. Halla has hands of light. A beautiful person. The best he has ever known. Pétur doesn't know when it was that he stopped loving her.

Everyone is sleeping. Including Eva, the apple of Pétur's eye, he and Halla's next-oldest child. Her laughter reminds him of happy lambs; she laughs and it's as if someone's tickling you. Except that she has stopped laughing altogether, and is sleeping in the earth twenty-three steps from her father's desk. She has slept there for ten years, nine months and ten days. Fell ill after she went with her father, contrary to Halla's advice, on official business around the countryside in the cool spring weather, which turned to sleet in the afternoon, a sharp, cold wind. They were both drenched, caught colds, developed coughs, he recovered, she didn't. Died eight days later in Pétur's arms as he said every prayer he knew, and in three languages, at that, but death stepped easily through them all. He came, took Eva, took her with him into the darkness and left Pétur behind in life.

It was then that I wrote you the first letter, Pétur had scribbled in his thirty-eighth letter to Hölderlin earlier that evening, having just come in after visiting Eva. He often goes to her in the evening, preferably in the dark because that alone can connect the worlds that life is incapable of bridging. Darkness flows between, it carries the words and the bereavement across the borders: I miss you, I'm sorry that I failed you, I'm sorry I couldn't die in your place, aren't you cold there, do you get enough to eat, is anyone taking care of you until I come, do you have something to read; my dearest, shall I tell you a short story – once upon a time there was a kitty that . . .

It was then that I wrote you the first letter. I had cried out to God from the depth of my love, with all the pain of my despair – he answered with death. Do you think it may have been then that life began to fade? Once I asked you, what should I do with my life? And you answered: ". . . und einsam/Unter dem Himmel, wie immer, bin ich" (. . . and lonely, under the sky, as always, I am).

What can I say to that?

I address God in despair and love – he answers with death.

I address you in despair and friendship – you answer me with loneliness!

Of course, what you wrote is beautiful, you're a mountain of a poet, but it's hardly a good example to console one's friend with loneliness, even if it's so beautifully composed.

Not a good example.

Pétur writes to a German poet who has been lying in his grave for decades, died before he was born. Writes the letters, puts them a few days later in the small blue chest beneath the bed. Maybe not exemplary. Only darkness can bring the words between worlds. But it's not a postman. Nor do the dead have a registered address. They're outside all postcodes.

I don't always feel good, poet, Pétur has just written, but writing to you brings me comfort. I feel fine when we're together, it's as if I'm standing on the border of life and death, looking into both worlds. As if I move nearer to Eva, hoping that she will sense my presence. But now I must stop. I have an article waiting to be read, and the letter accompanying that article. From a common woman. It will hardly be enjoyable. Why should it be enjoyable? Of course, I'll be forced to finish the bottle. And then there will only be two left. Life is truly a slope, poet, truly a slope, at least for those of us who are so misfortunate as to be alive. You're dead, and therefore have come further. Excuse me, but don't go too far.

Fate is as old as the world. It has seen many things, possibly every-thing, which is probably why it has an unquenchable need to mix up the cards in the hope that something unexpected happens.

Something to help it pass the time. Some call it the humour of the gods. Mix up cards, mix up lives, entertain itself by tying knots, throwing in an unexpected turn here, breaking down a bridge there, stirring our hearts, giving existence a flip so that what is standing still and secure is toppled. That's why you can see a beautiful woman crying behind the wheel at a red light on the most ordinary of Tuesdays, a bricklayer standing there at a loss over a new mixture and staring into space, a maths professor bursting into tears on a bus and only because the driver said good morning to him; now some-thing's happening, says fate in delight. And it was probably fate that saw to it that Guðríður's parcel to the journal *Nature and World* came into Pétur's hands. Jónas, one of the editors in Stykkishólmur, had forwarded the article and the letter that accompanied it to Pétur, unsure of what to do with it: "This completely uneducated woman writes about earthworms, and then writes an interesting letter to justify what she has written. What do you think of that!?"

Do you hear that, poet, Pétur mutters to the book of poems by Hölderlin that he usually keeps on his small desk, published in 1846, and that Pétur bought during his years in Copenhagen – when I was alive, as he sometimes words it to himself. Do you hear that, Pétur mutters after finally opening the parcel, two hours and just over half a bottle of red wine later; she has written about earthworms, you know them, right there in the ground. Darwin apparently liked them, he wrote a book about them, but to my knowledge few others have got the idea of writing about that blind traveller of the soil. Maybe there's something to this, after all?

He takes out the sheets of paper, smooths them, reads the beginning:

The earthworm is of the family of hermaphroditic annelids, and it helps the soil breathe. Without it, the soil would probably

71

suffocate, and then the grass would wither, and the flowers would
wither, and what would then become of us humans?

Pétur looks up as if in surprise, takes out the letter accompanying
the article, intending to glance through it, but its content, the writing
style, how the letters are drawn, the thought in it – all slow down
his reading. He reads it slowly to the end, and some sentences he
reads twice:

Many people seem clearly to dislike them, undoubtedly because
they are at home in the darkness of the soil and are completely
silent. That description bears no small resemblance to death.
Does it perhaps explain the antipathy towards this remarkable
animal? . . . I would call the earthworm the thought of God if
I dared.

Would call the earthworm the thought of God if I dared, what do you
say to this, poet, isn't this something, mutters Pétur, staring blankly
for quite some time as the night continues to sink in the darkness
outside. Finally, he takes a deep breath, reads the letter again. Reads
it for the third time.

WE HAVE NO OTHER CHOICE, THEN, BUT TO LOSE
OUR MINDS

Guðríður begins the letter, as common folk usually do when they
dare to or cannot help but step forward, by apologising for herself.
That she, a completely uneducated woman, with clumsy handwriting,
would let it cross her mind to send her reflections on the earthworm to such a prestigious journal – and she would like first of all
to hasten to express her gratitude for the journal, which she always
tries as best she can to purchase or to borrow. She really does not
understand how she can dare to send in these sparse and of course
clumsy reflections on the earthworm, but sometimes she cannot
contain her zeal, which has unfortunately got her into an excessive

amount of trouble in this life; she asks for forgiveness if sending them the article might be interpreted as hubris. Yet she has no arrogance in mind.

I have always endeavoured to acquire all the knowledge that I can, which is certainly not much. Possibly more than a smattering, on the scale of the people around me, but not at all of those who are truly educated, like the good people who publish the journal.

Not much, she writes, albeit more than a smattering. And I have always regretted people's low opinion of the earthworm, how they judge it, if not condemn it, for its simple form and blindness. Many people seem to dislike them, undoubtedly because they are at home in the darkness of the soil and are completely silent. That description bears no small resemblance to death. Does this perhaps explain people's antipathy towards this remarkable animal? Yet I have discovered, both through reading and my own observations, that few creatures may be more important to the cycle of life than the earthworm. As I write in my article, they seem to help the earth breathe, which is why I am tempted to say, although only in this brief letter and never in an article in your prestigious journal, that in that sense, the earthworm's contribution to life is more important than the contribution of human beings. This is why I would like, why I find myself compelled, to send you these poor reflections of mine, in which I seek to inform potential readers about the contribution of the earthworm to life. It is so important that people also recognise the importance of the small things in life. That they realise that all things count equally, women as much as men, earthworms as kings. That nothing is big but life itself. If I dared, I would call the earthworm the thought of God. Please try to judge my effort, rather than the result. Excuse my presumption. I know that every person should know his place. But who decides that place? And is it a sin to have an opinion on it, even doubt that that place was chosen correctly, or fairly? I hope that I do myself no shame. Yours sincerely, Guðríður Eiríksdóttir.

*

Pétur rubs his eyes, thinks, I would call the earthworm the thought of God. He takes out his letter to Hölderlin, intends to write something, wants to describe the unexpected emotions he experienced while reading the article and the letter, lifts his pen, stops abruptly, mutters, forgive me, friend, as he pushes the letter aside and reaches for a blank sheet of paper. On it, he writes quickly and resolutely, Dear Guðríður, it is growing dark and I was just now reading your letter and your interesting article. It will be a pleasure to publish it in the journal. It crossed my mind to loan you two books that I have here. I shall be happy to send them to you – if you would agree to receive them. I am sure that you will enjoy them. It is so clear that you are a seeker, have an open mind, a consciousness that desires knowledge. It is so beautiful. I envy you.

He puts down his pen. Am I going too fast, German poet, he asks the book of poems on the table – and I did not even address her formally! No, the poet answers, you are not going too fast, one should seize life and never address it formally when it reveals itself in this rare way, seize it without concern for the consequences. Finish the letter. But if you send it, everything will change.

Why should I heed you, Pétur asks, didn't you lose your mind, didn't you spend your final years in a tower, mentally unfit? Besides, you're dead, so what do you know about life?

I became mentally exhausted because I understood life. And I've long wanted to confide in you that in my life, love was a rainbow that glistened eternally before me but moved away from me every time I tried to touch it. Because of that, everything broke, and there was no other option but to lose my mind. What need does a loveless man have for his mind, anyway? All of this proves that it is safe for you to trust my advice.

This is of course completely irrational, says Pétur, yet he continues to write the letter and feels something that he hasn't felt in many years. Writes the letter, sends it, and sees to it that the postman delivers it to her alone. She receives the letter, and she reads it. She is surprised, elated, proud, confused; she is frightened. Two weeks pass before she dares to answer him. But she does, which is surely a mistake.

A mistake?

We know nothing.

AND JUST WHERE DO YOU THINK YOU'RE HEADED?

It crossed my mind to loan you two books that I have here – the next day Pétur asks the postman to take the letter with him to Guðríður. The postman has come from Reykjavík and is on his way out to Snæfellsnes, with two horses. It's a bit out of the way for him to deliver the letter directly, as it's customary to leave letters and parcels for Uppsalir at the estate farm of Bær, where they sometimes have to wait for weeks until someone has business in the vicinity of Uppsalir, or if one of the heathland farmers has errands down in the lowland.

Guðríður Eiríksdóttir, Uppsalir. The postman knows the name, has left shipments addressed to Guðríður several times at Bær.

A bit out of the way, three additional hours at least, and the postman's time is always precious. He says so, too; it's out of the way, he says, but, in the end, takes the letter.

A good two months later, Pétur himself travels the same route, with three, not two, books for Guðríður, having just received her reply, which took ten days to reach him. She is not a priority, unlike him. First, she had to take the letter down to Bær, and from there it went to Stykkishólmur, finally to Pétur. I thank the priest for his letter.

I thank the priest for his letter, which touched me deeply, she writes. I am, however, a bit shy about writing to you so directly. You are so learned. You have such beautiful and intelligent handwriting. It must be a trial for you to have to endure my scrawls – I dare not call them writing. Some of the letters are like badly trained dogs. I'm afraid that some of them, especially the F, the R, and probably the P, too, might start barking in your face – that they won't behave themselves in your fine abode. Gratitude is far too weak and dull a word to express my feelings regarding your warm generosity, to offer to loan me books from your collection. I would gladly accept them!

But would you dare to send them here to this cottage – into its blessed darkness, its accursed damp?

Blessed darkness, accursed damp – the history of Iceland?

Pétur saddled his horse, Ljúf, and rode for six hours to get to her.

Which, however, was considerably less time than it took the postman in February. In general, he rarely travels much faster than at a walking pace; his second horse carries the post and provisions and they stop at different farms to deliver it, or else to gossip, tell and hear the news, pick up new letters and parcels and carry them onward. Every person has his own role. Or gives himself a role. Pétur rides quickly, stops nowhere, hardly looks around, is of course forced at times to ride near to farms in order to avoid soggy ground, twice has to pass almost right before the farmhouse door. Now then, where might the priest be headed? people ask, burning with curiosity. And spring is in the air. It's late April. Spring is the season between winter and summer. It's the time of growth.

And the time of year when we're most severely punished for having settled here.

But the month of April is bright, you can say that about the bastard, surprisingly bright and always full of unabashed optimism. The migratory birds stream out from the horizon with their singing and the promise of summer in their wings – it must be one of the wonders of the Earth that they come here voluntarily year after year, century after century. Or what in the world drives them northward into the cold and light, from warmer and more merciful lands down south; are they simply stupid? Because if Icelanders had had wings, the country would have been emptied no later than the sixteenth century.

But there Pétur rides, and rather swiftly, at that. Ljúf scares up a snipe, and shortly afterwards Pétur hears a plover and is so overcome with gratitude to the migratory birds for never giving up on us that he feels like singing. It's so wonderful that they come here to us, fill the sky with their singing and optimism and make everything lighter, we should thank them better and more often than we do. For this reason, Pétur halts his horse, dismounts, and thanks the birds. Thanks them for displaying to us, undeservedly, that beautiful devotion of theirs, to come here year after year from a warmer and better existence; thank you, smartly dressed plover, long-legged godwit, thank you, you loquacious redshank and you, snipe, who can resemble a fist as you hide yourself between tussocks, among reeds, under riverbanks, springing up when someone approaches and changing into a note of the Lord in the air. Thank you for not giving up on us but coming year after year with your optimism, and the unwavering belief that life always wins, that no forces can bring it to its knees, thank you for assuring us that no darkness can overcome the light of spring. Thank you, says Reverend Pétur, before sitting down on a wet tussock and bursting into tears.

Shameful, he thinks, if anyone were to see me, crying on a sopping-wet tussock – and just where do you think you're headed?

Where are you headed; he doesn't try to answer this.

Or doesn't dare.

Simply allows the pain in his chest to have its outlet. Very seldom does he allow himself that, afraid of . . . giving in. Is fearful of what will be released when he does. Is fearful of breaking, as now. Fortunately, he's alone, at least; no-one can see him.

Alone? No, that's not right, because there is his horse, sandy grey, a beautiful mare, a good companion, with that beautiful name, Ljúf (Sweet, Gentle).

Ljúf stops plucking at the grass, which is still rather scanty and tasteless following the winter, saunters the three or four steps to her master and nibbles at his shoulder, lovingly and concernedly. Nibbles at both of Pétur's shoulders, then blows a little in his ear when his crying seems as if it won't subside, because the tears continue to flow from their deep well of pain and loss.

He cries because spring is in the air.

Because life is picking up after the long, slow winter months, heavy with darkness, hostile weather, cries because the snipe is back, so charmingly optimistic but seemingly sorely vulnerable to the cold spells that are doubtless yet to come. He cries because even if the light wins now, it will eventually become darkness again, cries because his wife, Halla, has hands of light and a delicate mouth and had looked strangely at Pétur when he saddled Ljúf and packed up the books, cries because he doesn't remember when he last took the initiative to hold her in his arms, to kiss her, hug her, or just whisper some amusing nonsense in her ear as he did so often in the past, a thousand years ago, as one should do, as one must do, and more often than often, at that, for it is the only way to counteract the thorns of life. He cries because he received a letter in which some of the letters written in it barked at him like dogs, he cries because now the grass will turn green, lambs will soon be born, birds will soon be laying their eggs and soon life will triumph, cries because the frost will soon leave the ground, which will make it easier for graves to be dug. Cries because Eva died in his arms, just seven years old, afraid of the darkness that awaited her while still being worried for her father.

She'd woken from her feverish stupor, opened her blue eyes and seen her father lying next to her, as he'd done since they came home, wet, bedraggled, cold. She opened her eyes, tried to smile, stroked his unshaven cheeks and whispered, as if to console him: Don't be sad, Papa, you mustn't be sad. She whispered it clearly and in a tone so laden with responsibility and concern that it was as if she'd aged by decades, matured in an instant and acquired a deep wisdom of life. Daddy, she whispered twice more.

An hour later she was gone and he lay there alone with his useless prayers, his worthless grief and her touch on his face – and for this reason, he has had a full beard ever since. As if he believes that, in this way, he can preserve Eva's final touch on his face.

TO WHAT DO WE OWE THE HONOUR?

No! This won't do, says Pétur, so loudly and abruptly that Ljúf starts in alarm. The priest wipes away his tears and stands up, his rear end drenched. It's all so wet and unpleasant, the frost is leaving the earth, it's as if winter is really letting go, that there is in fact some gentleness to be found in the world, at least the sun rises higher with each passing day, the migratory birds stream out of the horizon like cheerful messages from life – but the cold will still shoot some of them down. Pétur embraces Ljúf, breathes in the smell of her mane, drinks in her warmth and trust, and the mare closes her big eyes for a moment, as if from happiness.

Just where do you think you're headed, priest?

Where the magnetic needle of the heart points.

The magnetic needle of the heart. Wittily put. But is that good, and do you think it's justifiable, couldn't it be dangerous, even wrong to listen to the heart? You know that it's intrinsically untameable and can easily contribute to disruption if you don't control it, don't hold the reins. The heart doesn't hesitate, if necessary, to split marriages, including families, it doesn't hesitate to take discord and difficulties over security and stability; he who follows his heart can end up deeply hurting those closest to him. Moderation is the anchor of life; it is the balance. One finds one's place in existence and stands there, keeps balance in an unstable world. Withstands trauma, temptations, earthquakes in the heart. This is how one finds a purpose, and then everything grows, then everything around you flourishes and you're blessed. Quite frankly: can this trip be justified?

No, probably not.

In some places the earth is soft and springy under horse and man, they make quick progress, Ljúf is spirited following their rest stops, or maybe just eager to carry the man she loves quickly onward in the hope of his taking comfort in the speed. Some horses find it hard to see people crying, but they have no way to comfort us with an embrace and because of it their eyes sometimes seem filled with sadness. In some places, the ground is so springy that it seems about to break open, rip apart, as if intending to swallow man and horse. Swallow and then send them straight down to hell to serve their sentence. Which, of course, is very unfair, because the mare is innocent of Pétur's sins, whatever sins they might be. Innocent of all the sins of the world; all she does is graze, rub herself against rocks, pee, shit, dream now and then of a powerful stallion, whinny when someone strokes her, scratches her behind the ears.

Reverend Pétur's betrayal and sins.

So is it always a sin and an unequivocal betrayal to follow one's heart, to go where its quivering needle points, even if it means that worlds will perish?

Horse and the sky, tell us, which is nobler, to suffocate the voices of the heart in the hope that the world will remain unchanged, or to cling to emotions, surrender to them and simultaneously transform existence into uncertainty? To suffocate one's heart, thereby sacrificing oneself, possibly betraying oneself, or to live in harmony with oneself, following the magnetic needle of the heart?

Somewhere it says – and has been taken as true: "It's impossible to live as a human being without breaking one's treasures at least once."

Is that so?

It's useless to ask, since neither horse nor sky answers, much less the earthworm – after all, Guðríður's farm is still surrounded by hard-frozen snow, the earth is still frost-laden, the earthworms are so deep underground that they don't hear the man's questions.

The farm stands at an altitude of about two hundred metres and is therefore closer to heaven than other farms in this district. Pétur has halted the horse a good distance from the farmhouse, or the cottage, rather; Uppsalir is an unimpressive sight, standing there in the hard-frozen snow. A large tussock, an abode of mice, hardly of men. The mare has begun to tire out, breathes heavily, and Pétur rises and falls with her breathing. The horse's large heart beats fast from exhaustion, but yours, from stupidity, Pétur mutters to himself, before clicking his tongue softly in one cheek. Ljúf raises her head and walks slowly forward, towards the cottage, towards fate, the tussock that takes on the appearance of a human dwelling when horse and man draw nearer. Windows appear, or screens, in any case; there's the door, and now two dogs come running towards them; one is barking, the other is silent, but both are exuberant: a visit, brothers and sisters; now this is something new! Shortly afterwards, three children rush out of the dark cottage and immediately squint in the glare from the snow, hold their hands before their eyes, eager to see

80

the unexpected visitor. Pétur rides into the farmyard, straight-backed on his Ljúf, with her erect mane, and then the farmer comes out, rather tall, thin, sinewy, dark-haired, with long, strong arms and sharp facial features. So sharp that he resembles a Greek sculpture. Probably a little younger than Pétur, but slightly stooping, as if the toil, the demanding heathland farm, is beginning to bend him a bit. His expression, though, is determined, and he waits until Pétur has dismounted before saying hello, perhaps uncomfortable about having to look up at someone to greet him. Good day to you, he finally says, and both dogs sniff eagerly at Pétur's shoes, which the farmer completely ignores, looking at them might come across as curiosity, even jealousy, because they are good shoes, a bit worn, of course, a bit damaged, but still good. Such shoes can never be anything but visitors here in this cottage. Yet Pétur is not well-to-do. The children, three girls, devour the visitor with their eyes, and the youngest, probably about five years old, sticks her thumb in her mouth, as if her finger is so shy that it wants to hide there.

I know your name. I've heard about you. To what do we owe the honour of this visit? the farmer asks, yet he doesn't look at Pétur, but the mare.

To what do we owe the honour – the heath farm Uppsalir isn't on the beaten path, it's hardly on any path; it's simply off the path. Maybe not extremely remote, yet it's a walk of just over three hours to the nearest farm, which is quite a distance, a good five, six hours in all if you don't have a horse, and it's rare that you have time to spare for such a trip. For some reason, Pétur hesitates in answering. It's even as if he doesn't know what's stopping him; his heart suddenly starts beating fast, what's wrong with you, he thinks, as another thought almost immediately cuts through his question: Is she inside, can she hear me, is she listening?

He looks down at his shoes, from there at the girls, smiles at them, the oldest, fourteen years old, giggles. He clears his throat, looks at the farmer.

Clears his throat and Guðríður bites her lip as she stands there in the farm passageway, so deep inside that the daylight doesn't quite reach therein; so she's hidden in the darkness, for the most part, but is close enough to the door to hear what's going on outside, she hears the voices, the clearing of throats, the mare's tread; she heard him dismount.

WHAT COMES NEXT, WHERE ARE THESE TIMES HEADED?

What's going on now? her husband had said, when Sámur, the older dog, began barking. Snotra was quiet, as usual, she'd never been one to bark and because of it came across as more thoughtful. What's going on now, who has come? said her husband, and he stood up and peered out the window, whose pane was made of membrane rather than glass. He'd just come in to eat, had been out at the sheep shed all morning. Yes, the ground up here on the heath is still frozen, but spring is on the way, lambing will soon begin, though it's far too early for it, as usual. Everything generally happens too early at this time of year. The spring, the birds, lambing, the light. Sometimes it's as if God, the devil, or fate is laying a trap for life up here in the north. To lure it out of its den – it lowers its defences, it bares its soul, but then the cold clamps its irons around the fragile spring vegetation or it snows over the newly hatched eggs. But now lambing will soon begin, and there is much needing doing. Guðríður's husband has in fact just returned home, had been working on a fishing crew down at Arnarstapi, fished from there in February and March, into April, on a boat owned by a well-to-do farmer in that area; relatively recently returned after a nine-week exile. Came home with thirty fish and slightly more credit with the merchant. Guðríður had seen to everything in the meantime, the animals, the girls, the house, leaving little room for thoughts or reading; some nights she just dropped off exhausted. Yet she had, silly fool that she is, used one precious day, wasted precious energy, to take her reply to the priest's letter down to Bær. This will certainly give them something to gossip about, she had thought. She hadn't wanted to stop at all, didn't even accept a cup of whey from them. Such a hurry! Jóhannes, the district manager, had said; he hadn't even got a chance to ask her about the letter – because writing to a priest in another parish, and to that particular priest, what might that mean?

Sometimes it's as if existence is suffocating her, sometimes it's as if her life lacks oxygen – but then Sámur started barking.

Her husband got up, peered out the window, well now, a rider, he said in surprise, and the three girls ran down the passageway. It's hardly the postman again, damn it, that would be a bit too much, Gísli had said, looking at her as if she were responsible for the unexpected arrival of the postman while he was away; Guðríður's husband's name is Gísli, a common name, yet fairly weighty. Gísli had been surprised when he came home from Arnarstapi and the girls told him enthusiastically about the unexpected visit of the postman. Who stopped for a good hour, drank an awful lot of coffee, the eldest girl had never seen anything like it, and it made her quite angry; in just over an hour, a weekly portion of the home's coffee disappeared into that talkative man.

Talkative, curious, thickset, brawny. So big that everything in the family room seemed to diminish in size when he came in, the home shrank and he grew larger and stronger-looking in proportion. He sat down on the edge of the bed in the middle of the family room, sat there with his legs splayed, and there was something immovable about him, as if he could withstand everything, that everything would break against this big man. He looked around as if he were taking the measure of the farm, then fixed his dark but small eyes on Guðríður and cleared his throat so vigorously that Sámur jumped up and barked.

It's out of the way to come here, he repeated, somewhat out of the way, he added, said it three times as he sat there, possibly to justify his tremendous coffee consumption, his devouring of all the pancakes that Guðríður served him, which whittled away at the household's quickly dwindling rye flour, but she spared nothing in the belief that Gísli would soon be returning with new provisions from the merchant. But Reverend Pétur is not a man one easily says no to. You don't know him? Yet here I have a letter to you from that man.

Tsk tsk. Some even say he's an atheist, did you know that? An atheistic priest, what comes next, where are these times headed, everything's turning upside down! Cities overseas are becoming so incredibly well lit that it's as if night will never fall over them again, is that good, I ask myself, and out west in America the steam trains have horns from which a booming voice communicates information to passengers. The machines have begun talking, so what comes next, when are they going to start ordering us around, good housewife, this hardly bodes well. And the people here continue to flee west across the ocean, flee so eagerly that our numbers are falling rapidly, soon we'll be down below seventy thousand, apparently, that's hardly positive, but anyway, damn it, then maybe there'll be more room for the rest of us who are steadfast enough to go nowhere, show the mountains and our ancestors loyalty. And to top it all off, some people want women to have the right to vote! I love women, you're free to write that down and underline and send it to any country whatsoever, it would be a miserable world if we didn't have them, everything would be rather poor and grey. But women have never had the right to vote simply because they don't have the minds for it. It's not in their nature to reason logically about the issues that require our vote. This isn't something I'm inventing, because women were placed by God himself at man's side, to help him – to help, take note. Not to carry burdens alone, not to hold them for him, no, but to support him if necessary. There's a big difference – I would call it the chief difference. And as far as I understand, the Bible makes it quite clear that God never gave women the right to vote; should we then go against God, the Lord himself, the commander of life, the emperor of heaven? And do you think that is perhaps why the priest is an atheist? The postman asked Guðríður, who filled his cup with coffee for the third time and added to the pancake stack in front of the guest, who enthusiastically helped himself to another one.

She bustled, listened, said yes when appropriate, you don't say, goodness me, quickly sensed that that sufficed, the visitor was satisfied that his big voice ruled the roost. But of course: he has a lot to say, the widely travelled man that he is. He'd come all the way from down south in Reykjavík. The three girls sat straight-legged on the bed opposite the postman. It's so rare to see a person who has been in Reykjavík, let alone just a few days ago; he may as well have been from another world. It was so exciting, in fact, that they chose to sit in the family room and listen to the visitor rather than be outside with the horses. But the eldest had had quite enough of the man's coffee-drinking and pancake-eating; she went twice to check on the coffee and flour supplies.

Do you think that's why the priest is an atheist?

Guðríður hesitated to answer, unsure of whether this question had been directed to her, whether the postman was really interested in hearing her views. Nor was she certain that Reverend Pétur's possible atheism could be connected in any way with the lighting of cities, fleeing the country, talking machines, women's suffrage; in any case, he didn't wait for a response, but went on after taking another drink of coffee. No, I am not saying that they're all like Reverend Pétur, all things considered; perhaps there are very few of them, in fact, judging by what I've heard. I can't say that I know the fellow; I'm just the one who passes through, knows everything, is familiar with no-one, and, unfortunately, I've never attended one of his Masses. I would like to attend one, though, and aim determinedly to do so sooner or later; apparently, they can be a bit different, so to speak, but leave no-one indifferent. Some people have rather strong opinions about them, in fact. Which is refreshing. Most priests are as inspirational as cow's asses.

The postman paused for a moment as if to consider this simile of his, then seemed to accept it inwardly, at least giving a quick laugh and shaking his head as if cheerfully.

But inspirational or not, the priest seems somewhat heavy-hearted. I can tell such things. I'm very sensitive, which is actually a flaw; I can feel too much compassion for others. And I've noticed that people usually do better, in every sense, if they have less compassion for their neighbour. It's a burden, compassion, and, naturally, kindness often makes it difficult for someone to say no to people, for example when I'm asked to go quite far out of my way to make a delivery to someone. Because that's why I'm sitting here with you now. No, it isn't easy to be sensitive and a person of the better sort. But Reverend Pétur can be sarcastic, so sarcastic that the Evil One himself avoids quarrelling with him. Do you know each other, then?

It wasn't until silence had subjugated the whole room that Guðríður realised that that had been a real question, that the postman had stopped in order to let her have her say; he put down his cup of coffee, with his twelfth, thirteenth, or fourteenth pancake half-eaten in his stocky right hand, his small, dark eyes in his rugged, weathered face looking firmly at her, enquiringly, curious. She looked at her girls: the youngest was asleep, had given up on the visitor's gabble, the second eldest sniffed, coughed, but Björg, the oldest girl, looked sternly at the postman. Guðríður smiled to herself, both at how much Björg resembled her father with that look and how shocked she was at the man's zeal for drinking coffee, eating pancakes. Know him, she said at last, rubbing her hips, suddenly feeling her heart beating faster; it would be overgenerous to say that.

Overgenerous, what's overgenerous? said the postman, sticking a pancake in his mouth, he ate seventeen, her daughter would inform her afterwards, and later her father, when he came home. The priest instructs me to go out of my way to bring you the letter, instead of leaving it at Bær, as usual. I would call that something.

Was he insinuating something? Fishing for something? Something he could perhaps carry from farm to farm, from parish to parish? Strange how her heart was beating. So quickly, so heavily. It was clanging, in fact. Why are you acting so, little creature, she thought, but her heart didn't reply, naturally; it just kept clanging. She exhaled slowly, looked straight at the postman and her temper flared when she saw the obvious curiosity in his face. If not the nosiness. Her anger gave her confidence, and then her composure returned. Guðríður gazed at the man icily, with a sharp, dry, impersonal expression. Knew from experience that it was an expression that could throw people off – and the postman seemed startled. He hid it well, of course, but she saw that he hesitated. I've never met the priest, she finally said, in that polite tone of voice of hers that is so neutral and controlled that it seemed to contain not a shred of doubt. No uncertainty or hesitation, just certainty, just irrefutable facts.

The priest is, as the postman is obviously aware, one of the editors of the journal *Nature and World*. You may recall that I subscribed to it several times. And you may possibly also recall that some weeks ago, a parcel addressed to the same magazine was waiting for you down at Bær. That parcel contained an article by me that will apparently be published in the next issue. The priest is handling the article, and his letter probably contains some comments on it. I don't know why he has asked that you deliver the letter to me directly; perhaps that is how it is ordinarily done, little do I know, this is my first article. The priest is educated, I am completely uneducated, so I doubtless need to be corrected. I am just a woman. Would the postman like more coffee?

No, he declined her offer, perhaps fortunately, because her daughter might have lost her temper and been unable to restrain herself from asking if he intended to finish the household's store of coffee. He declined but asked, almost as if alarmed, so the housewife has an article in the journal? Yes, she said, I'm publishing an article. Was going to add, reflexively, which is of course shameful, but just managed to stop herself, bit her lip, didn't want to lose her advantage and hand him back his self-confidence on a platter. Might I ask about what? The earthworm. What, about the earthworm? exclaimed the postman, so surprised that his deep voice became almost a shriek. Yes, she said, narrowing her eyes a little, making them cold again. The postman knows, of course, that earthworms are hermaphroditic, which is why the problem of women's suffrage would never need to be discussed by them. In that, they have come much further than human beings. Of course I've written about them, wouldn't the postman have done so as well? she asked, in her neutral, almost impersonal voice and the postman, that big man, scratched his beard, gave a quick laugh, fidgeted a bit on the edge of the bed, looked down at his feet, she's quite something, your mama, he finally said to the three girls on the bed opposite, one of them asleep.

What a pity to have missed the postman, said Gísli when he came home from Arnarstapi, I understand that he's an interesting man with a lot to tell. But I certainly didn't expect him to make a detour here, and that carrying a letter to you from none other than Reverend Pétur Jónsson. People say he's an atheist, but that he's still able to provide solace. I have always found that curious, and have difficulty accepting it. And he sends you a letter, which is carried all the way here, and which you say has to do with the article; is that the usual procedure?

I don't know, I've never published an article before.

And was it because of the article that you answered, then? Jóhannes said that you hadn't wanted to stop, as if the devil was biting at your heels, he said.

I know nothing about the devil, but I felt I needed to answer quickly and well; it's not every day that I get to publish an article, I didn't want to keep them waiting too long for an answer.

Might the priest then come here in person if you send him another article?

I sent the article to the editorial board in Stykkishólmur, but apparently he is also on the board despite not living there, Guðríður had said, as she continued to wash Gísli's clothing, the oilskins that are also useful for the outdoor farm work, quite rainproof, protecting him quite well from wet, blowing snow, the devil's spit. She wanted to get the fish slime and fish smell out of them – she disliked that smell. Her husband muttered something she didn't catch. The priest has offered to lend me books, she said, as if addressing the clothing, the water, the soap. He can obviously see that they would do me some good.

It's quite generous of him, but I still don't understand why the postman had to bring the letter all the way here, and I expect that people will generally be surprised about it. So have you become some sort of penfriend of that reverend?

She kneaded the oilskins vigorously, grimaced at the odour of fish guts that rose from them, muttered, what do I know, hardly knowing herself whether that was an answer – which was at the same time no answer – to Gísli's question as to whether she and the priest had become penfriends, which is of course a ridiculous thought; it was astonishing enough that he had taken the trouble to write to her. She knows no better than Gísli why the post had to be delivered by the postman to her personally, as if it were from the king himself, God himself, instead of leaving it, like all other letters and parcels, with the district manager at Bær. As he has, until now, done without exception with letters from Gísli's brother in Canada, or Guðríður's mother in Norðfjörður and occasional periodicals for her, *Nature and World, Skírnir, Andvari, The Agricultural Digest,* sometimes even the Norwegian popular-science periodical *Kringsjaa,* when they could afford it or when she was insistent enough that he agreed to the expense. The postman has always left their post at Bær and taken from there whatever they have had to send, for example Gísli's letters in reply to his brother's. They're short letters, not so much news to tell from here at Uppsalir, mainly the same old refrain, today I cut turf and trussed it, Guðríður and I raked the heavy hay all yesterday, dried it and just now raked it into hayricks; it's autumn now; it's winter, dear brother, and I managed to increase my flock by two gimmers this autumn, we had an excellent hay yield, and I ventured it would last the winter. Hopefully I won't be punished for my arrogance with sea ice, cold and a shortage of hay next spring. Sometimes it worries me enough to keep me awake at night.

He has lain awake at night worried because he added two lambs to the usual number he keeps over the winter, in the hope of increasing his flock and increasing his income accordingly. Two lambs that grew into those fine gimmers and will hopefully bear two lambs each, if God allows it. Yet let's not expect too much, it's arrogance and ingratitude to ask for too much. God grant that I won't be punished for my imprudence and arrogance with a hay shortage and snow-storms this spring, he wrote in his last letter to his brother, who had settled in Winnipeg twelve years earlier and recently established an undertaker's service along with a German and a Swede.

The most reliable business in the world, dear brother, it said in the last letter from the west. Death never fails us, it's tireless, never rests, it's as busy in the sunshine as in dark, cloudy weather, in famines as in times of plenty, its share prices never fall, but rather rise quite frequently. The business is going to flourish, brother, that I can tell you for sure. There are a great deal of both Swedish and German people here, and a slew of Icelanders as well. Plenty of future customers, we sometimes say when no-one else can hear us. Mark my words, in ten years I'll be wealthier than a merchant in Iceland, with a paunch and a top hat – why are you still hanging about there on that little farm of yours? Independence, you say. Yes, all Icelanders dream of being independent, naturally. Of not needing to take orders from others, waking up and being their own masters. But the obsession with independence is more often than not so overriding that it enslaves us, condemns us to lives of hard labour and makes us old before our time, and also, which I feel to be even worse, makes us so dependent on the merchant that all talk of freedom is a ridiculous delusion. You lie awake at night worrying about having kept two lambs more than the number your farm has normally been able to accommodate, you toil by the sweat of your brow so as not to have to take orders from others, labour so zealously that when you're finally able to stand up straight financially, you've grown so old, worn and bent from the strain, so broken from the struggle, that you can no longer straighten your spine. That's how most independent men in Iceland end up, stooping, bent-backed. The only ones in Iceland who achieve independence can't stand straight-backed. Come here to the west. I can easily lend you the money for the fare. There are excellent opportunities here for hard-working men like you!

Maybe we should just go, Guðríður had said when Gísli read her the letter, there will be a school for the girls there, she added, and her mouth went dry and she felt a tickling in her tailbone, as sometimes happens when she gets very excited or nervous about something – her tailbone is like a sensor or detector that picks things up and alerts her, making it hard for her not to start fidgeting. A school for the girls, yes, quite right, and at the same time, she thought – and a new world of knowledge for me. I'll learn English, have constant access to books, not like here, intermittently, coincidentally. But Gísli showed little interest, just muttered something that sounded like, not all journeys are profitable, and the matter was not discussed further.

Gísli answered his brother's letter the evening before he went south to Arnarstapi. Sat for over an hour writing the short letter, one must apply oneself to whatever one does. Sat there half-hunched, his brow furrowed in concentration, holding the shaft of his pen like a little rake.

Tsk tsk tsk, I think I'll let America be, or else Canada, I really don't see any need to distinguish between them, it's all one and the same viewed from here, and everything under the sky looks the same in the eyes of the Lord. I have no doubt that it's good to live there. You're free of the damned sea ice, and of course that lummox of a district manager, Jóhannes. But someone has to catch the fish here, someone has to look after the sheep. I know very well, brother, that Uppsalir will never be considered among the more noteworthy of farms, I'll hardly grow fat and ruddy here, and will likely never own a fine hat. However, I firmly believe that in just five to seven years, if I manage properly, we'll be able to move to a better, easier farm. Even down by the sea. Then I'll be able to supplement the farming by fishing from a dinghy, and maybe later my son will help me, should the Lord bless me soon with a beautiful, hardworking boy. Let me tell you, brother, that here in Iceland possibilities finally seem to be opening up. Yet I have no space here to prattle on about this, my energy is nearly spent, and I'm on my way to Arnarstapi for the fishing season. Good luck dealing with the dead, dear brother!

He took the letter with him, left it at Bær. Stopped only briefly, didn't want to go in and listen to the grumbling and boasting and ostentation of the damned district manager, yet accepted two ladlesful of whey at the farm door. Well then, so I'm on my way south to the fishing station, to do my nine to ten weeks there. A man's got to

91

do what he's got to do, otherwise everything goes to hell. The weather? Well, that, you know, when is it ever really good around here? Maybe at night, but then of course everyone's asleep! But apparently our countrymen in Canada often have the finest sunshine, warm sunshine for days at a time, so warm that you really have to wear fewer clothes. It's downright incredible to think of. I can hardly believe it. Yes, which reminds me, here's a letter that I need to get to the post-man, there are actually two of them, said Gísli, after quaffing the whey and on his way out the door, saying mm hmm and ah ha to the housewife's prattle, hardly bothering to respond to Jóhannes' blather, and having almost forgotten his errand when this about the sunshine in Canada sprang from him. Two letters, in fact, he said, handing them to the housewife as he said goodbye. Because he was in a hurry. A full day's walk south to Arnarstapi, and the days are shamefully short in February. As short and dreary as this crochety month that has been stuck in between the two longest months of the year, January and March. They're as long as death, it says somewhere, for much has been said and written about the two, but little about February sitting there between them like an excuse, like a hesitation, living not much longer than a fly and its days accordingly short. So Gísli has to hurry if he wants to take advantage of the sparse daylight, which he definitely wants to do; to have made it down to the sea by the time it gets dark. Nor did he care to linger after handing the letters over to the couple. Fine with the letter to Canada, nothing to be ashamed of there, but then there was the other one – to the journal in Stykkishólmur. Guðríður had written on the envelope: To the editors of *Nature and World*. Gísli knew well that Guðríður's letter would raise questions. Knew well that the couple would look hard at the envelope, trying to guess its contents. Imagined the look of astonishment on both their faces. The blessed housewife, who is little but kindness, let it be noted, just overly curious, and that damned district manager with his double chin and staring, bulbous haddock eyes. No, he doesn't have haddock eyes, of course, and they aren't particularly bulbous, either, it's just so much fun to consider them so. But now people will talk, first at Bær, and then throughout the entire bloody countryside – about how the cottagers at Uppsalir sent a letter to the fine folk in Stykkishólmur.

THEN SHE STEPS INTO THE LIGHT

When Gísli returns home from Arnarstapi, with thirty fish and renewed credit with the merchant, the entire village knows that the postman had needed, on the instructions of Reverend Pétur Jónsson, to make that considerable detour of his in order to deliver Guðríður the letter. And that she herself had, not terribly long afterwards, come all the way from Uppsalir with a letter to the priest.

So have you become some sort of penfriend of the priest's?

How am I to know, she muttered, bending over the laundry, the smell, the stench of her husband's nearly nine weeks of fishing. Hid herself in her work. Knew that he was waiting for her to show him the letter, which she didn't; she just couldn't bring herself to do so. For some reason, she wanted it to be hers alone. Even though she knew that it would hurt Gísli.

And then the priest himself comes to Uppsalir.

News of his visit will spread.

I know your name, says Gísli, when Pétur introduces himself. I've heard about you. Although he had first asked, to what do we owe the honour of this visit?

Guðríður didn't come out to the farmyard. I'll prepare something, she had said when Gísli went out, yet she didn't do anything at all, but rather followed her husband soon afterwards, but stopped inside the passageway where the darkness meets the daylight.

She stands at the divide, on the border, hidden by the darkness, drawn forth by the light.

She heard the visitor dismount, heard her husband greet him. Heard the visitor clear his throat and then realised that she was holding her breath, so eager to listen, to hear his voice, his tone, excited, nervous, because what if it's anxious, she dislikes such voices,

93

what if his voice is tinged with arrogance or – which is possibly even worse – if it's sharp, birdlike? How silly you are, you fool, she said to herself quietly, shaking her head, what does the tone of this man's voice matter, he's not a part of her life, her everyday existence, she'll hardly ever associate with him to any degree; and why are both Gísli and she so convinced that the visitor is Reverend Pétur? What does he look like, then, if this is he; how does he comport himself; does he move his hands much, are his eyes warm, his nose too big, his teeth in decent condition, is he as fat as a seal, short, of somewhat average height?

The man clears his throat again. I'm not certain it can be called an honour, he says. Forgive the disturbance, my name is Pétur Jónsson. The priest at— I know your name, and your parish, I've heard about you, interrupts Gísli, making Guðríður wince; it's so unlike her husband to interrupt others, let alone in that way, almost discourteously, as if throwing a punch at Pétur, even . . .

So this is him then, God help me, she mutters, half wanting to hit herself, slap herself in the face. Hidden there at the intersection of darkness and light, as if eavesdropping, she hopes that he speaks again . . . which he does, his voice a bit hesitant, perhaps in surprise at Gísli's reaction. Yes, right, it's not quite your parish, that's true, but I had some business to attend to, various errands that I'd gathered into one trip, so to speak, and then I remembered that Guðríður lives in these parts, and I brought along the books that I'd promised her. Made enquiries down there at Bær, about the precise location of your farm and the best way to get to it. The people there asked me to give you their regards. I really don't like sending books by post, they can be so fragile. To tell the truth, books can be more sensitive than both letters and people. So, since I was passing through this area, I decided to stop here. I assume you're her husband?

Apparently, Gísli answers, apparently.

Why does he answer in this way, and . . . what might Reverend Pétur look like? Is he similar to his voice, a bit gruff, warm but also with a sort of undertone or foundation that she doesn't quite grasp, not immediately, yet which likely matches his handwriting; how does that voice look, or rather, does our appearance always match our voice, or vice versa?

Pleased to hear it, says Pétur. Your wife has much to commend her, which you of course know better than others. Her article is fascinating. It made me think differently, which happens, I can say, far too seldom these days, unfortunately; I feel as if I have read so much, yes, but in doing so have lost the ability to be surprised. Man is overly inclined towards stagnation, to becoming trapped in his own arrogance, prejudices, all sorts of dross that diminishes him. And the earthworm; we tend too easily to regard that which is much smaller than us as insignificant or of less worth, let alone if it has a form or shape that seems unpleasant, if not repulsive – besides the fact that it is blind, and most at home in darkness – which earns it our contempt, the sister of arrogance. But some are given the ability to see more and deeper than others, see through prejudices, traditional views. Such people are less bound by their contemporary world and can therefore open their neighbour's eyes; can see what is hidden from the rest of us. They have the ability to enable people to see everything with new eyes. The environment and themselves. Your wife has that ability – the least I can do is lend her books. And since I am passing through the area, the least I can do is deliver them in person. And here you have three children, three beautiful girls. Sometimes God gives us treasures. How foolish and misfortunate of me not to have brought anything for you. Or what? Who knows what might be hidden in one's inner pockets? Now wait, let's see, and what do I find here but these pretty, bright sweets, three different types! How they got there is a complete mystery to me – but perhaps you don't want this sort of thing?

The girls don't answer, don't dare, are shy towards strangers, maybe also shy because of the way Pétur speaks, but then Gísli gives a little laugh, well, luck has certainly found you – you're perfectly safe to accept it, I hardly think the priest bites . . . except very gently, like a fly, says Pétur, with a brighter tone to his voice.

You've got to go out there now, you fool, she says softly to herself, startled by her own voice, stifled in the passageway, as if the house itself is talking to Guðríður, driving her out. It's simply shameful just standing there, eavesdropping, in hiding. Shameful. And silly.

Perhaps the priest would like to come in? says Gísli, his voice so loud now that he doubtless hopes it can be heard inside the house. Of course, he doesn't suspect that she is eavesdropping, there where the darkness meets the light. That she's standing there unseen a few metres from them, her tailbone so itchy that she's having a hard time standing still.

Thank you for the invitation, Pétur replies. If you'll permit me just to unsaddle my Ljúf first.

Somewhere here is a handful of hay for the horse; girls, go bring the horse some hay.

Guðríður hears them scurry light-footed away, run off, eager to be useful, to get to feed the horse, cuddle it, besides being over the moon about having sweets to suck on. It's no ordinary day here at the farm, having something so delightfully sweet melting in their mouths. It's like having a mouthful of sunshine. Or kisses, she thinks inadvertently in the passageway – and she doesn't have her husband in mind. When she realises this, she is startled, frightened by the thought, and is even more frightened about going out to the two men, which she, however, must do, it's unbearable to think of meeting the priest for the first time in the family room, where the cramped quarters, the sloping ceilings, create a closeness that is difficult to escape. She takes a deep breath and rattles off, in a low voice, as if praying: "Organic substances are those compounds that contain a vital force, plants or animals, but inorganic substances are all elements and compounds that are of a non-living nature."

Then she steps out into the light.

But hopefully, I'll leave the darkness behind, she thinks.

HOW DOES ONE LEAVE THE DARKNESS BEHIND?

She steps out. And a hundred and twenty years have passed since then.

She steps out and he cries on a tussock, his rear end sopping wet.

96

She steps out and something happens in the world when she smiles, are you her husband, apparently, apparently, but what is your wife's name? Her name is Hands of Light. Is that why you sat there crying on a tussock, your rear end sopping wet, and your horse couldn't console you? Pish, don't ask, she steps out, does she manage to leave the darkness behind?

She scratches her tailbone, then she smiles, shouldn't someone investigate that smile and then submit a report, is it permissible to smile in that way, can smiles change lives, shouldn't we discuss it, deliberate it, are you her husband, apparently, but you correspond with a poet who died half a century ago, is that good, is that a good example, life corresponding with death, and are you expecting an answer?

Everyone dies in the end, earthworms and people. You're dead, and therefore have come further. She steps out. How do you leave the darkness behind?

She steps out and everyone is dead.

Miss You Baby, Sometimes:
Man Invented the Devil
to Bear His Sins

EVEN IN SUNSHINE, DARK VALLEYS CAN BE FOUND
WITHIN US – BUT MR ÁSMUNDUR IS HERE!

Suddenly I feel so terribly dizzy that I have to lean on the reception desk so as not to lose my balance; for a second, I'm entirely uncertain of where I am – in what place, at what time, in what life, and yes, in what universe. Slowly, however, my surroundings come clear, no longer concealing themselves in my dizziness – and I'm still in the foyer of the hotel that was once the area's elementary school. In the years when the fjord was more densely populated and the sheep were scattered like beautiful words about the slopes. Did I fall asleep, did I lose consciousness? And where is my beer? I mutter, before setting eye on a number of densely written sheets of A5-size paper covering part of the reception desk, numbered at the bottom though seemingly unorganised, almost as if they had bled over the desktop; page twelve lies athwart page thirty, page fifty-seven next to the first: "Eiríkur of Oddi. The man who has an electric guitar, dogs, three dead puppies, a shotgun to fire at lorries or perhaps fate. What more does he have?"

Hesitantly, I shuffle through a few of the pages, catch names . . . there, pistols become more and more accurate, there, the magnetic needle of the heart quivers and the earthworms are blind poets in the dust. "Good luck dealing with the dead, dear brother!" I read on and slowly recall the contents, they come to me in fragments, like sheep returning from the mountains in the autumn. "She stands there where the darkness meets the light . . ."

Where did this come from?

Wasn't the idea just to write something about that Eiríkur whom

I watched disappear towards the mouth of the fjord – as the opening lines suggest?

Yet I have no idea where Eiríkur was going, and I honestly know almost nothing about this man. Except that from a distance he looked like a sad rock star, who has dogs, a shotgun, three dead puppies, and probably fired his gun at lorries because of them. I would really like to know where all of this comes from. These stories, and why the need to put them on paper was so urgent that I had no choice but to comply.

Where does what we don't understand come from?

But man knows so little. It's scientifically proven, remember; I read an article about it in a reputable periodical. We're constantly adding to our knowledge, of course, yet it seems that the more we know, the less we understand.

That's the paradox, and we live within it.

In the dining room, Sóley laughs.

It's good to hear her laugh. Something about her laughter makes the world brighter.

But she's still on the phone.

Yes, she's still on the damned phone.

I look over the papers. At least seventy pages, albeit only in size A5, but filled with small, dense handwriting, so unreadable that at first glance it looks like code. It must have taken quite some time to write down all these stories, all these destinies, breaths. Weeks, one might have thought. Which, of course, doesn't add up – because I hadn't written a single letter of it when I was sitting in the cosy lounge before, drinking beer, reading an article postulating that humanity is trapped in a web of ignorance. Then I came here to the reception desk, a little disconcerted by the article, even alarmed, and noticed that it was about eleven in the morning. Right now . . .

. . . I look up at the line of twelve clocks on the wall behind the reception desk, showing the time in New Delhi, Hong Kong, Tokyo, Moscow, Sydney, Los Angeles, New York, Budapest, London, Paris,

Addis Ababa, Iceland. Eleven cities, one country. And three hands on each clock, because it takes at least three to keep track of time. The thinnest hand is constantly in motion, it never stops, dashes bewilderedly, breathlessly, even desperately around and around, pursuing what it can never catch, what perpetually gets away, though always just barely. Thin, if not emaciated from all the toil. The medium-sized hand moves slightly slower. It appears calm, but that's an illusion, because it's constantly quivering with inner tension. Knows that it can never rest, driven along by the restlessness of its thinner brother. The third, however, moves so slowly that it has put on weight in its leisure. Twelve clocks that measure time devotedly, accurately, yet which all appear different.

Accordingly, time is never identical, nowhere the same, and thereby is everywhere unlike itself. But the clock that measures time in Iceland has stopped, it looks to me, it doesn't move, the thin hand, the emaciated one, has given up, hangs there exhausted, maybe lifeless in mid-air, no longer measuring anything. Except possibly its own death.

Here you are, talking to yourself.

Sóley is in the doorway to the dining room, with her phone in one hand – the phone is warm, of course, from all those words – and she looks at me with that smile of hers. You were on the phone, I say, mainly just to say something, buy myself time while I think of a way to hide the papers on the table.

Aw, yes, sorry for taking so long, but that was Dísa. You hardly know her; it hasn't been terribly long since she came here to the fjord. She met Ágúst of Hof and fell for him. And he for her, he had no choice, you should just see her, beauty itself! You're so pretty, my sister said once as we three sat here one winter night killing a bottle of grappa, that I'm half sorry I'm not a lesbian. Dísa was the city child personified when she came here with Ágúst, with Westside Reykjavík written all over her – she won't last long in the country-side, people said. Do you remember Gústi, by the way?

Oh, I say, we remember as long as we can, and then we forget, and it isn't always certain that that forgetfulness is fair.

Sóley laughs softly, no, and you don't have to remember everything, and don't you have to forget something, anyway, to make room for something new? Poor Gústi has never really been what one might call front-page news, yet has a certain radiance or magnetism that some women latch on to and become addicted to. I've never understood his charm, I suppose I'm just not receptive to it, and felt that he never deserved Dísa. And in any case, it didn't last long between them. Yet it was Gústi and not her who gave up on the rigours of farm life three or so years ago, moved south, got a job at a large warehouse in the city, works mostly in the freezer, I think; he's frozen there and well preserved. Still, they managed to hang together for five years, had their girl Védís, who is a treasure, but by then that city girl and Westsider Dísa had become so attached to the fjord, the animals, the sparse population, that she couldn't think of moving away and took over the farm when Gústi gave up. Plunged herself into debt in order to buy his share in the place. Took over not only the farm but his mother as well, because the old woman stubbornly refused to leave Hof in any other way than horizontally. Shouldn't Dísa have got a discount on the farm's price for that? But no-one can criticise Dísa's farming; it's exemplary.

I saw that, I say, glad to remember it, glad to have noticed it as I drove past the farm. Took note of the apparent abundance at Hof, how stately it all seemed, the buildings beautiful, the door to the farmhouse wide open, as if everyone was welcome. And a great fortification of hay rolls.

Yes, she's so industrious, my dear Dísa. Of course, she gets help from most of us, if needed, she's just there by herself with Védís and the old woman, Lúna . . . who has seen it all, as you might vaguely recall. Was a member of parliament for the Progressive Party for one term, a long-time columnist for Channel Two. People enjoyed listening to this cheeky, elderly countrywoman with opinions on everything, her gruff camel voice saturated with life experience. She turned seventy last year, enjoys a splash of sherry most days, learns languages online and has become remarkably adept at French and Spanish. And has a boyfriend in his eighties, none other than old Kári of Botn – one could never have seen that coming! But no-one is safe from love, of course, as the two of us could probably testify. Dísa often calls me or comes here when she knows that I don't have many guests – only three at the moment, and the first foreign guests since January! You may have seen them out in the pool: a Canadian couple with their daughter. The mother and her daughter are related to Eiríkur; they got in touch with him this spring and he invited them to his and Elías's dinner party, which they're holding for the second year in a row. They arrived just over two weeks ago, got out of quarantine this morning and have barely left the pool since. Just in time, to get out of quarantine I mean, because the party is tonight, just so you know. But Dísa manages my bookings page, so she knows that it's at least an hour until the coach arrives with the first group of the summer. Well, the first group of the year – and maybe the last. The virus has hit us pretty hard. But Dísa can be so pleasantly enthusiastic, she's passionate about so many things, politics, world affairs, global warming, the latest books, and now, last but not least, this power-plant project here in the north that's been ratcheted up to full swing to mitigate the economic impact of the virus, or so they say. Using the virus as an excuse. "We Put People First" is their mantra. Did you get another beer, by the way; would you like one?

Huh, another, yes, no, I mean no, two is enough, especially in the morning, and I drank red wine with your sister Rúna before I came here, but thanks anyway, I say, sorry that she stopped talking. Her voice is both bright and husky and seems to come from deep down in her throat. She looks at me now, as if thoughtfully, with a touch of sadness in her eyes, but then smiles.

Can a smile be a drug? I think – but then remember the clock. It has stopped, I say, pointing above me; the clock that measures the time here in Iceland has stopped.

Sóley: That's right! Acting up, I see . . . well, at least we won't age in the meantime. Still, this won't do, hold on, she says, disappearing back into the dining room as I watch her, watch her walk away, look at her slender back and think what I think. She returns with a long pole, knocks softly on the Icelandic clock, wake up, time, she says, and is maybe a witch or a god, because time wakes up, it gives a start and commences passing again. The birds sing anew, the world starts to grow older once more.

Well, what should I do with you, my poor thing? says Sóley, having put the pole that wakes time back in its place. The clock appears to have stopped for only one or two minutes, hardly any noticeable difference between it and the others, the medium-sized hands all in the same place, but none displaying the same time.

There's a coach on the way, full of Japanese tourists, forty or so, and when the three of them out there in the pool are added, then . . . and my Ómar will of course come out soon, she says thoughtfully.

Ómar?

Who might that be? So is she married, can that be? Is it justifiable for one person to have such amber eyes, that nearly invisible hesitation, that smile that's a drug?

I feel jealousy gnawing at me from the inside as she looks down, muttering something, and then looks up. Oh, what is this? she says in surprise, goes to the reception desk, pushes aside the sheets of paper. I recognise your handwriting, she says. Remember, you called it the devil's handwriting. Said you'd learned to write in hell, always so amusingly dramatic. Hell, of course, is the perfect place for a writer to develop his craft; isn't human nature on clearest display there? Oh, don't be so stressed, I'm not prying, I won't even try to read this, how would I be able to, anyway, no-one but you can under-stand these scribbles, you and the devil, of course, if what you say is true. But that's quite a lot of pages, the equivalent of a novel, I'd say. So you've started working again, oh, how happy that makes me! You once told me that you existed only while you were writing – according to that, you're back in existence. But I must admit that I was half insulted when you said that to me back in the day . . . no, what prudishness is that, half insulted? It really hurt me. If you only existed while you were writing, what was it then to be with me; half an existence, padding? You probably saw how shocked I was, and hurried to add, in an attempt to defend yourself, as sweet as you could be: I don't exist if I can't write. I'm not sure it was a great consolation. I could be so stupid at the time, and wanted to be your everything. But you know, it's as if you've changed. You're so quiet, which seems to make me want to talk more. Rúna also mentioned this, and that it had the same effect on her, she said she'd blathered as if life itself were at stake. When I think of how talkative you were! But tell me to shut up. It's as if I can't stop. You've got to say something.

I smile to hide my insecurity. Feel my heart beating heavier, feel that my blood has begun streaming at an alarming rate, gushing towards my heart – that it will soon hit it with great force, turning my heart into a ship in peril at sea. Little chance of rescue.

She laughs softly . . . goodness, what look is that? she says.

Sorry, I say, manage to say it unashamedly, clear my throat; but I'm just not myself, and . . . what, I ask, because she's looking away from me, staring at the scrawled-upon pages on the reception desk, obviously surprised. Isn't this, she asks, without looking up . . . yes, I'll be darned, all of these pages are written on the hotel's letterhead. Can that be right? Because it's completely impossible that you wrote all this while I was on the phone just now. Dísa can talk a lot, but not that much! I'm astounded, I must say. Even the devil himself couldn't write so fast!

She strokes the pages, carefully, the sun moves a few centimetres in the blue sky, manages to shine in through the large window above the front door, and fills her blond hair with sunshine. We're so close to each other that I can hear her breathing. She smiles when she sees how I'm looking at her. It's as if she has a luminous core or highly contagious power, yet with something of a melancholy air.

Life is always difficult, perhaps. Even in sunshine, dark valleys can be found within us. Is that the price for being human?

Maybe so.

I breathe in. Now I've got to say something to divert her attention from the pages, which are impossible for me to explain. Maybe I should . . .

But then the front door is unexpectedly shoved open and a deep, strong male voice fills the foyer, sweeps away all hesitation: Mr Ásmundur, reporting for duty, and with him, the tiny Mundi – both ready for action!

NATURE IS ALWAYS WORKING OUT, BUT ON THE MOON IT'S IMPOSSIBLE TO LISTEN TO JOHNNY CASH AND WATCH WOOD OIL DRY

This is Ásmundur, says Sóley, seemingly amused, a tree farmer here in the fjord. And here you have Mundi, who comes here when he wants to take a break from the world, wouldn't you say that, Mundi?

You can say anything you want about me, you know, Sóley, replies this Mundi, a thin man, shorter than me, even considerably shorter, and yes, a shrimp in comparison with the tree farmer Ásmundur. Tree farmer, grizzly bear, hefty body, with thick shoulders and arms that could probably tear up the most sizable of trees by the roots.

We were both shocked by Ásmundur's booming announcement, but she was quick to recover, laughed, said, your presence isn't likely to escape anyone's notice, Ási, and then introduced them. A tree farmer, I say, half-surprised, not knowing that they existed in Iceland, let alone in this remote fjord, so far north in the world. A tree farmer, I repeat, probably with surprise in my voice, because this Ási or Ásmundur shakes his head and says in his booming bass voice, yes, people would hardly have believed it in the old days, when we were just runts – more like science fiction. Back then it was considered a real feat to be able to boast of four to five rowan trees right next to your house, planted in its shelter; hardly anyone would ever have thought of planting trees out in the open. We were quite convinced that everything that tried to grow here would die if it wasn't called grass, moss, dwarf birch, progressive conservatism or conservative greed. Times are different now. I was a sheep farmer here back in the day, like almost everyone in the fjord, with more than five hundred sheep in the end, but then gave up. The surest road to poverty is to be a sheep farmer in Iceland, despite the sheep having long been considered almost sacred – it was they who kept a spark of life lit within us when it was toughest here in centuries past, so tough that we should have been wiped out, according to all reason and common sense. But what's more beautiful here in this world than to see a well-kept sheep in a pasture? It truly touches a string in your heart. But of course you can't pay debts with that string, you can't pay the taxes on your car, can't buy a tractor or groceries, can't deposit it in a bank. No sir, I won't be made a fool of, not for years and years. That's why I said goodbye to my five hundred sheep in the autumn eight years ago. Asked them for forgiveness. You can believe it; I never exaggerate about such things. I took the head of each sheep in my hands, looked in its eyes and apologised for the world's stupidity, apologised for having to send them to death far too early. Since then, I've been growing trees.

A tree farmer, I say again, as if I no longer knew any other words.

Yes, my man, says Ásmundur, that's the right term.

Are you mainly watching trees grow, I ask, and Ásmundur laughs, laughs like a tractor would probably laugh, and my organs practically tremble within me. This I've got to tell my Gunna! What's your job, well, I watch my trees grow! And who would have believed that I, of all people, had the patience for that? But watching trees grow grants such deep serenity that, over time, you become so calm that arctic terns can use you as a nesting place. But Sóley here can testify that I've been an Independent since birth. Since birth, my man. Gunna often said to me, Ási, you're nuts to vote for the party that has always despised farmers, and never as much as in the last fifteen, twenty years after the liberal powers took it over. Liberals despise poverty and, consequently, despise almost all farmers in Iceland, most of whom are either poor or eternally broke, in dire straits, rattling around in old cars and never going abroad, except on farmers' trips to Norway, which liberals despise almost as much as they do the farmers. That's why I grow trees. They grow so slowly that no one can be bothered to hate them.

Ási isn't an Independent, Sóley tells me, he just says that to shock people or annoy them. But he sent a message to the US Congress when Donald Trump was elected president, suggesting that a good portion of the American people be shipped off to the moon, and preferably the dark side. And again last winter to the British parliament when the British voted for that liar Boris Johnson.

They didn't answer, the bastards, says Ási, throwing up his hands. Still, I'm a landowner in Iceland. I own a huge tract of land. I own part of a river and the salmon in it, I own half a mountain, there are trees growing on my land and the trees breathe for the Earth. I ask, is it possible to ignore such a man, Mundi, what would you think?

Mundi, that thin man, the shrimp, shrugs, I come here to the north, he answers, so as not to have to answer questions like this. Some people say that when you look at everything and consider it carefully, it's hardly possible to conclude otherwise than that humanity is a monster. And the more you study the history of man, the better you observe current events, the easier it becomes to accept that conclusion. Maybe it takes a little blend of immorality, selfishness and incorrigible optimism not to be filled with pessimism. Maybe you need to be on drugs to care for humanity, or have faith in it. Still, I know good people. Even very good, which tells me that nothing is for certain, and therefore it's natural to send messages and emails to the US Congress, the Pope or the United Nations and demand justice. Suggest that this person or that be shipped off to the moon. But yesterday I was oiling my deck and listening to Johnny Cash. Then drank a bottle of red wine while I watched the oil dry. I don't think people can do that on the moon.

You drank a whole bottle? Ási asks, seemingly surprised, if not worried.

It was full when I opened it last night, empty when I woke up. Something made that happen. But you've often told me that this fjord is quite haunted – maybe someone got into the bottle while I was in the loo.

I certainly hope so. You're good at thinking and should have worked as a philosopher, instead of selling damned jet engines to dubious parties, but then of course you would never have been able to afford to buy a summer cottage and have it transported here.

Those in Iceland who think deeply can rarely afford to buy summer cottages. But I hope and trust that the dead will look after you, such a slender body as yours can hardly bear more than two glasses of wine in one night. You're too important. I would immediately call an ambulance if I saw you drinking more, or rather the Coast Guard helicopter, it would get here faster and I could maybe go with you, too. I've always wanted to fly in those helicopters of theirs, but to do so I guess it would mean putting myself more at risk than I do watching trees grow. But of course it's haunted here, says Ási, now looking straight at me while Mundi, the slender one, who owns a summer cottage and possibly sells jet engines, sits down on the windowsill and takes a thin book out of his jacket pocket. He's dressed in light, thin trousers, woven of fine cloth, grey-speckled, along with a high-quality blue-speckled jacket, as if he's on the way to a sales meeting with jet-engine manufacturers. He fishes a pair of glasses from another pocket and starts reading, leans up against the large windowpane so the sun warms his back. Sóley has crossed her arms and is leaning against the reception desk, smiling.

Ásmundur: Of course it's haunted here. But that's because there have generally been so few of us that we're instinctively reluctant to let go of those who die. Except for the ones we're downright happy to get rid of. But tree farmer, yes, I'll sign to that. I think it's almost as noble as being a sheep farmer, just much more profitable. You get more generous grants, better loans, are held in higher regard, and don't have to slaughter your friends in the autumn. Yet Gunna says that she misses hearing the sheep chewing their cuds in the sheep sheds in the winter, hearing the lambs bleat in the spring and seeing them gambolling around. I agree wholeheartedly. I would often go out to the sheep sheds in the winter just to listen to them chew their cud, sigh, and hear the wind whine on the corrugated iron. But you know, it's as if the trees are in a love relationship with the state; I'm actually a subscriber to funds from there. And what do trees do, yes, they breathe for the Earth. They provide shelter from the winds and attract birds. A tree farmer. I ask: can a person be more useful, can a person live better? I don't think so. Maybe I should send a

111

new letter to the US Congress and point that out to them, or what do you think, Mundi?

I'm reading, says the thin man sitting on the windowsill, where he's baked by the sun, I can't do two things at once, read and form an opinion about trees and the US Congress, I've got to choose, and I choose to keep reading. Ask Sóley, she's smarter than the two of us combined.

I don't know if it can be called a compliment to be considered smarter than the two of us combined, says Ási, shaking his head. You may be brainy, but I pull us down; Gunna takes care of the thinking for me. I have three brain cells, one for prattling, one for growing trees, the third for sending messages demanding justice. I used to have four, but the fourth one was so saturated with libido or downright horniness that I was eventually forced to get rid of it. It took a lot of effort, you know – a real hurdle! Someday I need to tell you about it.

He stops and regards me, as if considering whether he should maybe tell me right away about the fourth brain cell, which was saturated with libido, with horniness, but then Sóley starts talking. I don't immediately grasp her words, their content, I lose myself in looking at her face, seem to be sucked towards those peculiar, amber eyes. But she was telling about . . . Ási, explaining something. That the brothers, Einar and Ási, had, by pure coincidence or the imaginativeness of fate, settled here in the fjord, just about a year apart, many years ago. Married to sisters from Hólmavík. Ási, however, hadn't been a complete stranger to the fjord, having spent a few summers in the countryside with the relatives of the brothers at Hof; he'd sold his small fishing boat up north and taken over the farm when his relatives gave up on the struggle, the distance from Reykjavík, their disappointment in global warming, the fact that it hadn't reached this far north and brought warmer sunshine, more days for wearing shorts . . . but this of course happened shortly after you were here last, she says to me. She seems as if she's going to add something and I hold my breath, hoping that she says more about it, for example when it was, where, for how long, but then Ási laughs and says, global warming, that's an excellent explanation and no worse than any other!

Global warming, poor Internet connection. It's as my Gunna has said, that anyone who intends to farm in Iceland must either accept semi-permanent poverty and hardly any trips abroad except perhaps farmers' trips to Norway, or run yourself ragged doing other jobs alongside looking after your livestock, maintaining your equipment, buildings, fences. Maybe take up construction work, become a member of parliament, immerse yourself in tourism, but then of course you've got to wear a woollen jumper, no matter what the weather, that's what the tourists like. And be careful not to get too fat, it doesn't fit with the image of a child of nature. Nature is never fat, it's always working out, lifting waterfalls and heavy mountains.

Yes, I say, feeling as if I'm expected to respond to the tree farmer's monologue, but, since I don't really know what more to say, I just say yes again, continue hanging on to that tiny word as I look at Sóley, which is of course a mistake because she has those damned eyes, that angel's hair and her upper lip rests on its sister like a kiss. Except that it's not resting there now, Sóley is smiling, you see, and I feel some organ inside me plummeting. Hopefully my heart. Hopefully, it will sink all the way down, combine there with the waste and be expelled with it at my next bowel movement. Then I'll be free of it and entirely lighter. Much easier to live without a heart. Except that my heart doesn't seem to fall far, unfortunately, but crashes in my stomach and thrashes there like a blind, helpless bird amid half-digested flatbread, bathed in red wine and beer. Yes, that's right, I repeat, now speaking into the air, between Sóley and Ási, I've heard a few things about that, but it's good, I mean, farms mustn't be abandoned. An abandoned, untended farm resembles a person who has lost all hope.

They all look at me, including the thin one, the philosopher who sells jet engines; he lets his book sink and looks at me over his glasses. Now I've said something stupid, given myself away, unmasked myself and will have to admit to my amnesia. That someone or something erased my life, switched me off, then restarted me in the front pew of the old church, where I woke up with no memory and the devil three pews behind me. With no memory of anything about myself. All I know is that I miss people sorely, and that I was in all likelihood in love with Sóley. In other words, whatever it was succeeded in radically erasing my life and memory, but not my love. Does that mean that love is stronger than death, survives everything, and is the only thing that can possibly move between universes? But she's probably married; should I borrow Lóa's rifle in order to get rid of that Ómar, or should I . . . They're still looking at me, all three. I've got to say something.

EVERYONE NEEDS A NAME, INCLUDING THOSE WHO MUST GO AWAY

The phone saves me. It rings in Sóley's pocket, demands attention and, in doing so, cuts through the peculiar atmosphere that seems to have filled the hotel's large foyer.

Never any peace, she says.

Mundi continues reading, Sóley fishes the phone from her back pocket, looks at the screen, says, oh, it's Elías, and smiles at Ási, so teasingly that it's almost a smirk. Ási looks down, appears to curse. She puts the phone to her ear, my dear Elías, to what do I owe the pleasure of your call? You need a spice, which . . . yes, we should have that, of course, I would be terribly surprised if the sisters, Wislawa and Oleana, didn't have that tucked away somewhere in their realm. Yes yes, just come over, though they're on the slope picking thyme, lady's mantle and the like, but will hardly be long . . . No, not yet, I think it's about an hour until the group arrives, so you have time. Good. I'll smile when you come, she says, puts the phone back in her pocket and I think, is it possible for anyone to say goodbye in a better, more beautiful way, I'll smile when you come. You're what makes me smile . . .

. . . and she's smiling when she puts the phone in the pocket of her jeans, blue but with a narrow silver stripe down the sides. Puts it in her back pocket, looks at me, with that smile that shows up on seismometers and I feel a slight hatred towards that Elías, for having the place in Sóley's life that evokes her smile – hopefully he'll drive off the road.

That was my dear Elías, she says, he moved to Vík almost three years ago, and will be here in fifteen minutes.

So you'll get to meet one more person here, which can hardly be a bad thing.

Ási: I'll stick to my own opinion on that, if you don't mind.

Wislawa, I say. That's familiar.

Sóley: Of course; it's the name of the poetess! You hopefully haven't forgotten that you gave me a book by her back in the day – you had two copies of it. Are you still in the habit of buying books you already own? Forget everything, forget yourself in the end, my sister Rúna sometimes said. A great book, you'd marked it in a few places. I knew you were fond of those verses . . . maybe that's why some of the lines stuck with me. Like this one: "Life on Earth is quite a bargain, Dreams, for one, don't charge admission."

Mundi: That's good. I wish I knew how to read poetry. I'm so stuck in prose.

I: Do you need to know how to?

Ási: Well, people used to sing "teach me how to kiss right and how to hug, but not too tight". It was a popular song. I expect that if you're not born with the ability to kiss, you need to learn how, so the same must go for poetry. You have to learn how to read it.

Mundi: Do you mean that a poem is a kind of kiss?

Ási: What do you think I know about that? Do I look like a guy who knows the answers to such things?

It would never occur to me to try to find words for how you look, says Mundi. You're way too big. In Japan and some Asian cities where the population is bursting at the seams, the streets bend beneath the weight of the throngs and the overcrowding is suffocating, which I've experienced first-hand; giants like you have to pay higher taxes and fees than others. It seems natural, fair, because you take up more space than others in this constricted world.

You're lying, says Ási, and I can't tell whether the tightness around the big man's mouth is caused by irritation or an attempt to stifle a smile. Hard to read this man, when he's being serious, when not.

I never lie, I read, says Mundi, sinking back into his book. I see Sóley smile out of the corner of her mouth and feel a mild sadness seep into my chest and mingle there with the uncertainty that suddenly seized me, maybe because for a moment I thought that Wislawa in the kitchen was the poet herself, even though I knew that the latter died a few years ago. This namesake of hers must be one of the Syrian sisters that Rúna had mentioned; they go out onto the mountainside in search of lady's mantle to use in cooking dangerously good food. But it's so tiring to know nothing about yourself. You become insecure, afraid to say something stupid, hurt people. I've lost myself so completely that I don't know what food I like best, what wine I prefer to drink, whether I have children or not, whether I'm married, cohabiting, what team I support in English football; but I suspect that I'm more inclined towards women than men when it comes to sex, though I'm not sure if I know how to kiss right, or hug not too tight, I know even less what . . . how I . . . act when I'm with a woman. When I have sex, am intimate with a woman, make love, when I fuck her. No, I reject that, to fuck; there is of course something titillating and brazen about that word but I like the others better, to be intimate, make love . . . but why did I have to start thinking about sex now, trying to remember how I act, whether I'm intense, gentle, rough, what I like, what excites me . . .

Sóley is still smiling at Mundi and Ási, she's saying something, I see her lips move but I don't catch the words, it's as if the volume on my surroundings has been turned down and I'm at a great distance or in another dimension, a parallel existence, another universe, in which Sóley is lying naked on her stomach, moaning softly, saying, my love, my love as I slowly enter her from behind, push deep inside her. My love, she whispers.

But then laughs.

Stop teasing us, says Ási.

Sóley looks smilingly at Ási and Mundi, says something as she turns and looks at me. I don't hear what it is, just feel her moaning and pushing back against me as I enter her.

I've got to say something, I think, and try panic-stricken to tear myself away from this memory, imagination, or whatever this is that's filling my consciousness . . .

But they're hardly related? I hear myself ask, looking into the air somewhere between Sóley and Ási.

They both say What? and Mundi, having lowered his book, looks at me over his glasses. He appears amused. I don't dare to look directly at Sóley, convinced that my face is an open book, that she'll see what just now filled my mind and consciousness; I try to think fast. To realise what women I meant, and why I asked. In a flash, I go over in my mind the women that I've seen or heard since I woke to consciousness in the church, but none of them seem to fit with my question. For some reason, the name Elías comes up, the one who's on his way here, and then the curtains are swept apart – Wislawa, I say. Of course, I know that she's dead, but are they related?

No no, says Sóley, and far from it, actually; our Wislawa isn't even Polish. But we all felt that the name suited her so well, didn't we, Ási?

Ási: It was you who suggested the name, and she accepted it immediately. Grabbed it as if you'd thrown her a lifebuoy. I remember it. For my part, the name could have been simpler; it took me almost a year to learn to spell it correctly. But now I've got it, and it's never leaving.

Sóley: Everyone needs a name, including those who must go away.

So did she have to go away, I ask, looking at Sóley, which I should probably avoid doing, because it's so hard to stop once I've started – safest just not to do it. Might that be a good description of love – when someone, due to happiness or despair, can't stop looking at another person?

Should we tell him, Ási? Sóley asks. About our Wislawa. May I?

Ási: Well, there are two things that weigh in as far as I'm concerned, and weigh in just as heavily. Can he be trusted and, if so, will we be able to tell the whole story properly before Elías arrives?

I would trust him with my heart, says Sóley, without looking away from Ási, and my eyes fill with tears that I don't dare to wipe away, afraid that it would only draw attention to them, to how deeply her words affected me. I blink my eyes so frantically that my eyelids resemble the wings of a small bird trying unsuccessfully to fly. I would trust him with my heart, and it's at least ten minutes to Elías, or fifteen, rather, he drives very slowly because of the cat, the creature gets so carsick.

Ási: Well, then. You choose. Where should I start?

HER LAUGHTER IS TITILLATING, SOFT BELLS

Ási and Mundi just managed to miss running into Elías, who drove at a snail's pace up the slope to the hotel in an old, black BMW; they were halfway down to the pool when the black vehicle eased into the parking space next to the Volvo. Elías stepped carefully out, tall but slightly stooping, skinny, bony, with shoulders so slender they resembled axe blades. Probably in his sixties and holding a cat, black with white paws, clutching it like something fragile. He threw up a little, Elías said to Sóley as he came in, but then he saw me, hesitated, looked at her and asked, in what language should I address that young man there? You can try Icelandic, she said with a smile, see where it leads you – he's an old friend, by the way. Ach, said Elías, petting the cat gingerly, an old friend, that's so beautiful, it's so wonderful to have old friends, you don't get so lonely in life. An old friend. It's actually better than sex, especially as the years start weighing on you. This is Alexander the Great, by the way, he gets so remarkably carsick but I didn't want to leave him at home with Eiríkur and the three dogs. Alexander's so shy around them, doesn't know how to behave. He's what's called an introvert in foreign languages and I suspect that those who are made so harbour all the world's fragility. The poor thing threw up a few times on the way here, even though I drove so slowly . . . aah, is that you there, my angel, he said when a young woman, hardly over twenty, black-haired, slim and short, came out of the kitchen with a bowl of cream for the cat, which began purring as soon as it set eyes on the woman.

118

Know, Wislawa, that Alexander loves you limitlessly. Sometimes I fear he'll run away from home, out of pure love for you.

It's nice to be loved, said Wislawa, in slightly broken Icelandic, the sound of the "o" in "loved" so musical that the word became even more beautiful in her mouth. So that's how languages expand, I thought. There was an unusual softness in the young woman's bearing, her movements almost boyish – and she had something of a light about her.

Smiling, Elías and Wislawa knelt next to the cat and the bowl of cream, Elías said something that made her laugh and the laughter resembled soft, titillating bells.

I looked up, met Sóley's gaze. She stared straight at me, firmly. I looked back, uncertain, but felt warm all over, maybe from the uncertainty, maybe because of her eyes, maybe because of love, maybe from shyness.

Obviously, existence is difficult.

And for a long time it was anything but easy for Ásmundur, Ási, who, along with Mundi, has doubtless started taking out his tools down by the pool, where the three of them float, the couple and their daughter – when she props herself up, the world grows restless.

I've had problems with my libido, Ási had said, ever since I reached puberty, overly young, barely twelve years old.

So began the story behind the name of the woman in the hotel's kitchen, the cook. It's a story of absurdity, humiliation, dark addiction, cruelty and affection. From darkness into the light. It's the story of humanity.

HAVE YOU READ *HARRY POTTER*, SEEN THE OLDEST TREE IN PARIS, IS SEX MORE DANGEROUS THAN MURDER?

Would you rather I tell it? Sóley had asked Ási, who hesitated, looked down, then at his watch, then out into the calm, but last at Mundi, who had lowered his book. Mundi nodded, almost invisibly, and then Ási looked at Sóley, no no, it's best I do it myself, he said, before drawing a deep breath: I've had problems with my libido ever since I reached puberty, overly young, barely twelve years old.

My Gunna sometimes said that God had given me this big body of mine so that it could accommodate and handle my libido, my damned horniness. But I can tell you here and now that even though my body has always been big, it was never big enough in that sense, for many years far from it. I'll spare you details, but be careful should you stop for any length of time here in the fjord, as some do – our fjord tends to hold people captive, there's something about it that calms them, eases their minds. Be careful, or rather, you should know that I can tend to go into details, especially when I'm drunk. It was also meant to be part of the recovery process, not to be drunk, but to talk things through. My psychologist said to me: Ási, just talk enough about it. Think of the words as cargo ships that you fill with libido, and then have them sail away with it and vanish. I must admit that I had limited faith in this method to begin with, but I can take instructions, and followed his advice. After all, most other options were closed to me. And you know what, it works. In the beginning, I actually followed it so eagerly that it was a sheer wonder that the fjord wasn't abandoned. People had started hiding when they saw me turn towards their farms or summer cottages. Hid in the farm buildings, crawled under tables, as if in great danger. But now you know the situation. So I'll continue with my story.

Ási stared at me as he spoke, as if he wanted to hold me captive with his gaze, or force himself to say everything, to hold nothing back, which we so often tend to do, rarely daring to go all the way in our confessions, our frankness, daring not to venture all the way into the shadows. But Ási seemed to dare. And he even plunged into the shadows. He left little space between his words, never hesitated, the sentences like a long train moving slowly onward, the cars locked together, propelled by a great, unshakable force.

Ási said that he obviously didn't know what sort of relationship I had with my libido. Said it like that, what sort of relationship I had with it. As if libido was an independent force, an autonomous character. Except, for a very long time, Ási's libido had had the upper hand over him.

I am, and always have been, he said, a fucking powerhouse, with the strength of three average people, it's just something I was born with and therefore can't possibly boast of, it's no achievement of mine. Strong, yes, as a bull, yes, but my libido proved stronger. I was an SUV, but my libido was better designed for an aeroplane. It couldn't have gone well. And it didn't, either. And yet . . . maybe after all the dust had settled. But it certainly didn't look good, and for a long time it was ugly, damned ugly. Yet we rarely see and understand life's events until they've passed, until their course has come to an end – as my Gunna has so often said. That's a name you must learn to respect! Without her . . . Well, I don't need to explain it or elaborate any further, just ask Sóley here, she can testify to what I'm saying. But I, like the poet, say that my happy years were those of my childhood. And they ended at puberty. Then that valley with its green slopes, good-natured streams and plentiful berries closed to me for ever. Everything changed! I became sexually mature and it was as if the world had been replaced. All laws changed. Fucking staggering. Everyone changes, including you, of course; I've read a lot on this subject. Sometimes I say I could write a doctoral dissertation on the libido. What a hard-core, phenomenal, dissertation that would be if I grafted my experience onto all the theories! Have you read Harry Potter?

What? I replied in surprise. I hadn't expected this, hadn't expected any question, in general, and certainly not about Harry Potter!

Yes, I know, said Ási, that was a bit abrupt of me, I admit.

Yes, quite abrupt, Mundi agreed, having laid the book in his lap. He looked quite comfortable on the rather wide windowsill; it was well suited to such a thin, delicate man. Quite abrupt. And no wonder this good man was bewildered. He's probably wondering what sort of madhouse he's ended up in. Where did the Icelandic rural idyll go, or since when did farmers start talking about the libido and Harry

Potter? But did Potter have a libido, or could he simply wizard it away if necessary? Forgive my prattle, I'm not used to talking so much.

I honestly didn't know you could put together as many words as you have today, you must be exhausted, said Sóley warmly as she leaned on the reception desk, arms crossed, and I allowed myself to watch her for a brief moment. I knew it was safe, no-one was watching me, knew that Ási would soon start talking again and that it would be fairly safe for me to watch her until then. As I did, I drank her in: her in her jeans with the silver stripe, a tight black shirt that revealed her slender build and a kind of hidden tension in her body. I would sacrifice a lot to see her bare shoulders, I managed to think before Ási began speaking again. Abrupt, he said, yes, but abruptly shall I speak all my livelong days if it can loosen Mundi's tongue. It suits you to talk so much in the space of a morning. But my Gunna told me to read Potter, so I put the whole stack in front of me, and just this morning I was reading about the library in that school of wizardry, where there's a department that holds forbidden, banned books. My doctoral dissertation would go there. That was the connection.

Mundi: I saw the movies. In them, people were killed, tortured and maimed. That was fine, apparently, but no-one had sex, and not a breast was to be seen, let alone a penis.

Sóley: If there had been, those movies would have been forbidden to anyone under the age of sixteen; you can just imagine how much income they would have lost.

So is sex more dangerous than murder, I said, or asked, it just came out, sprang up from my uncertainty, and anxiety trickled through me once more when Sóley gave me a mischievous look. Now I've said something stupid; now I'll be found out.

Sex, Mundi said, is the most popular content on the Internet, yet very few people admit to looking at it.

There you have it, said Ási, or rather, shouted, fixing his eyes on me again. The fucking Internet! Aren't you a poet; that's what I recall. Have you managed to describe that phenomenon, are there any poems that have managed to capture that monster, that god? I would really appreciate reading such writing, such poetry. My Gunna says that only poetry can capture the essence of man. I wonder if that's the case. I'm not made for poetry. I'm too restless for it. I was born with a pinworm on my arsehole, it's constantly wriggling there, and because of it, I've always got to be doing something, I can't bear to stand still, I'll probably be an unruly corpse, won't lie still in my grave. And if I stand still for a long time, like now, I absolutely have to talk, otherwise I'll burst. No, I'm not going to burst, but I feel as if that fucking pinworm has started gnawing at my tailbone, is hanging on to it like a dog to a fish skin. I tried once to read Einar Benediktsson, but his poems are like huge storms made of words, me and my tailbone just got lost in the storm and came close to dying of exposure! So read Stefán Hörður, said Gunna. I tried to, but there's so much silence in his poems that the pinworm in me went berserk, rushed up into my abdomen and gave me diarrhoea.

Mundi: And people say that poetry has no effect.

Shut up, said Ási, without turning round, there's no room for sarcasm here. But you said the word earlier, the Internet. Do you know what it is, my Gunna once asked me, a long time ago, when the world was just beginning to realise what sort of phenomenon the Internet was. No, I said, no idea. The Internet is chaos, she said. Aha, chaos, I said, that's probably true. No, not chaos, she corrected me, before quoting some old Greek book she was reading. She's always reading and sometimes tries to share it with me, as if there were any use in that. But the Greek book says that in the beginning of time, Chaos came into being, and Chaos was some kind of person or god. I'm bad at details.

Mundi: Still, it's necessary to have a decent grasp on Greek mythology in order to be a proper farmer.

Shut up again, said Ási, unfazed. But that was what my Gunna meant by the Internet, that there might be something mythological about it, both a void and the beginning of everything. Which in fact it has turned out to be. Hasn't it? The Internet is like a new sky above us – and of course new underworlds. I've given this a bit of thought. Would even say that I've weighed it carefully. I think that anyone whose job is watching trees grow turns into a kind of philosopher.

Mundi: And that's why philosophy has never really taken hold in Iceland. Philosophers here have been like white ravens.

Sóley: Because hardly any trees grew here for seven centuries?

We didn't need philosophy, said Ási, we had our quatrains. There's magic in them.

Mundi: But they prevented Icelanders from doing any actual thinking.

Sóley: Or fit extremely well with our tendency always to find the shortest path to a goal.

Just listen to you two, saying such shameful things about the quatrain, said Ási, with a snort. But stop interrupting me; I was talking about the Internet, a new sky, I said, new underworlds. These are huge changes. So huge that, for the first time, man doesn't have to die to find out what hell is like. It has risen to us and is now flooding the digital world. The devil is exploiting the technology. People tell me that there's a powerful Internet connection in hell.

That would have been something for Dante, I blurted.

Ási hesitated, Mundi smiled faintly, but Sóley said in a tone so cordial that it tickled my entire nervous system, made me so incredibly happy: you and your Dante again!

You don't know Dante? said Mundi to Ási's back. You can't grow trees in Iceland if you don't know him; you can hardly get better fertiliser. Gunna has let you down there. Ask her about Dante. As good as Snorri Sturluson.

Bullshit! No-one's as good as Snorri Sturluson, said Ási, or announced, it was a ruling; he couldn't even be bothered to turn round. No-one can match Snorri. Never. He was a kind of mix of Iron Man, Captain America and Óðinn.

Mundi gripped his face in his hands, Sóley laughed, but Ási didn't let it bother him. One must, he said to me, constantly be updating one's comparisons. Haven't you seen those superhero movies? Enormously fun, and I'm certain that Snorri would have enjoyed them. Dante or not, I'll ask Gunna about him, but there are two dark comets in my life, my libido and the Internet, and they connect well.

I don't have time to go into detail, tell you the whole story, I'm skipping over huge swathes of land, keep that in mind, and maybe you're lucky there, not everything in my life is beautiful, I'll spare you many things. We'll have time for more later. That is, if you stop for any length of time here in the fjord with us. Now I'm going to say a few words about my libido.

You're not going to dump all that on him, a person you know nothing about, said Mundi, having put down his book, but unfortunately it was impossible for me to see the book's title, and it bothered me. You first met him about twenty minutes ago and now you're going to pour your whole life out over him. One doesn't do such a thing; you can't. Even if you are a tree farmer and have written letters to the US Congress and British parliament.

Ási had turned so that he could see all three of us; stood there with his legs spread wide, a bit hunched, his big shoulders jutting forward, he resembled a giant, or a mountain.

I can't? Who's entitled to make such a pronouncement? Gunna always says that each time period has its own customs and opinions about what's permissible, what's proper. Later, it may turn out that those customs and practices that were considered the only proper ones turned out to be bullshit at best and, at worst, the most outrageous prejudices and misanthropy. How did most white men view blacks, say in the eighteenth century – and wasn't it considered normal, if not a natural law, for women to have few or no rights? Wouldn't Mundi, at that time, have rebuked me harshly for advocating for women's equality, or for claiming that slavery was cruelty, prejudice, a sin against life, huh, wouldn't he have said, no no, that's not how one speaks; you can't speak that way? I'm a tree farmer, trees grow slowly. You learn a great deal by watching trees grow. I've been to Paris . . . not that look, Mundi, I've got to take this side road . . . Gunna and I went there last year, as you two know. We sailed on the Seine, went up the Eiffel Tower, wandered around the Marais. I can absolutely recommend that city. If I weren't an Icelandic tree farmer, I would probably live in Paris. Except what I wanted to say was that while Gunna went to the famous bookshop, Shakespeare and Company, I sat with my beer in the sun in a small garden next to the bookshop and the café. And there discovered the oldest tree in the city. It was planted in 1601, more than four hundred years ago. I was completely captivated by it and was standing there spellbound in front of it when my Gunna returned, tottering under the weight of the books she'd bought. We sat down, I handed her a beer from my backpack and we looked at the tree, which has grown so decrepit that it's supported by concrete crutches. I feel, Gunna said to me, as if I'm looking at time itself. Just think, Ási, of how many different worldviews, beliefs and theories it has grown through. When it was planted, the Earth was considered by most people to be flat and the centre of the universe, and it was utter nonsense to claim otherwise. And my Gunna was right. She's always right. But the tree just grew and grew through the ages, heeded its own thoughts, headed upward, free and independent. Knew innately that man's views are often little other than dayflies. Correct behaviour today is considered wrong tomorrow. And vice versa. But I watch trees grow, and therefore am free.

Mundi: Someday I need to write a book about your theories, analogies and beliefs. It will cause an uproar and controversy. And people will argue long and hard about how to categorise the book. As deep philosophy, bullshit, a new type of surrealism, a handbook for comedians.

You don't write books, Mundi, said Ási, unwavering, still standing there wide-legged, with all three of us in his field of vision, well over a hundred and ninety centimetres tall, and weighing no less than a hundred and fifty kilos. The man is a force of nature, I thought.

No, you don't write books and never will. But I understand that this man here's a writer, and writers need to know about everything. Need to be familiar with everything. Life supposedly streams to them and fills them with its stories and power while the rest of us are obligated to inform the writers about the main things that stand out in our lives and the lives of others. Of course, everyone picks and chooses what to tell, but, once you've started, you can't leave anything out. Gunna says that in the eyes of writers, we're all naked. And once they've started writing, they can't ignore any shadows, detour around any pain or difficulty. Everything must come out.

Mundi: Tell everything? I forbid you to include me in that narrative. I want to live my life in peace. I don't want some writer to start fiddling with it. Even if it is a friend of Sóley's. I want my life to remain outside of fiction. And Elías should be coming soon, so you need to do some serious shortening of whatever it is you have left to say. And spare us details from the world of your libido.

I'll speed up, then, said Ási, straightening up, a descendant of giants. I don't want to be standing here when Elías arrives, we'd just start arguing. Wasn't there a door frame that needed fixing, a shower and some loose hooks?

Yes, said Sóley, seemingly having a hard time containing her amusement. There's a problem with one of the showers in the women's changing room, a few hooks need replacing, and the door to the pool doesn't close properly, the frame has swollen and come loose. That building is shoddy, poorly built, and is a constant headache. But you have another fifteen minutes, nearly twenty, I would think. I texted Elías while you were talking, told him to drive slowly, said that you were in the middle of a story. Suits me fine, he answered, Alexander the Great just threw up, we're sitting at the riverbank, composing ourselves. So go on, tell him about your libido and how it relates to Wislawa, but skip the details about sex. We have our imaginations. There's no need to spell it all out for us.

SO WHERE DID THE PROMISE ABOUT SPARING US DETAILS GO? Oh, the boy must be feeling the pangs of puberty, my parents said when they noticed that I, barely twelve years old, had started reading Kristmann Guðmundsson's books. Mum owned his collected works; she was a fan of his, which Dad was hardly happy about – I think he was just jealous. You know Kristmann's reputation, married multiple times, there were eight or nine marriages and countless stories of his womanising. Some claimed that he had learned to hypnotise women when he lived as a world-famous author abroad, and, for that reason, they hadn't been themselves when they ended up in bed with him. Others went even further, claiming that Kristmann was in the habit of slinking around under the cover of night in the cemetery on Suðurgata Road in Reykjavík, concealed by darkness and trees, to dig up newly buried women and— Yes. You know. I promised to spare you the details. The thought alone is disgusting. But . . . still . . . maybe a tiny bit exciting? Which I find even worse than the deed itself. What does it say about you if such an abomination turns you on slightly?

No, naturally you don't want to answer that! I'm not surprised. Or as Gunna says: our blood harbours many dark things. On the other hand, I say that it's a damned hard job being a human. But stories went around about Kristmann, no small number, either, and I couldn't help but hear some of them at home. Something that I, as a child, certainly shouldn't have heard, but heard all the same. Because Kristmann was often discussed there. Well, there are discussions, and then there are discussions, I should say – I delved into Kristmann's writings after hearing Dad and Mum arguing yet again one day about him and his books. It was an out-and-out row, and my father concluded by saying that Kristmann was no author, no writer, but a lout who wrote his books with his cock alone. In other words, it wasn't literature, just lust. They were both quite hot with anger, and quite drunk as well. Mum responded by saying, doubtless just to provoke him: Not literature, just lust? You're a fool, a damned fool who knows nothing. Don't you know that literature and lust are two sides of the same coin – why do you think people read?

I found that a revelation. Sexual desire had snuck up on me, literally like a thief in the night, stolen the child in me or rather destroyed it altogether, and put itself in its place. I went to bed as a child, woke up as something completely different. That night I dreamed I was aboard a trawler sailing the streets of Akureyri and I helped pull in a large net, heavy with fish, and a naked woman was tumbling through the wriggling catch. We'd finished pulling the net in, the fish wriggled dying on the deck and she lay there naked among them with her eyes closed. We all stood there astonished, just staring. Then she opened her eyes and looked straight at me. With those strong, hypnotising eyes, and then drew me to her with her gaze alone. I remember how the men around me seemed to disappear, they evaporated and I was suddenly close against her, the squirming fish from the deep rubbing softly against me in their death throes. She pulled down my pants, gently grabbed my rock-hard penis, which just a few weeks before had reached full size. And it was, I can tell you, a considerably large size. I found it terribly big. Felt like I had a monster on my front side, was actually horrified of it. I myself hadn't started growing to any extent, had a noticeable growth spurt about half a year later, but my damned penis was so comparatively large that I could hardly keep my balance when I got a hard-on. My proportions were skewed. But the woman grabbed it gently, pulled me all the way to her, looked deep into my eyes, spread her legs and steered it in. God help me, I'd never suspected there could be anything so soft, warm and wet! I slipped into her, my penis plunged all the way in, I gasped, whispered huskily, I think I'm dying. And she whispered back, even more huskily, of course you're dying, and isn't it good? Yes, I whispered, as something exploded inside me and I woke to my first ejaculation. My pyjamas soaked with semen. That night, the child inside me died.

Mundi: Where did your promise about sparing us details go?

These weren't details, but part of a story that simply wouldn't have held together if I'd left it out. The dream was still very fresh in my memory when I heard Mum and Dad arguing. Both piss-drunk, that damned liquor turned the house even more on its head than blessed Kristmann. On the other hand, I was completely spellbound by my dream. By that new feeling, or emotion, that new life. Yes, I think it's safe to say that I lost my childhood overnight. I no longer cared about my tin soldiers, despite having the entire army. Gave them to my brother. He's never grown out of anything. But for a long time, I didn't go to bed without hoping sincerely that I would meet the woman in the dream again. I wanted so much to be inside her again that I trembled, twice I ejaculated at the thought of it alone, and . . .

Mundi: Hmm.

What, is that what you'd call a detail, too? Well, she never returned. That was that. But then I heard Dad say that, that Kristmann had written his books with his cock, and Mum reply that all literature was lust. Said it to wind him up, naturally, but I was so young that I didn't understand sarcasm, didn't know that such a thing existed, so I plunged myself into reading his books in the hope that in them, I would meet the woman from the deep.

And did you find her? I asked.

No, I read five of Kristmann's books before I gave up.

Sóley: I can't keep Elías away for ever.

Is he coming? Ási asked, turning around, looking out into the bright day, over the large car park where the three flags hung limply, like a declaration that nothing was happening in the world anymore. No, he's waiting, answered Sóley. I slipped him another text message earlier, saying that you were still in the middle of your story. He replied that it must be a long middle, but added that he would continue to wait quietly by the riverbank with the carsick Alexander the Great. Yet everything has its limits. And the coach is on its way here and Elías wants to have picked up the spice before it arrives. He's going to cook for the annual dinner party in honour of Páll of Oddi, Elvis Presley and life.

Alexander the Great?

Mundi: Elías's cat.

I know, I was just thinking about the name.

Sóley: He has two. That one, and a she-cat called Cleopatra. She's always having adventures, disappears up the mountain for hours at a time, lies around there, hunts for food, thinks she's a mountain lion. Elías is a great cat lover and names his cats after characters from human history, having long been an enthusiast about it. An enthusiast, what nonsense, the man has a doctorate in history, no more nor less, a former professor at the University of Iceland. And to a certain extent, it was the history of mankind that brought the two of them together, Elías and Páll, their burning interest in it, and . . . but . . .

She fell unexpectedly silent, Ási looked down, Mundi at Sóley. There was some pain in the silence, so deep or difficult that the three of them didn't seem to know how to get past it, or through it. Sóley bit her lower lip, placed one hand on her hip, and I felt a mild lust. Your sister Rúna's puppy, I forced myself to say, both to try to curb the lust that grew fast, and also to break the silence – Rúna's puppy is called Cohen . . .

Sóley smiled, Ási looked up, the silence had passed. Yes, she adopted that from Mum after the fucking Norwegians ran over her old dog. You may remember that Mum always named her dogs after musicians, Dylan, Piaf, Beethoven . . .

Mundi: Cats named after famous people, dogs after musicians. People keep themselves entertained in this fjord.

Ási: Maybe I should name my trees after musicians. This tree is called Clapton, this one Bowie, there you have Chopin. A whole forest of music!

Sóley: Or after porn stars. You would get into the news for that. The BBC would even do a piece on you.

Ási: Don't tease me. I'm sensitive.

Mundi: I would like to know how you define sensitivity.

Sóley: I second that, but let's forget about it for now. You, Ási, have gone too far off track. And I'm a bit leery of where your definition of sensitivity would take us. Just about . . . a quarter of an hour ago, you were going to explain why Wislawa is here, but you've only talked about Kristmann Guðmundsson, about the Internet and your first ejaculation. You can have five minutes, and then I'm giving Elías the signal that he can get going again. Remember, I'm expecting a coach with forty Japanese tourists. We're hardly going to be offering them an account of the first ejaculation of a tree farmer who has written letters to the US Congress and British parliament demanding justice.

Mundi: A coach of forty tourists. A coach full of money.

Sóley: I prefer to view them as people in search of experience, and consolation in the midst of the Covid pandemic.

Stop this prattle of yours, said Ási, I only have five minutes.

But we didn't get past my libido. We've got to get through it, Ási began. Or get out of it. I don't know which fits better.

Mundi: In the beginning was the libido, and the libido was God.

Ási: That's fine. But maybe it's even better to twist it a little and say, in the beginning was the libido and the libido was with God. I find it more fitting. But don't interrupt me. We just wasted twenty seconds. It was diabolical, my libido, I mean. I felt like I would burst. In the pangs of puberty, my parents said. Pangs of puberty! Absolutely not. Those were no innocent pangs – I had a roaring T-rex inside of me! Forgive the descriptions that are coming now, but, just so you understand the situation, I could be so rabid as a teenager, so utterly beside myself with those urges, that I shoved my penis into all the holes I saw, exhaust pipes, loo rolls, plastic cylinders, two sheep in the fjord just outside the village. God help me, it was as if all the holes in the world were shouting to me. No, it was more as if they sang so seductively that no living power could stop me. They were like . . . aw, those ones in *The Odyssey*, whose singing deprived men of their senses and self-control, and . . .

Mundi: Sirens, they . . .

Ási: Thanks! I can never remember such things. Gunna told me about them, an amazing phenomenon, magnificent. He was a real corker, that Homer, inventing this; a mesmerising song that deprives you of all your will and you sail smiling to your death. The things that people can come up with!

Sóley: The Sirens have of course existed at all times, only rarely in the same form. The form changes, is adapted to the times, but their nature is always the same.

Mundi: And they play effortlessly on those siblings, jealousy and prejudice. But in a village in the north of Iceland, they put a great effort into making a pubescent half-giant fuck exhaust pipes.

Ási: Libido was my Odysseus.

Mundi: I'm not sure about that analogy.

Ási: You sell jet engines, what do you know about analogies? Leave mine alone. Especially now because the second hand is quickly slicing up the time I have left.

Like an onion, I said.

Ási: What?

Slicing up time like an onion, until there's nothing left. Except the tears.

Sóley: There's the person I knew.

Ási: I just met him for the first time here a little earlier, I don't know anything about him, can I finish?

Sóley: We're waiting.

Mundi: If it goes on like this, we'll come face to face with Elías before we get out of here, and . . .

. . . that can't happen, Ási agreed, hitching up his trousers. No, that can't happen, he repeated, I'll jump ahead in time, from my trembling adolescence to here in the fjord after the Internet conquered the world. It was, of course, very slow here for the longest time. It took for ever to download pictures, and half a day or so to download videos – hence the utter hopelessness of getting properly into porn. It got lost somewhere along the way, drowned in the ocean, died of exposure on the heaths. But then a member of parliament for this constituency saw to it that a powerful Internet connection was put in place here. To strengthen the community and keep its young people in it, he said, naturally hoping first and foremost for grateful votes; it was during the run-up to elections. And – bing – the gates of hell opened! I could sit spellbound for hours at a time watching that damned stuff. I just couldn't get enough! Video after video. I plunged into that pit, that quicksand that closed around me. You could even say that I moved my legal residence there. I masturbated so much and so hard that my penis swelled up and became sore. But I'm a farmer and know how to treat that condition, I've milked cows, the same principles apply as for excessive masturbation. I got some udder balm and applied it regularly to my friend. And it got better, so I could keep on masturbating, which was a relief – I refuse to interpret this as an unnecessary detail, Ási said to Mundi, but as a necessary part of the story.

Mundi: Jump ahead again. The second hand is speeding up.

Very well, very well. My horniness kept me from sleeping; that's just how it was. The songs of the Sirens kept me awake. They lured me deeper and deeper into cyberspace. The porn sites I was sucked into were bad, but things really got out of hand when I started on the social networking sites. Then I was undone. For the moment, I'll spare you a description of the effects that damned stuff had on my home life, I'm not going into that now, it was difficult for everyone, a married man with three children. There were incidents, I can tell you; it was terribly heavy. The libido, I read somewhere, can open the door to both beautiful moonlight and hell itself. I've always found that quite a good description, although I don't fully understand that about the moonlight. But I expect that sex with those who— okay, Mundi, I'll speed up; the social networking sites led me into the world of prostitution, plain and simple.

I created an alter ego, entered the chat rooms to chat, talk dirty, or post stuff. I cooked up fantasies as if I were some damned mass-production machine. They poured out of me. I was barely fit to be around people, did my job with little conviction. Was hardly present at home. Utterly useless. That's when I probably came closest to becoming a writer; I should have applied for an artist's grant. But bloody hell, it was ugly! On my part and many others on the sites, because the others were no angels. And I, the mad yokel, thought at first that behind all the made-up names were just people like me, looking for an outlet for their urges. No deceit, so to speak, no lies, just horny men, nymphos. For a while I corresponded quite a bit with Katherine the Great. There was a spark between us, so when she suggested we meet, I was quick to bite. She slowly pulled me in, took her time doing so and, before I knew it, I'd agreed to "help" her with sixty thousand krónur, she didn't have enough to pay her next month's rent, some bullshit like that. My fucking penis made all the decisions in that case. As if it had its own bank card. When it's quite incapable of managing its own finances! I came up with the story here at home that I needed to go south to see a dentist, so I had both an excuse and an explanation for the expense. But little by little,

I realised that behind some of the made-up names was some soulless scoundrel pimping girls, some in college and desperately needing money, some on drugs, and finally the foreigners stuck in the hell of sex slavery. But I was so sunk in sexual addiction that I didn't give a fuck about right and wrong – believe me, addiction to sex is little better than to drugs and booze. Without any hesitation, you'd sell your soul and mother for your next hit. But what woke me up, you naturally ask; and I'll answer, but speedily because Elías won't wait the entire day by the riverbank.

Sóley: And with a coach full of tourists on the way.

Quickly then, quickly then, said Ási, pulling up his trousers once more – I joined the Progressive Party and used that to justify my frequent trips to the capital, became active in party work. Or as Mundi here once said, sarcastic as he can be: people join that party either to climb the social ladder faster or to hide their sexual addiction. Wislawa was the eighth person I met.

Through those forums?

Ási: Yes, six women, two young men. It was all the same to me what sex they were, and that's how it still is with me, as there are so many beautiful and exciting people of both sexes that it's a waste as well as stupidity to distinguish between them. But I'd started feeling awful because of it. My Gunna moved to Hólmavík, my children were grown, had moved to Reykjavík, and hardly spoke to me. Yes, you might even say that I stopped seeing any purpose in life. And that's the state of mind I was in when I took one more trip south, for a date with a woman who called herself "Your wet dream". You see, I didn't want to go, but it was like I was dragged away by the monster that wanted to control me. I arrive in the city late one evening, check into my hotel, try to fall asleep but can't, toss and turn until I give up, take out my computer, had thought about watching a movie on Netflix but then see that I have an email from Gunna. A long message in which she went into various things in our lives, our years together, wrote with such warmth about what a good and beautiful soul I was that I was moved to tears. Attached to the message were photos of some of our kids' drawings from when they were little. Gunna had been going through old stuff, she wanted to share these things with me, and the innocence in the drawings, the deep joy of life . . . it simply overwhelmed me. I collapsed, cried my eyes out. Cried about my lost innocence. I cried because my libido had ruined everything beautiful in my life. I cried and didn't sleep that night. The next morning, I opened my computer and read the message that I'd got from that "Your wet dream", a message that would previously have appealed immediately and vigorously to the lowest in me, but now just filled me with deep sadness and heartache. I called Gunna and to my surprise she encouraged me, or actually ordered me, to go on the date, but then to apologise to her, whoever she was. I should make her a representative of all those from whom I'd purchased services and doubtless abused in some cases; apologise and offer to help her, if it were in my power.

I went to the hotel room where we had arranged to meet – there waited our Wislawa, and something happened as soon as I walked in. I don't know how to describe such things; something big just happened. I felt as if fate had brought us together to save each other from the hell in which we were both trapped. I was there with her for two hours and she told me her story. That of a girl from Syria who loses her parents and both brothers in the war, one of the brothers just five years old, the poor thing. I won't tell you how her parents were killed, I just can't, it's too awful. Then just the two of them were left, she and her younger sister, their home levelled by bombing, their city a battlefield. They fled along with others from the city, made it down to the Mediterranean Sea and then, completely destitute and in poor physical shape, over to Greece, two hundred people together in a rubber raft meant to hold no more than a hundred. In Greece, the hell of the refugee camps awaited them. The camps had been built in the name of humanity, and then the devil was got to manage them. A few months later, however, luck seemed to find them when they met a distant relative of theirs in the camp. He said he could find Wislawa work up north in Iceland; he would take care of all the paperwork. Well-paid work at a hotel. She could doubtless save up enough money to return and get her sister. This relative of theirs came across as nothing but kind and caring while coldly selling his own family member into sexual slavery, with her sister held as a guarantee. Now I say, like the writer whom Mundi here is constantly quoting: Man invented the devil to bear his sins.

Mundi: Of course, you've bungled the quotation, as usual, but maybe it's even better that way.

Ási: God supposedly created man in his image – what does that say? Whoever lets himself be led into the dubious pursuit of reading the history of mankind must think: this isn't the history of man but the annals of hell.

Maybe, I said, it was the devil who created man and, when God saw that it was too late to undo it, he gave us guilt and music.

And gave us Icelanders hot water, said Ási, but that's pretty good, Mundi, guilt and music; we'll have to remember it.

I've already written it down, Mundi said from the windowsill, but now you've got to finish your story, Elías is on his way. He has a doctorate in history, which means he must have a doctorate in the devil, too.

I'll speed up, said Ási. Wislawa was picked up at the Leifur Eiríksson terminal by a cheerful fellow, an Icelander, who said he knew her relative, an upright man, he said, who could be trusted; and he spoke non-stop all the way to Reykjavík. About Iceland, Icelanders. Had brought a sandwich for her, a Coke – she dozed off near Straumsvík. They'd apparently drugged her Coke and she didn't really come to her senses again until days later, woke up in some miserable room with three men who showed her a video in which she, dazed, stupefied from the drugs, was having sex with them all. Brutal, degrading sex. They'd taken her passport from her, said that the video of the four of them would be streamed on the Internet if she didn't . . . She told them to go to hell and not bother to come back. They pulled out photos of her sister, standing there smiling next to their relative, that had been taken the day before . . . her sister would be ruthlessly forced into prostitution if Wislawa didn't cooperate. Or, as you said, maybe the devil created man. Afterwards, I began reading up on human trafficking and found that it's as lucrative as drug trafficking and dealing in illegal arms. You make as much from selling children and women into sex slavery as trading in fighter jets – in Europe alone, thousands have been sold into sex slavery in the last ten years. Our Wislawa is one of the very few who has escaped. What scares me the most, however, is that this information is readily available; it takes hardly any work to access it. We know about this, yet we do nothing. What is that? Aren't we all going to go to hell? Mundi, you've travelled a great deal, read books, sold jet engines; how can this be?

Mundi: Because kindness is too demanding, it's a guarantee of wasted work hours, and in the end it just fills you with despair – as a result, about ninety per cent of humanity will probably go straight to hell. To the fires there.

Ási: We need to discuss this further. I need to write the US Congress and British parliament new letters. But that's my story. It's finished, for now. Later I'll tell you the last part, which I call the rescue mission. I can assure you that most people here in the fjord took part in it. Including my idiot brother. But now I'll stop; I see Elías's car. Mundi, to work!

MISS YOU BABY, SOMETIMES, AND THEN I JOIN A PROTEST
MARCH AGAINST LONELINESS

At the bridge, I meet the green coach full of Japanese tourists. They're on their way to the hotel, and I to the caravan that Sóley is letting me use, and which I noticed when we were standing in front of the hotel. A small white shape standing in the marshland across the river. I meet the coach full of travellers, tourists, full of money. There are many ways to look at the world, and your perspective probably reveals your inner person. Tell me how you see the world and I'll tell you who you are.

I slow down as I approach the single-lane bridge, park the Volvo at the side of the road and put on my right-turn signal, a message to the coach driver that he should cross first. In return, the driver flashes his lights, signalling his thanks. No, signalling her thanks, because the driver turns out to be a short-haired woman wearing sunglasses. As the coach crawls by, I see the silhouettes of several smiling tourists, two holding up cameras, one of whom appears to take a photo of me. So I might end up in a photo album in Japan, become a world traveller. But up at the hotel, Sóley, Wislawa and her sister Oleana are waiting for the coach, its passengers, driver and guide. The name Oleana means brightness, light, she who sinks ships. Some names are poems, if not planets. The three women are waiting for the coach, along with Ómar, Sóley's husband. Or at least that's how it sounded to me, that Ómar was Sóley's husband. That's what her wording implied.

Which means she's married.

Of course.

It stands to reason.

But is this Ómar worthy? She has amber eyes, they're rare stones, they're like moorland in gentle sunshine. She has an irresistible hesitation in her bearing. And when she smiles, the world has to be reset. Of course she's married. But does Ómar deserve all that? Where do the dragons that he defeated to win her lie buried, what mountains did he climb, what storms did he overcome, and does he remember in the mornings, when he stirs from sleep, to send messages of thanks to the gods, to fate?

I think I hate this Ómar.

Which is not a good feeling, it isn't noble, not at all clever, since jealousy doesn't ask questions, it couldn't care less about intelligence, wealth, happiness, kindness, fairness, logic. Jealousy is the dark sister of love, wanting only to rule and take what she covets.

My Ómar, Sóley had said in the hotel foyer.

I cross the bridge slowly, turn on the car stereo, and look down into the river's gentle current, hoping to catch sight of salmon. The stereo has chosen a new song for me that opens with broken but catchy piano notes, and then Regina Spektor starts to sing about being so lonely that she goes to a protest, just to rub up against some strangers.

That would be something, to take part in a protest against loneliness. Could I maybe find a purpose by going out into the world and organising a protest march against loneliness?

But first I need to get out to that caravan. Go in, look it over, make coffee and think a bit as I drink it.

Oh, I start to miss you baby, sometimes.

Miss you, baby, sometimes – and I'm approaching the caravan. There's Einar and Lóa's farm. All's quiet there. No rifle being aimed. I'm only going to stop briefly at the caravan, have to get back soon – like an ass, I'd promised to attend the dinner party that Elías and Eiríkur are holding in honour of Páll of Oddi, life and Elvis Presley.

This fellow here is a real Elvis fan, Sóley had said, when Elías's cat, Alexander the Great, was done lapping up the milk and cream mixture that Wislawa had given it and followed her into the kitchen. The three of us were left in the foyer, Sóley, me and that Elías who came for spices; he's preparing the dinner.

This fellow here is a real Elvis fan and someone has to give him something to eat, you can see how thin he is. What's more, he should be able to help you find new words to describe Elvis. He's always been good with words. They obey him like the most loyal dogs.

Anyone who has new words for Elvis is always welcome in my home, said Elías – and I didn't dare not to accept the invitation. Still, I don't want to be around people. People are usually overrated.

I drive past Einar and Lóa's farm and soon have to slow down to turn off the gravel road and onto the barely visible track that runs through the soft, tussocky ground down to the small caravan. I roll down the driver's-side window to let in the month of August, sunshine, the smell of the earth, the sea, the tall birch thicket that shades the farm, the whinny of the snipe, the blaring of the redshank and the screeching of the tern that will all soon leave this fjord.

But Regina Spektor is done with her song. A good song.

Miss you, baby, sometimes.

Shouldn't I write her a letter and thank her for the song; isn't that something one should always do? Write thank-you notes, my sincere thanks for the song, the album, the poem, the story, the radio programme, the movie, the speech you gave . . . shouldn't people send such letters, messages, wasn't that why post offices were built to begin with, isn't it the reason for the work of postal carriers, the idea behind email: to carry words between people, their thanks, encouragement, news, confessions of love?

But there's a new song now. A husky, emotionally charged voice has taken over from Miss Spektor, singing of things given that will always stay broken but will never be thrown away.

Tom Waits. We could hardly get through life without him accompanying us.

And now I've arrived at the caravan.

Which seems so small that I'm not sure anything can fit in it but one coffee cup, maybe, one loo roll and three arctic terns. The three take off with screeches into the air when I stop the car but wait before stepping out, wanting to listen to the whole song. Summer is gone, but our love will remain. Summer is over but my love for you will live through everything. It will live through autumn, winter, darkness, disappointment, all the heaviest of burdens:

> I love you,
> and am saved.
> I love you,
> and grief embraces me.

Then the song is finished.
Because everything has to end so that something else can take over.

> One love gives way to another.
> I die to make room for new life.

I put the guitar down so that someone else can pick it up.

*

The caravan is directly opposite the hotel and I think I see Ási by the pool – maybe talking to the daughter. Did she prop herself up in front of him, expose her breasts, transform herself into a Siren song, so that Ási has now forgotten all about repairing the door? Did her breasts distract even Mundi, the philosopher who sells jet engines, comes to the fjord to free himself of the world's questions?

Several of the tourists are wandering around in front of the hotel, most of them wearing masks and strolling happily in the sun, in the calm, fifteen degrees Celsius, you couldn't have much better summer weather in August so far north in the world, nor does it need to be much better. Fifteen degrees and the stillness so deep that it calms the blood. I reach into my pocket for the key to the caravan. It isn't big, Sóley had said, but it's very cosy, gives you a hug. Just come to me if you need anything, you can have your breakfast here, of course, but there should be coffee there, some rye crispbread, I'll give you some butter, goat's cheese and a bottle of single malt Scotch. Then you should be protected against everything. Won't that be okay . . . my love . . . she had added.

My love.

It came after a moment's hesitation. As if she wasn't sure whether she should say it. Whether it was safe. Whether she was allowed. But said it, all the same.

Here's the key to the caravan, and I'm holding the whisky bottle, Macallan, eighteen years old. Now all I need is a glass and music and I'll be completely safe. Miss you baby, sometimes. I stick the key in the keyhole.

I call the caravan Utopia, Sóley had said as she handed me the key and the whisky bottle. Smiling at the same time, and the gods were hastily summoned to readjust the world.

Utopia, that's good. The place that doesn't exist. It's highly appropriate.

I open the door, and have almost shut it again right away and locked it securely when I see the man from the church, the priest, the coach driver, unless it's the devil himself, sitting at the small circular table at the back of the caravan.

So, you finally made it, he says.

CALL ME SNATI. OR: I'M SO GLAD YOU CAME.
I'LL NEVER FORGIVE YOU FOR IT

It's as if the caravan grows in size when you step into it. I thought it was much smaller, I say as I sit down at the circular table, opposite the man from the church.

I immediately decided not to ask myself who this man was or what he was doing here. But it's surprising how cosy it is inside the caravan. Care in every detail. Curtains, simple tableware, furniture. A few old black and white photos on the shelves above the circular sofa; people doing haymaking, helping with lambing, at the sheep-sorting corral. One of them of a smiling couple and two young boys in front of a beautiful, corrugated-iron-clad, two-storey wooden house with an attic that looks like a smile. Can it be, I think, surprised . . . can it be that these are . . .

Yes, says the man, that's correct. It's Hafrún and Skúli, with their boys, Halldór and Páll.

I lean forward; I have goosebumps and am too disconcerted to wonder how the man from the church knew what people I was think-ing about. The couple have an unusually bright aura. They are holding each other tightly, obviously happy, obviously in love, and their two sons, Halldór and Páll, probably around eight to ten years old, are sitting sprawled at their feet, Halldór smiling, Páll serious. The four of them are a small, bright universe, full of happiness. A universe that is possibly extinct now, gone, nothing left of it but this black and white photograph, kept in a small caravan in a remote fjord.

But how did the man from the church know what people I was thinking of? And what— no, I'm not going to mull that over at all, it isn't always good to know the answers. Ignorance can set you free. Instead, I mention that the caravan seems to have grown larger just by my stepping into it.

143

Maybe it adjusts itself to you, or vice versa, says the man, but then he repeats what he said when I opened the door, you finally came.

Were you expecting me, then, I ask, actually against my better judgement, because I don't want to ask this man anything. His answers seem at best outrageous, at worst dangerous, or full of uncertainty.

Were you expecting me, I ask for the third time, and then add, because two questions might be more likely to elicit an answer than one: And who are you, in fact?

Then the man smiles for the first time.

Smiling suits most people. Something beautiful happens in their faces. A smile is a spice, an ointment, a joy, a door that opens. I'm not quite sure about this smile.

Finally a proper question, says the man, almost cheerfully. But didn't I warn you – sometimes the questions are life, the answers death?

You must at least have a name, because everything is called something. Mountains, animals, lakes, foodstuffs, people. God called the light day, the darkness he called night, the firmament sky, the dry land earth. In other words, it wasn't enough to create the world because it didn't begin to function, didn't come properly into being, until it had been named. Nameless, therefore, you hardly exist. I'm speaking to air.

Names get in the way, but you can call me Snati or Dingdong. One is a dog's name, the other is nonsense.

I could quite easily turn the question round and ask you your name. But I'm more tactful, and will let it be.

It's pointless talking to you. You're air. And they're waiting for me, too. I'm on my way to dinner with Elías, Eiríkur and Elvis Presley. I'm sure others will be coming as well. I'm not going to make them wait for me, that would be rude. You're not invited, as far as I know. Mankind can be divided into two groups, you see. Those who are invited and those who aren't invited. It's pretty obvious which is which here. And you'll have gone, of course, disappeared, evaporated by the time I return. So goodbye, I say, and I get up to go.

Don't you want to know what papers these are, he asks, laying his palm on a stack of A5-size sheets of paper beside him, which, for some reason, I hadn't noticed; don't you want to know what's on them?

I couldn't care less about those papers of yours, and couldn't care less who you are, where you're from. I'm assuming you're a priest who abandoned the faith, got your PCV licence and drive tourists. Moved from religion over to tourism. Lots of money in both. Money and power have always followed in the footsteps of religion and eventually taken it over. God always becomes a devil in the end. But now I'm going, and taking the bottle with me, naturally. It wouldn't do you any good. Nor can you be drunk if you come across your coach. Remember to lock the door behind you and try to behave yourself when you go. Lóa here next door owns a rifle, is constantly practising shooting and looking for targets.

You can't go right now, says the priest with the PCV licence bluntly, almost as if he's sorry, almost as if he's sad, at the same time as he turns a few of the pages over so the written side is facing up. The dark side, I think, and sit down again. Or rather, plunk into my seat and place the bottle on the table in front of me. I must not be looking very well, because the man pushes a glass over the table, an old, cracked glass that has shown up from who knows where but that I simply can't worry about right now; I uncork the bottle, pour myself a whisky. I take a good sip, close my eyes to enjoy the taste better and feel the whisky spread like a soothing whisper through my chest. Then I open my eyes and look down at the sheets of paper. Recognise my own writing, of course.

I'm not even going to try to understand, Snati, how the hell you managed to get these pages; I won't even let it cross my mind.

I'll be darned, you're learning, he says. So maybe there's hope.

Hope for what?

Nope, there it went. And there I'd thought you were beginning to understand things.

May the devil take you and swallow you in one bite. I'm on my way to a dinner party. Some are invited, others not.

That may well be, but you can't go right away; we have to finish certain things first. Or rather, to let fate take its course. That's the only way; otherwise we can't move forward. Nor can you shirk the task you've begun. You know that.

We? What bloody we, there's no "we" here, just me and then you – and you've got nothing to do with any of this. Fate? Mine is to go and listen to Elvis Presley. And then I'll know I've lived.

You know very well what I'm talking about, says the sanctified coach driver, calmly and with such conviction that my temper flares. But probably because he's right, unfortunately.

What about Elías and Eiríkur, are they just supposed to wait for me? I ask, trying to sound sarcastic and shaking my head as if to say, what a bunch of bullshit! But of course it's unconvincing, I just mumble the question, suspect that that's the deal, that whoever starts a story has to try to finish it. Including the stories that never end, or those that really shouldn't be written. I think it's a question of responsibility, I mutter, looking down at the table, at all the pages the man has spread over the tabletop. And I also think it's about going faster than death.

You're probably right. About responsibility, and that everything that matters is directed against death. You read that article about the multitude of universes at the hotel.

Is that a question or a statement? I ask, trying to sound harsh. It annoys me terribly to be in agreement with this self-satisfied clerically trained coach driver. And how do you know about the article, are you spying on me?

Pass me the whisky; sometimes you're so horribly stupid that I just want to drink myself into oblivion. So that I can get away from you. But you know that alcohol has a dual function: on the one hand, it's used for celebrating, and on the other hand to get away. Those who believe that they're one and the same are in considerable danger. But they can wait, don't worry about them, not now.

Those, what those who are in such danger, who think that alcohol is the way out?

Of course I meant Elías and Eiríkur; you're having a terribly hard time keeping up. The reason they can wait – says the sanctified coach driver, lifting the index finger of his right hand and maybe trying in that way to silence me because I'm unsure that the two men can wait, because Elías has come home, started to prepare dinner and the cat has fled to the top of the fridge, offended that Elías has let all those stupid dogs into the house, Eiríkur has carried the audio equipment out into the farmyard and is going over the two Spotify lists for the party. The Elvis list and the general one. It will be beautiful when Elvis is playing at high volume in the sunshine. And it won't be any worse when Eiríkur plays "In My Heart" by Bubbi Morthens, "Where is My Mind" by Pixies and "SOSA" by AZ. The mountains, those sleepy giants, will be moved!

You should come too, Sóley, Elías had said. You see, the sky is making a show for us of all the best that it has: calm, sunshine, gentle weather.

I would give anything to be there with the three of you, and with Elvis, she said, smiling her surprisingly bright smile. But you know I can't promise anything. There's a lot to do here. Forty Japanese tourists are on their way. I'm counting on you to take them on the usual excursion tomorrow morning, no need to remind you of that, of course. Hopefully you haven't got rusty or forgotten anything, despite not having taken a group for me since last November.

Never been better, I'll tell the story of the fjord and a little about Ási, said Elías, smiling.

The sky is clearly fond of Elvis, I'd said in the car park outside the hotel as Sóley and I watched Elías and the cat drive down the road; are they inviting anyone else?

Besides you and the sky, you mean, yes yes. My sister Rúna, of course, and my dad. Granted, he says he's dead, and it's hardly fun for the living when the dead come to their parties, but he'll be there. Dísa's invited, old Lúna, Kári of Botn and his family, the relatives from Canada, Mundi and Ási, because, despite the latter's comments about Elías, the two have a lot in common and visit each other during the winter months, when everything here in the fjord is so still it's as if the world has fallen asleep. Yes, they're all invited, along with us here

147

at the hotel, but no-one will be turned away and I wouldn't be surprised if many more showed up. I suspect that some will come unexpectedly, and from far away. We here in the fjord have been waiting for this party, and the sky has definitely blessed this day, thinking the world of Presley as it does, not least "Suppose" and "Can't Help Falling in Love", since you need to have been dead for a thousand years not to adore those songs as sung by Elvis.

You know that I was happy when we danced to them, she said, after we'd stood there silently for several moments. But I managed to convince myself that I was relieved that you disappeared from my life. Even though it was the worst and most difficult thing that has ever happened to me. I actually thought that I would die. For many days it was as if I literally couldn't breathe, and I couldn't eat a thing, just lived on coffee and became terribly thin. My poor Ómar was deeply worried about me. He wanted to send me to the doctor.

Afterwards, as I drove away from the hotel, it dawned on me that Sóley had, of course, been waiting for me to say something, to react. But I didn't say anything. Just stood there and saw the coach appear on the verge of the mountain like a phrase with which the heath addressed the fjord.

But what was I supposed to say?

Because we had once danced together to songs that were specially written and performed for the sky. We had loved each other.

But it's all wiped out. As if it had never been anything. That's why I said nothing but thought that it would probably be best for me to go to Einar and Lóa's and ask her to shoot me, preferably at short range. But then the back of her hand stroked mine, softly, the touch was a gentle, warm electric current, I got a lump in my throat and longed terribly much to live.

Maybe a person can seldom remember happiness without feeling pain, she said. But I'm just such a stupid failure and haven't been able to stop thinking about you. Ever since you disappeared. Time hasn't helped me there. My first thought almost every morning has been you. I've lain there next to Ómar thinking about you. We've made love, he's a beautiful person, a splendid lover and loves me, but even in the middle of our lovemaking I've had to concentrate on not whispering your name. It's so ugly. But then you came. As if nothing were more self-evident. Acted as if nothing unusual had happened. I nearly died when I looked up and saw you in the foyer. I don't understand how I managed to stay upright. To greet you, talk to you, give you a beer, calmly, as if I were just meeting an old acquaintance. You should be ashamed of yourself. Oh, sorry, you probably were. Of course, you haven't changed, it's as if you don't know how to grow old. All the same, you're different. My sister said so too. And even said she thought that grief had paralysed you. Or that you seemed both distant and vulnerable, as if you wanted nothing more than to snuggle up to someone. And you got her to blather all that stuff – the same goes for me, as I haven't talked so much in years. And so you know, I want to hug you as much as kick you. But has the grief paralysed you, the pain muzzled you? You don't have to answer me. Or yes, you can, of course, but not right away, I'm just not prepared for it. It's enough for me that you're here. I can't handle anything beyond that. Go to the caravan, look it over, settle in, it's there in the marshier area across the river, you can see it from here, I can keep an eye on you through the binoculars. But don't hang around there too long, hurry on over to Elías, Eiríkur, Elvis and the sky. Get drunk. Dance with Rúna. Dance with Dísa. Maybe I'll come, maybe not. Dance, but not while our songs are playing. I'm so glad you came. I'll never forgive you for it. Now I'm going in to prepare for the arrival of forty tourists from Japan.

And soon afterwards, I met the coach at the bridge.
Love has many faces and can travel unharmed through hell, create considerable unrest in heaven.

Miss you, baby, sometimes.

The clerically trained coach driver still has his index finger in the air. It's the finger that was supposed to silence me and my doubts that Elías and Eiríkur could wait – the latter will of course soon be hurrying out to the yard with the things needed there, plates, glasses, cutlery, red wine, white wine, beer, and setting the two long tables beneath the large canopy that Ási and Mundi helped to build yesterday.

Hurrying, no, he won't be in any rush, why would he be? Elías has just started cooking, two, three hours before the food is ready, things are done calmly and deliberately here.

But right now they're sitting together at the big dining-room table, going through a stack of photographs and papers. Eiríkur is holding an old photograph of four men and two women in a richly furnished living room: one of the women is in her upper middle age, big and tall, wearing a strong, determined expression; the younger has brilliant eyes and a very charming smile. Everyone in the photo is smiling. It has an air of joyousness. Festiveness. So this is them? Elías asks, and Eiríkur nods, smiling, like those in the photo.

The calm outside the big living-room windows, which look out over the fjord, the marshland bordering the river, and Nes across the fjord, is so deep that it seems to protest all haste, silently. Life tends to slow down in dead calm, it wants to enjoy the moment, to drink it in. Drink in this fjord in which the surface of the sea is so still that it has transformed into a mirror that softens the crags on the mountainsides; their acrimony takes on a dreamy air. Mountains think in centuries and you understand them best, sense their thoughts erode, either in deep calm or storms.

And it suddenly dawns on me that I simply may not hurry. The Fates are waiting to be tended to, and one does not offend those proud and noble ladies. Besides, I have a view of the road from my seat and I will hardly miss it when Rúna drives into the fjord, on her way to Elías, Eiríkur and Presley; then and only then will I need to get going.

*

The priest with the PCV licence smiles, lowers his finger, I see that you're beginning to understand. That's good. It saves me from having to explain things. Explanations slow everything down too much, make it cumbersome, ungainly, unexciting. And I have no inclination to address you as child. There's enough stupidity in the world; no reason to have it thrown in my face right now.

Okay, maybe I'm starting to understand. But I still have no idea who I am, where I'm from, what my life was like before I woke up in the church, where it went. Yet I feel that I have loved, feel that I am loved. Do you know how much it hurts to have forgotten those you love?

Who you are is completely irrelevant. Where your life went. Your love and betrayal don't matter here. What matters is that you continue with the stories you started. Hopefully, you've realised that you slow down time while you're writing. But you've got to pay the price for it. That's the deal. And that you mustn't hesitate once you've started. Death, says an old poem, is the sister of waiting.

You can tell me all sorts of lies, as you doubtless know. Something's happened to me. Maybe I'm simply dead, but for some reason have been forbidden from leaving life. Maybe I was just thrown from one universe to another. What do we know of what's possible, what's out of the question? But I readily admit I found it highly suspicious that I managed to write all of this that you have in front of you at the hotel while Sóley was on the phone talking to Dísa. There's no way; it doesn't add up. Slow down time, you say. Time, what are we supposed to do with it? I think time is a loaded pistol, a landslide that's about to fall over your life, the yesterday that never came. The old people said that time was a quatrain with a bad end rhyme, says the priest with the PCV licence. Bad end rhyme, yesterday that never came, loaded pistol – the rainbow loses its magic when we try to explain it. You won't feel the wonder of a kiss by analysing it. And it's always more important to feel things than to understand them.

Why don't you write? You seem to be on top of things. You write, and I can head worry-free to the dinner party, have beer, red wine, ice-cold schnapps, listen to Elvis . . . what?

He who knows everything can't write. He who knows everything loses the ability to live, because it's uncertainty that drives people onward. Uncertainty, fear, loneliness and desire. Not to mention the paradox. You don't know much, that's true, but when you're writing you see through walls, through hills and mountains. You see how the cells divide, see the president of the United States betraying his people, hear words of love whispered on the other side of the country, hear someone crying in another part of the city. You see the wife leave her husband, and when the husband cheats on his wife. You hear the world's sobs. That's the paradox, that's the responsibility, and that's the deal. You can't escape it, and therefore must continue.

To write?

Yes, what else? Write and you'll be able to go to the dinner party in honour of Páll of Oddi, Presley and life.

Write. And we won't forget.

Write. And we won't be forgotten.

Write. Because death is just another name for being forgotten.

Here, Spring Comes as Late as in Hell,
but Lord, Chasten Me – I'm So
Glad to Have Come

BE CAREFUL, MY LOVE – WORST OF ALL IS TO DIE SO
SLOWLY THAT YOU'RE HARDLY AWARE OF IT

It rains over Pétur and Ljúf on their way back home, after leaving three books at the heath farm Uppsalir, including two in Danish on biology and astronomy. In a nutshell, he had said in the small family room, having been shown to the seat where the hefty postman had sat a few weeks before and made a significant dent in the home's coffee supplies – in a nutshell, these two books are about life in the soil, the little creatures there, and about the expanses of space. Yes, they take us from the soil into the darkness between the stars, where man finds great mysteries.

If only I were better at Danish, said Guðríður, sitting opposite him, hunched over the first book, flipping slowly through it, her fingers trembling slightly, her eyes bright with enthusiasm. They literally shone. He thought, I've never seen eyes shine like this before.

First, though, coffee had to be made, refreshments prepared.

Pétur isn't even asked if he wants anything, this is just how it is, as long as there's a grain of coffee, as long as someone is alive to make it, it shall be served – the black drink that has for a good hundred years helped people to survive in this harsh, beautiful country. And, on top of that, made it easier for people to talk together.

Let's go inside for coffee, Gísli, Guðríður's husband, had said in the April light outside, when she had just emerged from the farm passageway, shielded her eyes with her hand, instinctively, due to the drastic change in light after standing in the tunnel for such a ridiculously long time. She greeted the visitor, a great honour, she said, and books for me, I'm at a loss for words.

And because of this, she said no more, just smiled.

It was the other smile, the dangerous one. Pétur saw it now for the first time.

He had received two letters from her . . . well, only one, strictly speaking. The first letter was addressed to the editors. Yet she had put all of herself into that letter, without intending it, without being aware of it. Which is probably the most dangerous. And had caused Pétur to write back, to answer it, and then to ask the postman to deliver the letter to her. It's a detour, the postman had said, that hefty man, it's out of the way. It can't be called life if we always go the same way, if we never take a detour, replied Pétur, before adding: Live. Which, of course, made no sense, as if I were dead, the postman would say later. Several times, and in various places. That's why many people knew about the letter, not its contents, no, of course not, but that Reverend Pétur had written a letter to the housewife on the heath farm Uppsalir, to she who would end up attracting attention from well outside her parish because of her article about the earthworm, uneducated yet still able to write such a thing.

Yes, he ordered me to live, as if I were dead, or dying, and then to make this detour. It's rather out of the way, I pointed out to him, and then he basically ordered me to live, as if that were one and the same thing, to live and to go places that are out of the way. Try to make sense of that! But the housewife in Uppsalir, yes, right, the one who wrote about the earthworm in the journal, courtesy and modesty in the flesh, and as slender as a girl, might I add, but I sensed something harsh, too, quite harsh. I'm so sensitive, that's my trouble. And because of it, I sensed that she can sting, she can bite, should she care to, if she's in that sort of mood, and then it's doubtless better not to tangle with her.

I wanted to be nowhere else but in that smile, Pétur thought, on the slope in front of the cottage at Uppsalir. Be nowhere else – as if he simply had no responsibilities in life, needed to be nowhere else.

The three girls led Ljúf behind them, they were supposed to give her a handful of hay and wanted to find a good one, the best hay in the barn, she's so lovely, they said, kissing the mare as the sweets melted like sunshine in their mouths. But their father stood between the smile and Pétur. He stood there in the silence.

I couldn't do less, said Pétur, but then he had to look away from Guðríður, to tear himself away from her smile. Get hold of yourself, man, he thought, remembering how Halla, his wife, had looked at him when he left early that morning, with three books and strangely vague explanations for the trip, which would take all day. Where are you going? she had asked, surprised, knowing that he had nothing planned; Pétur habitually let her know well in advance when he had to go somewhere, on official business here and there, or to Stykkishólmur because of the journal. But the decision for this trip was made late last evening, at nightfall – it was made in a letter to Hölderlin. He had written it down, then leaned back, excited, frightened by his decision – he slept barely a wink that night. And completely forgot to come up with explanations. Because he could hardly say, there's a woman, on a farm, a considerable distance from here, several hours on horseback, completely uneducated but wrote a fascinating article about the earthworm. Of all the world's creatures. There's something unusual about her. Something that calls to me. I wrote her a letter, asked the postman to deliver it, knew that it would be somewhat out of the way for him, which he pointed out as well, but then I ordered him to live. As if I have any say in that. I who couldn't stop death when it mattered most. Since then, no day has ever really dawned in this world.

He had thought all these things while Halla looked at him and waited for explanations, the reasons for the long day trip. He had wanted to say that about Eva. That it was as if no day had ever really dawned since she died. That even the light from God had faded. But why say that, it doesn't explain why he packed the books so carefully, why the thought of this unknown woman from the heath and her writing style had had such a strong effect on him. Maybe she was ugly, almost toothless, with a sunken chest . . . That didn't explain why love had begun to fade in his heart . . . fade so slowly that for a long time he wasn't aware of it, didn't suspect it. And when he finally noticed it, he initially thought it was related to some general malaise, perhaps due to his longing for life in Copenhagen, the possibilities there, perhaps the monotony of the countryside or growing older and coming to the realisation that he hadn't yet managed to pursue the dreams of his youth. Didn't understand what was happening until it was too late. The worst of all, and the most horrible, is to die so slowly that you aren't even aware of it. That's the defeat, that's the tragedy. You're defeated without having an opportunity to defend yourself. Such defeats seldom find their way onto the front pages of life, and even less into the work of writers. Few take up the cause of those things that die so slowly that we don't even feel it. No heroic poems are written about them, no tragedies. It's the dull Tuesdays, the bloodless Wednesdays.

Which can still be the source of the sadness that paralyses you.

The self-reproach that eats away at you.

Because Halla had made him a better person. It was because of her that he managed to establish himself in life, and that they have this home together. Three wonderful children, the fourth, Eva, is dead, she sank into the silence of the soil. But it was both of them who lost her, Pétur and Halla. I lost her too, she once said, not long ago. What right does he have to grieve more over it than Halla, with her poignant sensitivity, but also a determination that few can bend, cheerfulness that makes the days lighter, and more honesty and sincerity than Pétur has ever seen in any other person. His partner in life. And people say that she has hands of light. But when, how, did the warmth leave her touch, where did the eagerness about living with her go, the joy of waking up beside her, where did it go . . .

It's his fault.

Why did it have to happen so slowly that he didn't notice anything until it was too late, and therefore never got a chance to raise his defences?

I don't know, Pétur had written to Hölderlin, how many times

I've gone to the church and addressed God there, invoked Jesus, and pleaded for answers: where did love go, why couldn't I hold on to it? Pleaded for answers, hints, signs or just anything – but never got any response; why is that, poet?

Hölderlin: Maybe because God doesn't respond to the questions that man alone can answer.

This answer, statement, conclusion, comes to Pétur for some reason when Gísli invites him to sit on the edge of the bed where the postman had sat weeks before, on his errand for Pétur. Gísli himself doesn't sit down, not immediately, but chooses to stand, slightly stooping as usual, as if he's constantly pensive, perpetually grinding something down to its core. He has intelligent eyes, Pétur thought, but then he has to answer the bent-backed farmer's questions. The priest has travelled a long way, what would compel a person to make such a long journey, time is precious, it could hardly be only to bring three books to this cottage?

Gísli had raised his voice somewhat, as he had done outside when he invited Pétur in, spoke loudly, doubtless hoping that Guðríður would hear it in the house, and then realised that she was expecting a visitor. He was of course surprised that she hadn't come out to greet him, it isn't customary to wait inside the house if a visitor shows up. In such instances, everyone goes out to the farmyard, people and dogs, it's polite, and besides, having visitors was too big of an event to stay inside. That is, if the weather is conducive to going outside, if there's no harm in doing so. He wants me to hear, she had thought, in hiding, in the passageway, spying; he wants me to hear, she thinks again, in the kitchen. There's really no need for him to speak so loudly for her to do so, the distance between them isn't that great. He wants me to hear, and wants me to listen for the answer. But again she discerns that peculiar tone in Gísli's voice, insistent, almost aggressive. She hardly remembers having heard it in his voice before. Why is that?

Man alone knows the answers, but sometimes he hides them from himself, Pétur thinks, without knowing where that thought comes

159

from, or why it has come now. Then he clears his throat, repeats his convoluted explanation from when they were outside, but now adds, trying to affect weariness, oh, it's a sheer wonder how many tasks can accumulate and pile up around a poor priest, I don't wish to weary you with my prattle, my good farmer, there's no lack of wearisomeness in this world. But you have just returned from the fishing down south at Arnarstapi, I heard at Bær, from your district manager— Yes, he keeps his eye on everything, Gísli interrupts Pétur, he gets some satisfaction from it, does Jóhannes, that's fairly obvious!

An uncomfortable feeling comes over Guðríður as she prepares the coffee and the refreshments, which are perhaps on the unremarkable side, she knows it, yet they're something – an effort, at least. Gísli had allowed himself to buy various small items before leaving Arnarstapi, Oxford and Harvard English biscuits, rusks, raisins, figs, dates. Various unnecessary things, he said when he got home, shocked at his own extravagance, acting vexed with himself, which he certainly was in part, but he'd also been looking forward to coming home and seeing the joy on Guðríður's face, seeing her smile, which shall always touch him just as deeply no matter how many years go by, no matter how forcefully hardship, disappointment and toil cut into their existence and days. And of course he looked forward to witnessing the girls' joy.

And now some of the best is served.

Guðríður works quickly but quietly, trying to follow the conversations as best she can, and a feeling of unease takes hold of her when her husband interrupts Pétur and so unhesitatingly and openly criticises Jóhannes; what's wrong with him, she thinks, and her hands tremble a little – this isn't like him. Fortunately, Pétur doesn't seem to be disturbed, but of course he doesn't know Gísli at all, doesn't realise how unusual this behaviour of his, or the tone of his voice, is; he just smiles and says, yes, there are always some who wish to keep track of everything, have their eyes everywhere. That's true. We may curse them but, still, we don't mind having them visit, so eager we are to hear the news – then we thank them for being as they are. Such a difficult thing is life. So difficult it is to be faultless; it is of course nearly impossible for most of us. We drag our faults behind us like heavy rocks. But hopefully the cod fishing was good, and the weather was not too much of an inconvenience?

Over the years, Pétur has learned to do the asking and thus avoid being asked, learned to divert attention elsewhere, he asks in order to shelter himself, asks to give himself peace, asks others about things that he knows or suspects they would like to talk about, even so much that they're immediately grateful to Pétur for bringing whatever it is up. He knows how to get people to shine – and, in doing so, can turn his own light off. He only needs to pay enough attention to grasp the gist of the topic, gain an idea of its outline, just enough to add a small comment or two, a concise question in the right and suitable place for stoking the fire, otherwise he can disappear into himself, remain there alone, sheltered. And now he plays this role of his seamlessly for Gísli, who enjoys talking about seamanship with those who know something about it, which the priest seems to do, he asks intelligently, asks with knowledge, intuition. And then talking about it becomes even more enjoyable. So enjoyable that Gísli becomes almost eloquent. His mistrust of Pétur, the surliness that he felt every time he thought of the priest after returning from Arnarstapi and hearing of the letter, just disappears, becomes nothing. Gísli talks, speaks with gusto, the big boat cuts through the waves in the family room, Gísli licks his lips, which taste of salt. He stands up again because it's better to stand when you tell of things, it flows better. Pétur watches him intently, interestedly, seems to immerse himself in what is being described, yet remain at the same time deep within his own thoughts. He is sitting in the family room, but is not there. I may be looking at you, yet am very far from you.

AND THERE IS NO WAY BACK

Why couldn't he answer when Halla asked about the purpose of his trip?

His only answer was to pat the three books that he had bundled so carefully, smile like a fool, or like someone trying to hide something unforgivable, and say, oh, it's always something, as you know.

Always something.

Of course that's the way it is, always something. Seeing to solicitations and obligations, priest to numerous farms, pastor to almost three hundred souls; he holds seats on the local council, the editorial board of the journal, the board of the ministers' association, which means trips to Reykjavík once a year, or twice – to name just a few of his duties. Tasks, errands, responsibilities. But Halla has always known about his trips, where, why, and Pétur had never left so suddenly before, let alone for an entire day, and now he replied with nothing, for the most part, when she asked. Or answered as if it had nothing to do with her. Answered as if she were just anyone. Answered as if their lives weren't intertwined at all. Answered by patting the books and saying, it's always something. Then kissed her on the forehead, tried to smile, and managed to do so. Because he's able, unfortunately, to divide himself in two. And as a result will never be whole. Halla also tried to smile, he saw it, but she couldn't, she's too honest, too whole.

But then she called out after him: Be careful, my love.

And he nearly turned back.

He could so easily send the books by post, except then the postman wouldn't have to make a detour, go out of his way, this time it would be enough to leave the parcel at Bær, this time he wouldn't order the postman to live. He nearly turned back.

Nearly.

But didn't.

Because it was too late? Six years too late? Seven? He doesn't know.

Be careful, my love.

My love. There's hardly a more beautiful way to address someone.

Say my love, as you alone can say it; as you alone can whisper it, and no darkness will ever frighten me again; say my love, and I won't drown; say my love, and I'll go out into the world and defeat dragons. Say, be careful, my love, and I'll sit down on a tussock next to my horse and weep, with a wet rear end. Say my love and I'll bleed

162

internally because I no longer love you and life without loving you isn't life, it's a heavy, wet snowstorm. I'm bleeding because I received a letter, it wasn't even addressed to me, yet it was written just for me. And then I felt frightened. Because when I finished reading the letter I wanted to live, to be happy again. Yet I hadn't seen her smile then. But now I've seen it, now I've seen her smile, and I fear that from now on there's no way back.

Is it possible to be happy in one's unhappiness, is that justifiable?

THERE, SPRING COMES AS LATE AS IN HELL – AND THEN HER TAILBONE STARTS TO ITCH

Men will never agree which bait is best to use, Pétur hears himself say, not quite sure if it fits entirely with what Gísli is saying, having sunk so deeply into himself that there was hardly anything left of him here in the family room. Except for the one-tenth that's the surface of every human being. But that fragment clearly did its duty, assessed correctly, sent the appropriate message to his language centre, which put these words together and sent them out into the world: men will never agree which bait is best to use.

Gísli is in such full agreement with the priest that he sits down. Sits down, heaves a sigh, reaches into his pocket for tobacco, says, so true, so true, Reverend. It's so true that I've seen men give up debating it in words and tear into each other, letting their fists do any further talking! Pétur shakes his head, smiling, and Gísli thinks, it's fun talking to him. I probably live too far away from everything. It's right what my brother sometimes says in his letters, that it can be damned fun talking to people, it simply must be said, it perks you up. I'm going to mention it to Guðríður afterwards, when the priest is gone. I think it will make her happy. No, I *know* it will!

Now I'm going in to them, thinks Guðríður.

Gísli's unusually lively narrative has slowed down a bit. She has listened as well as she can, and it has been a long time since she heard

163

him describe his sea trips in such a lively way: for a time Guðríður felt as if she herself were out on the open sea, was crossing the waves up there on the heath. Too few people come here, she thought, probably for the thousandth time this year, and it's only April. But as enjoyable as it is to hear Gísli so enthusiastic, her mind is constantly wandering. Gísli's voice recedes, becomes a distant murmur, a meaningless mumble, and she starts thinking of the visitor. Just inadvertently. Unintentionally. But it's also hard to believe how little self-control she has. Over her thoughts, let alone her emotions, which can resemble a flock of sheep racing wildly over slopes and moorland, climbing up the steepest scree, rushing out into a hot-tempered, frenetic glacial river, unheedful no matter how zealously the shepherd dogs of reason bark.

Not that she's out of control in any way in the kitchen, there off the family room, the coffee's been made and everything's been placed on the fine tray that Gísli had been so lucky to acquire a few years ago, bought from English sailors for three pairs of woollen socks, two shirts of homespun, two pairs of seaman's mittens, a three-weeks' supply of tobacco. Wasn't it hard to be tobacco-free for so long? she had asked, and to give away your garments? No, not when I thought about how happy you'd be with the tray, Gísli had said, looking down, probably because it's very much unlike him to speak in this way, show his feelings so unhesitatingly, and she was moved, tears welled in her eyes. Because there was love behind the gift. Love and sacrifice. She knew very well how difficult it was for Gísli to have had no tobacco for three weeks. And then to have sacrificed his clothes. She recalls that sacrifice every time she takes out the tray. Remembers his words and how he had looked down, beautifully shy at his own words.

But there's no reason to wait any longer to go in to them.

She is composed, it has grown fairly quiet inside of her, except that she feels guilty about her attention wandering so often while Gísli was speaking. His narrative has wound down and now Reverend Pétur is saying something about . . . she moves closer to hear better . . . the problem of choosing the right bait. Yes, she's familiar with that controversy, Gísli has told her about it. Opinions on it can be passionate, to say the least. But she has everything prepared. There's the coffee, there are the refreshments from the merchant at Arnarstapi on the tray. She can receive guests unashamedly, even if their farmhouse is small, hardly more than a cottage here on the edge of the heath, lacking most of the luxuries that the modern world has begun to offer, coal stoves, kerosene lamps, more spacious rooms, chairs for visitors to sit on in place of the beds, nice cups for the coffee . . . yes, they really are too far from everything . . .

Up there, spring comes as late as in hell, Björgvin, her father-in-law, had told Gísli when they wanted to buy the farm, which had been deserted for a few years; the only farm they could afford.

Spring comes as late as in hell.

Björgvin tried hard to get Gísli to spend a few more years working with him in his trading business and at sea with an acquaintance of his during the winter fishing seasons. Patience isn't just a virtue, it's the sister of reason. But Gísli's need to be his own master, the Icelanders' old, importunate dream of independence, like a persistent itch, and the fact that decent farms rarely came available, compelled them to move up here. Those were bright days in Guðríður's life.

Almost fourteen years have passed since then – and her hands have stopped trembling.

She grips the tray. That nice tray of refreshments that she has nothing to be ashamed of. Even if the visitor is practically a famous man, a highly educated priest, intelligent, accustomed to fine houses. She is completely calm. Poised. And steps into the family room. After having glanced quickly into the small mirror she keeps behind the partition. Keeps it there so that she can check her appearance before walking out in front of the few visitors who make their way here. Vanity is a stern taskmaster. But, yes, she looks fine. As fine as she can. You're just fine, my dear, she thought, addressing her reflection, the creature that always meets her in the small mirror. She adjusted her expression, knows how to do so, is good at it. Is good at putting on her affectionate look, her friendly smile, making her peaty green eyes cheerful. No, not cheerful, that's too much; more like affable. You're ready, she said to her reflection, which smiled back.

Guðríður holds the tray. No need at all to be ashamed of it. She steps into the family room with her friendly smile, steps into her husband's speculations about which bait is best to use. I've literally seen people fighting about it, Gísli is saying, but then she comes with the tray.

Then she comes with her eyes. Then she comes with that slender body of hers.

Pétur looks up, meets her eyes for a second, and smiles. Not in a friendly way, like her. His smile comes from deep within his blood, everything he is, is in that smile, his entire existence is there, his consciousness, dreams, sadness, zeal. She is startled, she feels warm all over, she's happy, she's frightened, but she tries to maintain her friendly, neutral smile and make sure that her hands don't start to tremble.

Damn it, she thinks, and her tailbone starts itching.

ONCE HE STOLE, ONCE HE COMMITTED A CRIME

The priest is of course used to better houses, says Gísli as he reaches for the small table that he made in the spring after he brought home the tray. Which he got on board an English fishing vessel, that is quite correct, although not quite in the way he had told Guðríður.

Everything has its explanations.

They had encountered a storm.

It had hit them fast as they were raking in fish, the sea literally alive with fish that seemed to be vying to bite.

The crew had been working like mad, every man toiling away; they thought of nothing but hauling in the catch, didn't look around, all their focus went into the fishing, to bring in as much as possible, to fill the boat to the brim and, because of this, didn't notice the weather piling up around them; but the south-westerly gale hit just as quickly, with violent gusts. They just managed to pull the

166

lines aboard but it was impossible to make it back to shore. All they could do was hold their own, stay afloat, stay alive. They salvaged the fishing gear, everyone managed to pull in his own line, full of fish – but then they were at the mercy of the storm. The raging snowstorm so dark that it was as if the world was dying. And the third gust struck the boat flat. The sail nearly plunged into the heavy waves, they barely managed to right the boat before the fourth and hardest gust hit them. They survived it, but the five-man boat that had been fishing about a kilometre from them did not – when the snowstorm subsided, they spied the boat's keel, like a heavy coffin. The air cleared, they sighted land, they could see far out to sea and everything became so wonderfully calm and bright. It was almost as if the sky had wanted to shoo the storm away in order to watch the five men who fought desperately around the boat in the heavy waves. And it seemed to think, oh, to see you struggle! You who are so tiny that it's almost impossible to spot you, such fleeting tidings – I blink my eyes once and you've been dead for a thousand years. Why are you fighting for the brief moment that is your lives?

Go to sleep.

And it suddenly darkened again.

The sky grew heavy and dim with blowing snow, the wind howled, and it was impossible for them to change direction, sail towards the sinking boat, attempt to rescue the drowning men. Everything disappeared; the world went pitch-dark. They could barely see just a few metres in front of the boat, the wind tore up the sea and blew them westwards along the coast of Snæfellsnes and it wasn't until they had reached Hellisvík, a large fishing station and excellent mooring place at the very tip of the peninsula, that they managed to find refuge, rowed there up alongside an English fishing vessel that, like them, sought shelter from the weather. The English were already quite drunk and somehow it happened that Gísli ended up aboard the smack, along with two of his mates.

And woke the next morning in one of the fishing huts at Hellisvík, with the tray under him. Hardly remembered anything, had no idea how he got into the bunk he found himself in, whether he'd hit on it by chance or some local had taken pity on him. With a piercing headache, he staggered out, found a pail of ice-cold water, and poured it over his head, and his memory slowly began to clear. The three of them had been down in the forecastle of the English smack with the piss-drunk crew, loud conversations in a kind of jumble of Icelandic and English, a few men were jostling and Gísli had set eyes on the tray when he crept away from the table and stuck it without a second thought under his coat. Without knowing why. He couldn't understand himself. He had never stolen anything. To commit such an act, such a disgrace, had never once crossed his mind. It was so shameful. Being drunk was no excuse. A man should be blameless, no matter what his circumstances. And weather all storms.

The first, and, God help him, the last time Gísli had stolen something. He was racked with shame as they crept slowly past the English ship, where everyone seemed to be sleeping soundly. But he couldn't bring himself to return the tray. It would have been so humiliating, and the deed would probably have become public knowledge. That he, Gísli Björgvinsson, that hardworking, reliable man, was just a miserable thief, after all. He couldn't look anyone in the face again. No-one would trust him anymore. He would never get out of that heath farm. And maybe it would reach his father's ears . . . No, considering everything, looking at it from every angle, it was clear that he couldn't return the tray. Done was done, and could not be taken back. He would simply dispose of the tray – but when it came time, he couldn't bring himself to do so. Yet it would have been so easy. Just let it disappear into the sea. But there's something so bloody wrong about throwing away a treasure that the fine folk in both Stykkishólmur and Reykjavík wouldn't turn up their noses at. Over time, one can forgive much, if not most things; life can be heavy enough, all the hardship, constraints, constant struggles, without a person having something weighing on him, or without burdening it further with discord, old annoyances.

While it was truly shameful of him to have stolen the tray, it was something he needed to deal with himself, a responsibility that he needed to bear alone – but to throw away an object that was in perfect shape, that was so splendid, such a thing could hardly be forgiven – the world would have to be in a strange place for such a thing to happen. That is why Gísli kept the tray. Hid it carefully from his boatmates, and then took it home. But it was painful to let go of the garments, the woollen socks, the shirt of homespun, the mittens, it hurt to see them lying there in a lava hollow halfway between Arnarstapi and Uppsalir. He pushed them as deep into the hollow as possible. It stung him, it was an unforgivable waste, yet it was the only way. It was the sacrifice, it was the atonement. Five years have passed, maybe six, and Gísli still feels a twinge of pain when Guðríður serves refreshments on the tray, the few times they have visitors, and then at Christmas, Easter. A mild twinge. It's his shame, reminding him of itself. His humiliation. Like now. A mild twinge. Then he looks down, thinks of his crime.

A FEW GENERAL REMARKS ON THE USES OF A SOCK

When he looks up, he sees that Guðríður has laid the tray on the small table and has gone back into the kitchen to fetch the coffee. He watches his wife go. Watches this woman whom he has had before his eyes every single day all these years, except for a few weeks each winter when he is at Arnarstapi. She is the most ordinary thing in his life. Months can go by without Gísli seeing any other person but her. Her and of course the girls, which, however, is different. She is the first thing he sees when he wakes up and the last before he sinks into sleep. She is everyday life itself. His everyday life is called Guðríður. And when the cramped conditions of their home are added, he and Guðríður constantly on top of each other, especially in winter when they can't get anywhere, the world is submerged in snow and it's hardly possible to go outside, it's an incredible wonder that the years haven't worn down the important things to the point of breaking. He does, in fact, after all these years, that endless, unbroken chain of practically identical days, still find it nice to watch her walk. It touches something deep inside him. How can he explain it? That it's just so pleasurable watching her walk? It's like poise itself, so noble, but it can also be downright girlish – and then there's that vague, captivating quality that he can't put into words.

It's so remarkable.

As angry as he can be at her sometimes. When she forgets her responsibilities. When she grows careless. When, out of nowhere, she suddenly becomes a subscriber to this or that periodical. Or more or less refuses to unsubscribe during hard times. And he has come into the house after many hours of toil, a hungry, tired man demanding his meal, to gain energy to keep going, even a bit abraded in his soul, it is perhaps spring and the temperature has dropped, it has frozen, snowed, he has been forced to bring all his livestock inside and feed them hay, and the meagre hay supply is running out, alarmingly quickly; one of the sheep doesn't look so well, or Gísli has noticed damage to the sheds – he comes in, tired, a worried man, and she is lost in her own world. Her thoughts. Her reading, her study. Is even still in bed in the middle of the day, which has happened before, and the girls aren't even dressed, completely neglected. It's as if God is punishing him. And something inside him has broken.

Most difficult, however, was when Guðríður lay for weeks in bed following the birth of their youngest daughter, little Elín, so sluggish and apathetic that she could hardly take care of the infant, let alone their home. Of course, it wasn't exactly her fault. But still. Or, as his mother pointed out, women have had children in this country for a thousand years without having to lie in bed for weeks afterwards.

Because in the end, Gísli was compelled to visit his parents.

He had to leave Guðríður behind, bedridden. Left all the responsibility to the oldest girl, Björg, young as she was. Made his way down from the heath to his parents' home and admitted his troubles to them. Owned up to his privation. It was heavy, it was a difficult bite to swallow. Then his mother said that about women having had children for a thousand years and not having had to lie there helpless afterwards – what would have happened to this nation, after all, if they did? It was a matter of opinion, he had to admit, though only to himself, said nothing. And his mother, of course, had to go too far, couldn't stop. As if she were triumphant. Now, I've always said, she went on, and said it from the start, hopefully you haven't forgotten it, I warned you, and in this your father can bear witness, that, as sweet and intelligent as Guðríður can be, she doesn't have the grit for this. She's not the kind of woman who—

Gísli had had enough. He got up and left without saying a word. Went out to saddle Faxi, who was still in full vigour, the very picture of health. It was around midnight, but he didn't care. He was going home, this would all work out somehow, he needed no help. But his father came out after him and managed to calm him down.

The next day Gísli left for home, leading Faxi, who carried Sigrún, one of his parents' three maids.

That was the day when diligence came to Uppsalir.

Over the next months, Gísli got to experience how much one woman can accomplish. Got to experience diligence. Because it was as if Sigrún could do nothing but work. She was with them for two months and he sometimes thought, without intending to, without wanting to, that his dream of a better farm, even down by the sea, would have been realised many years ago had he had a woman like Sigrún at his side.

This thought just came, uninvited. Actually forced itself into his head.

And twice he saw Sigrún take off her nightgown in the early morning.

Both times, he pretended to be asleep, with Guðríður breathing heavily next to him. She had grown thin and pale. But there was Sigrún, sitting with her back turned to Gísli. He looked at her bare, strong back as she sat there unmoving for several moments, as if thinking. Then she stretched out her hand distractedly for her clothes, having to turn slightly to reach them. Which is why he saw . . . more. And just watched. He drank in Sigrún's nudity. She was sturdier than Guðríður. Stockier. Her breasts were much larger and seemed to be . . . calling to him invitingly, and it was as if he could actually feel them in the palms of his hands. Soft, big and buxom, and, as far as he could see, the nipple facing him had swollen. A warm, restless current passed through him and it was very difficult to lie still. Then

171

she got up slowly, and he saw that she was completely naked. She stood there motionless, one side turned completely towards him; he saw her swollen nipple and caught a glimpse of the dark hair between her thighs. Then she turned so that her naked back, broader than Guðríður's, was visible to Gísli, and, when she bent forward and down to reach for something, her buttocks parted and he saw . . . But then she was dressed. She went to the kitchen and began to light the stove, leaving him lying there. Breathing heavily. He closed his eyes and before he knew it he had slipped his hand under the blanket, it just found its own way there, grabbed his swollen penis tightly and Gísli had grown so strangely excited that he nearly came immediately. He just managed to grab his sock and moaned as he emptied himself into it. This happened twice. And for the next few days, it was enough for him just to think about it to become excited again.

Yet he was relieved when she left.

I HAVE NEVER SEEN EYES SHINE LIKE THAT BEFORE – BUT HAS HE EVER BEEN AS HARD?

Sigrún is the picture of diligence. But she simply talks too much; diligence and prattle go badly together – there's something wrong with that combination. And it was never exactly fun to watch her walk or move.

Diligence?

The folk down in the lowland should just see Guðríður rake grass! Then there would be no talk of incapability and dreaminess. Then his mother wouldn't find fault with her. Because sometimes she can work so hard that she would easily rake all the Sigrúns out to sea! God in heaven, he's so proud of her at such times. And it's also a sheer wonder how she has managed to grow birch trees at the south side of the house, or how she manages sometimes to get potatoes and swedes from her small vegetable garden, what great ingenuity she shows in making food from the little variety of produce available to them. I adore your cooking, Guðríður, said his mother when his parents stayed with them for a few days last summer. And my mouth

172

began watering as soon as we caught sight of the farm. His mother's words warmed Gísli's heart. And he filled with pride.

But still.

She tends to lose herself. For hours at a time. To drop out. Which happens very often. When she no longer seems to understand that life is a struggle. That one must never really relax, nowhere, and not at all up here at nearly two hundred metres above the sea. Spring may come late and badly, the delicate spring grass freezes, they're forced to feed the sheep hay well into lambing and life is on a razor's edge. At such times, one truly counts each straw. And the number of them depends entirely and mercilessly on how decidedly and ceaselessly one worked over the summer, keeping one's head out of the clouds, depriving oneself of sleep, pushing aside everything but work. No time for reading. No time for thinking about things that are far away. Because when spring is late and capricious, one needs hay, not deep thoughts. Still, Gísli is so proud that he has a hard time keeping it hidden when the people down in the lowland praise her in his hearing. Because that happens, too. Saying things, perhaps, such as one might think she'd attended school, or that she should even be got to teach the local children; after all, their girls outshone the others when they went for two weeks each winter to take lessons from the travelling teacher down at Bær. They could hardly learn anything new from those lessons, so well taught they were by their mother. And to watch her walk, with that slender back of hers, to see the curve in it, it's still . . .

This is quite something, says Pétur.

Gísli asks, What? He'd dropped out, hardly knows where he went, which is shameful. One should always be present, completely in the moment. One should be firmly rooted in reality. He asks, What?, vexed with himself. Looks determinedly at the priest.

These are such fine refreshments that I feel like the bishop himself, if not the Pope!

One can only offer the little one's got, says Gísli, refusing to allow himself to smile – one should always accept compliments humbly.

173

And then Guðríður brings the coffee. The coffee and her affable smile, the less dangerous one, and picks up the thread for her husband; hopefully, the priest can forgive us for how small and dreary this place of ours is here on the heath; he's naturally more accustomed to better houses. Our coffee, however, is authentic, and black as it can possibly be. But I see that the girls haven't given a thought to coming back in; they're out with your mare, of course. Hopefully, the priest will forgive them that. They're so young and unaccustomed to visitors that they don't quite know how to behave and probably find it more exciting to have a horse come to visit than a human being. They're hopeless; I suppose it would be best to disown them? In their defence, I must admit that we were forced to put down our horse, Faxi, last autumn. They miss him so much that they've chosen the mare over the man.

No need to apologise for them, no need at all, says Pétur, smiling broadly; he simply can't stop smiling around this woman, making a fool of himself. No need at all; my Ljúf surpasses me considerably, in terms of both intelligence and company.

Ljúf, what an incredibly beautiful name for a horse, says Guðríður, so warmly that Gísli gives her a look of surprise as she sits down next to him, sits down so softly that his longing to embrace her practically burns his arms. But Gísli composes himself. They have a visitor.

So here is the coffee, completely authentic, at that, says Guðríður as she pours Pétur a cup, poised, affable, polite, smiling. Black as a January night, as it should be, he says, taking a sip and sighing contentedly; then he reaches for the bundle that he had placed on the bed next to him, unwraps it, and hands Guðríður two of the three books, which she accepts. She intends to do so with a smile, grateful, restrained, but is suddenly gripped with shyness, insecurity, and a slight redness appears on her white neck. Gísli recognises this sign. Her skin always gives her away, which is why she is unable to hide her feelings from those who know her, that has always been the case, her skin can't lie. She accepts the books, immediately hunches over them, starts flipping through the pages, silently asks her fingers not to do her the disservice of beginning to tremble, it's enough that her skin betrays her, enough that she sits there with a red neck, red in the cheeks like a teenage girl. Don't tremble, she asks in silence, but mutters, if only I were better at Danish, then sinks herself into the text, forgets time and place. Her index finger runs along the lines, she moves her lips, almost invisibly, and her eyes shine, they literally shine. Pétur thinks, I've never seen eyes shine like this before.

She moves her lips, seems to be gone from the other two, immersed in the world of the text, and there's silence in the family room. Dead silence. Outside, one of the girls shouts cheerfully, Sámur barks; otherwise, there's only the faint sound of her running her finger along a line, as if she wants not only to read the words but also touch them, feel them, physically. The two men watch her, having forgotten themselves, as well, Pétur the visitor's courtesy, Gísli the host's duties, they just watch. Each in his own way. Two wrinkles have formed between her eyes. A wonderful thirst, Pétur thinks, wonderful, and suddenly Gísli feels like a visitor in his own home. What nonsense, he tries to think, he prefers to shake his head to confirm it, but instead sits as if paralysed and feels a strange sadness. He looks at the tray. Once, he stole. Once, he committed a crime. But it was only because he loves this woman sitting beside him, longed to please her, this person who sometimes seems out of place in his world, yes, sometimes he even feels as if he just borrowed her. That one day he'll wake up here in the family room and she'll be gone, she will have evaporated.

Thrice, in fact, he has dreamed that he wakes up in their bed, sits up in the half-darkness and sees that it's not Guðríður lying next to him but Sigrún, with her buxom breasts beneath her nightgown, diligent, tough Sigrún whose only flaw is talking too much. And not being Guðríður.

The girls are lying in the other beds but all look like miniature versions of Sigrún. He looks down at her, senses the power emanating from her, and the memory of her swollen nipple, her large, ample backside, her buttocks that separate, gives him a near-immediate erection. He looks and longs to undress her, longs to slip inside her. But he also thinks, now the hay will never run out. Now I'll never have to count the straws because I know there will always be enough.

175

He hears the ocean outside and notices the fourth bed, where his long-desired son is sleeping and is now big enough to go with him to sea to fish. Yet he is going to wait a bit to wake the boy, because Sigrún is awake and she's naked, and there are those big breasts, strong thighs, and she starts fondling his penis with her fingers. Isn't it nice? she then whispers as he slips into her. Yes, Gísli whispers. Has it ever been as hard? No, he whispers excitedly. It was never as hard when you were with Guðríður, she says huskily, she says triumphantly, she says and spreads her legs further apart, but then for some reason he becomes so sad, feels so hopeless, that he starts to cry. Wakes up crying. Wakes up as he's coming. Orgasms in tears next to the sleeping Guðríður.

THE DEVIL'S BROTHER IS AN OLD BOOKSELLER IN COPENHAGEN

When Guðríður, begins Gísli, before having to clear his throat, clean it out, trying at the same time to tear himself from that silly dream. He clears his throat well, because his voice had been so piteous that he sounded more like a bedraggled chicken. Pétur looks at Gísli with a polite, interested expression. When my Guðríður reads, Gísli begins again, having regained his voice, smiling as if to remove any possible bristling from his words, it's as if she disappears from me. Sometimes so completely that I feel on the verge of going down to the lowland and gathering people to go and search for her!

Pétur: An admirable quality, I must say, to be able to concentrate so fully on one's reading and observations. Such people may disappear, but they often return with something new for the rest of us who are shackled to our environment and the moment. Bringing new knowledge, a new perspective. And I understand better now how she could write her article in a way that conveyed so much knowledge, learning. Unfortunately, I can assure you that it isn't common.

Gísli laughs softly: Disappears, yes; sometimes she does so literally! I might come in and there's no meal, the girls have been neglected. Where is your mama? I ask. She went out, they say, and know nothing more about it. And she herself is surprised at my dissatisfaction when she finally reappears, maybe hours later. Even chilled to the bone after watching the loons on the lake here further up the heath. She once spent two days digging into the peat to determine how deep the dampness went, how the colour of the earth changes the deeper it is!

Those who are born with a living and clear mind, says Pétur, long to broaden the horizons of those of us who are shackled to habit. You're well married.

May I remind you gentlemen that I am here with you, says Guðríður, having looked up from the second book, but with her finger under the line, as if she doesn't want to lose touch with the world it contains. The two wrinkles of concentration between her eyes are gone, but one lock of her hair had come loose as she sat hunched over the books – as if to declare that it wouldn't let itself be restrained. Her neck is still flushed, that beautiful neck, Pétur thinks, but Gísli gives a quick laugh, refills his cup sharply and then pours its contents down his throat. The black drink is so hot that he has to concentrate hard not to spit it out.

They are good books, these two, Pétur hears himself say. He is sitting directly opposite Guðríður; or, rather, she is sitting directly opposite him. She was the one who sat down; he was shown to his seat. Her neck is flushed, she's sitting upright, one lock of hair is hanging loosely at her temple.

I have seen beauty, he would end up writing to Hölderlin. Did you ever see it, somewhere other than in the world of words, when you were alive? But you know, I think it's true what has been said, that beauty can make you unhappy, because life almost always comes off badly in comparison. Who said that? then asks the German poet. How should I know, and what does it matter, besides, because I saw beauty, I sat before it, it entered me and played me badly, you should write a poem about it, poet! I have done so, Hölderlin answers, but you're still alive and therefore haven't come far enough; for you, the language of death is illegible darkness. That may be, Pétur answers, but you should have seen how upright she sat, with her finger under a line in the second book. Her husband, who is probably descended from trolls, poured burning hot coffee down his throat – I actually had to wait to take a sip, let it cool down, while he just splashed it into himself like a cool drink. He drank his coffee fast, gulped it down, but I looked at his wife, thought some nonsense, and then heard myself say, they are good books, these two . . .

Guðríður looked intently at Pétur. They are good books, these two, he had said, but then his voice faded out, he seemed deeply thoughtful, as if he were trying to recall something. The lines on his forehead deepened. He's wearing a dark jacket, not entirely new, but made of good material. No-one in the district dresses like that.

She smiles.

She takes her finger off the book, moves her hand to the side and quickly places it on Gísli's arm, leaves it there for a few seconds. The men's eyes meet. Pétur clears his throat. They're rather good, he repeats, these two books.

Of course, I haven't read them cover to cover, as my head isn't fashioned well enough for science. One of my acquaintances in Copenhagen is kind enough to fear that I'm languishing here, that I'm too out of touch, that I— but you read Danish quite well, don't you, he interrupts himself, or may I call you Guðríður, he adds like a fool, embarrassed. What in the hell should he call her but Guðríður, that's her name, and nothing else. He's not going to start calling her Ásgerður, Hulda, Anna, hardly "good housewife", and even less the one who writes about the earthworm, he's not going to call her that; she who writes letters of the alphabet that bark like dogs. But she has begun smiling again, has again begun transforming the atmosphere with her dangerous smile. She smiles and nods, confirms that it's a fine idea to call her Guðríður. And that she reads Danish quite well.

Languages, he practically blurts, trying to hide his embarrassment, it's so necessary to learn languages. I have always been convinced that becoming accustomed to hearing other languages helps both nations and individuals to mature. It is detrimental to be so locked within one's own culture that you cannot see beyond it. That is a type of poverty that can eventually trigger all sorts of prejudices. One can escape by speaking another language. Besides— Lord forgive me, he interrupts himself, just listen to me prattle! Don't take note of half of what I say, I can tend to do this, to get so far ahead of myself that I fall on my face.

He ruffles his hair, angry at himself, because the obvious had struck him in mid-sentence – here he sits, in a confined family room two hundred metres above sea level, blathering about the importance of escaping to a couple marked by hard work, hardship, especially Gísli, his hands so rough and calloused that they're reminiscent of two weathered boats. These are people who are fighting for their independence, their lives, to be able to stand upright, and who dream, of course, only of moving to a gentler farm, and here he sits, indolent, blathering about language, the importance of escaping . . . Mustn't you first be able to stand upright in order to escape? And how do you escape if all of your energy goes into surviving? When the fight itself is to raise your children, bring them to adulthood, and never lose your independence?

Gísli is looking down, as if having noticed something interesting on the family room floor. Something much more interesting than the prattle of the visitor, who is taking up their time, drinking away their coffee, eating up their luxuries, such as dates.

I need to get going, thinks Pétur, it was a mistake to come here, sheer stupidity. Perhaps all that one can expect from someone who desires nothing more than to get drunk after others have gone to bed and writes letters to a German poet who has been lying dead in his grave for half a century. He thinks, my wife has hands of light. He thinks, I'll go home and hold her in my arms. I haven't held her in my arms for so long that I should be shot. I'll hug her and say, my love. Those are words, that is a form of address that can keep us alive. I'll say, thinks Pétur – but then he senses something, looks up from his thoughts, and is met by Guðríður's smile. Is met by her eyes. What colour are they, actually? And how many languages does one need to know to be able to describe that smile? He thinks, as stupid as he is, as hopeless as he is: I would be willing to journey in darkness for a thousand years if, in the end, I were to be rewarded with this smile, with these eyes. Lord, chasten me, I am so glad to have come here.

The priest is shy about helping himself to the refreshments. It's unnecessary. There's no need for him to hold back. We have plenty here.

Says Gísli, placing his right hand next to the tray; his palm rests firmly on the tabletop. His fingers aren't very long, but are sturdy-looking and for some reason he has spread them out, as if wanting to display all their power, to show that each of them has the power and strength to stand alone if need be.

Guðríður looks at his hand. Those fingers that she knows so well. That hand that has accomplished so much, lifted so many things, has an indomitable tenacity but can also touch her with almost painful softness. Why did he put his hand there, she thinks, and in that way . . . he could easily strangle me, rushes through Pétur's mind.

It's impossible to complain about anything here, in particular the refreshments, he says at last, reaching for a biscuit, instinctively hesitating. Gísli's hand is still lying on the table, as if he had forgotten it there, and for a moment Pétur's fingers are only a few centimetres from the farmer's own, thin, delicate, if not fragile in comparison. Pétur bites into the biscuit, pulls out the third book, strokes it as he would a cat, looks thoughtfully to the side; the lines on his forehead deepen. The couple looks at him, with their different eyes, in their different thoughts.

I gathered from your article, says Pétur, that you have acquired a decent command of Danish, or else Norwegian – there is not a great difference between the two languages; sometimes it's as if one is just a slightly distorted version of the other. But since I am very familiar with reading in a language in which I am constantly running into unfamiliar words, constantly losing the thread and the meaning, and wandering aimlessly in the fog of incomprehensible words, it occurred to me that this book here could be a companion and assistant to you on your journey through the two books I let you have earlier.

Pétur runs his hand over the new book, thicker than the others, *Icelandic–Latin–Danish Dictionary*. It's a bit old, the poor thing, he says apologetically, a bit weary, having lived a long life, almost a century old. I found it at an antique bookseller's in Copenhagen when I lived there. The bookseller may have been even older than the book itself. You should have seen him, so round-shouldered that he reminded me of a tussock or clenched fist. At least two hundred years old, according to my Danish friends, but his mind was razor-sharp, and he had the most incredible eyes I've ever seen. They seemed to penetrate everything, human flesh as much as the thickest of walls. He read every person like an open book, all the way down to the spine, and needed no dictionary to understand them. Something of a legend in Copenhagen. There were those who asserted that he was the brother of the devil. A claim that arose, I could believe, because of those eyes of his. I found it disconcerting when they looked at me, and I don't know of anyone who attempted to haggle over the price of the old man's books. People simply paid the price he asked, or left his shop empty-handed. A few days after I bought this book, an acquaintance of mine saw it at my place, recognised the copy, recognisable by these two stains on the cover, which cannot be washed off, it seems, resembling two eyes, don't you think, one sad but the other childlike. They're the very history of mankind, I had to say as I looked over the book in the old man's shop. My nonsense may have pleased him a bit, because that same acquaintance of mine had just a week prior intended to purchase this particular book, but decided not to when the old man named a ridiculously high price, at least six times higher than what I paid for it. Yet now I think, says Pétur, smiling as he hands Guðríður the book, almost shyly, that it wasn't due to my twaddle about these stains, but rather because those piercing, all-seeing two-century-old eyes saw at a glance where I would bring the book in due course, that it would go where its knowledge would best belong.

Some People are Fenceposts, Others
Put Together Playlists for Death

MAYBE ONE EXISTS IN ALL TIMES

I don't know why I had to leave my narrative mid-scene – Pétur having just handed Guðríður the dictionary that the devil's brother had sold to him at a reduced price. How did she react, or Gísli?

Guðríður accepted the book. Always more books, said Gísli, placing his hand, strong, calloused, on the small table. As if he wished to add, yet we need this here to get by, so that books can be written, and so that someone has a chance to read them.

But then I was yanked back.

And am sitting again in the caravan. With my mysterious companion, the sanctified coach driver.

I feel for Gísli and am worried about him, I say, looking up from the pages and seeing that my companion is now wearing gaudy shorts and a white T-shirt, standing there at the stove, stirring crêpe batter. A picture of the British-American musician MF Doom on the T-shirt, along with the opening line of the song "Accordion": Living off borrowed time, the clock tick faster. Good sentence. Strictly speaking, the picture isn't of the man himself, since MF Doom never appears without a mask covering his entire face, because of which very few people know what he looks like. I prefer not to mention how very appropriate I find it that the priest with the PCV licence chose a shirt with this musician on it, both wearing masks, except that one is obviously hiding something while the other wants art to be more important than the artist.

Worried, about Gísli, asks the clerically trained coach driver, holding the black, worn crêpe pan like a dark statement. Are you only worried about him, not the others, Guðríður, Pétur, Halla, and yes, mankind in general – especially that? But have you noticed that man seems to go out of his way to tell of imbalances and unhappiness, uncertainty and sadness, if not grief; few people have sought to describe the abode of heaven. I think the reason for this is that you don't tell of happiness, but live it. Just ask Hölderlin, he lost his mind and could therefore confirm what I say. Things may turn out fine for Gísli, or not at all, but everything dies in the end and then it's too late to wish for happiness. But you can always make crêpes. Times are only bad if you can no longer comfort yourself and others with lukewarm crêpes. But then, of course, he who has never been harmed by love doesn't know life. Has never lived, even.

But these are all just theories, he concludes, before pouring the first ladle of batter onto the pan, and the aroma of freshly baked crêpes fills the little caravan. I look down at the pages; I want to plunge back through the years, disappear into the past and find out what happens next; how did the visit end, in what direction did fate lean, did Halla's hands turn into darkness? I look down but the past is gone, it has retreated into the darkness of time, and instead I see myself next to Rúna of Nes in the front seat of her blue SUV. We're on our way to the hotel for three bottles of grappa and dark chocolate for French chocolate cakes; then it's the party in honour of life, Páll of Oddi and Elvis Presley. The convex caravan recedes in the rear-view mirror and finally disappears behind the broad thicket separating it from Framnes.

I'VE BECOME SO OBEDIENT THAT IT'S SHAMEFUL – THEN
WE PUT "I LOVE PARIS" ON DEATH'S PLAYLIST
Sóley had asked Rúna to give me a ride. Haraldur is at home at Nes, but had promised to come later, with Ási and Mundi, who had appeared unexpectedly at Nes with cold beer, both with a ten-song list of the best songs in the history of music, starting with the Beatles' *Please Please Me* album, and wanted Haraldur to make his own. Ási

said that he had high hopes that Haraldur's list would confirm that his own list was better than Mundi's nonsense.

Dad was happy when I left, says Rúna, and smiles so deeply that the sadness at the corners of her mouth almost disappears. She plays "In a Sentimental Mood" by John Coltrane and Duke Ellington. There's no good day without Coltrane, she explains – he wanted to change the world, unite humanity in music and thereby create harmony on Earth.

Rúna slows down as we approach the sharp turn near the head of the fjord, and then has to stop completely because a beat-up old Bronco Jeep reaches the turn, slightly before us, from the opposite direction. An elderly driver behind the steering wheel, with a thin, sharp face, grey, ragged hair, leaning so far forward that his grooved forehead almost touches the windscreen, moving at a snail's pace. He's acting like he doesn't see us, I say.

That's because he doesn't, says Rúna. That's Kári of Botn, who obviously hasn't found his glasses. It's happened before. He can't find them at home or can't be bothered to look for them. Points out that it's difficult to find glasses without glasses. He can't see much without them, which is why he drives so terribly slowly, staying in the middle of the road, which is so narrow in some places here in the fjord that it's impossible to pass him, meaning we're stuck behind him until he turns down to Hof and borrows Lúna's extra pair of glasses. Of course they aren't strong enough for him, but are better than none.

Rúna takes the turn so slowly that I have enough time to get a good look at the fjord's wide head, which opens up to one there; the two farms, Skarð at a distance, Ási's Sámsstaðir nearer, where the young wooded area spreads out, already starting to change the landscape, reaching well up the mountainside and over the hayfields closer to the river. Mundi's yellow summer cottage, located a few hundred metres lower than the farm itself, perched atop a low hill, is likely to be subsumed by trees within a few years. Skarð stands beneath a verdant promontory, at the junction of two valleys, in fact – the one, quite rocky in appearance, disappears into the landscape to the north, while the other, greener-looking, is mainly hidden behind the promontory. Skarð is still a working farm. I count twelve cows grazing in the marshland below it.

We've just crossed the bridge when we're forced to stop. We can't get any further due to Kári, who has stopped on the narrow road. Rúna gets out to check on the old man, but quickly returns. Kári had stopped to answer his phone. It was his daughter who had called. For the last few weeks, she has been at her house in the short, grassy Sunnudalur Valley, and was picking berries on the mountainside when she saw her father driving slowly down the valley, so slowly that she realised he hadn't found his glasses. Or hadn't bothered to look for them. Not having her phone with her, she hurried down to the house, called from there to stop her dad. Said that she was on her way up to Botn with her children to find his glasses and would then bring them to him. Got him to promise her he would stay put in the meantime. I've become so obedient that it's shameful, Kári had said to Rúna, who promised the man's daughter that she would stay there until she came and make sure that he didn't move. It's useless for us to offer to drive him out to Hof where a cup of coffee awaits him; he's too proud to accept help. Says that worrying about him and fussing over him is little other than poorly disguised pity.

So we, Rúna adds, but is unable to finish the sentence because her phone rings. She answers; her phone is clearly connected to the stereo because Elías's voice fills the car, and then his laughter, deep and heartfelt, when Rúna explains the situation.

It could be quite a wait, he says, but Kári, of course, has earned the right to be waited for. Besides, everything here is in full swing and there's really no need for you to hurry. Still, Alexander the Great is asking about you, terribly offended that I'm letting dogs roam the house. Otherwise, I am at this very moment on my way out to Eiríkur with the first beer of the day, says Elías – and shortly afterwards I hear Eiríkur's voice for the first time. The voice of the man who plays guitar, shoots at lorries, is on his way to jail. And talks to his dogs in French.

He does that sometimes, Rúna explains when I look at her questioningly – says he wants them to be bilingual.

You're with the writer? asks Elías's voice over the device.

I'm here with the writer, Rúna answers.

Does the writer know French?

I shake my head.

No, the writer doesn't know French, says Rúna.

That's too bad. Until now, I actually believed that all writers knew French. Isn't it the mother tongue of poetry?

Hölderlin, I say, but I have to clear my throat, start again: Hölderlin might claim that it was German.

Elías laughs. You don't say! So you have a deep dispute there – and you've probably given us the real reason for all the wars between the French and Germans! But Eiríkur said that he's translating lyrics into French for the dogs – what song is it, Eiríkur?

Eiríkur answers indistinctly, but that's okay, I knew the song right away, of course. "Wake Up" by XXX Rottweiler hundar.

Damn, what a name for a band, says Elías, but then he asks What? I didn't quite get what you said, Eiríkur, from which playlist?

Eiríkur's voice comes through the stereo system, but is so intertwined with the intense music that we can't hear his answer clearly. Elías laughs, and it seems to spread to Eiríkur, because I hear him laugh, too. Laughs infectiously. I honestly didn't expect that.

Death's playlist, says Elías – and I mean Death with a capital D. The song is on Death's playlist, which Eiríkur has put together for the occasion. You can find it on Spotify – under Eiríkur's name. According to Eiríkur, death desires nothing more strongly than life, but is doomed to destroy it every time it tries to embrace it. It's Death's bitter grief, and music is the only thing that can soothe that grief. This playlist is Eiríkur's contribution.

Death's playlist, here it is, says Rúna, after saying goodbye to Elías; she connects to the list via her phone, so we can listen to the same songs as the two friends out in Vík. The troublemaker with a guitar, shotgun, dead puppies – and now I can add infectious laughter – chooses the music for us while we're stuck behind a farmer in his eighties who takes advantage of the delay to find the CD *Ella Fitzgerald Sings Cole Porter* in the car's glove compartment.

Wake up, wake up, sleepwalker, wake up! You've got to stop living dying . . . enjoy your time, those few years that we walk the earth . . . don't dream, be the dream . . . rap and sing, the intense, audacious Rottweilerhundar.

Be the dream, don't live dying, live now. Great song, says Rúna. But the lyrics are actually like a message to me and Eiríkur, we've . . .

Her voice ebbs out. I don't know if it's because she wants to listen to the song better, or if its message has hit her so hard that she can't say more.

Wake up, wake up, be the dream, don't live dying . . .

In some respects, her life came to a halt the evening that the stiletto heel of her mother's shoe hit her in the eye, she lost control of the car on the ice, shortly afterwards hung unconscious upside down, like a sleeping bat, as her mother, broken, asked Haraldur to hold her. My love, she whispered, hold me, don't let go. You must never let me go.

Never let me go. Her last words, which is why . . .

I look up from the pages and ask What?

Which is why, repeats the sanctified coach driver, having made a hand's-breadth stack of fragrant crêpes, Haraldur couldn't go, and move south; who else was to hold Aldís? Unless he used it as an excuse, hadn't had the strength to start a new life without her. And so, the lives of the father and daughter came to a halt. To a certain extent, they're at as much of a standstill as Kári's Bronco, he adds over his crêpe-making, before pointing with his spatula at a black and white photo of the foster-brothers, Kári and Skúli, in a beautiful but faded wooden frame. In the photo, Skúli is hardly more than seven, eight years old, he's smiling but there's a shadow in his eyes; he'd recently come from Snæfellsnes, having had to leave everyone he loved, left and took nothing with him but nostalgia. Sent north to this unfamiliar fjord, which, however, became his home, his embrace, over time.

Kári, two years old, stands next to him, leaning against Skúli's thigh, practically holding on to it and looking at the camera with a focused, serious expression.

I look down at the pages. Kári's daughter has found the glasses and set off with them to her father, who is two years old in the photo but an old man behind the wheel of the Bronco in the middle of the road. Waits there obediently for his youngest daughter to bring his glasses. Waits quietly; the old farmer is nice and comfortable, having found his Ella Fitzgerald CD and started listening to "I Love Paris". Of course he does, because it's one of the songs that Ella sings every night in both hell and heaven – some artists are put together in such a way that they can travel freely in between.

"I Love Paris" is of course on Death's playlist.

Now something's going to happen.

WHO WAS ENWRAPPED IN HIS OWN THOUGHTS, AND THEN HE BIT THE CIGARILLO IN TWO

Skúli at Oddi. Remember, not from here in the fjord. Came to Botn as a child with the postman, who delivered him like any other parcel. He's a tough one, this one, said the postman. The two of them had had a very difficult journey, foul weather, but Skúli never complained. He's a tough one, this one, said the postman when the two of them arrived, bedraggled, at Botn. Tough, yet with those gentle eyes, the housewife, Kári's mother, said then.

Skúli was definitely determined and self-assertive, but his personality was by nature too bright for him to become a tough guy, and he never cared for the postman's pronouncement, which the housewife at Botn had softened, and, in mentioning his eyes, had perhaps saved Skúli from a reputation for feistiness. Yet, so gentle. They were dissimilar, the foster-brothers. Skúli with his infectious life force that captivated people, and Kári with his heavier, sometimes darker disposition. Right around 160 centimetres, fully grown, yet nothing but sinew and tenacity, his eyes generally screwed up, making them appear smaller and to lie deeper than they actually did. Secretive by nature, cared little for company, few knew what he was thinking, but it was clear early on that he was a born farmer and would take over his parents' farm; he had barely begun to walk before he started slipping out to the sheep shed to help, completely fearless in the face of horned, surly rams, even though their heads were half the size of the child. Stubborn, firm and secretive as the mountains, but unexpectedly turned out to be a man of the future, showing an interest early on in innovations in farming and later adopting the ones he liked best. Whether it was in the cultivation of fields, their drainage, innovations in sheep farming – or the breeding of cows.

When Kári was eighteen years old he heard about a farmer out west in Djúpidalur who had cultivated his own breed of cattle through hybridisation, and was so successful in it that his cows gave a third more milk than they generally did, and he had started to invite farmers from near and far to breed their cows with his bulls, at a fair price. Kári asked his father to call the farmer in question, and a few weeks later the father and son went west to Djúpidalur to learn more about these improvements, and to be present when a neighbouring cow was bred with the farmer's main bull.

It was in early March, and the snowy roads made the trip west a lengthier one than it should have been. The father and son set off early in the morning, trudged along in their newish Willys Jeep with chains on all the tyres, equipped with shovels and having to use them several times to dig the jeep through the most difficult sections. They arrived at their destination around noon and everything was ready. Böðvar, the farmer and owner of the bull, met them in the farmyard and then strolled with them east of the sheep shed, where two men stood smoking: a neighbouring farmer, who owned the cow, and his adolescent son. But Böðvar's eighteen-year-old daughter stood in the corral with the cow on a strong lead while the bull bellowed deeply inside the sheep shed. The men greeted each other, introduced themselves, but the daughter was silent, stood there motionless in the corral, holding the cow and looking down. My

Margrét is the only one who can control the bull, Böðvar said to the father and son from Botn, as if to explain or justify why his daughter was in the corral, exposed to the animal.

Then the door to the sheep shed was opened and out came the bull, bellowing.

Kári took an instinctive step backward. He had never before seen a bull so big and boisterous. Much larger than the cow, it seemed to emanate power and rage, and stomped when it noticed the men out of the corner of its eye. Turning towards them, it scraped at the ground and bellowed so deeply that it was as if the sound came from down in hell as it regarded them with its small, bulging eyes, seemingly weighing whether it should attack the fence protecting the men. Then the daughter whistled, the bull turned around, saw the cow, shook its big head, snorted, trotted over to the cow, and began to lick its hind end while its slender, long, light-red penis emerged and grew, quivering with excitement under the bull's belly. The young men – Kári and the neighbour's son – stepped right up to the fence and Kári felt uncomfortable having him so close as the bull licked the cow so eagerly that it moved forward, and Margrét, who had braced herself with one leg, had to push back hard.

After eagerly licking the cow's hindquarters, the bull curled its upper lip, its throat rattled a bit, its eyes bulged even more, and its slender penis trembled and swung beneath its belly, then the animal lifted itself up. Heaved itself up, rested its weight on the cow, which swayed beneath the weight and mooed, either out of anticipation or fear as the penis plunged into it. The bull thrust four or five times with such force that the cow was thrown forward, but Margrét pressed her heels into the ground, stood firm, and pushed back hard, as if to ensure that the bull's penis went in as deeply as possible, and her strong body trembled with the effort. The young men at the corral and the adults standing at the wall of the sheep shed didn't take their eyes off the bull and Margrét, each enwrapped in his own thoughts.

The father and son from Botn couldn't stay long, they wanted to get back over the snow-covered heaths before it grew completely dark, but they made an agreement with Böðvar to borrow the bull for a few weeks in the spring – two months later, Kári goes and picks it up in Botn's three-year-old International tractor, with a hay wagon attached. Because the bull was so hot-tempered and unpredictable, it was thought best, and necessary, to send Margrét along with the animal, and she would stay at Botn for the weeks that the bull was there in order to control its temper and hold the cows beneath it when it came to it.

Kári had set off from Botn in the night, had reached his destination around noon, and couldn't refuse having lunch there and getting a little warmth in his body after having rattled all night in the cabless tractor up on the heath in a biting-cold wind; have lunch, answer questions about the weather conditions and farming methods in the fjord. But then the bull was put in the wagon, tied securely for the long journey, and they set off, Margrét and Kári.

Since the tractor had only the driver's seat, which was a backless iron bowl lined with old sheepskin, Margrét had to stand for most of the way, stooping to hold on to the wing and sometimes also to the seat. It was a fourteen-hour journey, tiring for her to stand stooping like that, and soon her arms began to ache from bracing herself, but she didn't complain. Halfway home it began raining, rather heavily, and both of them were soaking wet. But Kári never slowed down and the tractor rumbled along against the wind, soldiered on in that way while the bright spring air dimmed, grew cloudy, turned almost into darkness within the heavy rain, which sometimes changed to sleet. Kári said little, making her feel it unnecessary to speak, except twice she asked him to stop, jumped lightly down from the tractor, disappeared behind a large rock to pee; then pulled herself up onto the hay wagon to pet the bull and chat with it for a few moments before they went on their way.

A fourteen-hour trip. Margrét took the opportunity, when the road was straight enough and sufficiently undamaged by the winter, to let go and stand up, legs spread for balance, and have a bite to eat from her packed lunch, hurriedly down a bite of bread; Kári's only snack was dried fish, pieces of which he tore off and munched

194

on from time to time. He was clearly enjoying himself and seemed hardly to be aware of Margrét. The only inconvenience was how hard a time he had lighting the cigarillos he kept in his coat pocket. The wind and rain extinguished the matches and the cigars quickly became so wet that the embers died. Still, he refused to give up and tried again every now and then. Once, when they were about halfway home and Kári had tried unsuccessfully to light a cigar, Margrét wordlessly shielded the flame with her hands, Kári managed to puff the cigar to life and she saw him smile for the first time. Or it looked to her as if the change in his features could be interpreted as a smile, and it suited him well. An hour later he tossed aside the soaked stub, took out a new, dry cigarillo and handed Margrét the matchbox. But as the tractor was jerking a bit on the rocky, uneven road, she was forced to sit down on one of his thighs so that it would be easier for her to shield the flaming match. This went so badly that she had to move a little higher, both to get closer to the cigarillo and to be better shielded by Kári, with the result that one of her buttocks lay over his groin and she felt, as he eagerly puffed life into the cigarillo, how his penis, which had for some reason slipped out of his underwear, swelled rapidly. Pretending not to notice, she sat there for a few moments longer, looking aside as if in thought while Kári stared straight ahead, concentrating on his driving. Finally she stood up, propped herself, and the tractor rattled on. Two hours later, Kári took out his matchbox again, she sat down on his upper thigh. And the day turned into night. They rattled up a heath, through a long valley, up another heath where the sleet gradually turned back into rain.

It was nearing midnight when Kári stopped the tractor on the edge of the heath, jerked his head to the north-west, towards a short, grassy valley that opened inland, and Margrét made out the lights of a few farms through the rain. So there's Botn, he said, with a touch of pride in his voice. Then he fished out his matchbox and a new cigarillo, but hesitated. Without a word, Margrét took the matchbox from him, sat down on his thigh, bore the flaming match to the fragrant cigarillo, and, for the third time, she felt his penis quickly swell, lengthen and harden in his trousers. But instead of sitting still and looking away, she began cautiously yet firmly and determinedly to rub herself against his penis. Back and forth. Not long afterwards, perhaps half a minute, he moaned loudly and bit his cigarillo in two as he came. She felt both the man and his hard penis twitch, and saw him bite the cigarillo in two. She lifted herself a little, laid her palm firmly on his thigh and felt the hot liquid. Two months later, they got married.

CONCERNING FENCEPOSTS

The days passed over the Earth, they became night, the two of them had four children and now Margrét is dead. She and Kári were never seen arguing. They were like two fenceposts here outside the world. Standing confident, silent, weathered by time. They never went abroad, rarely to Reykjavík. Their story could easily fit on one sheet of A4 paper, with large lettering, double-spaced. Kári got drunk twice a year with Skúli, his foster-brother, who was also the only man he respected. Then Skúli died. People are always dying. Kári and Margrét's bedroom overlooked the valley and they saw the lights of the other farms go out one by one, the fields grow wild, until they alone remained in this snowy yet grassy valley. Margrét often sat with binoculars by the window on clear winter evenings, counting the stars over the valley, observing what was going on in the sky, and enjoyed going out to Oddi to discuss it with Skúli, who was so wonderfully knowledgeable. And as she observed, Kári lay in bed, under a dim light so as not to bother Margrét, perused the *Agricultural Review*, read farmers' biographies, new crime novels, books by Halldór Laxness and Gunnar Gunnarsson. If it was too bright or cloudy for stars, he read aloud from Halldór's or Gunnar's books to his wife, who laid her head on his chest, listened to his voice coming from the depths, and fell asleep that way – she died in her sleep about a decade ago.

Kári didn't let anyone know until the following evening. Sat all day with his wife, held her hand, felt her body go cold. Their children wrote an obituary together, which was short, barely more than ten lines long, yet it took them an entire evening to compose it. As it turned out, there was just so little they could say. So few stories that had any business outside the valley, and then they had difficulty finding a decent photo of her – none of the photos bore a good enough resemblance to the person they had known. She lived for seventy years and it's impossible to say much about her. Except that she'd been a fencepost, knew how to handle bulls, enjoyed counting stars, listened to her husband read aloud from Gunnar or Laxness. Some lives seem so uneventful that they can hardly be described. No more than fenceposts. Yet they hold the fences up for us.

THEN I LAUGHED LIKE A GIRL

We plod along behind Kári, who now has his glasses. His daughter had rushed down with them and stopped for a moment to say hello to me and Rúna. A cheerful person, shaking her head at her father, as they all do regularly, the four siblings. Three of them have built summer cottages at Botn, but the cheerful woman and her husband bought one of the valley's abandoned farms and have renovated the old farmhouse, which is delightful news, because, as you remember, little is as melancholy as an abandoned farm with empty buildings that time has begun to erode – it's like a depressed or sad person left in the open to die.

See you later, said Kári's daughter before leaving us; because she, too, will be attending the party in honour of Elvis, Páll and life. Rúna smiles as we drive off, following Kári's car. Smiles because of the woman, because of Kári, and maybe because she's expecting something from Paris?

Why, oh why do I love Paris – because my love is here.

If I dare to love you. If my heart is strong enough. If the socks you choose make it impossible for me not to love you. If you don't send socks but yourself.

Will the French journalist bring the socks in person, and is he even on his way north in a rental car at these written words? Will a fairytale occur, then, will happiness triumph, are we then, when all is said and done, within a touching love story? Oh, hopefully! But what will become of Haraldur and the farm at Nes if a journalist from Paris wins Rúna's heart? We can hardly expect someone from a big city, accustomed to the hustle and bustle of life, theatres, cinemas, literary events, daily interactions with people, someone who lives and moves in such a world, to become a sheep farmer in a sparsely populated fjord on the edge of the inhabitable world, where it's sometimes so uneventful in winter that people go out with a shotgun and shoot at fenceposts? The Frenchman comes and Rúna sends the sheep to the slaughterhouse; so do the sheep have to pay for love with their lives? And what about Haraldur?

Is it one of the laws of nature that the price of happiness in one place is unhappiness in another?

The smile has faded at the corners of Rúna's mouth and the reluctance has returned. She knows, of course, that Haraldur wants to be nowhere but at Nes. To be able to lie down to sleep within earshot of Aldís's grave. Who will stay with him if Paris wins Rúna's heart? That is perhaps why she's afraid to love again, to open her heart . . . because sometimes the dead refuse to let go of us – unless it's we who are unable to let go of them. Drag them behind us like dark, heavy rocks. Let go of us, they ask, allow us to sink into the existence to which you have no access. And keep living, for only in this way is it possible to comfort us who are dead.

But Aldís had asked Haraldur to hold her. You must never let go.

Never is a long time. Much longer than life. I die and your life stops.

Until someone comes from Paris wearing mismatched socks, and your life becomes a sundial?

We trundle along behind Kári, who listens once more to Ella proclaiming her love for Paris. He turns down the road to Hof, where Lúna and Dísa are going to give him coffee; and Lúna will quiz him on English sentences before he heads up to the hotel to practise on the Canadian family and Japanese tourists.

Kári, who bit the cigar in two; the secretive, taciturn Kári, learning English in his old age?

Margrét dies in her sleep, Kári sat beside her, held her hand, spoke to her, didn't eat or drink, then called Hafrún and Skúli late the following evening, and said, well, Margrét is dead.

And the dark years came over the mountains.

Dark with bereavement, dark with meaninglessness because Kári's life became like a fence that has fallen down and the grass has begun to grow over. He seemed completely indifferent to living anymore, and neither his children nor the folk at Oddi, when they were alive, could rouse him from his torpor. He became more irritable, quieter, more aloof, didn't even talk to his cats, and would probably have disappeared ungracefully into the nearly lifeless winter grass if Margrét hadn't appeared to Lúna in a dream.

An unusually vivid dream. Margrét began by greeting her old friend; she apologised for the disturbance, but said that since Kári's dreams were so closed off that she couldn't get in, despite having tried for years, she had come now to her friend for the purpose of asking her to go to Botn, chastise Kári, and bring him to his senses. For it was a terrible shame and nothing but humiliating to witness him let himself waste away. Lie there like a broken-down fence in front of everyone. You don't do that to yourself, and certainly not to your children. You should give them joy, not burden them with worries and sorrow. Does he want his grandchildren to remember their grandpa as a broken-down fence, or an old, half-dead ram that they avoid winding up alone with? Go and tell him that he should be the person our grandchildren long to be around and pester their parents about going to visit, summer and winter. He should be a trusty corner post in their lives.

But unfortunately, Margrét said to Lúna, Kári has never believed that there is anything of note in dreams, let alone that the dead can appear in them with messages from the beyond. I see no other option, she said, suddenly becoming shy, the dead woman, not even daring to look her friend in the eye, than to confide in you that Kári and I enjoyed most, from the very start, or ever since he came in his trousers on the edge of the heath, making love in this way: I would take off all of my clothes except for my tights, get myself a cigarillo, smoke a bit in front of Kári, then get down on all fours and ask him to take me from behind. But in our final years together, my knees had grown so weak that we had to do it in bed, and once I wasn't careful and set the duvet on fire with the cigarillo. We had to run down naked to fetch water. Kári with his beautiful penis erect, which made me laugh like a girl. Tell Kári about all of this; you mustn't leave out or forget any of it, otherwise it won't work.

Look, I'm not saying these things to Kári Guðjónsson, Lúna was about to inform her friend, but then she woke up and Margrét dissolved into thin air. And Lúna, who had never hesitated to express her views – on the contrary, never knew how not to express them – became so shy at the thought of conveying to Kári this description of his and Margrét's sex life that weeks passed before she gathered the courage to go to Botn, and her heart was beating so fast with anxiety that she nearly drove off the road three times.

When she went to see Kári, he was unkempt, unshaven, his hard stubble poking out like menacing knives, and, when Lúna opened the fridge to get milk for her coffee, there was little in it but a stack of microwave dinners. Lúna poured milk into her coffee, then pulled out the gin bottle she'd brought with her, fortified both of their coffees, emptied her cup – and told him about the dream. Repeated what Margrét had told her, that Kári mustn't be like a broken-down fence, but she hesitated to mention . . . the other thing. Simply didn't dare to. Hoped, too, that it would be unnecessary. And Kári seemed to listen intently, even nodding when he recognised Margrét's manner of speaking through Lúna. Yet when Lúna was finished, he looked up and said that he was astonished that she believed in dreams; superstition and old wives' tales, he said. Old people shouldn't humiliate themselves with such nonsense.

This angered Lúna, which was fine, in fact, because her anger swept aside her hesitation and she dared to tell about the dream's conclusion or, rather, what it was that was meant to convince Kári

200

that the message had indeed come from Margrét – despite her having lain in her grave for six years.

An orgasm on the edge of the heath, a cigarillo that set fire to a bed, tights, Margrét on all fours, take me, and Kári enters her from behind.

Then there was a long silence in the kitchen at Botn. Kári stared at Lúna, his stubble poking out menacingly towards her, as if he were angry. Then he got slowly to his feet, went and got a cloudy-looking glass, filled it halfway with gin, downed it, and cursed.

So it was her? Lúna asked, hesitantly, shy again. He didn't answer, just poured himself more gin. Then she also went and got a glass, took her own big drink of gin, intending to announce right afterwards that she'd come here to raise the fallen fence into which Kári had turned, but spoke so inarticulately because of the strong liquor that Kári clearly misunderstood her words, or misheard them, because he said What? and then asked hesitantly: Did you say you've come here to find out whether I can still get it up? What do you expect, woman, I'm old and worn out   I seldom get an erection more than twice a week!

Then Lúna blushed and at first acted as shy as a teenage girl, but had more gin, took a deep breath, and said: Kári, you've been a widower for eight years, I a widow for twelve. We're both in our seventies and our days on this side of the grave aren't increasing in number. Twice a week, you say. Wouldn't it be a great sin if we two, in this last stretch of life, let such a thing go to waste?

Four years later, Kári turns down the road to Hof to have coffee and let Lúna quiz him on the English sentences she'd assigned him. Later today they're heading to the party. Yes, even Kári is going, he who was never one for crowds or parties, instead changing into a stubborn horse whenever Margrét so much as mentioned a dance or some other gathering. When a large crowd of people gathers, they get so stupid, he said sometimes. Which is in some respects true, although it's also true that man's joy is in man, as the saying goes. In other words, when all is said and done, we probably know almost nothing.

Except that Bubbi Morthens' song "Afgan" is next on Death's playlist, and he's singing as Rúna and I approach Oddi: When I knocked on the door your ghost opened, she said, you were only a dream, a vision of you is all I've seen.

Is Eiríkur punishing us, me and himself, I mean, says Rúna, shaking her head. We actually talked about it just last week when Dísa, Elías and I sat drinking and listening to music with him well into the night at Oddi, that the two of us both experienced a period in which we went through life like ghosts, as if we were dead, had stopped living. Or does a person not die if his life stops, is life not movement and death a standstill? But then things changed . . . she falls silent when Kári stops his car above Oddi, steps stiffly out of it, goes and stands behind it to pee, shields his wrinkled old penis like a cigarette. I look down at the farm, the unpainted farmhouse that Halldór built after the old, beautiful wooden one burned down. Two terns glide over the ruins of the old house, which stood closer to the river.

All ruins, churchyards, houses, villages, cities, trains, planes, everything, even blowing plastic bags, hold stories or fragments of destinies.

Destiny, fate – we create it by living.

It's the fabric of the gods.

Or the blind shot of chance.

Skúli trips and falls over his father in March; a few weeks later the postman brings him to Botn, two hundred kilometres from his childhood village. Then he and Hafrún take over Oddi – and almost seventy years later, Eiríkur is living there alone with three dogs, hot-tempered chickens, a guitar, a shotgun, he puts together a playlist for death, fires the shotgun at a lorry and is possibly on his way to prison, what will become of the dogs then, he can hardly bring them with him to his prison cell . . .

I didn't think about it then, Rúna is saying, and I didn't realise until much later that around the time of his confirmation, Eiríkur became more mysterious, more closed, even for many years towards Sóley and me, who were almost like his sisters. Still, I think that for a long time no-one was really worried about those changes. There had always been what you might call a serious string in Eiríkur; it was apparent even when he was a child. No, maybe not serious, but . . . maybe it was sadness. Because of his mum, of course, but it was also from something else. We didn't give it much thought, though. There were all sorts of kids in the fjord, and Eiríkur was just Eiríkur. He could also be so wonderfully cheerful and imaginative that we didn't let it bother us if sadness came over him now and then. I do know, however, that Hafrún sometimes mentioned to my mum and dad that she feared that Eiríkur had what she called the string of sadness. Or the family string of sadness.

SO IS THIS ALL HAPPENING INSIDE MY HEAD?
The family string of sadness?

Kári has finished peeing and we trundle off. I look over the ruins of the house that Skúli and Hafrún built when the world was much younger – yet many things had already happened then. What will happen to all the world's stories, who will look after them?

The rapper Mac Miller, taking over from Bubbi, starts singing about spending the entire day in his head, and wondering if he should wake up instead.

Yes, maybe I should just wake up.

Don't dream, become the dream.

So is this all happening inside my head?

That may come to light, but just not right away, says . . .

HERE IT COMES
. . . the priest with the PCV licence as he pours new batter onto the pan, still in those silly shorts of his. But it must be time for Eiríkur.

203

Remember, you once wrote, and it was a long time ago: "Eiríkur of Oddi. The man who has an electric guitar, dogs, three dead puppies, a shotgun to fire at lorries or perhaps fate. What more does he have?"

And is the answer coming now?

Why should I have an answer to that, and, besides, it isn't certain you'll want the answers; that isn't always so desirable – some answers do little more than bring you new questions. On the other hand, it's the first and last questions that drive life onward – tell me what questions are burning inside you and I'll tell you who you are!

I'm not so sure I really want to know anymore, I mutter, looking away from the coach driver, who seems rather pleased with himself and his incomprehensible answer, and down at the pages where the SUV holding me and Rúna trundles off; she's telling me about the string of sadness inside Eiríkur, which had also sounded in Páll, even to some extent in Skúli, who always tried to focus on the positive sides of life, driven by optimism but nevertheless went in for melancholy music: Chopin's nocturnes, Mozart's Requiem, Chet Baker. And he played Pablo Casals' interpretation of Bach's Pastorale in F Major daily for the sheep at Oddi. That's why they stand out from other sheep, he used to say.

The same string sounded loudly in Skúli's father, who, piss-drunk one night, rolled over onto his back to try to see a newly discovered galaxy in the sky over Snæfellsnes; and in Eiríkur's great-great-grandma, Guðríður, who once wrote an article about the earthworm and whose tailbone sometimes itched, who had a dangerous smile, eyes that had an influence on both the Earth's tilt and Hölderlin's poetry, even though he had died before she was born – when she wrote, some of her letters barked like dogs.

So it happens that an article about the earthworm, written at the very end of the nineteenth century in a small heath farm under straitened circumstances, is the cause of a pie-eyed fisherman in the nineteen-thirties rolling over onto his back out in his farmyard in the hope of seeing a newly discovered galaxy, his six- or seven-year-old son stumbling over him in the early morning and scrambling, covered in pee, to his feet – all of this leads to Guðríður's great-great-grandchild ending up, long afterwards, alone with a guitar, a shotgun, three dead puppies and Death's playlist.

Once she stepped out of the darkness, and now everyone is dead.

And time's chief task is to kill people?

Pétur handed Guðríður the dictionary that the devil's brother sold him, Gísli placed his hand on the table as if he wanted to display his strength to Pétur; be careful, my love, Halla had said to her husband, she has hands of light.

Was he careful?

And what does it mean to be careful, does the heart beat carefully, do I kiss you carefully, did Gísli use his sock carefully when he emptied his semen into it, and is it true that Eiríkur, who looks like a sad rock star, hasn't slept with anyone since he returned three years ago, does he make do with a woollen sock; that can hardly be healthy. Is this symphony of fate, which grows and changes like man's world-view, not, then, about amnesia and love, betrayal and death, the search for happiness and the true universe, but first and last about a lack of sex, is it about emptying oneself into a sock?

*I Can't Really Imagine Life
Without You*

LOVE MUST NOT BE KILLED

Eiríkur came to the fjord when he was three months old.

Bundled up in a child's car seat in the front of a worn-down Datsun.

It was early winter, but the weather was mild. Heavy snows had been followed by a continuous thaw that lasted over a week; the snow was gone from the fields but a sagging drift or two remained in the ditches. The roads all clear, and the heaths above the fjord no obstacle. As if fate wanted to clear the route north for Eiríkur – two days after his arrival, storms hit, snow fell hard, the heaths were closed for several days and Strandvegur Road, which runs through the village of Bjarnanes, was nearly impassable – under such conditions, the dented brown Datsun that stopped in the farmyard at Oddi would hardly have been able to make it here to the north.

Stopped in front of the two-storey wooden house with its tall attic, built by Hafrún and Skúli, the attic always seemed to be smiling. A beautiful house, pride of the countryside.

The weary Datsun stopped with a sigh in the farmyard and a young, slender woman stepped out, holding an infant in her arms. Beautiful, straight-backed, but with a peaky face and dark circles under her eyes. Both of the farm's dogs came out to meet her, sniffed at her, sniffed at the car's tyres and marked them. Hafrún greeted the woman from the door, short, delicate as an elf maiden, with her boyish haircut, bright forehead, dark, almond-shaped eyes that were lively and warm. Alone at home. Halldór was on a herring boat based in Þorlákshöfn down south, the giant Páll was at university, studying philosophy, working on his thesis on Søren Kierkegaard, Skúli away from Botn helping Kári with construction.

Bless this day, said Hafrún, after stepping out into the farmyard. To what do I owe the honour of this visit, and who might you be?

The young woman looked down at the child, then at Hafrún. You must be Hafrún, Halldór's mother?

Hafrún nodded, and suspicion awoke inside her. The woman held the child tighter, took a deep breath, and said: My name is Svana and I'm the mother of Halldór's child – this is Eiríkur, our son.

Then we should probably have coffee, said Hafrún impassively. You're not standing with your baby out here in the cold.

A few minutes later, they're sitting opposite each other at the kitchen table. Hafrún makes coffee, serves crullers and marble cake. The young woman talks; tells her story.

The previous autumn, she had been working along with Halldór at the slaughterhouse in Búðardalur, and there they had an affair.

A forbidden love affair because she's married, and the mother of two children.

I'm five years older than Halldór and I want you to know that it has never crossed my mind to look at men other than my husband. We've been married for seven years. I promised him loyalty, trust, and you don't betray such vows. You don't go back on your words. I've always found adultery both filthy and unforgivable. Something that can neither be washed off nor justified. Of course, I have feelings and desires. I'm human. But it's up to us to control them; it shouldn't be the other way round. I've always viewed it as a matter of self-control, plain and simple, and that adultery is the result of a weak will or unforgivable selfishness and irresponsibility. I'm not irresponsible, hopefully not selfish, and have never been accused of a lack of will. But how well does a person know herself in the face of the powers and forces that are far stronger than herself? How . . . oh, I'm sorry, I've already begun to apologise, to try to justify everything; that wasn't my intention. But I want you to know that this wasn't some trashy affair on my part, or negligence and thoughtlessness on the part of Halldór, though I know very well that he's just too cheery and carefree to have a strong sense of responsibility. I think you know what I mean. But this was . . . I want you to know that this all happened because I love your son. That I . . . I just wanted to say that I never suspected that I would be with someone besides my husband. And more than once. Much more. A person doesn't do that. It's so wrong, and probably can't be forgiven. Still, I would do it all over again. I suppose that sometimes it's wrong to fall in love. It's probably criminal, sometimes.

Shouldn't one keep control of oneself? Svana asked Hafrún, who had listened silently but said, when Svana stopped, that she had always felt that it was a testament to a dull life, not to have made mistakes at some point, in one way or another.

Especially when one is young. I think that fate would find it quite dull if we never did anything wrong.

Or if love were to start to act rationally.

Svana smiled, looked down, stroked Eiríkur's head, kissed his hair. Still, I've always kept good control of myself, she said as if she were talking to her son, before looking again at Hafrún, and I have downright condemned people who have poisoned or blown apart their marriages through adultery. Adultery is a terribly ugly word. Did I say that already? But it certainly can be an ugly word, because it's ugly to betray your spouse. Extremely ugly. Do you really think it's possible to forgive such a thing? I just couldn't control myself at all, yet the entire time I knew what I was doing. I was just out of control. I felt . . . as if I'd been hit by a meteorite. I know it's not at all logical to say that, because no-one gets hit by a meteorite. Still, it's how I felt. A glowing meteorite that hit me, passed through me, and I simply burned with uncontrollable, wild, irresponsible happiness.

I had no idea that it was possible to love so utterly irresponsibly, she said, looking again at her son, as if she were talking to him, that silent child, apologising to him. It was as if I had never loved before, and that thought was as wonderful as it was awful. You see, it wasn't just that I was betraying my husband by being with another man, but that I loved Halldór more intensely and passionately than I've ever loved my husband. I almost felt as if I could die of love. Which, of course, isn't possible. You get hit by a car and die. You develop cancer and die. No-one gets hit by love and dies; you don't develop love like cancer and die. That's just nonsense. That must be nonsense.

Unfortunately, I think that there's no-one like your Halldór, she added. He's so full of life that it spread to me. And that liberating nonchalance of his seems to be capable of opening all the doors of life.

The coffee cooled in the cup in front of Svana, the corner of the marble cake lay untouched next to the slice on the plate, and Hafrún nodded, bowed her head, as if to confirm, agree, that there was no one like her Halldór. I know, my dear, she said, I know. But she said nothing about how, for many years, she'd feared that that same charming nonchalance would sooner or later have unpleasant consequences. It had already done so, yet not in this way. Never on this . . . scale.

Hafrún looked at Eiríkur in Svana's arms, met his brown, limpid eyes and felt a deep, intimate affection wake inside of her, stream forth and fill her heart. It was so obvious that he was Halldór's son. The family resemblance was plain to see. The same peculiar and irresistible space between his eyes and her Skúli's. A space that seemed to give their faces a new and mysterious dimension.

No need to apologise, child, said Hafrún. No need to justify anything here. And we don't want to live in a world in which young people always have perfect control over love. It shouldn't be an obedient dog. Thanks for coming. Your Eiríkur is also our Eiríkur; he'll always have a home here.

Then Svana wept. She wept into her coffee, the marble cake she tried to eat, maybe to please Hafrún. Wept softly, almost silently, into the dense, soft, downy hair on Eiríkur's head, yet while clearly trying to compose herself, her slender shoulders trembling with the effort. Wept, chewed her cake, then went on talking, looking alternately down at the child in her arms and at Hafrún across the kitchen table. Coffee, marble cake, crullers between them, soft notes from the radio, a sonata for violin and piano by Handel.

*

She and Halldór had tried to restrain themselves around others and pretend that nothing was going on but, before long, people started whispering; stories were spread, which female acquaintances of hers let her know about. They met every night at the home of an old widow in Búðardalur from whom Svana rented a room. The old woman, who had been widowed for fifteen years, soon began to switch off her hearing aids when Halldór came. Just so you know, I can't hear anything, she told her tenant, grinning as if the two of them were colluding against the world.

I didn't know, said Svana, that love could be infinitely beautiful and deeply physical at the same time. I couldn't get enough of him. My body drank in his skin like a desert celebrating the rain.

It went on for four weeks. Four weeks of boisterousness, carelessness, betrayals, unbridled happiness.

Then she fled.

Could love be a kind of mental disorder? Because when I was with Halldór, I didn't care about anything else. I was completely irresponsible. The only thing that mattered was him and me. I was prepared to throw everything away, my entire life, just to be with him. I even forgot about my children. I didn't recognise myself anymore. I've never been so happy. I was just waiting for him to ask me to come with him. Anywhere, my love, I would have said.

That is why she fled.

I fled home, south to Hella.

Left without saying goodbye. Snuck away, hastily. It was a Thursday and a dance was being held that weekend. Halldór hurried home, here to the fjord, for better clothes. For you, he said, I'm going to dress up for you. Left in the morning, came back in the evening, with the clothes but also photos of his family and the fjord, to show Svana. But then she was gone. Vanished.

Something told me that if I didn't leave immediately, didn't seize the opportunity while Halldór was away, it would be too late. I was so frightened of my love. I feared that it would ruin my life and cause my family unbearable harm. I'm married to a good man. He's kind and trustworthy. We have a good life. A beautiful home. I thought that that was enough and felt good, I was happy in life. I couldn't imagine it otherwise. I had probably never considered that even though I care so much for my husband, I've never loved him. Maybe I just thought that all this talk about love and the necessity of it was just neurosis stemming from books and movies, or something that wasn't meant for everyone. Who really needs a burning love when everything is secure and stable, when you have two wonderful children, a good husband who loves you? I think Halldór is the man in my life. No, I know that he is. The only one I can love. But that wonderful, liberating nonchalance of his also frightens me. I'm a mother of two, and children need security. I love Halldór and I know that he loves me. But sometimes it's not enough. Sometimes responsibility is more important than love.

She fled home to save her marriage, prevent the destruction. Came home numb with grief, transfixed by guilt, but with the steadfast resolve in her heart that her relationship with Halldór would be a forbidden adventure that she would take with her to her grave. Two weeks later, she realised that she was pregnant, and that changed everything. But in some strangely contradictory way, she found the thought of admitting her betrayal easier, as if the growing life in her womb would justify everything. Isn't life sacred?

Svana's husband listened silently to her confessions, stared down at his hands silently for a long time, and then got to his feet without looking at her, went and got his shotgun, and drove up into the mountains. Didn't return until early the next morning, when she was nearly out of her mind with fear and anxiety. Came back with sixteen bloody ptarmigans, sat down in the kitchen to pluck them. She watched in silence, waiting for him to say something. You'll have an abortion, he finally said, on the third ptarmigan. Said it calmly, as if he were talking about the weather or something self-evident, some mundane thing, then reached for the fourth ptarmigan: And we'll never speak of this again. You've humiliated me and no-one can ever know of this. If you respect me at all. We will never discuss this again. I'll leave you if you so much as think about that wretch again.

I thought I could trust you. When I think of you together, I feel as if my guts are being ripped out. How often did he get to fuck you? Didn't you know that I love you? Didn't you know that you're the only woman I've loved? Did you take him in your mouth? Was it good? How could you? Still, I'll forgive you everything because I love you. Didn't you think about our girls while he was fucking you? I can hardly believe this. Did you think of me when he entered you? You must never think of him again. I love only you and I'm nothing without you. You'll go to your mother and have the foetus aborted. And gradually, everything will be fine between us again.

He spoke slowly, with his hands bathed in blood, focused, his expression stern, yet so vulnerable, fragile, that she wanted to cry.

I couldn't imagine hurting him more. I felt responsible for him, for his and my daughters' happiness. I knew that the girls needed him. They need the security. They need a father who is always there. But for me, abortion was out of the question. In that regard, I took advantage of the fact that my husband's family is religious. I said that abortion is a sin against life. I couldn't imagine destroying that life. It was as if I were going to . . . kill love. And love must not be killed.

Love must not be killed.

That's how she put it, while the coffee cooled, grew cold, on the table in front of her and the month of October filled the outside world with its evasive light.

My poor child, Hafrún said so sincerely that the woman was moved to tears, her shoulders began to tremble again, almost invisibly, and then she wept, silently into Eiríkur's downy hair.

Svana went to her mother in Reykjavík before her pregnancy became noticeable, under the guise that she had unexpectedly got a well-paid job in Copenhagen through her Danish aunt; her father was Danish, and they could use the extra money, were aiming to move to a bigger house – that's why she'd got a job at the slaughterhouse in Búðardalur. She wrote letters thrice a week to her family, but sent them to her friend in Copenhagen, who then forwarded them to Hella, with the correct postmark.

My husband is a good soul and loves me dearly, but can also be so jealous that it frightens me. I know he'll never forgive me for this. That's the price I have to pay. But worst is that it's why I can't keep Eiríkur. My husband will remember my betrayal, and what he calls his humiliation, every time he looks at Eiríkur. I fear . . . no, I know that's why he could never love him. On the other hand, I fear that it would be too hard for him to hide his disgust, if not hatred, and that it would poison our home. That's why I decided to give birth to Eiríkur without my children or my husband's family suspecting anything. But I quickly made the decision to bring him here as soon as I could, preferably no later than a week after his birth. Yet I've been unable to come until now, when he's three months old. I just couldn't let him go right away. I wasn't strong enough for it.

She'd thought this through. From the things that Halldór said about his parents, Svana felt she knew them and was therefore sure that with them, Eiríkur would have a refuge, and would grow up enwrapped in warmth and security. I love your Halldór, she said, and was so strangely free when we were together. Everything became so much fun and exciting. Still, I doubt that I would have come to leave Eiríkur here if it weren't for you and your husband. I think you know what I mean.

But Eiríkur must never know that his mother exists. In his eyes . . .

. . . I have to be dead. It will prevent pain. I have a middle name that I've never used, but will start doing so now so that it will be harder for Halldór to look me up. I called him after I came to Reykjavík, didn't tell him that I was pregnant, so he doesn't know about Eiríkur, and made him promise that he wouldn't come after me, never try to find me. I said that I loved him, but explained to him that I had to choose, that I couldn't imagine losing my girls. He promised, but he is as he is, and loves me. People who love break promises. You understand that I had to choose between keeping my Eiríkur and taking the risk of turning my home into a hell for all of us, or coming here to the north and leaving him with you.

Here with you, the young Svana reiterated, passing the whimpering boy like an ordinary cup of coffee over the kitchen table, and

Hafrún accepted her first and only grandchild, who, just a few minutes before, she had had no idea existed.

The woman sat there silently for a moment, motionless, with her hands in her lap, and didn't take her eyes off Eiríkur in his grandma's arms. Little could be read in her expression. But then she asked, calmly, and Hafrún could just barely distinguish the tremor in her voice: Might I say goodbye to my child?

I KNOW THAT NOT A DAY

will pass when I don't think of you. Without my thoughts being with you. I also know that one day I won't be able to resist driving here north to the fjord, a stranger whose only business is to turn down to your farm to ask for a glass of water. I know I'll recognise you immediately. I'll always recognise you, anywhere in the world, and at any time. I'll come here only to ask you for a glass of water. Just one glass of water. And then only to get to drink from the glass that you were just holding. The bottle will still carry the warmth of your palm. Maybe it will be in six years, maybe eight, ten, maybe twelve years, I don't know exactly. But I will come, and ask you for that glass of water. And then slowly drink it while the warmth from your palm goes into my palm. Forgive me. For that moment, my love, I will live.

SUCH TIMES! OH, AND NOW GONE

He remembers this incident. When the woman came to Oddi to ask for a glass of water. It was unusual. Not necessarily that she should ask for water, but that he had been sent out with the glass and no one had come out to bid the visitor welcome, as is customary when someone shows up, stranger or not. But he was only seven years old, of course; the world could be incomprehensible and the adults could be so serious or preoccupied with insignificant things that Eiríkur had asked God several times to make it so that he would never grow up, could always remain a child. But he remembers this incident. Hafrún had gone and got him from the recording studio that Halldór had set up in the large barn, and that day Halldór was working on writing a long interview he had held the week before with elderly sisters in the countryside north of the fjord – the interview was then published in three parts in the *Strandir Courier* and, in addition, Halldór had sent it in its entirety, clipped from the paper, as he often did with such material, for preservation in the National Museum. But Hafrún had come, said something in a low voice to Halldór, who nodded and bent again over his interview, and she asked Eiríkur to come with her. Said she needed to talk to him, yet spoke not a word as they walked across the farmyard and into the house. There she began asking him strangely random questions, looking constantly out the kitchen window, then poured a large glass of cold water, asked Eiríkur to take it out to the woman. It was then that he noticed the car in the farmyard, and the woman standing beside it. The woman who smiled as she watched him come over to her, thanked him for the glass of water, said his name twice, then drank from the glass without taking her eyes off him. He doesn't remember any more; the rest of that day, insatiable oblivion has swallowed. Yet something inside of him often kindled when he saw an unfamiliar woman, and he could lose himself in his thoughts looking at her, imagining that she was his mother. That she wasn't dead at all; it had just been a misunderstanding – there she was, and would never leave him again.

Otherwise, he was happy. Otherwise, it was fun to be alive.

"To think," wrote his grandma in her card to Eiríkur on his sixth birthday, which was waiting for him in the kitchen when he came down in the morning for crêpes and hot chocolate, waiting there with his presents: a large racing track with electric cars from Páll, a child's-size guitar from Halldór, a Playmobil house from his grandparents . . . "To think," she wrote in her steady, neat handwriting, "that just six years ago you hadn't been born, and your grandpa and I had been living for nearly half a century and had no idea that we lacked the most enjoyable thing in life – our little black-haired boy! To think that it had crossed the world's mind to be without you, that it had actually felt like that at all! We're so indescribably grateful for you. With you, every morning is bright. Every morning I listen for you and maybe say to your grandpa: Well, won't our Eiríkur be waking up soon? Sometimes you come to me in the kitchen just to hug me for a few seconds before going back to playing, and then I'm so grateful to have been allowed to exist and to have you as part of my existence. Our beautiful, wonderful boy, happy birthday!"

And below, Skúli had written in his messy handwriting: "I agree with your grandma's every word!"

It was so much fun to exist, enwrapped in the warmth and affection of his grandma and grandpa. In a secure bubble, of sorts, and the distance from the world seemed to slow down time. It was in less of a rush here in the fjord than elsewhere, as if it felt there was no reason to hurry, wanted to enjoy life, and especially in the kitchen at Oddi, where the kitchen table was a kind of centre point of the district. People from the fjord and the surrounding countryside came almost daily for coffee and refreshments, to chat, discuss various aspects of farming, dinner parties, fences, balers, the animals; this sheep was limping, some damned breathlessness in another. Probably few problems that weren't solved over this table, that weren't smoothed over, whether it was confirmation preparations, a breathless sheep, or a malfunctioning tractor. Hafrún took care of the latter, the tractors, and everything that was mechanical, having from the very start been fascinated by machines and technology, televisions and lorries, balers and radios, how everything worked, was built, as a child unscrewed all the equipment she got her hands on in order to study its workings; so if a hay loader, baler, tractor, or car broke down somewhere, which happened all the time, and the farmer in question was at a complete loss, the emergency contingency was to go and get Hafrún. Skúli said that he hardly knew the difference between sparkplugs and pistons, but on the other hand was an utter magician when it came to construction and knew the mind and spirit of all animals. So the district turned to Hafrún regarding machinery and parties, to Skúli if something was plaguing the livestock.

And so childhood passed. Eiríkur woke each morning in his attic bedroom, clonked down the stairs to the kitchen where his grandma baked, cooked, made jam and blood pudding, sewed, knitted, went over the accounts to the murmur of the radio, over which the leading articles of the newspapers were read, current affairs were discussed, and *Patients' Song Requests* were played. Hafrún stood up with a smile when he came down, three years old, five years old, seven years old, welcomed him with a firm, heartfelt hug, served him toast with cheese and blueberry jam. Then Skúli came in for his morning coffee, with the pleasant smell of the sheep shed and the winter hay clinging to him, shook his head at the tastelessness of the *Patients' Song Requests*, told Eiríkur that the two of them would probably have to be admitted to hospital so that better music would be played. Then they all sat there with their slices of bread, a cruller or piece of marble cake, hot chocolate or coffee, but Hafrún with only her cup of coffee before her – Eiríkur hardly remembers having seen her eat.

Wonderful mornings; that's how all the world's mornings should begin.

Life in the shape of happiness, time lying curled up like a tranquil dog under the kitchen table at Oddi, his grandma and grandpa knowing the answers to most of the world's questions; they were the world's most trusty cornerstones. He was a cheerful child, earnest, enjoyed little better than when his grandma, Aldís, and even the sisters combed his hair. Then, he would shut his eyes like a purring cat. All was right in their world. The only shadows were his dead mother and his longing for a father who was absent most of the year, at work here and there around the country.

Here in the past, when life was smaller in size, in a sense, when people got by with considerably less, or there was simply little available, fewer options, Oddi easily sustained two to three generations of the family, ten to fifteen people, children as well as adults. One of the fjord's better farms, with decent hayfields, respectable pastures, rich berry land, fish in the heath lakes, and several possibilities for fishing at sea. But by the 1980s, the farm could hardly support more than two adults. Which, however, may not have mattered, because neither of the brothers seemed to be inclined towards farming. Halldór often said that Páll was too smart for the sheep, having been the first of the fjord's residents to attend university, first earning a BA in history, then a master's in philosophy, wrote a 200-page thesis on Søren Kierkegaard, then taught, mainly at the comprehensive school in Keflavík, where he lived for a time with a fisherman's widow and played the role of father to her three children. Halldór himself graduated from Ísafjörður Junior College and then spent a year studying at the Icelandic Musicians' Union Music School in Reykjavík. But he was so overflowing with passion and energy that he had a hard time staying in any particular place for long. Played as a young man in bands in the summers, at dances around the country, then worked in construction or went to sea in the winters. But he always came north for the lambing and tried, after Eiríkur was born, to stay at Oddi for the better part of the summer. Helped with the farm work when he wasn't in the studio, which he started setting up after Eiríkur's birth. Went around the countryside with a tape recorder to record old folks' stories, verses, poems, old nursery rhymes; to save memories from insatiable oblivion. Sometimes old bandmates came to visit and jam in the studio, even hold impromptu dances in the school auditorium. And although Eiríkur wasn't much taller than a guitar, they dubbed him their roadie; he got to help set things up for the dances, hang around with them in the studio, listen to them rehearse and tell endless stories of domestic and foreign musicians. And he noticed how Halldór's voice changed, how his eyes shone in a special way when he mentioned names such as Nick Drake, Tom Waits, Bowie, the Beatles, Nina Simone, Chet Baker – spoke of all of them as if they were dear friends whom he missed – and Eiríkur vowed to practise the guitar more often and better, become so good that he could eventually be the friend with whom his dad would want to start a band. He also dreamed that his father would get a job in Hólmavík and could therefore be more or less home all year at Oddi. Though he never mentioned this out loud. He was afraid of hurting his grandparents – afraid that it would come out as if he were saying that it wasn't enough for him to have them.

221

And that he considered his father more important than them . . . so for that reason, he hid his longing for his father, couldn't bear the thought of hurting them, but went to the kitchen and hugged his grandma when the sense of loss bit most painfully. Did so to seek comfort in her warmth, but also because of his guilt over . . . feeling bad despite having his grandparents there.

So Halldór was the one who came, and the one who went. Came like the migratory birds in the spring, went around the time the darkness returned. But also came most Christmases and Easters.

You can drive the car up to the road if you've managed to learn "I'll Follow the Sun" on the guitar when I come for Easter, said Halldór when he said goodbye to the seven-year-old Eiríkur after the Christmas holiday.

Well, said Halldór four months later when he came home the day before Holy Thursday, and Eiríkur sat with his child's guitar on top of the kitchen table, focused, and played the basic chords of the Beatles song that McCartney wrote when he was sixteen, after having had the flu. Leaned over the guitar, causing his dark hair to fall over his eyes, plucked the simple, plaintive song and sang over and over again the only lines he had managed to learn, his voice, which later became like dark velvet, still bright with youth, and his English harsh, brittle: And now the time has come, and so, my love, I must go.

Damn it all, you're going to make me cry, boy, said Halldór, taking Eiríkur in his arms and allowing him not only to drive up to the road, but all the way up to the school, where he had his son drive a few laps in the big car park where the kids in Aldís of Nes's class could certainly see him; envied by the school's younger kids for driving a car, and by the older ones for having Halldór as his father – the man who often appeared at the school's Christmas, Easter, and spring celebrations with his electric guitar, always knew the most popular songs and performed them with such conviction and drive that the kids danced on the tables. Having Halldór for his father was like walking around wearing a medal.

And so, his shadowless youth passed.

*

222

He was so sweet as a child, Eiríkur, Rúna says to me as we slowly pass Oddi, sweet, sensitive, sincere, quick to laugh, imaginative. Sóley and I did all we could to stay overnight at Oddi. We were terribly jealous of Eiríkur, getting to live with his grandma and grandpa. You just felt as if time didn't exist around them. They were so warm, so much fun, Skúli was a real prankster. Like Eiríkur, actually. They played tricks on each other and Hafrún and then both laughed like idiots if she fell for it . . .

A prankster; he poured salt into his grandpa's coffee, caught mice out in the sheep shed and let them loose in the kitchen because Hafrún was so scared of them, woke his giant uncle by pouring cold water over his face, hid his shoes from his father so that he couldn't leave that autumn to do construction work in the east, go to sea in the south. He hid the shoes so well that it took Halldór three hours to find them. No-one said anything about it. Halldór just searched, finally found the shoes, said goodbye to his parents, said goodbye to Eiríkur, work hard, boy, this winter. Be kind to your grandma and grandpa. Help out as much as you can. I'll call. I'll write. Learn "I'll Follow the Sun" on guitar before I come home next. Learn "Bell Bottom Blues", "Rock 'n' Roll Suicide". Then Halldór left, and it was just the three of them, Eiríkur, Hafrún and Skúli. The Three Musketeers, said Skúli, where's your sword, boy? And Eiríkur smiled.

Of course he smiled, for in Eiríkur's childhood years, this fjord was high on the list of the world's top-ten places for growing up – it would have required a special talent to be bored here. Fourteen working farms, if those in Sunnudalur are included, children on all of them, in some places a large number, and, when school began in the autumn, dozens of children from the surrounding countryside were added, among them the weekly boarders whose homes were farthest away. High on the top-ten list; no hope, of course, of spotting a celebrity or a foreigner, getting on TV or being asked the Question of the Day by a newspaper reporter, there was no toyshop here, no ice-cream shop, no shop at all, to be honest, disregarding the three shelves in the pantry at Oddi for the first ten years in Eiríkur's life, a tiny branch of the Co-op in Hólmavík, managed by Hafrún, necessities that people could purchase on credit if the road to and from the fjord was impassable or there was simply no time to make a trip to town for supplies due to lambing, haymaking, fence work. Here, there are plenty of tussocks and hollows and hills and cliffs that can easily be turned into battlefields or distant lands, streams where Eiríkur played with his ships, built by Skúli from driftwood, and from Oddi it wasn't far down to the shore, which always held unexpected wonders. Strange fish or mysterious sea creatures that death had disfigured, shellfish that could be cooked at home, this and that from ships or boats, some foreign, and then the driftwood, fallen trees from Siberia or, as people thought in ancient times, from the great underwater forest at the bottom of the sea – tidings from another world. High on the top-ten list. Even if the world was far away, no cafés, theatres, concert halls for the adults, no amusement park, playgrounds, or proper football fields, and no cinemas.

The latter isn't entirely true, however, because once a month Hafrún drove Eiríkur and the sisters from Nes to the movie show at the community centre in Hólmavík, letting neither storms nor heavy snow hinder them. They enjoyed driving in dark, cloudy weather, soldiered on through poor conditions with chains on all four tyres of the old Land Rover, inched their way over dizzying ice in bright winter weather, when the low winter sun rolled silently through the icy blue sky, fuzzy like a ball of woollen yarn, so low in the air that they heard it when it grazed the crests of the mountains.

He alone is truly happy, it says somewhere, who both relishes the passing day and looks forward to tomorrow. Eiríkur looked forward to the mornings in the kitchen with his grandparents, looked forward to meeting the sisters at Nes later in the day, and he looked forward to the evenings, when Hafrún read to him, told him stories, recited verses or rhymes. But if the winter sky was clear and the multitude of stars sparkled over the white, silent fjord, Skúli would lie next to him in the bed under the attic's big window and the two of them would go on a journey between the stars. Skúli taught his grandson about stars, star systems, told him about black holes, explained the structure of galaxies, described the distance between them, what the northern lights were made of, where meteors came from, how, through the centuries, they had hit the Earth as if sent by the gods and changed everything; told of the comets, which are giant fists of ice hurtling through the darkness of space, like gods rushing through the cosmos, and in ancient times were considered heralds of great events. Yet they themselves are the greatest of events, said his grandpa; they're the fairytales of the heavens. They appear and change everything around them, then disappear and leave behind a trail of melancholy yearning in the human heart . . .

So Dad is a comet, Eiríkur thought as he lay there beside his grandpa, with his head, as so often, on Skúli's chest, drinking in his serenity, his deep voice. Thought it, but didn't want to say anything.

And started school as soon as he was old enough.

Then came the slow winter evenings, which drift like islands of bliss in the sea of his memory, when he sat over his homework at the kitchen table, the dogs drowsing beneath it, licking his bare feet, Hafrún busying herself with something, endless chores, cooking, baking, making jam and blood pudding, knitting, ironing, mending clothing to the murmur of the radio. Choirs, current affairs, a piano concerto by Frédéric Chopin, the evening reading from *Witchcraft and Will-o'-the-Wisp* by Ólafur Jóhann Sigurðsson, *The Bridal Gown* by Kristmann Guðmundsson. Hafrún helped him with history, geography, languages, and Skúli with mathematics and science. His grandpa, who had barely attended school, had always enjoyed reading about scientific subjects and wrestling with mathematics, and he made them into games for Eiríkur, turned the numbers into dance partners, army divisions, or footballers, depending on the operation. But sometimes, when the evening's mood lent itself to it, or a piece of music on the radio called up some memories in Skúli, he took a break from his instruction, leaned back and began telling Eiríkur about his childhood out west in Snæfellsnes. Described the glacier that towers eternal over human life, told of friends who disappeared from his life after the postman brought him here to the north, of their games and capers; told of his parents, his enthusiastic but erratic father, his unhealthy but strong-willed mother and her three sisters. The eldest, a little older than Skúli and who left when she was ten years old to live with relatives in Canada, to relieve the burden on their home, the other two younger than Skúli, one still living, the other died young from tuberculosis. Recounted how his mother laughed, how she tilted her head and pouted her lips when she was concentrating, how her natural joy made even the greyest of days sparkle; how his father could become so deeply immersed in his reading that even God couldn't have reached him; when Skúli's sisters crawled into bed with him at night, maybe scared, or else it was just so abominably cold in the house, their dad away from home, their mum so ill that she could barely get out of bed, and then the three of them lay close together, Skúli told them stories, turned the bed into a ship, sailed it to distant lands where the sun always shone, where the weather was so clement that no-one fell ill, where no-one got drunk and there was always plenty to eat . . .

Hafrún would then sit down with them; she sat idly at the table, her hands as if asleep in her lap, listened with her eyes half closed, but opened them all the way when Skúli's voice changed as he said the names of his sisters. Eiríkur's only clear memories of his grand-mother's hands are from those evenings. Otherwise, he only ever saw them working, so interwoven with endless tasks that he didn't notice them, yet there they lay, petite but strong, delicate but calloused in her lap, motionless, almost as if sleeping, while Skúli talks about his youth, speaks slowly, looks away or pats Eiríkur's head as if distractedly.

Later, much later, with both Paris and Marseille behind him and Eiríkur back in this sparsely populated fjord, it dawned on him that that was the only time he had heard his grandfather talk about his youth out west in Snæfellsnes – about his life before the postman brought him like any other parcel through storms and over difficult heaths down here into this fjord. Skúli sat close beside his grandson, spoke softly, an underlying hoarseness in his voice, which became a bit strained when he spoke the names of his sisters. He chose his words carefully, sometimes pausing the story while fiddling with his pipe; in those years it was fine to smoke indoors, and around children; nothing dangerous about it. Such times! Oh, and now gone . . .

IF YOU'RE SOUR, BE SWEET – BUT THIS MOMENT, I WANT TO
AND AM GOING TO REMEMBER, EVEN IF I REACH THE AGE
OF ONE HUNDRED AND SEVENTY!

But weren't those the best days when both brothers were at home at Oddi?

Páll seemed to be able to calm the unrest inside Halldór, who, in the summers, could spend whole days roaming the countryside or show up out of the blue out west in Ísafjörður, up north in Akureyri, and be away for days at a time. Páll calmed everything around him. He was like a sun. Like a heavy but perhaps slightly dark sun that emanated more warmth than light, serenity than joy. And the best times in the world were when the brothers took Eiríkur fishing with them, out in the bay in their small diesel-powered boat. Barely more than three years old when he got to go for the first time, partly against Hafrún's will, but the brothers promised to look after him and Halldór took this so seriously that he tied Eiríkur to himself. The next day Hafrún went to Reykjavík and returned with a life jacket for her grandchild.

From the beginning, sea-fishing had been interwoven with farming in this fjord, and for a time in the 1950s a small freezing plant was in operation at the tip of the peninsula below the church. Sea-fishing is an important supplement in a poor agricultural area; lumpfish and seals in the spring, whatever can be caught in the winters. But for the most part, in Eiríkur's youth it wasn't done any longer, and the brothers went to sea for fun, to catch fish for the dinner pot and keep up the old boat that Skúli and Kári had built back in the day; for fun and to enjoy being together and free out at sea. Out in the wide bay that neither knew nor had any interest in man's everyday life, his trials and tribulations, endless obligations and demands. And after the life jacket came, Eiríkur could go with them whenever he wanted, which was almost always, even if the brothers left early in the morning, when the countryside wasn't fully awake, the mountains in a deep sleep and wrapped in morning fog, as if to protect themselves from the cold.

Eiríkur sat bundled up between the brothers, like a tussock between mountains, but they were bare-headed, bare-handed, seldom wearing anything besides jeans and a woollen jumper, with generous lunches prepared by Hafrún, hot chocolate for Eiríkur, and sometimes Halldór snuck a bottle of red wine for himself into his lunchbox, to spice up the day, as he put it – and finally the powerful tape recorder back in the stern, wrapped in several layers of plastic, because life without music is no life, it's just poverty and heavy, wet snowstorms.

But out of consideration for the fjord's residents and the morning stillness, they never turned on the tape recorder until they were out on the wide bay, where the waves breathe heavier, more deeply, but then they played it loud as they laid the lines, as they pulled in the fish and bled them. Halldór was in charge of the music selection, he had used the day before to copy them onto a cassette, each song specially selected and preceded by a short introduction, read by Halldór: Here you have Pink Floyd. They rarely tell jokes, and their friends would call a doctor if they saw them smiling, but their music can breathe as deeply as the sea.

And listen now, because here we have none other than Etta James, a voice that, with its sad beauty, fills us with longing for life and love, "I'd Rather Go Blind", And baby baby, I would rather go blind, boy, than see you walk away . . .

Later, much, much later, when it was possibly too late, Eiríkur realised that his dad hadn't just been entertaining them and himself with those introductions, and educating his son, but also and perhaps no less addressing him in the future, saying, remember these songs, they were my inner landscape, listen to them and then you'll know how my heart beat.

Remember me, don't forget me. Listen to these songs and I'll be with you. Listen, and then I'll dare to be wholly with you.

*

"Eiríkur Halldórsson, able seaman on the *St Mary*" was written on the envelope holding the birthday card waiting on your bedside table when the sprightly notes of the *Eniga Meniga* album woke him at six thirty, and it was difficult to see who looked forward more to Eiríkur's birthday, himself or the adults. Able seaman, a better birthday present couldn't be imagined, not in this universe. It was as if Batman had told Robin that hereafter, they were equals; and the fjord celebrated his birthday by pulling from its savings drawer one of its best summer days. Dead calm, twelve degrees Celsius when the brothers woke Eiríkur. Páll had come the day before, solely to be there on Eiríkur's birthday. Two weeks until haymaking, the grass grew, that green song. July and the light still supreme. The sky hasn't shut its eyes for weeks, it being unnecessary to rest or sleep in the summer. The sky wide with light, with the songs of moorland birds as the three of them drove down the fjord towards the boathouse where the inhabitants of Oddi had launched their boats for centuries.

They sailed and their boat, the *St Mary*, which Páll had painted in the spring, yellow like van Gogh's sunflowers, except the prow was so red that it resembled a kiss, clove the placid fjord, they sailed out onto the still bay with the sun over everything like a bright, warm trumpet. Truly one of the world's great days. A day they never forgot. The three of them together with packed lunches, fishing gear and music. Three seamen, and one of them having just turned eight. Twelve degrees on land, it would grow warmer over the course of the day, climb to seventeen degrees, but was cooler out at sea, which is why they had coffee, hot chocolate and sandwiches made by Hafrún. Sailed the sea, sailed the silence, and the blazing sun rose higher and woke the birds that were still asleep. Of course, there were no stars to be seen, because the light had destroyed them all early in May and it was weeks before the brightest ones would return. But that's alright, because as it says: If the stars are the birds of the night sky, then the birds are the stars of the Earth.

Who said that? Páll asked, I don't remember, his brother replied. And I remember so little nowadays, unbelievable what little is left. Which is a great sin because what's forgotten has in a sense never existed. Has never happened. But don't worry, he said to Eiríkur, this moment I want to and intend to remember, even if I live to be a hundred and seventy! And besides, it's our duty to remember, said Páll; to forget is to betray life. Which Kierkegaard knew, of course. If one generation succeeded another like birdsong in the forest, he writes in *Fear and Trembling*, and "mankind passed through the world as a ship through the ocean, as the wind through the desert, without thought, fruitless; if eternal oblivion were forever lying greedily in wait for its prey and no power were capable of snatching it away – how empty and hopeless would life then be?"

Amen, said Halldór. Those are sentences to fish with, and this you remember, down to the last comma, I who can hardly remember the simplest of rock lyrics nowadays, unless I'm holding my guitar. It's so good that I should compose a song with it so I don't forget it.

Kierkegaard is my guitar, said Páll.

Are you sure he's not a cello, instead?

Who's Kierkegaard? Eiríkur asked.

Halldór: A Danish philosopher who wrote letters to God, and received answers. My brother's an expert on him. Søren Kierkegaard. Kierkegaard apparently means "churchyard".

Eiríkur: Like the one out at Nes?

Exactly, like the one out at Nes. The poor man was called churchyard – what a burden to bear! A name full of death, crosses and dead people. Maybe no surprise that the man was sometimes a little down.

Páll: He knew death and could therefore write about life in a way that none other could. Still, he was always trying to write himself towards the light; that path must undeniably be dark sometimes.

Halldór: Towards the light, as it is around us? I don't really know about that. I've got to know him relatively well through you and your writings, and, if I remember correctly, he says in one place: in life you usually have two paths to choose from, and you can either choose this one or the other. In all honesty and with your well-being in mind, I say: Do it, or don't do it, it doesn't matter which you choose – both choices will fill you with regret. It's not exactly the kind of music you can dance to, or use as flippers to swim towards the light!

Give me darkness, and then I'll know where the light is, but now Eiríkur and I want cake, said Páll, inching his way back to the stern, to the storage trunk there, from which he took three good-sized slices of Hafrún's chocolate cake. The boat swayed on the tranquil, slumbering bay, the land gleamed with sunshine, it literally sang and they had coffee, hot chocolate, and the best chocolate cake in the world, and it was the birthday of one of them, he was eight years old and had just been made an able seaman. That's big; it doesn't get much bigger.

They sighed, they squirmed, this is good, man, they said to each other, so happy to be together that the dead smiled. Finished their slices, made ready their lines, slid them into the deep, sat and waited for the fish to bite down there in the dark. The sea breathed quietly, at home Hafrún waited for the catch that would become the birthday dinner. Grilled, fresh fish. I prefer cod, Hafrún had said when they got themselves ready that morning. Then we'll ask the cod to bite, and we'll turn away the other idiots, Halldór promised; and now they're waiting, lines in hand, in the rocking boat, happy with the moment, the tape playing the songs that Halldór had compiled in the studio for the birthday trip. The sun is a fire in the sky, it burns like life, because it's supposed to burn, it must always burn, otherwise the world will grow cold. Halldór plays three songs in a row from the *Eniga Meniga* album for Eiríkur, "If You're Sour, Be Sweet". The last song was played at full volume and they sang or shouted along: "We need boards and we need a saw/we need paint and lively songs!" They sang so loudly that the fish dove deeper to escape. It isn't working, said Halldór, we'll put on Miles and let him blow the fish up to us. And of course he did, of course Miles Davis blew the fish up from the bottom, the biggest, a big, solid cod, it took Eiríkur's bait, saying: I'll give you my life as a birthday present.

Now we can sail home, said Halldór, pulling his line aboard, and he started the engine, asked his brother to steer, knelt down to the tape recorder, poured himself a glass of wine, lowered the music, fast-forwarded, stopped the tape, listened, rewound it a little, then stood back up, glass in hand, and announced: Boys, this here isn't a song but a mountain range. And it will be our song. We'll remember this day, this moment of ours together, every time we hear this song in the future.

Then Halldór pushed play and they sailed home with their birthday dinner, listened, happy to have had this moment together while Paul McCartney sang for them, the bay, the fjord, the sun, and the land that gleamed, the land that resounded and the five seagulls that hovered over the boat, eternally hungry:

And when I go away ...

What can be said but: Such times!

Why do days like these have to end, why can't happiness stop when it comes to us, and we could carry it through life as the tortoise carries its house; like an unbreakable shield against the arrows of unhappiness?

GIVE ME DARKNESS AND THEN I'LL KNOW WHERE THE LIGHT IS Wherever I go, my heart will remain with you, happy birthday, Eiríkur, I'll give you my life as a birthday present, youth wrapped in warmth, security, love – but now at the age of forty, Eiríkur lives alone at Oddi, looking from a distance like a sad rock star with his electric guitar on his back, a loudspeaker in his arms, fires, piss-drunk, a shotgun at a lorry or perhaps fate and is possibly facing up to twelve years in prison; what happened, why did life go in this direction, where did the security and the warmth go? Does one get drunk on Calvados, empty a shotgun at a lorry or fate after having sung "eniga meniga" and "my love", been happy on your eighth birthday, where are Páll and Halldór, by the way, why do they no longer speak to Eiríkur . . . yes, that's right, Páll is lying under the heavy shore rock and the words of Kierkegaard in the churchyard out at Nes, it's regrettable, it's sad, but where's Halldór, then? Did the world that Skúli and Hafrún created around themselves and filled the house at Oddi with dissolve and turn to nothing after they died; can happiness not endure, does it bear life so badly, and death not at all? Can't a person change happiness into a tortoise or even a dog, rather, that follows at one's heel, does happiness not know how to heel, is there no way to train it, does it have no loyalty; and it's all finished, just Elías's party remaining and then it's finished, twelve years in prison – Kierkegaard failed to write us into the light and darkness alone is ahead, please fasten your seatbelts because now the darkness is taking over?

Let's wait a bit with this. Eiríkur is still only eight years old.

Then he'll be nine years old.

Then ten.

Because time passes, it always does, it's an expert at passing, has a doctorate in making us age, and then die, then disappear. Time passed and so did Eiríkur's youth, mostly shadowless. Halldór came home with the spring birds, at Christmas and Easter, spent more and more time in the studio, slowly made progress on his guitar, the old Hammond organ, sometimes jammed with his old bandmates, and went on with his endless project of recording the stories of the older folk in the fjord and the countryside north of it, saving the past from oblivion; for if eternal oblivion were forever lying greedily in wait for its prey and no power were capable of snatching it away – how empty and hopeless would life then be? By the age of ten, Eiríkur felt so at home in the studio that he gave his dad a hand whenever he could, and, in the farmhouse, Hafrún awaited them with homemade bread, rhubarb tart, crullers, marble cakes, maybe strolled up to the studio, Skúli often with her, to fetch them for coffee and see what they were up to.

But the spring before Eiríkur went south to junior college, Páll moved back to the fjord, and then took over the farm at Nes. Came alone. It hadn't worked out between him and the widow. He was loved by her children, they sometimes came here to the north, stayed for a while, and their mother loved him. But sometimes she said, and meant it every time, that Páll demeaned himself by living with her, that she didn't deserve him, she who drank, was irresponsible,

233

couldn't even give him a child, barren now, after having given birth to her youngest child with great difficulty.

I don't deserve you, she said, and sometimes I fear that you pity me rather than love me. I fear that this is kindness, not love. I fear that I'm ruining your life. Sometimes I even think you're too good to love.

Páll had found her in bed, or rather on the couch, with an old friend and shipmate of her husband's. A cheeky, self-assured first mate who seldom referred to Páll as anything other than the soft, pale giant. He's ten thousand times better than you, the widow told the first mate, his little finger is worth more than your whole miserable life. Shortly afterwards she looked at the clock, lifted her long skirt, look, she said, no underwear; then leaned over the back of the couch and ordered him to fuck her. If you're the man you claim to be, then come and take me, take me hard, properly, fuck me like no-one has fucked me before.

And that was how Páll found them when he came home from teaching. She was naked below the waist, with her skirt up on her back, the first mate humping away at her like an excited dog. Despite the first mate's panting and loud moans, she heard Páll coming up the stairs. Maybe she was listening for his footsteps. She looked up, he looked in her eyes and understood everything. Turned around and left. The first mate is too excited to notice anything, until he comes out, rather satisfied with himself, intends to get in his car, drive home to his wife who is waiting with his lunch, but finds his car turned on its side, lying up against the pavement like a helpless turtle. And Páll comes here to the north, says little, takes over Nes that autumn. Sad but also somewhat relieved to be done with teaching. He loved sharing philosophy and history with the kids, but would sometimes stutter so much that his classes could turn into nightmares.

Give me darkness and then I'll know where the light is.

There are so many layers to life.

But it's time to talk about sex. Or the libido.

Which is the light and darkness of the world.

We can't avoid my libido, Ásmundur would later say at the hotel, before adding, in the beginning was the libido and the libido was with God. The same goes for Eiríkur, that we can hardly avoid his libido, which was fortunately not the same tremendous force in his life, never a roaring Tyrannosaurus rex, he didn't fuck exhaust pipes, the sheep had no need to fear him. Yet it did change everything. His libido, or rather, sexual maturity. It changed everything and drove him, thirteen years old, to scan the four bookcases in the living room in the hope of finding overt descriptions of sex. After flipping through several books with little success, he happened upon the biography *When Hope Alone Remains*, and his heart skipped a beat as he looked at the cover image and read the subtitle: *A Prostitute Tells of Her Life and Environment* – the Icelandic translation of *La Dérobade* (*The Life: Memoirs of a French Hooker*) by Jeanne Cordelier.

It was a rainy day in July. The rain pounded the mountains, the fjord and the buildings, it was barely seven degrees, the cows at Skarð stood like depression itself up against the fence gate, staring towards the cowshed, mooing from time to time and finding the world unfair. A few days before, Halldór had gone north to stand in for a friend of his in a dance band who had suffered a broken arm, Skúli was out in the sheep shed replacing the mangers, Hafrún was visiting Botn. Eiríkur had been helping his grandfather, going to fetch tools, holding boards, when the unrest awoke inside him: his mind filled with vague, exciting images, he got a rock-hard erection and fled to the farmhouse to hide his condition, hoping at the same time to find a remedy for it. Which had until then been his main problem: on the one hand finding exciting pictures and texts, on the other hand giving vent to the urges that had woken in him a few months before – he simply didn't know how he could . . . uncork himself. He fled into the house, locked himself in the bathroom and took off his pants, and just standing there naked with his penis rock hard and quivering in front of him was strangely exciting, something forbidden. But it wasn't enough. Then it occurred to him to go to the living room and rummage through the books; he vaguely recalled seeing a half-naked woman on one of the covers, and found the book after a bit of a search: *When Hope Alone Remains.*

The cover image was of a woman with long, curly hair and long, bare legs, wearing a short, thin dress that accentuated her alluring figure. She had her back to the photographer and looked to the side. Eiríkur stared at the woman. He made what sounded like a desperate whine and his penis was so hard that it ached. He stared at the image for a long time, then ran with the book up to his room, laid it on the bed, tore off his clothes, pulled them away without taking his eyes off the cover image, trembled with agitation, practically distraught with the desire to give his aroused urges an outlet and staring almost pleadingly at the woman on the book cover. Her short dress was slightly hiked up, wasn't her arse showing a tiny bit, hadn't she turned her head even more to the side to see him naked? Eiríkur trembled. He was so worked up that he actually felt sick, his hard penis ached so much that he grabbed it in the hope that his warm palm would ease the pain. His penis's skin had stretched so tightly that its ugly, bald head was revealed. He tried to pull the skin back over the swollen, one-eyed head to cover it, repeated it three times and orgasmed. He gave a little cry as he felt a warm, wonderful flare deep within him, near his arse, but, as the semen squirted jerkily over the bed and the book, it struck Eiríkur that his mother may have looked like the woman on the book's cover.

In fact, maybe she *was* his mother.

He looked down at the book and met the woman's eyes, clouded by his semen and brimful with sorrow.

He lay awake that night, tossed and turned, couldn't sleep. Gave up around two o'clock and snuck down to the silent living room. He wanted to look at the two photo albums in the living-room cabinet, especially the first one, containing photos that went back to Halldór and Páll's childhoods and ended when Eiríkur was five. He longed to immerse himself in the world in which his sexual desires didn't exist. He'd looked through the album countless times, knew every photo, but that night he saw everything with new eyes. Yet noticed what had always been obvious, so clear that he didn't understand how it could have passed him by – that his family seemed so much brighter before he was born. This was especially noticeable with Halldór. As a child and young man, he's smiling in all the photos, and, although they're black and white and some blurry, joy emanates from him, his infectious zest for life. But he's slower in the photos taken after Eiríkur's birth – he has become the man that Eiríkur has always known. The zeal is still there, but his smile isn't as absolute, there's an uneasiness in his eyes, and he no longer seems so open.

Eiríkur sat in the living room in the rain-grey light of the July night and it slowly dawned on him that he'd not only killed his mother, but to a certain extent his father, as well, murdered his joy of life.

It rained the next day, too, a heavy rain as the cows mooed their dark poems. They mooed, it rained, he killed his mother, he suffocated his father's joy of life. And it was clear to him that he had to get away. It was clear as day. There was no other way.

He thought, now I have no home.

Which is why he left as soon as he could, at sixteen.

South to Reykjavík, to junior college. He left in early September, ten days before the sheep round-up, the first round-up he'd missed.

He wanted to take the coach from Hólmavík but Halldór, who had been in Oddi for a few weeks at that time, wouldn't hear of anything other than driving his son all the way to Reykjavík. They left early in the morning.

One of those quiet, cool autumn days. The fjord calm, the mountains gentle giants. The most beautiful days of the year, the world puts on a good face despite being full of sadness because that summer is gone and will never come back. That birdsong has been silenced for ever.

Oh, said Hafrún as she hugged Eiríkur for the third time, it's incredible how ridiculously sensitive a person can be over little, but I've always been a bit sensitive at this time, when summer turns to autumn, isn't that so, Skúli, and then, of course, I've begun to grow old, when the rigor in one's bones softens. Forgive me, she added, holding Eiríkur's head and leaning back to see him better; she had to look up. Goodness, how tall you've grown! You were tiny when you came here, and now, when you're leaving us, you tower over me. And I can't really imagine life without you. But don't listen to my nonsense, and get going now, before I say more, God help me, you might think I was drunk, she said, letting go of her boy, turning him round, pushing him gently away. Towards the car where Halldór was standing ready; he'd opened the passenger-side door and bowed as Eiríkur approached, smiling slightly, his greying, dark hair falling over his eyes. Then they set off. When they reached the road, Eiríkur glanced back. Hafrún was standing in the same spot, but Skúli had gone to her, they held each other, watched the car drive away, and, for some reason, seemed to age as they receded. Soon they'll be gone, Eiríkur thought, looking towards the heath and fighting back tears.

Soon they'll be gone.

They drove south. Eiríkur was gripped by deep sadness, because he sensed or suspected that in a certain regard, he would never come back. He thought, now I have no home. But then, can't I live wherever I want?

They drove up the road that lay in wide, steep curves up the hill. Halldór shifted down, the car's engine struggled, over the last few days he'd filled three 90-minute cassette tapes for the trip and marked them as *Me and Eiríkur's Songs*. Each song carefully thought out, and he looked forward to playing them for his son. Put the first tape in on the edge of the heath and Morrissey sang "All the Lazy Dykes", Touch me, squeeze me, … and my love, when you look at me you see me as I really am.

The journey south took seven hours. It takes seven hours to drive between lives. The Lord created the world in six days, blessed it the seventh. Everything that is important must therefore happen seven times.

Say I love you seven times, otherwise your love won't live.

It takes seven hours to escape oneself.

*You Don't Make a Decision
and Are Paralysed*

It took seven hours to drive to Reykjavík and Halldór managed to play all three tapes of the music he'd chosen for the trip. Each song carefully chosen, but Morrissey's song still the only one Eiríkur remembers, touch me. Otherwise, the entire journey was swallowed by insatiable oblivion, the black hole in the centre of all universes.

Seven hours, repeats the sanctified coach driver in the middle of his crêpe-making, dressed in a new T-shirt, *Anthology 2, Beatles*, the lyrics of "Real Love" scattered over the shirt, and all my little plans and schemes, lost like some forgotten dreams. This Beatles album was released six months before the father and son drove south, and the world got goosebumps when it listened to "Real Love", which Lennon had sung onto tape almost a year before his death, and the surviving Beatles completed and released many years later. Of course, the world got goosebumps because they were reunited, twenty-six years after their break-up, the four friends, John, Paul, George, Ringo. The world's broken friendships glued together again – even though Lennon had been dead for sixteen years. We seek all means to overcome death, to capture lost friendships or moments that have disappeared deep into the irrevocable past – sometimes we succeed, even if natural law says it's impossible.

And that's why we must never stop trying.

But it was autumn, 1996.

They drove south and the music no longer streamed like oxygen between them. There were seven hours between them, mountains of unspoken words and a dead mother.

Seven hours, the sanctified one says for the third time, while simultaneously using his crêpe spatula to tap on the bottle of single malt whisky that one of us has placed on the small table next to the stove, tapping it as if to ask to be heard. I look up and the car with the father and son and the silence between them that even the music can no longer bridge disappears into the fog of time, like the entire year and most of those who were living then, and so many dead. Harrison is dead, and Bowie, and Cohen, and Prince, and Amy Winehouse, too, who was of course only thirteen years old when they drove south; otherwise songs of hers would have been on the tapes, definitely "Back to Black", which Halldór would later play at the countryside dances and make even the toughest farmers and gruffest female fish workers cry. We only said goodbye with words, I died a hundred times.

We only said goodbye with words and since then, death has cut into me.

Everything begins with words, but they can be completely useless if not followed by an embrace.

But what had happened, why is there so much distance between the father and son, where does Eiríkur's melancholy come from, where did his shadowless youth go, was Eiríkur not allowed to come over the French book, the prostitute's autobiography? My mum's autobiography, he thought as the semen spurted over the book and obscured the cover image. Did Halldór find out, and could never forgive his son . . . for having masturbated? Thirteen years old?

Damn it, says the priest with the PCV licence, it can't be. Enough is enough! Human history would have never amounted to anything without masturbation. The human brain would have just boiled away or turned into a cactus. Even Jesus masturbated when he was a teenager, and then a young man. He closed his eyes and thought of Mary Magdalene or Jesus' friend Pétur. But are you finished, may I say something?

I look up from the pages again, put down my pencil and the year 1996 is extinguished.

Seven hours, he says for the fourth time when he sees that I've come back to the present, today the trip takes a maximum of four hours, and Halldór would have put his playlist on Spotify, which would have been less inconvenient, taken less time. Everything takes less time now, except maybe sex, football matches and Wagner operas. Yes, everything takes less time, our knowledge is expanding, we've reached the moon, sent spacecraft out beyond the solar system, we live longer, we can communicate with the whole world from the couch, yet humanity is no happier. Shouldn't that fill us with sadness, doesn't it suggest that mankind's journey is a failure? Without happiness in life, all victories are trivial, all wealth is meaningless. Might we find happiness first and foremost in simplicity, in effort-lessness, he asks, handing me a photo of Hafrún and Skúli that had hung above the stove, taken during their first year of marriage. They're standing close together outside the old turf house where Hafrún was born; a year later they had built the house with the smiling attic.

I scrutinise the photo, probably longing to see and experience their happiness; the old Framnes farmhouse is just barely visible in the background, the turf house that had been enlarged with a wooden extension, clad in corrugated iron. As was the custom then. People hesitated to demolish the turf houses, and chose instead to enlarge them with wooden structures. Which was beautiful, because then it was as if the old and the new times merged, became one, embraced the people, giving them the feeling that the times were inextricably linked, were interdependent. The past nourished us with its constant presence, breathed stillness into the turmoil of our century, helped us to keep our balance in an ever-changing world, provided security, it . . .

. . . held us captive, says the priest with the PCV licence. We dragged it behind us like chains, iron balls. There you see again, and once more, how man's existence is ruled by paradox, and always has been. Nothing is obvious. Put the person immediately into quarantine who claims to understand the big picture, how everything is connected, don't let that person out until she or he has realised and accepted the paradox, written a novel in which the world is incomprehensible. But Eiríkur went south to junior college, Hamrahlíð JC, no surprise there, an artistic soul, engrossed in music, and with an interest in theatre and cinema; perhaps Hallgerður's movie night in Hólmavík sparked that interest?

Yes, no doubt. I forgot to tell about those important evenings in Eiríkur's life. Hallgerður, who was once a chubby cashier at the Co-op, founded a film club and showed films by directors such as Bergman, Kieslowski and David Lynch at the community centre. Eiríkur attended most of the shows, usually going to see them with the folk from Nes. By the time he was thirteen, his interest in films was so great that Halldór gave him a VCR and a small television as a Christmas present. Then Eiríkur disappeared into both movies and music, and weeks could pass without him coming out of his room, except to eat. Sometimes, when Halldór was at Oddi, he stood silently next to the door of his son's room, trying to find out what Eiríkur was listening to, and then he would buy the album or CD and listen to it in the car, during haymaking, out at sea . . . it was his way of connecting with his son, of experiencing the same things as him. Maybe Eiríkur knew he was listening at his door and chose the songs accordingly; they were a message to Halldór, and even to his mother who had to die so that he could live. I will kiss you, I will kiss you, and we shall be together.

I'll kiss you and we'll always be together. Those who lose their mother at a young age, let alone at birth, bear inner wounds that heal late, heal badly, probably never, that tend to reopen every time life rubs up against you, or cuts at you. Oh, he'd had no idea that she was alive, that she who died still lives, that she'd come here to the north to ask for a glass of water, to say his name twice while Halldór lay under the baler. Why didn't they say . . .

Wait, I say, we aren't there yet.

I'm just trying to help. It's the job of us who make crêpes, drive coaches, work for God or run errands for the devil, to help. To help, urge you on, fill you with uncertainty, push you off the precipice, and become the safety net that catches you – but don't put too much faith in that. You're judged by what you do, not what you intend to do. But Svana brings Eiríkur to the fjord, hands him over the kitchen table because love must not be killed. Sixteen years later, Halldór drives him south, hold me, never let me go, sang Morrissey, at that time, they hadn't hugged for many years. Maybe you'll never do so again? I can only greet you with words, but sometimes they're useless if not followed by an embrace. Were things never again the same between them, the closeness gone, wasn't that difficult for Skúli and Hafrún to live with?

We can, however, call it a kind of embrace when Halldór and Eiríkur sat opposite each other in the living room at Oddi with the large windows that framed the mountainside, the sky, the school-house, the farms Hof and Skarð, both with guitars; only coffee or soda in front of Halldór. This happened thirteen times, and always on the day after Christmas. The first time when Eiríkur was eleven, the last time the Christmas before he went to Paris. Thirteen times, Halldór remembers the number, not Eiríkur. Sat facing each other with their guitars, Halldór guided his son the first few times, though they eventually became equals, Eiríkur's technique having developed over the years, having become even better than Halldór's, who, though, had the advantage of experience, yet there was never any competition, only a longing for harmony; two souls talking together through the music. They sang when appropriate, Halldór in his high, bright voice, Eiríkur's lower, his voice possessing its dark touch from around the age of fifteen, dark, velvety, and the harmony between them could be so perfect that Hafrún had a hard time holding back tears as she sat on the couch, her greying head leaning against Skúli's shoulder. Eiríkur serious and focused-looking, while Halldór sometimes had a hard time keeping from smiling. Stop smiling, he ordered himself, Eiríkur finds it embarrassing to see me smile like an idiot . . . but he was just so happy. The last five times, they ended up playing "Ashes to Ashes" by Bowie, a song they both liked very much . . . The only shadow over these happy moments was how Halldór sensed to his very core that when the moment was over, the magic gone, they'd put down their guitars, that everyday life would return and the distance between the father and son would grow again.

That's how it is, we have our moments in which happiness blesses us, and then they pass, change into the past, and the past never returns. Sadness is our memory of past happiness.

It's the history of mankind.

Everyone grows old, loses life. We live bright moments, experience happiness, and then they pass, time never slows down, it couldn't care less about us, this one dies, that one falls into unhappiness, disappointment, drinking, and in the end everyone goes away and doesn't come back. From life to death; that's our trajectory. We come out of nowhere, disappear into nothingness, and, in the end, everything is erased. We gain happiness, then we lose it. We're faced with two options and no-one knows for certain which is the right one, maybe both, maybe neither, and it may even depend entirely on one's vantage point. You don't make a decision, and are paralysed. Pétur hands Guðríður the book, the light in Halla's hands fades, did they eventually become darkness and turn into two black holes, is betrayal forever the reverse side of love because everything has at least two sides? Halldór and Svana's lives intersected one autumn in Búðardalur, she betrayed her husband out of fidelity to love. Halldór knew that she was married, a mother of two in a stable, warm marriage. Don't kiss me, she asked, you mustn't kiss me, if you respect me, if you care about me, if you love me then you mustn't kiss me, then you mustn't look at me like that, I'm afraid, you mustn't kiss me. Trust me, my love, said Halldór, and kissed her. I'll kiss you and we'll always be together. I will kiss you, I will kiss you, and we shall be together.

Maybe fine for the Cure, but not in this story, not in this universe.

They were granted happiness, then they sacrificed it and Eiríkur was born with a black hole inside him. Because they betrayed, because they weren't allowed to marry each other, because they didn't dare it, couldn't, because she didn't dare to sacrifice everything for love? Usually, you have two paths to choose from, but it doesn't matter which path you choose, a black hole always forms somewhere. How, then, are we to live?

Eiríkur left with a black hole inside him. It was seven hours. Touch me, squeeze me, hold me tight. The only song he remembers from the trip, from the three tapes Halldór had spent an entire day putting together, each song with its own meaning, each text its own message, but it was all erased at the edge of the black hole. Eiríkur sat up against the passenger-side door, began immediately to miss his grandparents, the landscape rushed by and Halldór had to slow down again and again, reaching 130kph on the narrow road without realising it. I don't know how to talk to my son, he thought, fighting back tears as he drove. Three years before, Sóley and Rúna had given Eiríkur a hammock as a Christmas present, Halldór hung it up in his son's attic room. "So you can dream in mid-air," Sóley wrote on the card.

Is it daring for us to dream if our dreams can never come true?

And all my little plans and schemes, lost like some forgotten dreams; you make a decision and something happens, this one falls into unhappiness, this one embraces happiness, but there's always a price. You don't make a decision and are paralysed. Now that I've seen you smile, what will become of me?

Now I No Longer Know if
I Dare to Exist

IT'S JUNE AND SOME SENTENCES EXPLAIN EVERYTHING.
UNLESS THEY EXPLAIN NOTHING AT ALL

Almost half a year has passed since Pétur paid an unexpected visit to Uppsalir with three books, one of them an old dictionary that an even older bookseller in Copenhagen, possibly the devil's brother, had sold him because he knew that in due course Pétur would take the book to where its knowledge belonged. Pétur handed Guðríður the book, the priest is shy about helping himself to the refreshments, said Gísli, it's unnecessary, we have plenty here. Pétur smiled, reached for more, added to his plate, while at home at the church farm, Halla waited, she has hands of light. But it can be complicated to live because sometimes you're faced with two options and they're both bad, what does one do then? It doesn't matter which you choose, says Kierkegaard, you'll regret both.

And we can add: you choose one and learn that sometimes the gap between happiness and unhappiness is just one letter of the alphabet. You choose neither and it paralyses you.

Pétur smiled, and said goodbye shortly afterwards. He had a long journey home and night would soon fall. Best to hurry. That was an interesting visit, said Gísli.

The couple accompanied the priest out onto the slope in front of the farmhouse, out into the clear air. Soon it would be spring. Spring is on its way here with its endless light, full of anticipation, optimism, but also hesitation because the frost will come and settle down on the birds' eggs, the newborn lambs. Gísli and Guðríður's daughters had hugged and pampered Ljúf while her master was inside and saw a dangerous smile for the first time. Now she doesn't have the heart to leave you, Pétur had said. He said goodbye with a smile. Rode off with a smile.

Torn by despair, fear, happiness.

He rode away, sat on his horse so finely, and something plummeted in Guðríður's heart.

That was an interesting visit, said Gísli, looking out of the corner of his eye at his wife. He's a priest, she said, as if that explained anything, which it didn't, so she added, I've never had the opportunity to speak to such a learned man.

Then evening fell . . .

. . . and new days come on the heath.

Lambing begins with its incessant vigils, when all your attention goes into watching over newly kindled life. You mustn't blink an eye, or death will snatch away the new life. Which the couple do not do, and life wins this round, this battle. The vast majority of the lambs survive and the blood sings with joy in Gísli's veins, he hugs his wife out of nowhere, pulls her quickly and tightly to himself, this secretive man who rarely shows his feelings, which you shouldn't do unless you're so old that no-one pays attention to you any longer. He hugs Guðríður after they've just finished setting up the pen for the lambs that they remove from their mothers so the latter can be milked. He takes her quickly in his arms and pulls her firmly against his body, almost passionately, with warmth, ardour – and for no apparent reason.

It's so nice how well we work together, he says after releasing her. Says it as if he needs to explain the unexpected embrace, and Guðríður's heart beats fast, she gets tears in her eyes and turns away so that Gísli won't see it. It's been six weeks since his visit.

Because she's counting the days.

She doesn't know why she's counting the days.

She has read the two books thoroughly with the help of the dictionary, does so surreptitiously when Gísli is out working, or deprives herself of sleep. And counts the days. Why are you doing that, my dear, she asks herself, what kind of idiocy is this? But she doesn't attempt to answer, nor does she have any time to lose herself in speculation, there are so many things needing doing. First, there's the lambing and its vigils, the constant watchfulness added to all the household chores: the laundry, the cooking, preparing lessons for the girls, quizzing them on the material, and yes, stealing away to read herself. Sometimes there are just too few hours in the day. But six weeks have passed, forty-two days, and Gísli hugs her so unexpectedly. Tightly, warmly, and then says this so openly and sincerely, that they work so well together.

Which means, we're so good together.

Which means, we have a good life.

Which means, together we can do everything.

Which means, I love you.

Pulls her so closely and quickly to him, then lets go, and she has to turn away from him to hide her tears.

I'm sorry, Gísli whispers. Maybe thinking she's angry, reaches out to touch her but stops and pulls back his hand. She looks over the lamb pen. Tomorrow she and the older girls will start milking the ewes and processing the milk. So that task will be added to the others. The palms of her hands will be sore for the first few days as her calluses thicken, her muscles become accustomed to the effort. Her heart beats. Six weeks. Which means that I love you. I'm sorry, Gísli whispers, and she turns away.

Why does it have to be so complicated to live?

So complicated that people like Kierkegaard have to write books about it.

Gísli had pulled her to him, quickly and tightly, so tightly that she could feel his hard penis. He desires her. That's why he said sorry. Why did he do that? After they've been through so much together.

She looks down, she slowly lifts her long skirt, ties it up, pulls down her underwear, glances at Gísli, then leans slowly over the stacked stones, it's good to feel the cold air on her bare backside. She looks back at him, take me, she says, quick, take me now, at the same time spreading her legs and bending over a little more, so that

253

he can see everything better, knows that it excites him, she hears him gasp. The girls, he whispers and starts fiddling with his trousers. It'll be fine, if you're quick about it, she says, is it very hard now? Yes, see, he whispers huskily, and then she looks back, knows that he wants her to, knows that it excites him even more when she looks at his erect penis. Take me, she says. Take me *now*, she orders. And then he enters her, slips easily in. Ardent, excited, he moans softly. Be careful not to make me pregnant, she whispers, she moves her hips and he grunts, thrusts, and his throat rattles as he pulls out his penis. *Look*, he practically barks. She looks round and sees his penis twitch, sees the semen shoot out of it.

Which means I love you.

Which means we're so good together.

It's June and so bright that it's incomprehensible. It neither freezes nor snows past the eighth of June, which is wonderful, a blessing, and everything is on life's side. It's raining, the grass grows vigorously. Guðríður plants potatoes and swedes as soon as the ground thaws. The grass grows, the lambs are separated from their mothers for the milking and bleat bitterly for days on end. I'll never get used to it, sighs Guðríður, the poor little things. That's life, says Gísli.

Some sentences explain everything. Unless they explain nothing at all.

The grass continues to grow, the lambs grow larger, most of them survive, the ewes give their milk. Good weather. Take me. Look how hard it is.

It's a fine summer, Gísli's blood sings and at the start of July his parents come to visit and stay three nights. Arrive during the gap in which all the work of the spring and first part of the summer is over but the haymaking hasn't begun, making it safe to breathe freely. It's alright to relax a little. At least when you're getting into your upper years and are lucky to have a fine farm and workers you can count on. Then you can ride around the countryside on horseback like the finest tourist. Soon we'll be speaking foreign languages, says Björgvin, Gísli's father.

They don't arrive empty-handed, but have brought small gifts, veal, biscuits, of course sweets for the girls, even a five-year-old mare; and finally a parcel from the postman, which had been down at Bær for three or four weeks. At the home of the district manager and his wife, who say hello.

SHE'S SO SWEET, BUT WHY SHOULD GOD WANDER UP HERE
TO THE HEATH, ISN'T EVERYTHING WITH A NAME DOWN
IN THE LOWLAND?

Oh, of course we should describe the girls' immense joy when their grandparents brought rarities such as foreign biscuits, caramels, fine silk ribbons, because it was just as if Christmas had come in the middle of summer. Or what's the use of plunging into the past to retrieve forgotten lives, lost moments, if we fail to describe the joy of three girls, sisters, on a heath farm, in a heath cottage, joy that they will remember all their lives? Over the gifts and the mare that their grandparents brought; a five-year-old, good-tempered, reddish mare with a blaze all the way down her snout, a broad white blaze that practically shines in the dark, as if her head is a lantern, is light. The mare is a gift to Gísli, and Guðríður. A horseless farmer is a peasant, says Björgvin. She's of good stock, strong, can carry heavy hay but is a beautiful saddle horse at the same time.

A gift. No, that's not the right word. The words must be chosen carefully here.

After all, Björgvin doesn't say that, that the mare is a gift, because in that case Gísli would have sent it back with his parents.

Do you have enough hay to keep my mare for me this winter? Björgvin asks his son.

I can keep her for you if you need me to, Gísli answers; no animal in my keeping has ever starved. Are you tight for space?

Tight, what's tight and what's spacious? I suppose this is what people would call a matter of definition, and it would all depend on your position. But I'm just asking if you could keep her here this summer, and preferably next winter. I thought that I was old enough and had been around enough not to have to explain such things anymore, finally. It's up to you.

The creature can certainly be here, says Gísli, clearly preferring to drop the subject.

The women, meanwhile, are silent, even Steinunn, as difficult as it is for that woman not to get to have her say. They fear that Gísli will take this request, or this disguised gift, badly. They fear that Björgvin will say something wrong that will get Gísli's hackles up, anger him, make him answer so testily that it would rule out the elderly couple being able to leave the mare behind.

So it's settled, says Björgvin, taking out the bottle of cognac that he'd bought from a French fisherman in Ólafsvík. There's the word of the Lord, says Gísli, and then the father and son go out to the sheep shed to get drunk, and there Björgvin says again that a horse-less farmer is a peasant.

A peasant, replies Gísli, is a man who envies others.

That may be, says Björgvin. But your brother is nagging your mother and me to come and join him out west in Canada. Death is earning him a fortune, there's always a good supply, he says, potential clients everywhere you look. But what should an old farmer like me do abroad where almost no-one speaks Icelandic? But I'll admit, if you don't repeat it, that sometimes I get tired of those damned sheep, it's true, they can be so terribly stupid at times, and more stubborn than any devil. And naturally, I'm getting on in years, which is fine, perhaps, but soon I'll be old, useless for most work, and then I'll just be in everyone's way. In the end even too old to scold my dogs properly. Old people have always been looked down on in Iceland because they're both no good at scolding dogs and useless for work. I would ask you to shoot me before I get too old, in the certainty that I could count on you to do so, but I guess you're not allowed to shoot people for humanitarian purposes, only for economic purposes. Everything in this world is so skewed and strangely screwed together that you can see how it might occur to us to pack up and move west across the ocean to your brother. He says that older people there are so highly respected that people doff their hats to them. How do you like that?

I don't have a hat, so I couldn't doff it to you.

You're so damned stubborn that it doesn't change anything if you don't have a hat. I even think you wouldn't doff your hat to God if he passed by here on his horse.

Why should God wander up here to the heath; isn't everything with a name down in the lowland?

What should I know of God's travels – in fact, I think he doesn't show himself much so far north in the world. And I wasn't talking about that, but the other thing – what you would say about me going like a worn-out old horse west to Canada instead of growing old here and becoming so useless that not even the dogs would show me respect?

I have no opinion on it. And have no experience of being old. Soon it'll be haymaking; what will Canada matter then? But apparently it's so warm there sometimes that people work shirtless – and all day long, at that. That's something. And it's thrifty, too; your clothing wears out slower.

So you're not opposed to Canada? Might even come with us?

Aren't I going to house the mare for you? I can hardly do that if I've moved to Canada.

Björgvin shakes his head, reaches for the bottle. It's just not, he begins to say, but then Guðríður brings them freshly baked pancakes.

Came out of the farmhouse, out of its dark passageway with the warm, fragrant stack, crossed the slope separating the farmyard from the homefield and felt a peculiar sting in her heart, or a strange feeling. Maybe because she has the pancakes on the fine tray that Gísli had given her, sacrificed so much for; he'd been so beautifully shy when he brought the tray home from Arnarstapi, and she always feels a bit sentimental when she takes it out.

Crosses the slope to the sheep shed. Blessed is the light of heaven, says Björgvin when Guðríður comes, and she smiles when she sees how drunk the men already are. They're sitting in the manger, Björgvin hunched, he's gained weight in recent years, has a big head and wears the expression of someone who has never had to apologise for who he is or doubt the obedience of his dogs. Gísli's head is shaped precisely the same, but he's much taller than his father, sinewy, so slender that he's downright skinny, and sometimes wears such a stubborn expression that even God and the devil realise there's little point in commanding him or trying to manipulate him.

Guðríður leaves the better part of the pancakes with the father and son, steals a swig of cognac from them, stops to see the girls, who are doting on the mare outside the storehouse, unable to bring themselves to leave her. There are seven pancakes left, two for each girl, and they're allowed to give the mare the seventh. I'll pretend not to see it, says Guðríður, taking all three of them in her arms, quickly breathing in their scent and holding the oldest the longest, Björg, who has grown so much in recent months that she is nearly as tall as her mother, who can feel the girl's growing breasts when she holds her close. My love, she whispers, needing to fight back tears.

My love, she says, her voice nearly breaking, because earlier, in the house, Steinunn had suggested to Guðríður that she take on Björg that autumn and have her there until Christmas, at least. The couple would be hosting the travelling teacher that autumn and, along with that, the district manager and his wife would have a young graduate staying with them that winter in order to teach their children, it's only an hour's walk between our farms, said Steinunn, and I'm certain they'll allow Björg to attend lessons with their children. What do you say to that? she asked Guðríður, who looked down to hide her expression. She wished that she could say no thank you, but knew full well that she mustn't deny her girl this opportunity, it would simply be unforgivable. Deny her that education and chance to experience more comforts, space, larger and much more modern homes, where she would meet more people. She knew that Björg would be so happy that she would lose sleep from sheer anticipation. But Guðríður also knew that if Björg said yes, which she would do, she would lose her daughter. Because whoever leaves a poor, remote heath farm for education never returns there, except as a visitor. She hugs her tightly there outside the storehouse. Holds her so tightly, fighting back tears, that Björg starts to laugh. Mama, she giggles, and

Guðríður lets go. She allows the youngest girl to dash to the farm-house for more pancakes, including one more for the mare. Just one, says Guðríður firmly. She's so sweet, says Elín, inhaling the mare's aroma. The girls are trying to find a name for her but have come up with so many suggestions that they can't possibly decide between them. Maybe we should call her Ljúf, Guðríður lets slip . . .

MAYBE GOD'S THOUGHT IS NOT PARTICULARLY BEAUTIFUL,
BUT AT LEAST SHE'S WEARING NEW SHOES, MAKING IT
EASIER TO PEE AMID TUSSOCKS

In early September Guðríður rides alone on Ljúf out to Stykkishólmur; it's a journey of several hours and she has to cross a heath.

Heath, it's a beautiful word. But heaths are the places where the land rises as if out of a desire for the sky. A beautiful word, though sometimes meaning the same as loneliness, bad weather, hardship, and fog you get lost in, but it also means freedom, tranquillity and dreams, and the best heaths have lakes full of trout and streams that cut quietly through tussocks and grass. Not much in this world that beats the feeling of lying between tussocks on an Icelandic heath, lying there and becoming one with the sky and the scent of heather, grass; then that person has lived, has existed, that is, if the ground isn't wet and cold, if it doesn't rain, or blow so violently that the person crossing the heath on horseback can thank her or his lucky stars for not blowing off the horse's back like some scrap of paper. And if there's no blowing snow or sleet, which there can be even in midsummer – but whatever heads for the sky, the landscape or a person, must of course endure more than others.

It isn't snowing or blowing, however, when Guðríður crosses the heath, sometimes frightening adolescent lambs, many quite fat after the summer, the first and only summer in most of their lives. Excellent weather and such deep stillness that the sky has moved closer, as if it's more interested in humankind than before, and wants especially to watch this woman with ashen-blond hair, a bright face, eyes that are either amber or brown, depending on how the light falls on them, and hands red from doing laundry, but still delicate beneath their calluses. Her long fingers, which loosely hold the reins of the good-natured mare, wrote an article a few months earlier about the earthworm, which hereafter will seldom be called anything but the blind poet of the soil. It's because of this article that she's on her way out to Stykkishólmur.

A fairly long way, probably eight hours, but don't take our word for it, we aren't locals. Except, there's this heath and Guðríður sometimes doesn't go faster than walking pace, both to protect the mare but also in the hope that the heath's deep stillness will soothe her restless heart; the world up here is so still that one would think it was happy.

Three days ago, however, there had been a storm that lasted for two days. The first big autumn low pressure system. High winds from the south-east that scourged the land with violent rain and it snowed in the highest mountains, which then shone white against the sky as the storm subsided. A white message from the winter. I'm on my way.

Strange, thinks Guðríður on the sauntering mare, that in the autumn the mountains can become so white and peaceful that they call to mind God's thought, yet hold this message from winter, that it's on its way with its cold and vehemence, the fear of hunger, isolation – maybe God's thought isn't as beautiful as we would like to believe?

She rides over the heath and approaches Stykkishólmur. Approaches slowly, yet draws closer with each step. The heath is so wet from the autumn rain that she waits to dismount to pee until she reaches the high heath, where the ground is rockier. There, she pees up against rocks piled as a waymark. When Guðríður lifts her long skirt she remembers that she's so unusually well-shod that she could have peed on the peaty ground without fear of getting her feet wet. But just to be safe, she removes her shoes, so they don't get sprayed on when she pees.

Because Steinunn, who had come the week before to fetch her granddaughter, gave Guðríður some newish clothes of her own that she'd altered to fit the younger woman, as well as these fine, ankle-high shoes, almost unused. Admittedly too big on Guðríður, but no-one needs to know that. All that will show is that you're wearing nice shoes, Steinunn had said. My daughter-in-law isn't going to meet such fine people in sheepskin shoes, not as long as I breathe here above ground.

It's the beginning of September, she's wearing good shoes, has just finished peeing up on the heath, is on her way out to Stykkishólmur, the town itself, to meet fine folk. She who is merely a housewife on a small heath farm. What would the district manager and his wife at Bær say about that, or the people down in the lowland in general?

But the article can hardly be the only explanation for her trip, and what about Gísli, is it fine with him that his wife is making this trip alone, will wear out Ljúf on such a long journey?

Except that this mare is named Blesa (Blaze). Gísli had put an end to all discussion of the mare's name, dismissed the name Ljúf, which seemed to be their daughters' preference. Her name will be Blesa; that's what the creature was called before she came to Uppsalir – why change it, Gísli had said and the girls know their father well enough to understand that nothing can move him once his decision has been made. The mare is just too sweet to be called Blesa – and that's why, for us, your name is Ljúf, they whispered to her, which delighted the mare, because horses like having beautiful names. But no matter what the mare's name, Guðríður is on her way out to Stykkishólmur. It's a three-night trip and an almost five-day absence, counting the trip back, and for what purpose? Because the article is written, it has been published, what more is needed? And who, might I ask, is to see to the laundry and meals at Uppsalir in the meantime, now that only the two younger girls are left, since Björg had gone down to the valley with her grandmother for the autumn and won't return until Christmas?

All summer, Björg had hardly been able to think of anything other than what lay in store for her. She was literally soaring, had a hard time hiding her eager anticipation, her expectation, but felt a constant pang of guilt, as well; wasn't it as if she were looking forward to parting from her family? She'd snuck out the night before she was supposed to go with her grandmother down from the heath.

Guðríður watched her, waited a few minutes, then went out after her daughter and found her with her face buried in the hay in the barn, crying; she'd begun to sense or suspect what Guðríður knew, that, strictly speaking, she would never come back. She cried because she was losing her childhood. Mama, tell Grandma I don't want to go, she pleaded. Shh, said Guðríður, taking her child in her arms, that big girl, swallowing her own tears and anxiety: Shh, it's just for a few weeks!

A few weeks. No less than fifteen.

An age-long train of endless days during which Guðríður would be confronted with Björg's empty bed, like an open wound. Fifteen weeks, and probably the same again after the new year. An entire winter for her girl in a large, crowded, modern home, brimming with life; how would it be for the child to return to the heath cottage, in the darkest month, see all the things that she'd never noticed before: the lack of space, lack of light, the monotony, the poverty? Wouldn't she try all she could to get away again? And therewith, Guðríður would lose her entirely, not just for a few months? The price for living in such a remote place is that you lose your children early.

Yes, that's the price. For independence. But now Guðríður is on her way out to Stykkishólmur. In shoes that are too big for her, in new clothes from Steinunn, is making this journey because of a blind poet in the soil. But for what purpose, and three nights, five days counting the trip back, who is going to see to the cooking in the meantime, might Steinunn return and stay with her son in the meantime?

No, that wouldn't go well. She couldn't bear the cramped conditions for so long, any more than she or her son could bear the close presence of the other, and for that reason sent the diligent Sigrún, she who dressed herself so slowly one morning that Gísli had to empty himself into a woollen sock. There are various things that a person has to endure, woollen socks, too, for that matter. But the purpose, the reason for this trip on horseback over the heath? Yes, the old couple, Björgvin and Steinunn, had come from Bær with a parcel for Guðríður. Steinunn just didn't remember it until the second day of her visit.

God in heaven, we forgot to give them their mail, Steinunn said to her husband the next morning. After everyone was up except the youngest girl, Elín, who was allowed to go on sleeping. Clear weather, the summer light seeped through the window membranes and Björgvin held his head as if he were deep in thought, so hungover that his wife's bright voice stuck like glowing knitting needles into his brain. Gísli, on the other hand, had gone out to pee and fart, after which he was just fine, and mainly free of his own hangover. Post, he said, for us, it can hardly be remarkable. Why did you bother bringing such rubbish all the way here?

I was supposed to give you the district manager's greeting, said Steinunn.

Gísli: That'll be added to the rubbish.

Steinunn: Don't talk like that in front of your girls. The district manager and his wife are good people. Hardworking and scrupulous, and they have a fine home.

Gísli: Good people, you call them – who hardly ever stop gossiping about others.

Steinunn: Yes, good people, whatever you may say! But they were of course surprised by the large envelope, the letter, and who the sender was, and by the fact that it was addressed to Guðríður. Well now, they said, if it continues like this she's going to end up bigger than all of us!

Gísli: Sheer curiosity is going to make his teeth drop out of his head one day, the blessed district manager. And what are letters but a waste of paper and time?

His mother didn't answer, probably not wanting to take a stand regarding this statement, or the question of the nature of letters, or to delve any further into the intrinsic qualities of the district manager and his wife at Bær; she knows her son and the fact that sometimes it's useless to argue with him, any more than to ask a mountain to move, a cod to swim on dry land, a dog to meow, so she took out the envelope addressed to Guðríður and the letter accompanying it, also addressed to her in the same hand. Learned and beautiful handwriting, and the sender, according to the reverse side of the envelope, was none other than Ólafur Ágústsson, a doctor and ship owner in Stykkishólmur, who once held a seat in parliament, has written about national issues in the Reykjavík newspapers, and is, in addition, one of the editors of the journal *Nature and World* – the latest issue was in the envelope.

Guðríður realised immediately what it was; she'd been waiting for the journal, but was surprised that a letter accompanied it. She hurried into the kitchen, pretending to need to check on something. Good God, she thought, what have I done? Her heart was pounding so hard that she had to lean against the wall and wait for the worst of her anxiety to pass, the Earth to calm down, her nausea to subside. So there's no article by her in this issue – of course, and that explains the letter with it! How did she even think of sending that stupid article that proclaimed her lack of education, her ignorance, who did she think she was . . .

The priest, Reverend Pétur, what he said . . . why pay any heed to that? Stories are told about that man; people about whom stories are told can hardly be taken seriously. The letter accompanying the envelope is addressed in the same hand and, accordingly, it's none other than the doctor, the wealthiest man in Stykkishólmur, a former member of parliament and one of the journal's editors, the best-known and most respected of them, who has written to her; doubtless a grave rebuke, spurning "any further writing of yours, good woman! Do you think, perhaps, that we have nothing better to do with our time than read your uneducated, shallow-minded reflections?"

Of course, she didn't stay long in the kitchen. She knew that they were waiting for her, not long, maybe one minute, hardly more than twelve years. She took a deep breath, gulped at the air as if suffocating. She glanced in the small mirror and cursed when she saw that her cheeks and neck were red. She hurriedly adopted a serene expression, which took some effort, but she managed it. Went with that expression into the family room to face what awaited her there, the shame, the humiliation.

But, no, of course it wasn't so, not at all, otherwise Guðríður would hardly be up there on the heath from which she was now beginning to step down, moving away from the sky, that treacherous beauty. Because the article was definitely in the issue, and even in a prominent place, on pages three to four. She'd opened the envelope with trembling fingers, Steinunn sipped at her coffee after letting it cool, she prefers to drink it half cold, lukewarm, which is peculiar and poor treatment of a good drink, still, let's celebrate the diversity, hell is the place where everyone behaves the same. She sipped her coffee and watched Guðríður, a little surprised, a little curious, noticed the blush on the skin of her unpredictable daughter-in-law, whom she'd gradually learned to care for, as well as to forgive the dreaminess that struck Steinunn as downright laziness and feebleness; over the years, she'd come to realise that Guðríður simply wasn't made of exactly the same material as the rest of us. She watched her closely, immediately having suspected that there was something unusual going on here. The district manager and his wife had implied much the same, by mentioning who the sender was. But she had wanted to wait until the day after her arrival at Uppsalir to bring out the parcel, knowing that they would have more privacy then, the father and son not wanting to get out to the sheds with the cognac bottle as soon as possible, and when she saw the redness on Guðríður's neck and cheeks, the trembling of her fingers, she knew that she'd been right to wait.

It's not every day you come across a woman like your daughter-in-law, has often been said to her – referring to Guðríður, who arrived penniless at her old aunt's home in Stykkishólmur about twenty years ago. Thinner than a blade of grass but well groomed, polite, clearly with few needs, either for food or anything else, which has always been thought appreciable in a domestic. Steinunn had been on the lookout for a young maid, preferably on a long-term basis, someone who wasn't likely, as had become too common in these extraordinary times, to rush off at the first opportunity to get a job processing fish in some village where wages were paid in cash, or even all the way to Canada. She had heard of this girl who had recently arrived from the east, and hired her. Had no regrets about it at first; the girl was quite diligent, conscientious, satisfied with her position, worked well despite tending to become lost in her own thoughts rather often, stand there motionless and stare into space, completely detached from her surroundings, or to stop to read one of Björgvin's books during her working hours, his library holding forty to fifty books. At first she'd been shy, aloof, never complained, but became more confident over time. Gradually began to smile, and her smile turned out to be one that people noticed, some perhaps more than others – no-one, though, as much as Gísli. Steinunn was quick to notice the changes, and that there was a connection forming between them; she tried unsuccessfully to oppose it, having had, of course, entirely different plans for her younger son than that he marry a penniless maid. These young people, however, had largely stopped listening to the advice of their elders, and it hasn't got any better since then; poor world, where are you headed?

Years have passed since then, what happens, happens, and we have to accept it. At the time, though, Steinunn and Björgvin certainly weren't happy that the young couple chose to eke out an existence up here on the heath; Björgvin tried to dissuade Gísli, convince his son to work for him and even take over the farm after fifteen, twenty years, but Gísli refused, more stubborn than any ram. But they've given them their three granddaughters, the apples of Steinunn's eye, now watching as her daughter-in-law opens the larger envelope, pulls from it the journal *Nature and World*. Guðríður looks at Gísli.

Well, well, he says, scratching his shoulder.

IT'S IMPOSSIBLE TO DENY THAT SOME PEOPLE SIT THEIR
HORSES BETTER THAN OTHERS

The envelope held two copies of the journal *Nature and World*, in addition to a card with the journal's name stamped at the top, her name written on the card in fancy calligraphy, the editors' thanks for the article and their four names beneath, each in its own hand; the thanks had obviously been written by Ólafur. Guðríður was so overwhelmed with shyness upon seeing this fine card, and upon seeing her name written in letters that seemed royal, that she instinctively handed it to Steinunn, as if in haste to get rid of it.

Well I'll be, says Steinunn, obviously surprised, if not disconcerted, when she reads the card. Well I'll be, she repeats, with such heavy emphasis that Björgvin sighs softly, knowing his wife and hearing in her voice that there is no way that he'll be left in peace with his hang-over. Go and get cold water for your grandpa, my love, says Guðríður to Björg, before sitting down at her bedside with the journal, laying it on her knees, using it as a kind of desk, running her hand over the cover sporting its usual illustration of Snæfellsjökull Glacier, with the titles of the articles and names of their authors below.

Guðríður looks up. Steinunn is still standing there with the card, Gísli is sitting on the couple's bed, looking as if he's thinking about sheep or haymaking, Björgvin, head hanging, is looking forward to the water. Guðríður smiles at her mother-in-law, it's the only thing she can think of doing as she waits for her fingers to stop trembling so she can start flipping through the journal's pages fairly shamelessly. Smiles, looks and feels as if time has stopped. But then Björg comes with a small wooden bucket full of cold water from the farm's creek, and time starts passing again. It didn't take long for Björg to fetch the water, because two years earlier Gísli had toiled for many summer weeks changing the creek's course, moving it nearer the farm, and then built a long, winding passageway out from the farm's main one over to the creek, which seldom freezes, thereby ensuring access to water in every sort of weather. Which is a great convenience, a luxury equal to the kerosene that the better farms down below now have. But Björg brings the bucket, freeing time and Guðríður from the spell that had bound them, and the latter hands her mother-in-law the extra copy of the journal, saying apologetically, there's some nonsense by me in it. Björgvin gulps the cold water, Steinunn sits down next to him with the journal, her rugged face, which can rarely hide the ups and downs of the soul, is gaping with astonishment. She opens the journal so hurriedly and excitedly that she practically tears off the cover. She leafs through it in search of her daughter-in-law's article, sees Guðríður's name written in capital letters, the title of the article and finally a short introduction by the editors, which they conclude with praise for Guðríður's writing, her keen observational skill and maturity of thinking, despite her having barely attended school and living under constrained conditions on a difficult heath farm. "Guðríður Eiríksdóttir is a shining example of the knowledge intrinsic to the common folk of Iceland, and which has survived indescribable hardships over the centuries. If we succeed in opening this up and putting it to good use, we shall have nothing to fear for the future of our nation."

Steinunn reads this aloud to Björgvin, then looks at her son and asks, sharply, why haven't you said anything about this?

Placing his hands on his knees, Gísli says, as if he can't be bothered to discuss it, how was I supposed to know that those fine men would write such things?

Of course I didn't mean that, but that my daughter-in-law has an article in a prestigious journal, and you don't see fit to let me know; was I supposed to learn of it from strangers?

Let you know? As if people don't talk enough in this world. But, yes, it's like that, that's just as it is.

As it is? Is that the only thing you can think of to say – why haven't you told us about it? Just look at what the editors have written about Guðríður!

As I said, I couldn't have known what they would write. How should I know what such people think, let alone what they'll write? I'm a farmer; what more do you want? Besides, I can hardly spend my time blathering about everything that happens; who would do the farming in the meantime?

I doubt many animals would have died while you sent me a line letting me know that Guðríður was publishing an article in this journal!

Well, says Gísli, squirming a little, scratching his neck. Maybe that's true. But on the other hand, it's hardly possible to deny that there have been an awful lot of articles written in this world.

That may well be, says his mother, almost angrily, but I have simply never, any more than you, any more than your father, known a person, let alone so well, who has published an article. And not only that, but the editors write, she adds, holding the journal away from her slightly as she reads: "The first, but doubtless not the last, article by this common woman, unschooled, yet so educated." Too worked up to sit still, Steinunn gets to her feet. Look, she says, holding up the journal; here's your wife's name. And here they're praising her, the editors, who are no ordinary people, as you should know. And I have the impression that reading this article can in fact make a person smarter. But you don't say a word about it.

Well, says Gísli, there's just so much. And of course there are all different sorts of people. Some people sit in the saddle better than others, many have strong opinions about what bait they should use, some think about moving to Canada, some write articles for journals. This is all true, and it's all correct. And is probably no small thing. But to tell about it? As I said earlier, don't people talk enough in this world? What would it have changed if I had sent you a line; I assumed that you would come to visit sooner or later. And there you have the article, too. So everything is as it should be.

Steinunn looks at Gísli, then at her husband, as if to ask, are you responsible for this? Björgvin sighs, waves one arm, perhaps to wave off all responsibility for Gísli and refuse further participation in this dispute, but then says, shouldn't we read the article? I'll make more coffee, says Guðríður quickly, and she gets up and hurries to the kitchen to make the coffee, but first and foremost to read the letter that came with the journals. And to escape while the others read the article. Gísli exhales, stands up, and peers through the window. It's summer outside. The summer in Iceland reaches from the soil all the way up to the sky.

HORSES ENJOY SEEING NEW PLACES; RESPECTFULLY,
AND FOREVER WILLING
It's the chief editor, Ólafur Ágústsson himself, the doctor, sometimes called Ólafur the Rich, Ólafur the Impassive, who has written the letter accompanying the journal – and which Guðríður reads in the kitchen. Reads it three times before trusting herself to return to the family room.

Thank you for your interesting article, writes Ólafur, nicknamed the Impassive because it seems that some incredible marvel has to take place in order for him to change his mood; Ólafur the Rich, because he and his wife Kristín have, over the years, acquired great wealth through the ownership of fishing ships, a popular doctor, respected, people trust him, he held a seat on the esteemed Alþingi and has often published articles in the major Reykjavík newspapers about Icelandic politics, medicine, education, upbringing, and most recently about the book *The Subjection of Women* by the Englishman John Stuart Mill, in which he encouraged the book to be translated and published. In short, a nationally known voice, a man of new times, and who has devoted a portion of his precious time writing to Guðríður, who is just a farmer's wife up on a heath, on a small farm, hardly anyone knows she exists, apart, perhaps, from three district poets who have written rather bad poems and verses about her smile, and a priest who corresponds with a dead poet, ordered the postman to live, and made a long trip to deliver her a book from the devil's brother. But Ólafur writes:

Thank you for your interesting article – forgive me for addressing you informally, but there is not a trace of disrespect in it, of that I can assure you. As you can see, we have given your article a distinguished position and accompanied it with a few introductory remarks. Such a thing is unusual for us, if not unique. I hope you will forgive us for pointing out, even underlining, that you, the article's author, are a completely uneducated common woman from a small heath farm. This, of course, we have not done to disparage you, but rather to show that there should hardly be any obstacle that cannot be overcome, no mountain too steep to climb, if one has the necessary gifts and a focused will, of which the author – you – are a shining example. Or, as we have written: "The editors are extremely pleased to have received this article for publication, for this journal was founded in its time not least in order to reach all of those individuals here on our long Snæfellsnes peninsula who are born with a desire for knowledge in their hearts, but who, due to circumstances, are prevented from pursuing studies or acquiring solid knowledge. In our poor and dreary society, in which, however, we are finally beginning to see the possibility of progress in the near future, it is vital to waken these souls to consciousness, and inspire them to action. In the opinion of the editors, Guðríður Eiríksdóttir of Uppsalir is an excellent example of such an individual. A woman who lives, like far too many a commoner in this country, under constrained, cramped conditions, in addition to being in considerable isolation, but who fosters this unquenchable passion for learning, and has with great determination managed to acquire a rich and varied knowledge – and to put it to good use! We trust that this first article by Guðríður of Uppsalir will be far from the last."

This we have stated in the journal itself. We would, however, like to add here, even enthusiastically, might I say, that we would be very pleased if you were able to accept our invitation to a seat on the editorial board itself. It would be a joy for all four of us to have you on board. For you, it would also mean better and increased access to all sorts of material and knowledge, new books, foreign magazines that we would send you free of charge. And it would doubtless be a pleasure to you to attend meetings with the three scholars who make up the editorial board with me. Finally, and immeasurably importantly, it would send the message to all those men and women who are in a similar situation as you, with good gifts and who foster a desire for knowledge, never to be discouraged. That sometimes will and perseverance are all that is needed. The editorial board meets twice a year, in September and April, here in Stykkishólmur, in the home of me and my wife, Kristín – who sends you warm greetings and hopes sincerely that you will accept our invitation. It is undoubt-edly just as well that you do so, or my Kristín might be likely to mount her horse and fetch you! I say this, of course, in jest, but also to underline how very hopeful we are for a positive response from you. If you prefer not to wear out a horse journeying here, we would of course be more than happy to send someone from here with an extra horse for your use. There is no shortage of horses here and, naturally, they would enjoy seeing new places. Otherwise, you do not need to bring anything with you but yourself. You shall have your own room here in my own and Kristín's house, we live spaciously, old couple that we are, and you certainly do not need for a single moment to think about food, because here you will eat as if every moment is the last! In addition, you will be paid a small sum for the inconvenience and the work – for although a seat on an editorial board will never be classified as a hardship, it still requires work. Please write to us as soon as possible, preferably with a positive reply, and we will welcome you joyfully. The editorial meeting itself will be held on the morning of the first Monday in September, so you should plan to arrive on the Sunday, and in time for the sumptuous supper, which begins at eight o'clock. If the weather and travel conditions are adverse to us, we will postpone the meeting as long as necessary. Respectfully, and forever willing to be of assistance, Ólafur Ágústsson.

A BIT ABOUT RIDING GEAR AND THE EIGHTH WONDER OF THE WORLD

It's not unlikely that Steinunn was considerably more impressed by the letter than the article itself, the greatest quality of which was to have been published, and it is naturally a bit difficult to be interested in the earthworm, which one sees rarely, it being a nearly invisible and rather repulsive being down in the darkness of the soil, something in which only the birds ever really take delight. But, of course, it's far from an everyday event to have one's article published in a journal, with the editors' praise as a foreword; it won't be unpleasant stopping at some of the farms along the way home and mentioning this, in passing, as if coincidentally; the article as well as the letter from Ólafur, which she read several times in order to memorise some of its lines.

The elder couple read the letter and the article while having their coffee, Gísli humming some nonsense, Guðríður braiding Elín's hair, taking refuge in that activity, listening with a smile to her chit-chat. Björgvin gulped down the black drink, each gulp a soldier sent to combat his hangover, then stood up, walked back and forth through the family room, which didn't take too many steps, of course, farted and agreed with his wife's wordy declaration that it was no small thing receiving a letter from Ólafur, but Björgvin added that, for his part, Ólafur was one of the few people to whom he would doff his hat without a second thought.

So he wouldn't need to move to Canada? said Gísli.

What?

You said you wanted to move to Canada so that others would doff their hats to you. So he would have no reason to move there.

Spare me your jokes; I have better things to think about in this life. But I will just say that you are lucky to have got this fine mare . . . for safe keeping, I mean, to have got her for safe keeping, Björgvin hurriedly added, following a sharp glance from his wife. Because naturally, you will ride the mare, Guðríður, to that meeting in September. No-one is coming to fetch my daughter-in-law as if she were some pauper. I will have good riding gear sent to you in time, yours was in poor condition, Gísli, the last I knew, and could hardly have improved since.

There's nothing wrong with my riding gear.

It's fine for here at home, but not for when my Guðríður goes to meet with the most important people in the district. Stifle your stubbornness, for once. Just pretend that you don't notice the riding gear from me. You can put the old gear on your obstinacy and ride it over mountain and dale.

Björgvin got his way regarding the riding gear, and it is new reins that Guðríður holds this September day, or September afternoon rather, because the light is starting to change, the mountains and sky are darkening, and faintly visible ahead of her is the town of Stykkishólmur, with its three shops, a dizzying number of buildings, life on the streets. A trip there is always an event to look forward to, to leave the monotony and sink oneself into the town's buzzing life. But she had never really imagined that someday she would go there alone, on a beautiful horse, with fine riding gear, in nearly-new clothes and elegant shoes, not as a nameless figure from up on a heath, but a woman with name, a woman with a reason for going. Maybe she had dreamed this or that, had had her silly, private dreams about what could happen in her life, but there are so many dreams, and, besides, in this country there has generally been such an immeasurable and utterly unbridge-able gap between dream and reality, such a depressing distance, that it's simply incomprehensible, and has never been possible to explain properly, how Icelanders managed to survive all those harsh centuries in their barren land – we're probably forced to call that fact the eighth wonder of the world.

SOMEONE IS TURNING INTO A CHURCH, AND THOSE PERSONS WHO OVERCOME VANITY CAN THINK GREAT THOUGHTS

The nationally renowned Dr Ólafur, who doesn't need to move to Canada to have others doff their hats to him, and who had written Guðríður that fine letter, is not at home when she arrives on Ljúf in Stykkishólmur and rides to the doctor's house, one of the grandest in town. Two spacious floors and a good attic, with space for drying the laundry and three maids' rooms. The house is so big that Uppsalir could fit in it three times, with room left over. She dismounted and then stood close against Ljúf, regarding the huge house and suddenly wanting nothing more than to turn round and ride back home, to the security, the shelter. How could she have thought of agreeing to come to a meeting with highly educated men who had more sense and knowledge in their little fingers than she in her entire body? I'll be struck dumb if I so much as open my mouth, she thought, holding tightly to Ljúf's reins as the horse rubbed its head against her like a giant cat. Let's just go home again, she said softly to the mare, but then the door opened and Kristín came out, as big as a frigate, and said loudly, smiling, you must be Guðríður, I can just see it! You know, I've looked out at least a hundred times today in the hope of seeing you, and there you are! May I give you a hug? said that big woman, and, without waiting for an answer, she hugged the young woman tightly, a head higher than her, big as a house. How delicate and slender

274

you are, let me take a better look at you, she said, turning Guðríður in a circle; and with those eyes! They're rare, I would say. But come in, Ólafur is making a house call but won't be gone long, I expect. Don't worry about your horse, it will be nice and comfortable. A mare, you say; I'll have her brought to Jónas, who has promised to house her and pamper her, though not nearly as much as I plan to pamper you!

No, Ólafur the Impassive is not at home. He had to look in on a certain Þorketill of Hólar who happened to step on some damned thing at the shore the day before yesterday, and his foot started to swell. The farmhand who came to fetch Ólafur said that the farmer's right foot was so swollen that it was starting to look like a steeple. Then we'd better hurry, before Keli turns entirely into a church, Ólafur had said.

But he'll be back before supper; he wouldn't miss the feast. He'll be seated at the table in time, just like Stefán and Jónas; it's not far for them to go – they live practically next door, after all! It's another matter with Pétur, said Kristín, that is, whether he comes in time. Not because he lives so far away and has to ride several hours to get here, but because the Lord completely forgot to imbue him with punctuality. Although Pétur says that life is more important than punctuality – and I don't know what to say to that.

Guðríður didn't know, either, so she said nothing, just smiled, and followed the big woman into the house, through it and into the bedroom at its western end. There she was to settle in; the room would be hers for the duration of her stay. Here is your kingdom, said Kristín with a laugh. But, oh, forgive me that it's not bigger; I did try, though, to make it comfortable for you.

Sorry that it's not bigger; the room is the same size as the entire family room at Uppsalir, where all five of them sleep, seven, in fact, when Gísli's parents are visiting. Kristín had sat with her for a good half hour, instructed the maids to serve them coffee, some finery from the bakery that Guðríður had never been able to afford even to enter, filled the big bedroom with her presence and the vital energy that emanated from her, talked so much that Guðríður hardly had to say anything; nothing, really, just listen. We're so excited to have you here, said Kristín, and that they have decided to offer you a seat on the editorial board, the first woman who will be on it. Stefán and Jónas will welcome you kindly, distinguished men, both of them, each in his own way. Still, you can expect that it will take them time to learn how to speak to you. I assume that you are nervous, which is very understandable, but, whether you believe it or not, those two are as well. In their own way.

We're so excited; *we* turns out to be Kristín and three gentle-women of Stykkishólmur who meet regularly to discuss literature, politics and various urgent matters of progress such as public education, school issues, the building of hospitals. And women's rights; one of them, Ásgerður, Jónas's wife, was lucky enough to meet Bríet Bjarnhéðinsdóttir herself, who subsequently sent her her lecture on women's rights.

I don't know if you heard of it, said Kristín, but it was the first time such a lecture was held in this country. We have been corresponding with Bríet for the last two years and she sent us a Danish translation of a famous essay by John Stuart Mill called *The Subjection of Women*. A remarkable essay, remarkable! We all devoured the essay, then had our husbands read it and I persuaded my Ólafur to write about it in one of the Reykjavík newspapers, and we have now offered to subsidise an Icelandic translation of this important work. I have put the Danish edition on the table there, along with some other books. Pétur told me that you read everything you can, using every free moment that you have to do so.

"Pétur told me that you . . ."

So he has spoken of her, here in this house. He actually bothered to do so, despite having so many other things to talk about. But the priest is right; she reads everything she can. That has always been the case. She can't leave a book alone, and steals minutes and hours from the farming and upkeep of their home to read when Gísli can't see her. But now, when she finally has access to books that she has only ever been able to dream of, as well as two hours to herself, no obligations, something that she hasn't experienced since childhood, she sits as if paralysed in the bedroom's comfortable chair. Sits there like a stupid sheep and lets time pass, lets it go to waste, lets it be worn away. And soon a tub will be brought to her, and it will be filled with hot water. She is to take a bath. Oh, it is just so wonderful to relax in a hot bath, Kristín had said. You feel like a new person! And don't worry, she added, you'll have plenty of time both to relax in the hot water and to read.

Plenty of time; almost three hours until Guðríður will be fetched for the dinner that Kristín had described to her. A three-course dinner with dishes that Guðríður has hardly heard of, let alone tasted, a feast that until now has belonged to another, distant world, in the company of highly learned men, with whom she is now to fraternise. An uneducated, stupid woman from a heath.

You'll sit next to me tonight, Kristín had said, holding Guðríður's slender but work-worn hands tightly, as if to reassure her. I'll be there for you as you become accustomed to your new environment and our dear gentlemen. About whom you need have no worries. My Ólafur is kindness itself; he is so thoroughly good that I sometimes think life would have long since crushed him if he didn't have his bright temperament, if he never took himself too seriously, and if he did not have me by his side. Stefán, the shopkeeper, you know of course by reputation. He can certainly be a bit grumpy, if not so downright gruff that he frightens people. But I think it's partly because he tries overly much to be like his father, whose arrogance actually sent him to his grave the other year – in my opinion, that is. But Stefán's moodiness and rough, brusque comportment are little more than a façade, no more than a thin film, really, underneath which lies a sweet man who is enormously good to his children. I think that God judges people a great deal by the way they treat their children, and then animals. But it may also be that he is forced to conceal his kindness, because otherwise some people would try to swindle him in business. Unfortunately, kindness has never gone hand in hand with business.

Jónas, on the other hand, studied law in Copenhagen, an intelligent creature but lazy and indolent as an old ram. For many years he was married to a woman who was so strict and serious that Jónas had, to tell the truth, completely lost his smile by the time the dear died ten years ago from tuberculosis. Soon afterwards, however, he had the good fortune of meeting his Ásgerður; they've been married for six years and she breathed new life into Jónas. It is thanks to her that he tries to keep up with the latest developments in the world and adopt modern thinking when it comes to issues such as public education and women's rights. You must tell no-one, but sometimes I suspect that his views in these matters are to a large extent Ásgerður's own. You have little to fear from Jónas. On the contrary, I think that he will be insecure at first in your presence, desultory in his zeal to display how unprejudiced and progressive he is, and accepting of whatever you might say. But he will settle down; don't worry.

Then there is Pétur, who is my favourite. The others have great respect for him, because of his knowledge and eloquence, but their respect is sometimes tinged with fear because of how unpredictable Pétur can be. It was Pétur, after all, who suggested that you be offered a seat on the editorial board. He mentioned it to me, and I quickly got Ásgerður to support the idea, after which it was as good as guaranteed. But now I shall leave you in peace. You must be exhausted after your trip. I'll leave you with the books, and send the girls to you afterwards with the tub and water.

Then Kristín left. That big, warm person who takes over her surroundings wherever she goes with her enthusiasm, and an inner strength that reminds Guðríður of the sea itself. She leaves and Guðríður sits there stock-still, a stupid sheep in the chair, and lets time pass. Lets it go to waste. There are two reasons why she wastes her time by sitting there in the chair instead of going and getting one of the books to read, now that she is completely alone, free from all obligations. The first is that it is because of him, then, that she is here. It was a shock to find that out. And she of course had been so ridiculously happy that her face probably shone, her neck became flecked with red, and she could hardly control herself – hadn't Kristín looked at her suspiciously? The second reason is the full-size mirror in one corner of the room. She is afraid that if she manages to get to her feet, it won't be for the reading material, but to go and stand in front of that mirror. She is paralysed because it has been a quarter of a century since she last saw all of herself in a mirror. At home at Uppsalir, there is only the one small mirror in the kitchen, which is, however, somewhat larger than the one at her parents-in-law's, yet not full-sized, besides the fact that she never has the opportunity to stand alone in front of it. Why should she do so, anyway? What is to be seen, and what does it matter what a person looks like? Is it not thought and character that shape a person; is not appearance just humbug? Besides, few others see her up there on the heath apart from the sheep and the sky, which all have as little interest in her appearance.

She sits there paralysed in her chair because Reverend Pétur is approaching Stykkishólmur, not punctually because it's more important to live than to arrive on time. Does that mean he lives more than others?

She sits there paralysed because she hasn't seen herself in her entirety since she was a child out east in Norðfjörður, when she'd stood with her father in front of a full-sized mirror at the home of the merchant and his wife. She remembers that she and her father held hands. She remembers the warmth of his palm, remembers how he winked at her in the mirror and smiled, filling her with happiness. She fears that it will be too difficult to recall this while looking in this mirror, because then he died. He said that he was going to swim to France; that was thirty years ago.

She sits there paralysed because since then, she has had three girls. Since then, all those days and nights have passed through her and doubtless been unkind to her.

But the person, Guðríður mutters as she finally manages to rise, who is more interested in her reflection than in books, is a person I have no interest in knowing.

Because there is that famous book, *The Subjection of Women*. And there is Guðríður, hunched over the book, flipping through it.

Of course she overcame the mirror's stupid vanity.

The book is in Danish. In her head, she translates one of the sentences at the start of the book into Icelandic: "It is my opinion that the arrangement that currently exists between the sexes, in which the one is subject to the other, is not only unacceptable but greatly inhibits the progress of mankind."

Those who overcome vanity, she says in the mirror, can think such thoughts.

Come closer, says the mirror, and tell me more about this. I'm so lonely, too.

And I am not so easily beguiled, she says mockingly. And continues reading.

THE DEVIL SCORES A POINT, HE READS DANTE,
THE SUBJECTION OF WOMEN, AND THEY'RE GOING
TO ARREST ÉMILE ZOLA!

But then it went as it went, and what of it? What hasn't happened on Earth, what hasn't that aged heart had to endure – meteors, countless gods, generations of lives – and the Earth's crust so heavy with events and stories that geologists are unable to explain why it didn't give in long ago. All that has happened under heaven, and little of it written down. Grief that could have torn the gods apart, kindness that brought the devil himself to his knees . . . Perhaps man, or humanity, is defeated, suffers a blow every time a destiny is forgotten, when a story worth being recorded, written in a book, sinks without a trace into oblivion.

If all this and more is kept in mind, it can hardly be considered newsworthy whether a woman looks or doesn't look in a mirror, even if she's as thin as a streak of rain, writes letters that bark like dogs, has a father who set off swimming to France from Norðfjörður almost a quarter of a century ago; his body was never found. He may still be tossing somewhere on the ocean waves, lonely, exhausted, sorely missed by his daughter – who put the book down, not to look at herself in the mirror, but to take a bath. As simple as that. No devil to score points.

Guðríður had barely looked up from the book when two young maids came with a large tub that they then filled halfway with hot water. She looked up quickly when they arrived, greeted them with a smile, then continued reading, so absorbed that they didn't dare to disturb her. Nor were they allowed to do so. You are not to disturb her if she's reading, Kristín had said.

But as soon as they're gone, Guðríður gets up, dips her hand into the water, locks the door, removes her clothes without looking in the direction of the mirror, steps carefully, hesitantly into the tub, then lets herself sink into it and starts laughing when she feels the hot water surround her. It's so ridiculously and titillatingly cosy that she simply laughs. Laughs, looks up – and faces herself in the mirror.

Here I am, says the mirror, come closer, I'm not that bad at all.

I'm taking a bath, she says, and you won't deceive me.

Yet almost half an hour later, she is standing in front of the mirror, naked, but with a soft towel around her narrow shoulders. So that's what you look like, she mutters.

A thirty-four-year-old woman who lives on a heath, working some days no less than fifteen hours, haymaking in wet weather, standing knee-deep in freezing peat in order to pick a few last blades of grass so that they can increase their flock by one ewe lamb next autumn, and thereby inch their way a little closer to their dream of having a farm down in the lowland, preferably adjacent to the sea. That work can be seen on her palms, on her hands in their entirety, in fact, the backs of her hands are cracked from a thousand washes, but she stands upright and proud, with her small breasts, her slender, curved back, and her soft, smooth skin appears timeless, somehow, as if fate, God, or something has commanded time to stop passing close to her skin, or else pass extremely slowly.

So that's what you look like, Guðríður mutters to her reflection, and continues looking, wasting time instead of educating herself, reading *The Subjection of Women*. She turns this way and that in order to see herself from all sides. Vanity won, the devil scored a point.

Oh, is that for certain? What do we know about right and wrong? Maybe this sort of vanity is part of a personal quest, a form of introspection, and maybe the devil always has a stack of books on his bedside table, an avid reader of new texts as well as old, with Dante and Jo Shapcott, Hamsun and Amos Oz beside him; to be honest, it isn't unlikely. Remember, the devil is a fallen angel, the rebel who couldn't accept the absolute rule of heaven – those who question and wish to see life from all angles, turn to literature.

She has not seen herself in her entirety in a mirror since she stood as a child next to her father, Eiríkur, in the merchant's house out east in Norðfjörður. Eiríkur, uneducated like his daughter, later, but who had learned both English and French so well that he sometimes got to teach the children of better-to-do folk in Norðfjörður, freeing him for a time from the toil that he hated but had grown up with. He learned English by ploughing through the novels of Dickens, which he borrowed from the drunken doctor in the village; but French from the captain he met through his barter with the French smacks that fished every summer in the waters off the Eastfjords. Eiríkur traded with the Frenchmen for cognac, which he then brought to the doctor to gain freer access to his library. The captain, no less bookish, heard about this business and contacted Eiríkur. They immediately became good friends, went for walks on the heaths, spent the nights there far from everyone under the open summer sky, and wrote to each other over the winters. But once during Eiríkur's stint teaching the merchant's children English and French, he took Guðríður with him to their big house. He knew that the family had all gone to Copenhagen. A maid let them in and Guðríður got to snoop all around that big house, look at the children's toys, which were so numerous that she couldn't see how any child could live long enough to play with them all. Eventually, she was drawn to the mirror. She doesn't know why she removed nearly all her clothes, maybe just out of curiosity. But she remembers the two of them, herself, scantily clad, and her dad, dressed, smiling, with his sharp nose, thick, brown hair, his restless but warm eyes, encouraging her to take a good look, examine her body, because the human body was a wonder, complex and simple at the same time, and we had been given a body to remind us that we aren't gods. To remind us that we tolerate time badly and therefore have a duty to make good use of it.

Eiríkur, do you want me to take off my clothes, too, the maid had asked when she found the father and daughter in front of the mirror, and gave Guðríður's father a look that Guðríður didn't understand, but which stirred up a mixture of anger and jealousy inside of her. She remembers that look a quarter of a century later, in front of another mirror, naked again; she remembers and understands. She remembers her father's voice, warm, a bit husky, often passionate. Remembers his smile. Remembers his eyes, slightly dark, slightly mournful but also loving. Half a year after they stood together in front of the mirror, she woke to find her father sitting over her, stroking her head and talking to her. But she was half asleep and remembers little of it. She only remembers him talking for a long time, then singing to her until she fell asleep. When she woke up the next morning, he was gone. He swam away that night. Said in a letter, which he left for her mother and her, that he was going to swim to France. A year later, her mother married a fisherman who could say such ugly things about Guðríður's father that she turned against her stepfather, then fled and ended up on Snæfellsnes, at the other end of the country.

Eiríkur swam away; he wanted to swim to his friend, the ship's captain, who had sailed home two weeks before. He swam away with his restless eyes but also that sad string that sounded many years later in Páll, and to some extent in his namesake, his great-great-great-grandson who shot at a lorry and is therefore on his way to prison – what will become of us, his dogs ask anxiously.

But we're not there yet, the dogs must wait, as must Eiríkur, too, in fact, since he isn't even born yet, and now Guðríður has to hurry to get dressed. Jesus, how time has flown, and she, the stupid sheep that she is, wasted it in front of the mirror. Scrutinised her body, was ashamed of being content with it, even happy, which is unforgivable, was even more ashamed to have crouched down, parted her knees, slipped a finger between her legs, examined herself there, caressed herself there. She should have used her time, read *The Subjection of Women*. She's probably always going to be stupid. Did the devil score a point? But she is sitting upright, reading, when the younger of the maids from earlier comes to fetch her; dinner is ready.

*

Guðríður looks up, smiles distractedly, so deep in thought over the book that the maid, an eighteen-year-old girl who, like others in the house, had been looking forward to the visit of this woman of the heath, she finds her so noble and proud, completely focused on reading, that she bows reflexively, as if Guðríður were a gentlewoman. Yes, that's right, dinner, she says, standing up, yet with her finger on the page and seemingly reluctant to tear herself away from the book.

Then they go up to the second floor of the house.

You start with the outermost fork and knife, the maid whispers to her as they near the dining room, but, before Guðríður can ask what she means, Kristín shouts: there she is!

And with a knot in her stomach, Guðríður steps into the large dining room.

There are four people sitting at the long table: Kristín, Ólafur, Stefán and Jónas. The chandelier over the table is so big and bright that it nearly frightens Guðríður; those at home will never believe me when I describe this, she thinks. The chandelier, the crystal glasses, the silver cutlery, the red wine in three large crystal carafes, and the food that has arrived on the table, a three-course meal. So tempting and wonderfully aromatic that the knot of anxiety in her stomach unravels and disappears, she's filled with intensely eager anticipation, making her smile deeply as Kristín introduces her to the men – it's her other smile, the dangerous one, that the district poets had written about, but not particularly well; unfortunately.

You should write about that smile, Pétur had said in a letter to Hölderlin, who replied, I have long since done so: You smiled, and now I no longer know if I dare to exist.

Is that a poem? Pétur had asked, but the German poet hasn't yet answered by the time Pétur approaches Stykkishólmur, which is located at the end of a long, wide strip of land, with an excellent natural harbour and overlooking the vast Breiðafjörður fjord with its countless islands. They outnumber the days of man, says old sources; freckles on the sea, Pétur thinks, clicking his tongue in one cheek. Ljúf raises her head and speeds up to a gentle trot.

Pétur must be on his way, says Ólafur after they are all seated, and Guðríður thanks and blesses the young maid in her mind as she looks down at the triple row of cutlery on both sides of the plate. I've got to tell them this at home, she says to herself over and over, like a mantra, like a prayer; to describe the dining room, the richness, the tableware, the table, the chairs, and the food! Because she is going to describe the food! Which we should also do – at least write down the names of the dishes. Guðríður had never eaten such excellent food. She simply didn't know that it was possible to create such delicacies. Still, she's constantly trying to prepare new dishes at home at Uppsalir, from the little that they have, to improve the taste by adding Iceland moss, arctic thyme, alpine and common lady's mantle, and birch leaves, trying thereby to create a little fantasy out of everyday life. Björgvin and I start to salivate as soon as we catch sight of the farm, Steinunn had said in the summer, as she watched Guðríður prepare the veal that the old couple brought; it's a pure wonder what you can conjure up!

But what was on offer at the doctor's house belongs to another world. The food is so good and so different from anything she'd tried before that she completely forgot her insecurity, her anxiety about not measuring up, about falling dumbstruck, about the men and Kristín realising that she is stupid, has nothing to offer; she spends time in front of the mirror, after all, instead of reading. She forgot everything as she ate. Sometimes closed her eyes to enjoy it even more. To bathe her taste buds, discover a taste she hadn't suspected existed. Each bite was an adventure, a new experience. How can a mortal person create such food, she asked, flabbergasted, overcome, in the middle of the meal, and Kristín, who had observed Guðríður's manifest delight with a smile, summoned the cook, a German woman who had been working for acquaintances of hers in Reykjavík, and whom she had offered a job seeing exclusively to the food; she would not have to touch any other work. The German woman came out; she was as tall as the housewife, and had a deep voice, eyebrows grown into one, a big nose, small but sharp eyes; she looked like a force of nature that people prefer to avoid provoking to anger. And this crusty-looking woman beamed, softened entirely when she saw and sensed Guðríður's admiration for the food, and then the intuition to which her questions testified. Shouldn't we write about this for the journal, Guðríður asked, and get her to explain how it's possible to turn food into a fairytale, dinner into a journey through the lands of delight? For example, I would think that there would be no reason to move to Canada if it's possible to cook such food in Iceland!

Of course we should describe it all, Kristín said, see now, you're already making an impact on the journal, and Guðríður looked down to hide her smile. We ought to describe it when the four of them moved to the drawing room, Ólafur, Stefán, Jónas and Guðríður, while Kristín withdrew; I'll leave you in peace now, she said; the frigate turned back to the harbour and made room for her husband, no longer overshadowed him. We ought to describe how Stefán and Jónas, both tipsy, tried in their own different ways to display their intelligence to Guðríður, their liberalism, modern thinking, so obviously enthusiastic and even excited about Guðríður's presence that it eased her anxiety, which had stirred again after dinner. Describe how the men relaxed after their first glass of cognac and started acting naturally, while she drank one cup of coffee after another to numb the effect of the red wine, wanting to stay focused, calm, prove herself, concentrate on taking advantage of this unexpected opportunity, this good fortune, to have been invited here, feeling as if she were standing in a doorway looking into a world she could only have dreamed of; a world that her father had also longed for all his short life. She feels that she must, for the both of them, maintain her focus, think clearly. We ought to describe it when she inadvertently downed the glass of sherry that Ólafur had brought her. All of these things, we ought to describe, but unfortunately there is no time for it, because now the door opens and in comes Reverend Pétur. He who chooses life over punctuality. Comes in and pays no mind to greeting the others but says unceremoniously, waving his hands, can you believe it, they're going to arrest Émile Zola!

Remember Me, and the Devils will Retreat from Me

I LOOK UP AND YOU ARE NO LONGER ALIVE

Is it because of Dreyfus, asks the sanctified coach driver, swinging his crêpe spatula like a sword, as if he sees himself as a soldier of justice and truth, perhaps thinking of fighting for Dreyfus and rescuing the French writer Émile Zola from prison, armed with a crêpe spatula in a small, convex caravan very far north in the world, actually all the way out on the edge of the inhabitable world. Still in those silly tropical shorts and in yet another new T-shirt. The new one black with a picture of Edith Piaf, the singer of sorrow, who was born under a streetlight early in the last century, vomited blood on stage, as tall as a bottle of wine but with a voice bigger than death, who, just then, was adding the song "Non, je ne regrette rien" to his playlist. The singer looks dreamily ahead of her, with an expression as if she has just sung: *Avec mes souvenirs, j'ai allumé le feu* . . . I set fire to my memories, worries, joys, sweep it all away, the good, the bad, because my life begins now – with you!

Non, je ne regrette rien, I don't regret anything. And only want you. To sweep away everything else. I vomit blood and choose you. I make a decision, and therefore am not paralysed but live on. Otherwise, yes, right, apparently they're going to arrest Émile Zola, the bastards – perhaps because he made a decision and wasn't paralysed, unless it was the other way round, because he didn't make a decision and was paralysed?

Is Zola going to be arrested because of Dreyfus, the sanctified one asks again, ignoring my muttering, stabbing an imaginary enemy in the gut with the crêpe spatula and Edith Piaf.

I look up from the pages and they all disappear. Are sucked like shadows into a long-vanished time, and it's as if they never existed.

They all disappear. Guðríður and the three men in the drawing room, and the house disappears, it no longer exists, that big, Norwegian wooden house in an Icelandic village around the turn of the next-to-last century; with the young maid who whispered advice to Guðríður, and the German who turned the food into a fairytale, made it worthwhile to live in Iceland, and even Kristín, the frigate, big and imposing in life, steadfast, vibrant with energy, she also disappears without a trace, as if she'd never walked on this Earth. Yet she ascended to the ground in such a way that it was noticed.

I look up and everything is sucked away.

Guðríður's girls, as well.

The eldest, Björg, who has just arrived at her grandparents' home down in the lowland, for a winter-long stay, eager anticipation and anxiety seesawing inside her. I look up and she disappears; the same goes for her grandfather, Björgvin, who can barely contain his joy at welcoming her into his home; they both disappear.

And Gísli with his big hands, his indefatigable diligence. Gísli, who for weeks has been looking forward to having Sigrún at home at Uppsalir. He is going to be sure to go to bed before her every night, even pretend to be sleeping by the time she starts getting ready for bed. He gets an erection every time he thinks about it. Over the thought of how she'll undress, taking off her clothing bit by bit, revealing her backside . . . then bending forward, when he'll see her buttocks separate and . . . he's looking so forward to . . . and desperately longs to . . .

. . . but now that she has finally come he has fled to the sheep shed, is sitting there paralysed in the manger, doesn't dare enter the house. Thinks of Guðríður who is out in Stykkishólmur among educated men. Gísli looks at his strong hands, as if wondering whether they're strong enough to hold on to Guðríður, unless, on the contrary, he's thinking about what they'll do when he sees Sigrún get ready for bed . . . he mumbles something that I don't catch . . . and I see Halla sitting at Pétur's desk, and she appears to be crying. I try to move closer but then they're all sucked away, she, Gísli, Guðríður, Pétur, they're sucked away along with that bygone time.

They disappear.

Are erased when the priest with the PCV licence asks if Émile Zola is going to arrested because of Dreyfus. Asks twice as he fights against injustice with Edith Piaf and a crêpe spatula. I look up, the connection with the past severs, everyone is dead.

WHERE, THEN, IS SHELTER TO BE FOUND?
Maybe Zola is going to be arrested for telling the truth, bearing witness to it isn't always popular, it can sometimes be a merciless mirror, I say, now with four warm, rolled-up crêpes in front of me. I take a bite of one of them, look out the small side window and see the ruins of the old farm at Oddi across the river, the ancient farmstead, where Hafrún was born and she and Skúli built their house. The new house, built by Halldór after the old one burned down, is further away; an unpainted, concrete house with a red roof. Halldór always refused to paint the house, saying that the concrete should be allowed to become weather worn and thereby gradually take on the look of the crags on the mountainsides. Perhaps the house would end up turning into a huge boulder topped with a red roof. And in that boulder, Eiríkur now lives. Alone with his dogs, three Border collies, a shotgun, three dead puppies, and the guitar he brought from Marseille. He left the fjord at sixteen, turned at the edge of the heath to look back, felt the pain when his roots snapped and sensed the freedom of having no home. He left, and seven hours and heaths full of silence arose between him and his youth. He lived in Reykjavík for ten years, rented a basement room from transplants from the fjord, immersed himself in the artistic life at Hamrahlíð Junior College, worked in a convenience store, mopped office floors to be financially independent, worked at a bar for a year after graduating, then enrolled in the Icelandic Musicians' Union Music School and after that studied in Paris.

But he came home regularly while living in Reykjavík, often

bearing gifts. Music from the record stores in the capital, art and gardening books for his grandmother, along with books on machinery, the history of cars, the history of tractors; but books on science and scientists for his grandfather – and helped him get through the chapters with the most abstruse English. One Christmas, for example, they sat together for days over *Bright Galaxies, Dark Matters* by Vera Rubin, the woman who proved the existence of dark matter. Hafrún baked a chocolate cake, she poured coffee, cooked chicken and lamb thighs, and at dinner they gave her a report on what they'd read that day.

The best and deepest memories of his life had to do with his grandparents, and he likely always missed them. Yet – as the years passed, for some reason it became increasingly difficult for him to return to the fjord. The idea of heading north to visit no longer sprang up of its own accord and, more and more often, he postponed it. And so, a whole year could pass without him making an appearance there. Or even three after he moved abroad. Which is so strange, because he missed his grandparents. Missed the fjord. The people there. Why . . .

. . . Because paradox has always been one of the mainstays of human existence. How often do I need to repeat it? You're probably not the sharpest knife in the drawer, but I'm stuck with you, says the bearded priest, the coach driver who offers trips to hell; he who has gone there and returned understands everything better.

Again, he taps the crêpe spatula against the bottle of single malt whisky, as if intending to give a speech, perhaps on how paradox is a recurring theme in human history, on how our history is all at once tragedy, soap opera, requiem, playfulness of the gods. Unless he taps the bottle again to cover over how happy he is that I've hinted that he understands the world better than others. And therewith, the paradox that human life appears condemned to be.

I'm not happy with myself, he says, and can hardly help it that I know more than others. I tapped the bottle just to keep you on topic, it was no more complicated than that: Eiríkur goes to Reykjavík, graduates from HJC, then from the IMU Music School, plays for a time in a jazz band, lives with a girl for almost two years, and goes to Paris; and then what? Eiríkur would pass through fire and brimstone, sacrifice an arm, if not his own life, for his grandmother and grandfather. Yet his ties to his childhood haunts are cut, or fray. Why is that, and where is Halldór, where did his life go, did he never manage to put down roots anywhere after having met, loved and lost Svana, Eiríkur's mother – can too much love destroy a person's life if that person is never allowed to live it, is it like a nuclear bomb in your heart, a flare that illuminates the universe for a short time before the radioactivity of loss and grief spreads through your veins and paralyses you? It paralysed Halldór so completely that he could neither live properly afterwards nor connect with his son; isn't that a bit too much? And Eiríkur, he hardly became homeless in this world just because he masturbated over a book and inadvertently thought of his mother just as he came; that could hardly have been sufficient to cut his roots . . . The person who cuts his own roots, who loses them and who flees the past, no longer has any refuge in this world.

SO IS IT BÚÐARDALUR ALL OVER AGAIN?

Each person has his own way in life. Some are open, others less so. Some people have a great need for companionship and a social life, others are inclined towards solitude. In whatever direction you lean, it doesn't necessarily imply anything about your disposition towards your neighbour, those who matter to you. Each has his own way, and no-one should go against his nature. And naturally, everyone carries his own luggage. His wounds. His knots. Some struggle with them all their lives. And it appears that certain knots can only be undone by death – his uncle Páll, the giant, barely uttered a word from the age of twelve until he was sixteen – almost as if he'd given up with regard to the stutter that had afflicted him from childhood, but which had grown much more pronounced in his teens. Was antisocial, shut himself off from others and few people, apart from Halldór, maybe, knew what he was thinking.

It's complicated to be human, said Hafrún, making hot chocolate for her son, baking a rhubarb tart, which Páll liked so much. He was allowed to break a horse when he was only thirteen, to contend with the heavy snow in the Land Rover as a teenager; he got stuck, went and got Halldór and the tractor, they worked hard to free the vehicle, and then only to get it stuck again. Skúli and Hafrún knew that he enjoyed it; it made him forget himself – which is sometimes a brilliant method, as effective as hours and hours at a psychologist's. To forget oneself, to get away from one's consciousness, away from the torments that can accompany the self. To be allowed to forget that you are who you are. It can be refreshing, a great relief, a welcome rest, but of course not free from danger because some people fall into alcohol or drugs, are caught up in sex or religion, travel endlessly in the hope of getting to a place where they never find themselves. It's not easy. But Hafrún and Skúli allowed Páll to break horses, get a vehicle stuck in snowdrifts. Knew that it was no solution, but a help, which is always a step in the right direction; which can make all the difference. Each has his own way.

But then it went as it did.

Went; yes, Eiríkur went south to Reykjavík. Ten years later, all the way to Paris. There were seven hours, seven heaths, and an entire ocean between him and those at Oddi. Too far for rhubarb tart, too problematic to send him a horse for breaking in Paris or a Land Rover to get stuck in the snow on the boulevards there. But each has his own way, no-one goes against his own nature. Those at Oddi let him know that they were there for him. Halldór sent him recordings from the Lonesome Town studio, as he'd begun to call his recording studio in the barn, after the Ricky Nelson song from 1959, which he liked best as performed by McCartney and Gilmour; we'll add it to Death's playlist. Sent recordings of the old folks' stories of the past that had begun to sink into the darkness, the recordings so well edited and the music so tastefully compiled that they resembled professional radio programmes, as well as Páll's readings of Icelandic literature and classic memoirs; so you don't lose Iceland and the Icelandic language out there in the world, he wrote to his son. Hafrún, on the other hand, called her boy every week, always at the same time, eleven on Saturday morning, when he was certain to be up. Eiríkur usually sat down at a café or in a public park and Hafrún told him what the old couple were up to. There was feeding the animals, there was lambing, haymaking, round-ups, fence work, berry picking, occasional fishing trips; she talked about what she and Skúli were reading, what was being said about the latest novels in the district's reading club, which they'd been hosting for thirty years, and that the old folks were taking a farmers' trip to Norway and Finland; the things that one gets oneself into!

Eiríkur appreciated these regular phone calls. It might even be said that he looked forward to them. Although he usually spoke less than Hafrún, and probably less still as the years went by, sometimes he closed his eyes while his grandmother spoke, as if he wanted to drink in her voice, calm, warm, with her smile in the depths of his soul, hearing the murmur of the radio, hearing his grandfather whistling or humming something in the background. He closed his eyes, became a little boy in the kitchen again, the world's dangers far from him. Closed his eyes and missed them. But, yes, he naturally said very little about his own life, and gradually it was as if the distance between them, all these kilometres of mountains and then the ocean, became palpable in the kitchen at Oddi following the calls.

He thinks of us as country yokels now, Skúli said once, when they'd been sitting silently in the kitchen for a long time following a phone call with Eiríkur. Oh, yes, Hafrún said softly, but he can't help it. He's young, there's so much going on in the big city, he's experiencing so much and finding himself as an artist and a person. Many things will have to give way in the meantime. It's alright. But maybe I shouldn't have sounded so excited about the trip to Norway, said Hafrún. This will all pass, said Skúli, holding out his hand to his wife.

It wasn't really that; he told them various things. They visited him in Reykjavík, he came one Christmas and one summer with his girlfriend, and then, from a distance, they watched him settle into Paris, grow into the language; sensed how his interest in his studies began to wane after the end of his first year there. So much so that the following year it waned entirely and he started working for a kind of experimental theatre – if they understood it correctly – which combined theatre, films, music, drama and social satire. Eiríkur always livened up when he spoke to them, first about music and later about the theatre; they could hear the same passion in his voice that they'd known since he was a child and talked about something that was close to his heart. They smiled when they heard his excitement, saw it in their mind's eyes, his fingers tousling his long hair, with a passionate glow in his eyes. In that theatre company, he met two French and two Arab musicians who formed a band with him, after which they played as much for theatrical performances as at bars and restaurants here and there in France – he met Tove on one such outing.

She's Danish and her name is Tove, like the poet, and she says hello to you.

Will we get to meet her sometime soon? Hafrún asked when Eiríkur had, as if in passing, said her name three times in the same phone call. He seemed to have a need for saying it. Yes, of course, when things have slowed down, Eiríkur answered, thereby confirming their relationship, but only in this indirect way.

What's a Danish woman doing in Paris? Hafrún hazarded to ask, trying not to let her voice give away how excited she was.

She lives in Nice, in fact, Grandma, and we met in the south of France when my band played for a few weeks in performances of two absurd works by Alfred Jarry. She's a cultural journalist, specialises in theatre, and wrote about the show. She has an enormous interest in Iceland and the Icelandic language and has long dreamed of travelling around the country. We're planning on coming to visit, of course, but it will be a bit tricky finding a time that suits us both. She lives there in the south, I in Paris, both of us actually in 150-per-cent jobs, and she's also mother to two girls, six and ten years old.

Two daughters, how nice! In which case, I suppose that makes me a proxy great-grandmother, completely unexpectedly, said Hafrún happily, but she bit her lip when she saw Skúli lay a finger to his; not too fast, the finger warned. Oh, said Hafrún then, dear Eiríkur, this is such good news. And hopefully you'll come and visit us much sooner than later! And Tove must be quite savvy in French, then, working as a journalist. She writes for the French newspapers, doesn't she?

Yes, and you can hardly hear that she isn't French. People here in Paris assume that she's from the south of France; no-one could imagine that she's from Denmark. She came to France at the age of sixteen as a language refugee.

Language refugee, is there such a thing?

Eiríkur laughed, as far as I understand, he says. According to Tove, their numbers will increase significantly in the coming years. People who come from countries where the language is being destroyed from within. As is apparently happening with Danish. Tove says that her mother tongue is sinking deeper into the throats of her countrymen and within a few decades won't resemble any of the sounds we'd normally connect with human language.

I had enough of it, she said, and came to France under the pretext of studying, but instead applied for residency as a language refugee and was immediately granted citizenship for humanitarian reasons.

The things you two say about Danish! said Hafrún. But it would be so wonderful to have you come visit.

We're determined to come, and she says hello!

She says hello, she says hello, says Eiríkur, but he doesn't say, doesn't dare to say, not wanting to sadden his grandmother, worry her, that the reason why it's complicated for them to come together to Iceland has nothing to do with where she lives, her 150-per-cent job, her two young daughters, but the fact that she's married, has been so for ten years. She loves Eiríkur with all her heart but doesn't dare to leave her husband. She fears the consequences. Her husband has been struggling with problems from his past for a long time, had trouble with drinking and Tove fears that he'll lose control of his life, that he'll start drinking again, sink into anger and despair if she leaves him. And that her daughters would then have to witness their father waste away.

She's married to a fragile man. Is the mother of two children.

So it's Búðardalur all over again?

The story repeats itself, bites its own tail.

ALL DANISH WOMEN ARE NAMED TOVE

Would this Danish woman, the language refugee, then later show up in the farmyard at Oddi, in a brown Datsun, a green Toyota, a blue Subaru, with an infant in her arms, which she would then hand to Hafrún over the kitchen table and say goodbye to with a few words about a glass of water after seven, eight or nine years? Búðardalur becomes Paris, Paris Búðardalur, is the theme of this symphony repetition, women asking for a glass of water, men emptying themselves into socks?

How, I ask as I look up, but without letting go of my pencil, letting its point rest on the last question mark so that the bearded coach driver from hell understands that I don't want to be bothered because I'm grappling with destiny and that he who isn't fully focused in that battle might just as well declare surrender, and I look up only long enough to make my one-word remark before continuing uninterrupted, how, I ask, pretending not to notice how smug he is about having changed his T-shirt yet again; I wouldn't dream of praising the new one, even though it's quite cool, dark red with a big picture of Nina Simone, who was as tall as a giraffe and was no less of a stranger to grief and heartache than Piaf – or drink and drugs, for that matter; the heartbreaking lines of the song, "Just Say I Love Him", under the picture of the singer, naturally, that song is going straight onto Death's playlist – it's not to be missed; how am I to put all these destinies on paper, in the hope of possibly giving the dead voices, life a new dimension, if you're constantly interrupting me? But to my knowledge, the Dane hasn't yet come here to the fjord, and certainly not with a child. As far as I know, they never had a child, although they certainly dreamed of it, toyed with the idea countless times while dwelling as refugees of love in their world behind the world. A world in which happiness and unhappiness constantly see-saw; deceit and lies clink glasses with happiness and sincerity; despair greets anticipation, irresponsibility embraces affection, and cowardice walks alongside sacrifice. Anyone can get there; the only entrance ticket is love. And its flip side, of course – betrayal.

So the Danish woman's name is Tove? asks the priest with the PCV licence, permitting him to drive us all to hell, and he turns on the radio, which has by then probably given up telling us news of a tired world, fatigued by the coronavirus, weary of housing the eternal adolescent that man is, and instead plays "Just Say I Love Him" by Nina.

Unless this companion of mine is simply calling the shots; is or was her name Tove, and how did their relationship go – badly, I suppose, because he lives alone in Oddi, with a shotgun, three dead puppies, big speakers, the guitar?

Her name was her name, and still is her name. To a certain extent, all Danish women are named Tove. They didn't have a child but lived together for four years in their world behind the world. Had their legal domicile in love.

And were they happy there?

YOU'RE BLESSED; HOW DO WE GET THERE?

Some months after their phone conversation, Eiríkur sent his grandmother and grandfather a photo of him and Tove sitting at a restaurant on a sun-baked square in Lyons, lifting beer glasses, smiling and obviously happy. And they suit each other. Complement each other. Half a year later, he even sent a photo of her daughters. Knew that it would make his grandparents happy. Knew that his grandmother would have them both framed, and then place them alongside other family photos. Which is fine, he thought, because it was unlikely that anyone who knew Tove would see the photo of the two of them happy together, as well as that of her daughters, in his grandparents' living room up north in Iceland.

Of course, he realised that it was wrong – if not unforgivable – to send the photo of Tove's daughters without asking her first. But when he sent it, he was convinced that he and Tove would be together within a year, or two years at most. Her husband had started seeing a psychologist, he had cut back on his drinking, he was getting stronger. Soon, Eiríkur thought – albeit a bit ashamed of himself at those dreams – the man would be strong enough to take the blow when Tove told him about Eiríkur, and file for divorce. Strong enough that Tove needn't fear that the divorce would devastate him.

And deep down Eiríkur hoped that, as long as the photos of Tove and her daughters were among the family photos at Oddi, it would significantly increase the chances of their lives merging one day. Logic is probably one of the first things we lose when we're in love.

Our daughter-in-law, Hafrún told visitors, happy about Tove and Eiríkur's obvious happiness, happy to see his eyes so bright – as if the shadows of the world had receded from him; and these beautiful girls are my great-grandchildren. How blessed Skúli and I are in our old age!

Your grandfather, Hafrún said when she called Eiríkur to thank him for the photo of Tove, muttered something about how he never suspected that such a beautiful woman could be born in mountainless Denmark, and would love to meet the woman who makes you so happy. He will, Grandma, he said, and hopefully as soon as possible! There's just so much going on right now. We're about to start on a six-month, packed theatre tour. You recall that Tove took over a theatre in Marseille last year, and then got me to help her produce Ionesco's *Rhinoceros*. We've just finished a month-long tour of France with it, with a multinational group of actors, each speaking in his own language, while the audience can read the French text on a big screen. It's been so successful that we're taking the performance on a six-month tour throughout Europe and beyond.

I won't be bothering you with phone calls then, said his grand-mother, so happy to hear the enthusiasm in his voice, at how much he was obviously looking forward to the tour; but send us postcards! Which he did, cheerful postcards from one city after another: Milan, Moscow, Athens, Warsaw, Oslo, Tel Aviv . . . and sometimes photos of the production, with him sitting with his guitar at the wings of the stage, dressed in black, so veiled in darkness that he seems like a suspicion or vague thought. An endless triumph, new shows were added, the tour was extended. The six months eventually turned into sixteen, the schedule sometimes so tight that weeks could pass without Tove coming home to her family. It was the best of times for her and Eiríkur. They didn't need to be constantly saying goodbye, living in eternal loss. The world behind the world took over their existence.

On the other hand, they didn't know, or perhaps avoided thinking, that this long, happy theatre tour made it increasingly difficult to travel between the two worlds. It became increasingly . . .

It could hardly end well, says the coach driver from hell, now holding the photo of Hafrún and Skúli that Skúli had sent to Eiríkur during that tour. A photo that followed Eiríkur from city to city, country to country, took five months to reach him, when he was in Amsterdam. Skúli is holding his wife close, their deep, quiet love seems bigger than the world. Hafrún is smiling, a bit as if she is saying it's alright, and leaning against her husband, who is looking seriously into the camera.

Eiríkur pulled the photo from its large envelope in his hotel room. Tove was sitting up in bed, having woken relatively recently, naked, with tousled hair. Aren't those your grandparents? she asked.

He nodded. Oh, they're so beautiful, Tove said, and so happy! They're clearly blessed!

(. . .)

It took the photo five months to reach him, says the bearded coach driver with a PCV licence that permits him to drive me between worlds, between times, areas of existence; gone is the stack of crêpes, gone are the gaudy shorts, T-shirts with musicians; now he is wearing dark jeans, a black jumper, a high-quality dark-blue jacket.

You mentioned somewhere that Skúli was brought here to the fjord at a young age by the postman, my companion adds, before looking up and saying, as if reciting a text from memory:

Came here because his father, Jón Gíslason, a fisherman, had been lying on his back outside their small wooden house, looking up at the clear night sky in the hope of spotting the galaxy that had been discovered a decade earlier out in the world, but which he'd first read about in an English newspaper a few hours earlier. So big and expansive, he thought, that it would take the fastest train in the world millions of years to get from one end of it to the other. How could something so big, so important, be hidden from the eyes of man for millennia – if something that size has been completely hidden from us until now, what else is lurking there outside our lives, outside the history of man? Can it be said, then, that the world we've all lived in has, strictly speaking, never existed?

What do you say, my companion asks, are you going to leave Jón lying there much longer – and have we, strictly speaking, never lived?

I don't know, I answer, and don't have time to think about it, or to go west to Snæfellsnes, because it took the photo five months to reach Eiríkur.

IN ANOTHER WORLD. AT ANOTHER TIME

It took five months for the photo to reach him. Skúli drove to Hólmavík and posted it to Palermo, where the troupe was to be for a week from its posting date. But for some reason, perhaps due to the sleepy slowness of the Italian postal service, the photo didn't reach Palermo until three weeks later, when the troupe was in Cairo, where the envelope was then sent; but by the time it got there, they were in Athens. This went on for five months, and the envelope had gone through eight cities and six countries when it arrived at Eiríkur's hotel in Amsterdam. What do you have there? Tove asked when he brought the large envelope up to their room. Just over an hour earlier, Eiríkur had slipped out as she slept, after jotting her a note and leaving it on top of her phone on the bedside table: "8.30: Went out to find a decent croissant in this city of canals, bicycles, marijuana. Who knows, maybe I'll see Chet Baker, who's constantly falling out his fifth-floor hotel window, with his trumpet and his heartache in his arms. Then I'll run, grab him, bring him up to our room and, in gratitude, Chet will play 'My Funny Valentine' for us: Each day is Valentine's Day, for us two, love!"

When he came back, he found her awake, sitting up in bed, tousled, naked, and warm. What do you have there, she asked when she saw the large envelope.

I don't know, or yes, I mean, it's a letter from home and has clearly travelled far, but the strange thing is that this is my grandfather's writing. I can hardly remember him having written someone's name on anything, not even on his gifts to my grandmother.

Oh, they're so beautiful, Tove said when she saw the photo, and so happy together! My love . . . this is how we would have become after thirty, forty years. If we'd been in another world. Or in another time.

She'd woken soon after he left, saw the note, read it, and smiled happily. At the words, the messy handwriting in which each line carried within it the presence and character of Eiríkur, the man she loved. She read the note three times, and then made ready to put it in the box she always kept with her, in which she had a large number of similar notes, little jottings, cheerful messages that Eiríkur had left for her here and there over the past few years. Little tablets of joy and happiness that she sometimes took out when she needed consolation, or if she just wanted to rejoice, smile, drink in his presence. But then she received a desperate text message from her elder daughter, who was having her first period and was scared, nervous, even though she knew what was happening. Tove had immediately called and talked to her for a long time, managed to comfort her, calm her down, even got her to laugh. She was smiling as she hung up the phone and reached for the note to put in the box – but then the tears started to flow. What is this, she said in surprise, wiping them off. But more came, streaming forth like an independent force, and then she started crying uncontrollably. Lying face down on the bed, her entire body shaking and trembling, and she cried so hard that she could barely catch her breath. She cried because it was obvious to her. What she'd tried to deny for too long. That this dual existence was tearing her apart. And Eiríkur, too. That despite their having always been happy together, despite their love, they were throwing their lives away. It dawned on her that the wonderful, titillating everyday life that the note carried with it could never become their everyday life. That's why she broke. And wept with bitter sorrow. But also with . . . a deep sense of relief? For it was as if a mountain had suddenly been lifted off her shoulders.

And she could finally breathe.

That's how we could have become after thirty, forty years – Eiríkur didn't really catch what she said. He looked at the photo, saw the lassitude in his grandmother's posture, the unusual seriousness in his grandfather's face, and an anxious suspicion awoke inside him.

He picked up the phone and called Skúli, who answered in Reykjavík, at Hafrún's hospital bed.

NOW YOU CAN COME

Your grandmother forbade us to tell you about her illness, says Skúli over the phone. She was diagnosed with cancer nine months ago, colon cancer. They call it the silent killer because you become aware of it only after it has rooted itself so deeply that there's little that can be done. We weren't to bother you. We had to promise her that. You were so busy, your time taken up with your show. And you were so obviously happy with the Danish woman that she didn't want to ruin anything. This will pass, she said. And Eiríkur should enjoy life. He's young, there'll be plenty of time for him to think about death. He must first be allowed to live. And I don't want him to see me in such bad shape, little more than a rag. Still, if I should be such a wretch as to leave, I want people to remember me at my best. It's enough that the three of you have to hang over me and see me in such poor shape. You know her, Eiríkur. This is how she's always been. The warmest person in the world, but can sometimes be so stubborn that she should have been included in the *Guinness Book of World Records*. But you got the photo only now, five months after I sent it?

Yes, Grandpa, it went through eight cities, six countries. I've never seen so many postmarks on one envelope.

Your grandmother would have enjoyed seeing it. She didn't want you to know. Did I already say that? First, because of what I think I said earlier, that she didn't want you to see her in such a wretched state, and second, because she'd had enough of our hysteria – as she called it – mine, Palli's and your dad's. She said that it was probably our worries that made her so ill, and that, on the other hand, it gave her strength and joy in the fight against cancer to know that you were so happy with the Danish woman. Tove, that's her name, right? And we saw that there was something to what she said, that it gave her strength. We saw that your postcards from countless cities in Europe, Africa and Asia delighted her. At times, I even felt that they managed to blunt the pain better than the morphine. I sent you the photo without her knowing, and had almost started to regret it. I mean, when I saw how much strength it gave her to receive only good news from you. I'll have to get on my feet, she said, so I can welcome our Danish daughter-in-law properly. Your grandmother is probably in control of everything, even without knowing it. Because you got the photo only when she wanted you to. Death shouldn't disturb life more than necessary, she told me, when I said that I was going to let you know what was happening. I've never made any decisions without her. But now you can come, Eiríkur. I was thinking of calling you today. She's taken a rapid turn for the worse. You've got to come quickly. I don't know how long I can hold on to her. I can feel that she's being pulled hard from the other side, and sometimes death just pulls harder than life. After all, I'm not that tough. Still, I've never pulled so hard. I'm afraid I'm not strong enough. I'm afraid your grandmother is leaving. And then I honestly don't know what will become of the world.

HOW AM I TO DIE IF YOU'RE NOT WITH ME?
Two hours later, Eiríkur is on his way to the airport. The only ticket available just a few hours before the flight was on Saga Class, expensive as death, Eiríkur thought involuntarily, and he sent a text message

to his grandfather from the train on his way out to the airport to let him know that he was coming.

Eiríkur is on his way, Skúli whispered to Hafrún. Whispered it into the fog that had been thickening around her for the last twenty-four hours. She was so deep inside it that she'd stopped hearing Skúli, no longer felt his presence, despite his never leaving her bedside. Talked to her, read to her, held her hand.

In fact, they'd always done everything together since they were children.

Had been as dependent on each other as the foot is on the leg and could always untie life's knots together. The painful, the difficult, the mundane ones, and lift each other up when knocked down by life's blows. Because there were blows, life is a long breath, something always happens. There were financial worries, fences needed fixing, they'd made the decision to put down a dog that had been their devoted, faithful companion for fifteen years, they had to paint the house, go fetch Halldór in the Eastfjords after he'd been drunk for a month and lost his job, had plunged into debt, took Páll in their arms when he came home broken following the shipwreck of his cohabitation with the fisherman's widow, and sometimes Eiríkur didn't answer when Hafrún called on Saturdays – she would let it ring out, and he didn't call back; those were difficult moments. But they'd got through everything and life always smiled at them when it passed through the fjord. They were blessed, Tove was right. They'd done everything together. But now a rift had formed between them and Hafrún sat alone deep in a dark fog, holding her knees and talking to herself in the hope that her words would somehow reach him. I've loved you for more than sixty years, she said.

I've loved you for more than sixty years. Remember, I was only eleven years old when I realised it, and you hadn't yet turned ten. We were sitting on tussocks in Gufudalur Valley, watching the ewes; it was the last summer that lambs were removed from their mothers for milking here in the fjord, even in all of Iceland. We'd been chit-chatting and daydreaming, as children do. I enjoyed watching you talk. Seeing your mouth move, seeing the light change the colour of your eyes that could turn so strangely blue – and then, for the first time, I noticed the space between them and all of a sudden I thought you were the cutest, most beautiful, most enjoyable thing in the whole world. You were so full of energy that your eyes blazed. I must have looked at you strangely because you fell silent and then asked anxiously and so solicitously if something was wrong. Is something wrong? You bet there is! I was eleven years old, and had a giant crush on a nine-year-old boy. It was just humiliating. I was so angry that I stood up and slapped you as hard as I could. So hard that you tumbled off the tussock. Confused and surprised and with a split lower lip, you scrambled to your feet, but I had already run off. I didn't stop running until I was well out of sight, threw myself down in a hollow, screamed and cursed furiously into the soft ground. I've loved you every single second since then and it's so terribly painful and unfair to no longer feel your touch, no longer hear your voice. How am I to die if you're not with me?

Then she cried.

My love, Skúli whispered when he saw the silent tears flow from her closed eyes and disappear into the sheets. He got up, dried the tears, wiped them away, whispering, I'm here and will never leave you! Held her hands tightly, bore them to his old lips, up to his old blue eyes, but didn't cry, wanted to be strong for her. Because if the one you love is vulnerable, scared, crying in pain and loneliness, you've got to be strong. And he'd promised his mother that he'd always be strong. She exacted that promise from him at the shore an entire lifetime ago. Promise me that you'll be strong, for me and your sister Agnes, because I can do anything, my love, as long as you're strong.

Be strong, my love.

ONE DOESN'T OFFEND THOSE PROUD WOMEN

Jón, Skúli's father, rolls over onto his back outside their house in order to spot a galaxy, says the priest with the PCV licence. You have to go there, you can't avoid it; west to Snæfellsnes, and deeper into the past.

There's no space, there's no time, I mutter, taking care not to look up so that he . . . doesn't get a hold on me, deflect me from my path. One must try . . .

Yes, right, that's the word; *try*. Because Jón is trying to spot the newly discovered galaxy. But I think you need a powerful telescope for that, so he never had a chance to see it, not in this life – but there are only four cloudy sips left in the bottle. Maybe five. Skúli is asleep inside the house while his father lies outside. Sleeps with his two sisters, six and three years old, on either side of him. It's so cold in the house that the siblings share the same bed to keep each other warm. Skúli wakes up early that morning, around six o'clock, with little Agnes practically in his arms. He badly needs to pee, and totters out half asleep, the cold of the floor bites the soles of his feet but he's too tired to muster the energy to put on socks or shoes. Opens the door, which had come slightly free from the door jamb during the night, steps out, trips, and falls over his father – and then answers the phone about seventy years later next to a hospital bed in Reykjavík.

Yes, I mutter, that's true, but I peer hard at the pages, in which Kári turns down the road to Hof, Lúna and Dísa come out onto the steps to greet him and wave to me and Rúna as we drive past, heading for the hotel where Sóley is waiting for me, or is not waiting for me, I don't know, I'm . . .

. . . irrelevant, says the coach driver, pouring himself a shot without offering me any. Your memories and your love mustn't hinder us. The Fates are waiting to be tended to, and one doesn't offend those proud women. Keep doing what you're supposed to be doing. If you do it well, and well enough for it to be noticed in the world around us, then maybe I'll tell you who you are. Not before.

MY LOVE, I'VE SEEN THE WHOLE WORLD
Only God knows the answers, it says somewhere, but God hasn't said a word for two thousand years, leaving man with his questions, his uncertainty, his fear of meaninglessness. God knows the answers

and the grand design, man dwells in uncertainty, and that's where the stories come from. But where, then, would you put the devil?

I scrutinise the pages, read this about God, the answers, the uncertainty about where to put the devil and see Jón, Skúli's father, convincing a bootlegger in the village to let him have a bottle, his hand is fine now, he'll go to sea soon and then he can pay for the bottle.

My companion turns his full shot glass from side to side between his long fingers. Those were difficult times, he says.

I give him a sidelong glance. He has the look of someone who has gone so far as to know how the roads end. It's possible that the same man was making crêpes here in the caravan not so long ago; can a person with that face, that expression, dressed in silly shorts, swing a crêpe spatula around like a timeless version of Don Quixote?

Those were difficult times, he repeats – the 1930s. The Great Depression and its repercussions still hacked like a merciless axe at the everyday lives of the common folk, and things had been very tight for Hulda and Jón that winter. The unpredictable weather cut hard into opportunities for fishing, and in addition, he had injured his hand and hadn't been able to go to sea for week – their debt to the merchant grew and grew. They had to be extremely thrifty with everything; the coal had run out two days before and it was freezing cold in the house.

Which was his fault.

That they hadn't moved into a better place long before. That they had no money set aside. I'm exactly like my mum, he sometimes thought, and wrote in a letter to his sisters, because no matter what a destitute state we're in, I can't help but buy books that speak to me, subscribe to periodicals, and Hulda and I have even gone to Reykjavík to attend lectures, go to the theatre. More than one person in the village has shaken his head in disdain. And there's little sympathy now when we're in such a serious pinch. It serves them right, people think. Did I tell you that my shipmates call me Jón the Learned when they want to be funny, the bastards?

Jón the Learned – he and Hulda had about a hundred books,

which was more than the number owned by the travelling teacher who stayed in the fishing villages, almost as many as that owned by the magistrate and his wife in Ólafsvík. But, yes, there was also this: he hadn't been completely sober when he cut his hand at sea that winter. And it was now so cold in the house that yesterday morning Hulda had woken with her long, dark hair frozen so firmly to the wall that he had to cut it loose. He was worried about her, had even begun wondering what books and periodicals he could sacrifice to try to get some warmth in the house. Because Hulda had contracted tuberculosis as a child, without it having caused too much damage, admittedly, but it had flared up last winter and prevented her from working much; she tired out quickly. Wasn't it due to the cold that it had reared up again?

But it's night and Jón is standing drunk outside their house and the front door, which tends to swell so much in wet weather that it has to be forced open, can't be budged, the house refuses to let him in. This is a sign, Jón thinks.

He'd gone early that day to try to negotiate with the merchant to purchase food and coal on credit, but came across English sailors in the shop and asked them, as he was accustomed to doing when he met them, if they might have any newspapers dating back a few weeks that they'd read and reread and might therefore be willing to part with. The sailors had invited him out to their ship, tempted him with beer. Just one, he thought, and then I'm going back ashore. But the beers kept coming and it was nearly evening when he finally did go ashore, but he didn't dare to go home immediately, empty-handed, drunk. He couldn't bear the thought of confronting Hulda's disappointment, much less seeing the anger in Skúli's eyes; he was old enough now to realise the connection between his drinking and their difficulties, the coldness of their house, his mother's illness, and Agnes' persistent cough. And Jón had, without even thinking, stopped by the bootlegger's, got a bottle from him for a pledge, and then hunkered down in a shed where nets were repaired, lay there well into the evening on an old pile of nets, read the papers, sipped at his bottle.

The English had given him a decent-sized stack of papers and in one of them was a long article about Edwin Hubble and his over-ten-year-old revolutionary discovery of the existence of another galaxy. Jón read the article three times. More enthusiastically each time, more joyfully, and in the end he was so elated that he couldn't wait to tell Hulda about the article and hurried home. So eagerly that he forgot he'd been drinking, that he hadn't been home since he went to negotiate with the merchant, that he would be coming home empty-handed and drunk. Had forgotten all of it. Which doesn't matter anymore – what does the ordinary matter when the sky clears its throat, he thought, and half-ran the last few metres to their house.

But the door was stuck in the jamb.

It had been raining the last few days and the door frame had swollen so much that it couldn't be moved. The house refused to let him in. Jón sighed, looked up at the sky, and realised that it was probably past midnight and Hulda was asleep. But he also saw that the sky had cleared for the most part, the temperature had dropped, and the stars were returning. This is a sign, Jón thought – this is a sign!

It was plain to see!

That fate and his mother Guðríður were sending him a message to the effect that hereafter, he should always raise his eyes to the sky where life and beauty reign. All he had to do was lie down on the ground where he could take in the entire sky at even a single glance, let himself sober up as he looked up until he spotted the newly dis-covered galaxy. For it would be, to a certain extent, the same as seeing eternity itself.

He pulled the bottle out from under his belt, tossed it aside contemptuously, and lay down. He who seeks eternity no longer needs to drink. He just needed to recover from the nausea that came over him when he lay down. It would soon pass. Then watch, talk to the sky, and listen to it. The night would pass, then he would go in, take Hulda in his arms, kiss her hair, kiss her neck, eyes, say, wake up, my love, for I have seen the whole world. And when I saw that life is bigger than death, I tossed aside my bottle, because I knew I would never have to drink again. My love. Now everything will be fine.

IT'S SO NICE TO LISTEN TO YOU, YOU KNOW THAT, DON'T YOU? In a windswept churchyard towards the tip of the Snæfellsnes peninsula, if not at the very tip, so far out that from there, you can see an incredible distance out to sea, can apparently still be found the beautiful and fairly large gravestone of Jón Gíslason, a large shore rock, shaped and rounded for centuries by the sea, weighing at least thirty kilos, found by his wife Hulda. Who had searched for a long time, gone far, walked kilometres of shoreline to find the right rock, and then carried it a long way home. The rock was so heavy and her arms were so thin, her lungs weakened by tuberculosis, that she had to sit down numerous times to catch her breath, had to rest, it started to snow, the snow fell hard and turned her into a sad angel who carried rocks for death.

Around eighty years later, the three of them stand over that rock, Halldór, Páll, and Eiríkur in the space between them, and read what Hulda herself had chiselled onto it, so deeply that time hasn't yet managed to blunt it to any significant degree: "Jón Gíslason (1901–1939), fisherman, beloved husband and father. Sorely missed."

Two years framing birth and death and then that little dash between them, supposedly containing his whole life, all his thoughts, dreams, the touch of his hands, his laughing, mischievous eyes that could become dim with sadness, could grow dark, containing his youth, his sisters' coddling of him, his dependence on his mother, loved by Hulda, loved by his children, despite having failed them all. This was all supposedly accommodated in that little dash, a fisherman renowned for diligence, resourcefulness, skill, who feared no storm, drank far too much but had an unquenchable desire for knowledge; a bleeding genius, that's what you are, his shipmates sometimes said. And he died outside his house under a clear February night sky, beloved, sorely missed.

Loss and oblivion.

Remember me, and the devils will retreat from me.

Forget me, and they'll tear me open.

*

312

They stood for a long time over the rock, the brothers, as well as Eiríkur, so long that their presence undoubtedly seeped into the ground, to the three of them, because Jón isn't alone in the dirt, in the darkness amid the blind poets – on the shore rock are also the names of Hulda and Agnes, the little sweetie, who always wanted to sleep snuggled against her brother. Agnes Jónsdóttir (1935–1939), Hulda Jónasardóttir (1905–1939).

Then the three of them continued onward to Uppsalir, where it all began. So it was a kind of a pilgrimage.

They followed country roads, took old paths, and had to walk the final kilometres, there being neither a road nor a path up to the farmstead, hardly a sheep trail. Then they stood over the sagging remains and collapsed walls and there was little, in fact nothing, left to remind them of the family room where Gísli and Guðríður had slept and woken many thousands of times and had their moments. Where two of the younger girls had been born and spent their childhoods, dull, perhaps, but full of love; where Gísli had had dreams of a farm down in the lowland, preferably a stone's throw from the sea. Where he'd emptied himself into a woollen sock and Pétur saw a dangerous smile for the first time. That family room is now gone, has been so thoroughly erased that it's as if it never existed. Gone, too, is the farmyard, where three eager girls rushed to see Pétur and Ljúf approaching, gone is the farmhouse passageway where their mother had stood hiding like a fool, where the darkness met the daylight, stood there waiting to hear his voice for the first time. The farm passageway that she would step out from with a stack of pancakes for Gísli and Björgvin and her girls, who wouldn't leave the five-year-old mare; she stepped out from the passageway and soon afterwards walked through Eiríkur as he stood over the farm's ruins almost a hundred and twenty years later – and her heart skipped a beat when she sensed him.

But her son, the apple of her eye, her last-born, the long-desired son that Gísli had dreamed of having and going fishing with, lay up against the front door, crosswise, when Skúli came out in the early morning, on his way to the privy. He'd woken up needing badly to pee and was in such a hurry that he tripped over his father. Tumbled onto the cold ground. It was still dark outside, starry, the galaxy somewhere up there in the darkness, but it wasn't moved by the sight of a seven-year-old boy tripping over his father, tumbling onto the ground so cold in the morning, so startled by his fall that his bursting bladder emptied itself.

Oh, no, Skúli thought when he felt the warm pee stream out and soak his pyjamas. He got up, drenched with pee, and saw his father lying on his back, strangely motionless, strangely stiff, with his head thrown back.

Dad, whispered Skúli, Dad, wake up! And he started shaking him when Jón didn't answer. He begged him to wake up because he mustn't be lying down like that when Mum and the girls woke up. Dad, he whispered, over and over. Dad, you've got to wake up! I'm sorry I was mad at you. I'll never be mad again if you just wake up now. Won't you tell me about something you've read? It's so nice to listen to you, Dad, you know that, don't you, and you know that I love you, Skúli whispered, trying to clean the vomit off his father's face. But Jón didn't answer. It was as if he didn't care about anything. Lying motionless, his head thrown back, as if in agony. Choked on his own vomit as he searched for another world in the night sky.

REMEMBER WHEN I SLAPPED YOU IN GUFUDALUR?
Two months later, Hulda walked with Skúli down to the shore. Under a cloudless sky. The whole time, he looked straight ahead, concentrating on listening to his mother, drinking in her words and presence and holding back his tears. He wanted to keep them inside him, wanted to be strong for his mum.

They walked slowly, lengthening their path, eking out their time together. She told him about the fjord that awaited him, and the small grassy valley where she'd spent just over a year as a child. Those were good times, among good people, and Margrét, who is now the housewife at Botn and is looking forward to having Skúli with her,

314

was her best friend. We write to each other from time to time, said Hulda. It will be alright, said Hulda.

And you're so lucky to be going on a trip! Just seven years old, and soon you'll be seeing beautiful countryside, different landscapes, and of course all the houses in Stykkishólmur! It's almost like going to Reykjavík. I know of no seven-year-old who'll have travelled as far as you after this trip. You're lucky. You'll become incredibly wise. I'm so proud of you. You're so beautiful, pleasant and kind. Everything is going to be fine. You've just got to be patient. Sometimes very bad things have to happen to allow for the best. I know you'll be happy. I envy all of those who'll get to know you and be near to you. How incredibly lucky they'll be! Maybe everything will be fine in a year and I can send for you. I'm already looking forward to it! But first you must be quite strong, can you do that, my dearest, will you promise me that?

Then they'd come down to the shore and she knelt beside him. Waiting nearby was the boat that would ferry him out to the fishing vessel. She held him in her arms, held him tightly for a long time, held on as tightly as is possible in this world. And he felt her tremble. Tsk, tsk, she whispered, such a fool I can be, getting your nice jumper all wet. My brave and handsome, handsome boy!

She opened his hand, laid it over her heart, closed it gently but firmly, and said softly, now my heart will always be with you. Take care of it, and be strong.

She stood on the shore, watching him, the ship sailed away, and she grew smaller the further it moved away. As if the distance was erasing her, little by little. As if distance were another name for death.

It sailed away – almost seven decades later, he's sitting by Hafrún's sickbed, holding her hand tightly. He'd fallen asleep, exhausted. His head had sagged, his forehead rested on the mattress. Falls asleep and finds himself on the deck of the ship as it distances itself from his mother. He watches her grow smaller, watches her die, but then it occurs to Skúli that all he has to do is climb down into the boat that the ship has in tow for some reason, and row ashore. Then he'll save not only his mother and Agnes, but also Hafrún. But no matter how hard he tries, he can't move, some huge, invisible force holds him fast. He struggles against it, exerts the utmost force, but doesn't move. He isn't strong enough. He cries bitterly into the mattress but wakes up to Hafrún stroking his neck, soothingly.

He looks up and meets her smile. So you're back, he whispers happily. She doesn't answer, her warm palm, her gaunt hand, strokes him affectionately. Do you remember, she then whispers, clearly needing to work hard to make her voice heard, do you remember when I slapped you in Gufudalur? He nods, she smiles, then lies back on her pillow, exhausted, but whispers, still smiling, oh, how could I not love you?

Skúli squeezes her hand and feels sobs beginning to fill his chest again, but he had promised to be strong, so he leans forward, kisses her hand, kisses his fingers, and manages to keep himself from crying. He sits back down on the chair, checks his phone, and sees a message from Eiríkur, sent two hours earlier: "Grandpa, I got a ticket on Saga Class (!) taking off in two hours, ask Dad to pick me up at the airport, will be there in six hours at the latest."

Skúli gets up, leans over Hafrún, and whispers to her that Eiríkur is on his way. She opens her eyes, smiles again, squeezes his hand, twice.

And then Skúli cries.

He cries as both a seven-year-old boy on a fishing boat distancing itself from his mother and an old man in a hospital in Reykjavík.

MAN COMPREHENDS ONLY THE INCOMPREHENSIBLE
And then Hafrún steps into the darkness whence no message has ever been received, says the sanctified coach driver, turning his empty shot glass between his long fingers. Says it in such a way that I get the uncomfortable feeling that he knows both this darkness into which everyone seems to disappear and the words that are stuck there and have never managed to reach the world of the living.

I look at the pages in the hope of escaping from him. My head clears and I find myself sitting in the SUV next to Rúna, on our way up to the hotel. She needs to fetch three bottles of grappa for the party, and dark chocolate for the French chocolate cakes. I long to go back there, hear the next song on Death's playlist and see Sóley, drink in her smile and that bright energy of hers that seems to make it easier for me to live. And I want so much to meet the Canadian family in the pool, find out how they're related to Eiríkur, why he has relatives there across the sea to the west – I suspect that the answer to that question could help me understand the big picture. If it can be found. The big picture.

I look down at the dense writing, the small, compressed, messy devil's handwriting, but I don't see Rúna anywhere; instead, I see Eiríkur coming out of the Leifur Eiríksson Terminal, the airport in Keflavík. Better put, out of the airport above Keflavík, located on the ancient rangeland of Njarðvík. Halldór is there to pick up his son. They haven't seen each other for . . . three, four years?

He's aged, Eiríkur thinks, half startled. Because Halldór has grown thin, his softness and boyish zeal have disappeared. His face has become sharper, darker, and it's as if his eyes have sunk deeper in their sockets. I hardly recognise him, Eiríkur thinks desperately, he's unable to say anything, barely greets him, just stands there in front of his father, holding tightly to his big suitcase, he's once again a six-year-old boy who fears that he'll never be good enough for his dad to want him in his band. You've brought your guitar, says Halldór instead of greeting him, nodding towards the guitar neck sticking up over Eiríkur's left shoulder – and the latter just nods. He's brought his guitar and the big, heavy suitcase that he's lugged with him all over Europe in recent months, south to Africa, all the way east to Baghdad. Tove had offered to take both the bag and the guitar with her and bring them to the small apartment that Eiríkur had bought in Marseille just over a year ago. But he declined her offer, choosing to take it all with him home to Iceland, without knowing why. And now he nods at his father's words, to confirm that he has brought his guitar, and also to say hello. They haven't seen each other for three, four years, and greet one another by one of them saying, you've brought your guitar, the other by nodding. Still, I could easily both play and sing "I'll Follow the Sun" for him, flies through Eiríkur's mind as he follows his dad. Grateful to him for not asking or saying more, apart from remarking that the car was outside.

They drive in silence from the airport, through the lava fields between Keflavík and Reykjavík, which has begun to dress itself in vibrant autumn colours. Eiríkur drinks in the surroundings and feels how badly he has missed Iceland. The light, the smell, the landscape. He looks out over the lava, the roofs of Keflavík and at Snæfellsjökull Glacier beyond the vast expanse of Faxaflói Bay. It's as if it wants to tell me something, Eiríkur thinks as he agrees with something his dad says.

They exchanged a few words, a few sentences, to begin with. Eiríkur asked about his grandmother, about his grandfather, and Halldór about the theatre tour. Then they were silent. It wasn't exactly a comfortable silence, but they still had a hard time breaking it. As if they no longer knew how to talk or be silent together.

Have we ever known how to do that, Eiríkur thinks as they crawl out of Njarðvík, turn onto the Reykjanesbraut highway, and pass all the car dealerships. Keflavík's surroundings are beautiful, Páll had once told Eiríkur, and maybe because sometimes it's as if there's no landscape there, just wind, wide-open space and seagulls. Landscape becomes so mysterious and captivating when it's absent.

The most incomprehensible explanations are probably the ones we understand best, Eiríkur thinks to himself, and agrees, almost too eagerly, when Halldór asks if he can go on listening to Páll's reading of *The Liar* by Martin A. Hansen, or the *Deacon of Sandey* as it's titled for some reason in the Icelandic translation. Palli came home, explained Halldór, to record novels for his mother. She's had difficulty reading these past few weeks, gets tired so quickly, but has no trouble listening and was very happy when we brought her Palli's recordings.

Eiríkur is so happy, so relieved that his father isn't going to put music on, that he agrees to his proposal to listen to Palli's reading with probably too much enthusiasm – the thought of listening to music, songs loaded with memories, while sitting there next to Halldór, is actually overwhelming. He was worried that his dad would have even put together a list of songs to play for them along the way. Songs that they'd shared. Their songs. Breathing easier, Eiríkur leaned back in his seat, listened to Páll read. "What was it again that I called you last night?":

Natanael! Now I remember. I needed to talk to someone, and then I called you, I don't know where from.

He listens, looks at the lava, the low mountains, the blue, ruffled ocean. Faster, go faster, he thinks, when he sees that his dad rarely drives much over 100kph. Go faster, as fast as you can!

Eiríkur closes his eyes, they approach Hafnarfjörður and he sends his grandmother one mental message after another, Grandma, dear dear Grandma, I'm coming, I'm on my way! I'm sorry for how long it's taken me to get here. But now I'm finally here and will never leave you and Grandpa again. Don't go. I don't know if we can go on without you.

But then Páll calls.

CAN THE DEAD SPEAK TO EACH OTHER?
And it went as it did. That's the way it is. Everything must happen as it does. Life is movement. We call it death when it comes to a stop. What was it again that I called you last night? Does life create fate or does fate shape life; did God create the world or the world God? What was it again that I called you?

You've never called me anything, and never Natanael, even less last night because you've only been around for about eight hours. If you add it all up, the result will be one hundred and twenty years. But you're right that it went as it did, because everything must happen as it does. Hafrún stepped into the darkness, left Skúli crying at her hospital bed, he who may not have cried since receiving the letter that his uncle sent to him up north at Botn, letting him know of the death of Hulda, his mother, and little Agnes. They died a day apart. Agnes first. Praise be to God, he added. Now they're at rest with your father. I hope you're in good health.

Did he write praise be to God because Hulda managed to keep death at bay long enough to be able to hold Agnes in her arms so that she wouldn't die alone – then hurried into the darkness after her? And did she find her little girl in that darkness; can you find someone after death? Did Jón even welcome them both? Can the dead speak to each other, can they comfort one another, or is such a thing exclusively in the purview of life?

You certainly can ask a lot of questions – in the year 1939, about a hundred people in Iceland died of tuberculosis. That's the way it is. Halldór and Eiríkur were at the aluminium smelter at Straumsvík when Páll called his brother. Mum is gone, he said.

So Eiríkur came too late?

It's not about coming late, but about being there in one way or another, and he wasn't. In that, he failed, and he knew it. That's why he wanted his dad to drive faster, to drive illegally fast, well over the speed limit, in the hope that getting there in time would somehow make up for things. Then it went as it did.

As it did, I think, and I look down, see Eiríkur and Halldór come to the hospital bed too late, and I realise that they both failed, each in his own way.

CAN FISH SWIM IF DEPRIVED OF WATER?

Three days later, they drive north with the coffin. In Halldór's pickup truck. He's alone in the cab, and Skúli, Páll and Eiríkur are sitting on a thick mattress in the bed, up against the cab, all the way north, a five-hour drive, as if they're looking after the coffin, or keeping Hafrún company. It's snowing on Holtavörðuheiði Heath and Eiríkur is so cold that he almost turns into an icicle. Which would be fine, because icicles don't feel anything, they just melt. But it's probably illegal to sit in the bed of a pickup truck on the highway, at a speed of 100kph. Perhaps corpses and coffins shouldn't be transported in this way either – the coffin is of course tied down securely, but the men clearly are not; they're shaken or jerked this way and that by the vehicle's movements, the bumps in the road. Some others who passed them were obviously alarmed, shocked, even angry; at least the police are notified about the trip and a highway-patrol car catches up with them just before they reach Borðeyri.

Catches up with them, flashes its lights, signals them to stop, pull over. Which Halldór does, he shuts off the engine, steps out and Skúli, Palli and Eiríkur hop down from the truck's bed. Two policemen in their early thirties step out of the police vehicle and approach them. Where are you headed? one of them asks, before immediately biting his lip while the other looks away; before them are the coffin and the men's faces, dark with sorrow.

And nothing more is said to begin with. The four men just look at the two policemen, who hesitate. The one who asked the question looks down, as if ashamed.

We're bringing my mother home, Halldór finally says. I hope that's okay. I hope there are no laws against getting home, even if you're dead?

No, not at all. Of course not, the embarrassed man hurriedly answers.

Still, you stopped us. So aren't we allowed to transport our dead mother home in the back of a pickup truck? You can see that we've tied it down securely. She isn't going anywhere. Although she's actually gone already. But I think that the dead don't fall under the laws you serve. You'd need to be gods to have any authority over them. And you're hardly – forgive me for being so blunt.

The policemen look at each other uncertainly. It isn't going as smoothly as they'd hoped. No, says the one who had kept quiet, no, while it may not exactly be forbidden to transport a dead person, one's mother, on a pickup truck, it's certainly highly unusual . . . on the other hand, of course, you're not allowed to sit in the bed of the truck, unsecured, travelling the roads of this country. That's just a given. It's reckless. A violation of the law. Surely you can see that!

So should my mother be alone in the bed of the truck?

My good man, the policeman begins as his partner continues to look at the ground, but then Skúli gets down from the truck, where he'd been standing between Páll and Eiríkur, and starts talking. Speaks calmly, softly, looks firmly from one policeman to the other: My wife and I have known each other for more than sixty years, and have been married for over half a century.

Or rather, we were married for over half a century. Now she's dead. I can't live without her. That's just a fact. I'm not complaining. I'm just giving you the facts. Her name is Hafrún, and she'll be called that for eternity, death can't change that. I'm not going to try to describe her to you, who are so young and also have plenty of other things to do than listen to me. Suffice it to say that the world would be a very beautiful place if more people were like her. It would even be heavenly. But God decided to call her to him early, and without me. That's a fact I need to learn to live with. I don't know how it will go. Can fish swim if they're deprived of water? Is it worth it for the Earth to keep turning if the sun goes out? You're young men. It's your job to uphold the law, to protect those in need, and it's a good job. Go and do it. There's nothing for you here, except an old, dead, farmer's wife, four grieving men. This is a job for the heavens, the gods, and time.

The policemen sit quietly in their vehicle for a good while, watching the pickup truck as it drives into the distance and disappears, with the three men on their wide seat in its bed. Wearing coats and hats, except for the old man, who is bare-headed, his grey, rather long hair fluttering. We'll just pretend we didn't find them, one of them finally says, the one who had asked the men where they were headed. Did you smell something on the driver? the other asks hesitantly. You mean alcohol? Yes, and shouldn't we have . . .

What?

Asked him to take a breath test.

His mother was in the coffin.

Yes, I know.

And you saw his dad, you listened to him.

Yes, yes, but . . .

Didn't you notice how wide-set his eyes were? I've never seen anything like it before.

Sure, yeah, that's right, but still, I mean . . .

It was as if the third eye itself was staring at you. The third eye, you know! I've heard that yogis concentrate their life force there at the moment of death.

Eeh, yeah, maybe, although I've never understood that yogi stuff. I leave such things to my wife. But I admit that there was something unusual about it. Which, however, doesn't mean the one who was driving . . .

You saw their faces, didn't you? Didn't you see that they were all like, I don't know what, maybe like tears. Yes, they were like tears. Or that's the only thing that comes to mind. Their faces, I mean.

Like tears?

You know what I mean. I'm no good at describing such things. But you saw them.

That's right, I saw it and it hit me pretty hard. Still, I'm fairly sure he had a smell on him.

Would you have wanted to ask him to take a breath test, do you think this was the day for it, the moment, his deceased mother two metres away?

No, maybe not. Or yes, anyway. Driving under the influence is of course an offence, plain and simple.

Nothing has happened, I say, we never saw them. And you . . . you can't measure the amount of alcohol present in grief.

The other looks down, obviously embarrassed. Then he reaches for the radio, probably to cover up the awkward silence that fills the car following his colleague's words. Turns it on, tunes it to the station The Wave and turns it up when he hears the opening notes of "Tragedy" by the Bee Gees.

But we're not adding any songs by the Bee Gees to Death's playlist.

No, of course not. We're not bastards.

BOY, YOU TURN ME ON!

They all smelled it, Eiríkur, Palli and Skúli. But nothing was said about it. None of them dared. Hafrún, however, would certainly have brought it up, and criticised it, but she of course had stopped talking entirely, was securely tied down to the bed of the pickup truck, and, not long afterwards, came to her place in the churchyard at Nes. Didn't say anything because she'd disappeared into the darkness from where no sound comes. No news, no milestones, no music. Disappeared into darkness and silence.

Into that which engulfs everyone.

We watch helplessly as loved ones disappear into it, we call out, we shout, we plead, but we get no answer. No response. The gap between it and us seems as unbridgeable as the gap between universes. Rather, you literally have to pay with your life to get there, and there's no chance of getting back, it's a one-way ticket only.

No response. Except perhaps when Kári of Botn had to be restored, when he'd turned into a useless, broken-down fence, a pesky eyesore, then Margrét returned and saw to it that the times he had an erection were put to good use. To our knowledge, this is the only time that has happened. No world thrives without exceptions.

Securely tied down to the bed of the pickup truck, then buried in the soil out here at Nes, and it was the old priest, Reverend Arnljótur, who officiated at the burial. Both her priest and a friend, it was he who had married her and Skúli, baptised and confirmed their boys.

Now you're gone, he said, and I feel as if a mountain has been taken from us. A gentle, grassy mountain, with plentiful berries and a calm but deep lake. A mountain that gathered light and sun. Which emanated the warmth that makes life around it gentler. Now you're gone, and the birds will probably start dwindling in number, and soon the birdsong will fade. Your presence made everyone better.

That's why we're all worse for your going. With no-one to repair our broken tractors. Thank you for being with us all these years. Now we must learn to exist without you, while the heavens, for their part, rejoice to welcome you. I'm looking forward to meeting you there, my friend.

Arnljótur finished his eulogy, delivered it without notes, his voice thin and broken by old age, yet strong enough for the small church, which was full; there simply wasn't enough room for all who had come. Álfrún of Skarð, who normally assisted Arnljótur when he held Mass at this church, went from car to car as it drove up and told the drivers where it was best to park, distributed the hymn books, and informed people what radio station they should tune to in order to listen to the service in their car. And Arnljótur delivered the eulogy, it came from his heart, then he sat down, tired, sad, and silence fell over the church, filled the cars outside. The priest stared downwards, as if waiting for the choir to sing the last song, a seven-member choir, five women, two men – the loft could hardly have accommodated a choir much larger. But he suddenly started, cleared his throat, stood up with difficulty, looked over the church, and said loudly and abruptly, it will be a remarkable experience for me to be dead.

Yes, it will be a remarkable experience for me to be dead, Hafrún said to me when she saw that the battle was lost. I've never tried it before. But the strangest thing, she went on, the strangest thing will probably be that I won't be able to have any influence on what happens in the district, let alone at home at Oddi. I'm a little scared that to begin with, the Heavenly Father will have to tether me like a stubborn sheep in order to keep me there on the other side. But the last thing that I ask for, the last thing that I'll stick my nose into in this district, is to see to it that my three boys, Halldór, Palli and Eiríkur, play one final song for me and Skúli.

Arnljótur paused, cleared his throat again, then directed his eyes and arms upward and said loudly: Let it down! And right away there descended, not from heaven, but from the choir loft, two guitars, a small guitar amplifier, two microphones, a single drum, drumsticks and a chair. The brothers and Eiríkur got up and caught hold of them. I wasn't allowed to say anything, Skúli, said Arnljótur to Skúli, who watched in surprise. But now, we'll hear one of your and Hafrún's favourite songs. A song she said she put on so many times when you had dinner on Saturday nights. And I was supposed to say to you: Remember how much we looked forward to cooking together and remember how I could dance like a fool to this song, yet you always loved it so much!

Boys, please – the church is yours.

The father and son arranged the gear in silence, tuned the guitars, then stood side by side for a moment and looked over the church, which was even fuller now. Few people had stayed in their cars when they realised what was happening, but instead came in quietly and filled the small vestibule and the narrow aisle between the pews. The people waited in silence, they waited expectantly, which they tried to hide, though, out of respect for the family's grief. Waited, watched the father and his son and the giant Páll. Halldór standing straight as a post, almost cockily, in a pinstriped suit, with his hair combed back, while Eiríkur had tied his in a ponytail, was wearing a black suit, a dark silk shirt, unbuttoned at the throat, and looked down and to the side. Páll, on the other hand, was just in his thick woollen jumper, his hair cut close, looking like a mountain behind the little drum. But then Eiríkur looked up and at his father. Looked at him affectionately. Behind them were rigorous rehearsals in the studio, without Skúli's knowledge, during which the father and son taught Páll the basics of drumming and how to switch up the beat when appropriate. Halldór nodded and Eiríkur took half a step forward, put his lips to one of the microphones, counted: one, two, three, four, one, two, three, four – and opened the song with its famous guitar riff, with such energy that everyone, both those in the church and out in the cars, gasped. And then the father and son began to sing at the same time. Their voices blended perfectly, Eiríkur's slightly dark, Halldór's high and bright. But they changed the lyrics a little, adapted it to Hafrún, because it was she who sang through them, sang for the last time to her husband:

Boy, you really got me goin'
you got me so I don't know what I'm doin' now

Boy, you really turn me on, you thrill me, deprive me of sleep, I love you so much that I slapped you, I've loved you so much that for almost seventy years your heartbeat has been mine, my smile has been yours, my dreams have been yours, and that's why these have been the Earth's best years since its beginning. I love you so much that I've never stopped getting a little weak at the knees when I see you in the distance, never stopped desiring you, longing for you, never stopped looking forward to waking up with you in the morning, smelling you, hearing you speak, you've always been my happiness and best friend, I could never have been able to imagine life without you, but now I'm dead. How can I die without you, how can I find my way through the darkness without you, see, don't ever set me free, I always wanna be by your side, always, always!

Forgive me, said death, as it stood darkly between them. Can you ever forgive me?

TO BE ALONE AND WITHOUT YOU, THAT'S DEATH
Can we ever forgive death?

My mysterious companion, the priest who abandoned the faith and got a PCV licence in order to drive me between realms of existence, stares silently at me. As if he didn't hear my question. But I'm not certain I asked it; and even more uncertain, then, whether I care to know the answer.

It's so hard, he finally says, looking out the gable window that frames the fjord where it opens and bleeds into the wide bay, out that window that seems to be getting bigger – it's so hard, so terribly difficult to lose the person you love and who has meant everything to you, that it has brought the most powerful people to their knees. But for many, the uncertainty of what comes next is even more difficult. If anything comes next at all. Other than erasure. Other than the futility of the void. But we know that Hafrún stepped into the darkness where time and space dissolve into nothing. We know that someone was waiting for her there. Some man, and, as far as Hafrún could see, he bore a strong resemblance to her Skúli. But maybe it was just because she misses him so much that everything on the other side bore a resemblance to him, in one way or another. The man came right up to her, took her gently by the shoulder and said, *Allein zu sein, und ohne Dich, ist der Tod.*

I don't speak German, said Hafrún, what does that mean?

To be alone and without you, that's death.

AND HE LAUGHED

Almost two years later, Páll calls Eiríkur in Marseille, where he lives in the small apartment he'd bought when Tove hired him for the theatre she ran, and where they still dreamed of having a life together. Páll calls. The slow Páll, the giant who, a quarter of a century earlier, had written a master's thesis on Kierkegaard, taught for a number of years at the comprehensive school in Keflavík, then temporarily took over the farm at Nes, but was now back at home at Oddi, along with Halldór, who manages the farm mainly on his own because Páll takes his small fishing boat out four to five times a week from Hólmavík along with Elías, the old professor of history.

Am I interrupting? he asks hesitantly, hearing a commotion around Eiríkur. No no, he'd just arrived for a band rehearsal. I'll go out, says Eiríkur, before stepping out into the alley outside, where the full moon pours its cold rays over the city. He lights a cigarette, listens to what his uncle has to say.

Skúli had got up unusually early that morning, before six. Fried an egg for Páll, who was on his way to the sea, toasted bread, made coffee. Then lay down on the couch to read Bulgakov's *The Master and Margarita*, which had been one of Hafrún's favourite books, but which Skúli had never read. Páll ate breakfast and smiled heartily when he heard his father laughing on the couch.

It was growing dark by the time Páll returned, and Skúli was still lying comfortably on the couch, the book open on his chest, the coffee so cold in the cup on the coffee table that he'd likely been dead for a few hours. At noon he'd made a Spanish egg dish for Halldór, whistling so happily to himself as he did that Halldór sent Páll a text message: "I think that Dad's coming back to us :)" Then the older son went out to the recording studio, immersed himself in his projects, suspected nothing.

And he was laughing? Eiríkur asked, looking down at his burning cigarette.

Yes, heartily. I was so glad to hear it. But I think Dad laughed, and then whistled over the egg dish, because he'd already decided to die today. Admittedly, I hardly believe that anyone can make such a decision, except, of course, if it means suicide. Still, I think Dad did. He was in good health. You remember. But his heart just seemed to stop beating. Yes, I think that Dad decided to die today. That's why he woke up so early to make breakfast for me, and then an omelette for Dóri. And that's why he could laugh so heartily over his book. He knew he would meet Mum that night, and laughed with the joy of looking forward to it.

ONLY FIFTEEN PER CENT LIFE

Behind everything, Skúli once said to Eiríkur as they lay together beneath the attic window, is some gigantic force that man has probably always sensed. A silent, invisible, mysterious force that we've either called God or fate – but these two, we've always had difficulty telling apart. But whatever that force is called, it seems to power all life. The big as well as the small. The life of man and the earthworm. The life of the Earth and the Milky Way. It powers the solar systems, it powers the galaxies and it probably surrounds the universe.

We all disappear into it eventually, my grandma told my dad – and now I'm telling you. We disappear into it, merge with it and become one with it. Do we completely cease to exist, then, I asked my dad worriedly, finding it a horrible thought that all of us, my mum, dad, my sisters and I, would simply cease to exist and merge without a trace with some invisible force that powers everything. To me, it sounded like a horrible nightmare. Of course, I worded the question differently, I was a child, asked my questions and came to my conclusions as a child. I probably asked whether the children who die never get to play again, whether they're never sung to again or read stories. Whether you never get to see your parents, siblings or friends again. Yes, whether everyone just ceases to exist because they turn into rays of sunshine, raindrops, or air.

And what did Grandpa say?

He laughed and said that he'd asked his mother similar questions. And that she'd also laughed and said that probably no scientist should present a theory without checking it with children first. But I know that they both often thought about this mysterious force, and I think they believed that our lives here and now, our thoughts and actions, have a constant effect on it in one way or another. And consequently, human beings, whether they like it or not, are not only responsible for themselves and their lives, but for the whole world. Or in other words – the world shapes us and we shape it with our behaviour and lives. And not just that, because what you do on this side will be waiting for you on the other side in one way or another. Do you understand, boy?

Not then, but I think I understand it now, said Eiríkur, about a quarter of a century later, over his grandfather's coffin, which stood for a day and night in the living room so that the three of them, Eiríkur, Palli and Halldór could all say goodbye to him, each in his own way. Which they did. Páll sat half the night by his father's coffin, told him why his relationship with the fisherman's widow in Keflavík hadn't worked out and about his relationship with Elías; Halldór also sat by the coffin for a long time, saying less but playing many of Skúli's favourite songs on the guitar and humming along.

I think I understand it now, said Eiríkur. And thank you for making the world more beautiful. Tell Grandma I miss her terribly.

Tell her I'll always be sad around eleven on Saturday mornings, when you used to call me. Tell her that I'm so sorry, and that I'm afraid I'll never be able to forgive myself for how, for a while, first in Reykjavík, then in Paris, I sometimes got angry, irritated, at those phone calls. At just knowing they were coming. Yes, for a time I was ashamed of you. I found all the news from the fjord, about farming and your everyday life, rustic. I found you rustic, Grandpa, and felt embarrassed when Grandma quoted something in English from books or song lyrics. Her pronunciation was so rough that it was like English was stones in her mouth. Four times, I just let the phone ring. Pretended not to hear it. And never called back. Yet I knew that it made you sad. Still, I was afraid you knew why. It hurts me, Grandpa, it hurts. I still remember the dates, all four times. They're burned into my memory. But I probably convinced myself that later on I would have the opportunity to make up for it. I think that people can be overly eager to convince themselves that later, they can . . . that later it'll be possible to . . . But Grandpa, sometimes that later never comes. And we pay for it the rest of our lives. Hardest of all is not being able to forgive yourself. But I dreamed so often of having you visit me. Dreamed of showing you Paris, taking you to my favourite places. I knew that you would enjoy sitting outside a café just watching life stream by, knew that Grandma would love to go to the museums and then sit under a parasol in the Luxembourg Gardens, sip chilled white wine, read a book, you with a cold beer, maybe, you teasing her a little bit and the city buzzing with life all around.

And I looked forward to introducing you to Tove. I was so incredibly proud of her and convinced that you would like her. But it wasn't possible. You weren't allowed to meet her. I was too cowardly to tell you the truth, that she was married and could not, dared not, did not have the resolve to leave her husband. For four years, Grandpa, I lived in two worlds. On the one hand, there was the one with Tove, a world that very few people knew about, yet which was the one that controlled everything. On the other hand, there was the world in which I lived in plain sight, in which I paid taxes and bills – the everyday world. For four years, everything there was at a standstill. Paralysed.

All plans put on hold because my and Tove's existence, the one that no-one must know about, had taken over my life. In the eyes of those friends and acquaintances who didn't know it, it was as if some invisible force had paralysed me, and many of them worried about me, of course. Some urged me to see a psychologist. Others to cut back on my drinking. I agreed to everything, but did nothing, except immerse myself in work, seek refuge in my music. But what do you talk about when you can't talk about what matters? When you're not allowed to talk about your love, what does that do to you? I wanted so much to tell everyone about the love that seemed to free me from the sadness that has been like a constant buzz inside of me for as long as I remember. Sadness because of Mum, and because of being unable to connect with Dad. The two are intertwined, and always have been.

And then there was my guilt when I felt your and Grandma's disappointment or sadness at my relationship with Dad. Or lack of a relationship. When I was a child, I blamed myself for it. That I just wasn't fun enough, diligent enough, smart enough, quick enough to learn the songs he assigned me, or didn't play them well enough. Now, of course, I know better. I know that it was, and still is, both of our faults. I don't know how to describe it, but something inside us just freezes up when we're together and it's only through music that we've managed to connect almost effortlessly. Until I was a teenager, it was enough for us to listen to something we both enjoyed. Usually music that Dad introduced to me, and I was so incredibly happy to enjoy the same music as him . . . so happy to . . . But later, in my teens, when I began to discover and make connections to music on my own, I unfortunately closed that channel. Poor Dad had probably been looking forward to getting to . . . know me through the music I liked. Maybe the music would have opened up something between us, lowered the barriers and made everything easier for all of us. But I failed. I just couldn't. I didn't want to let him in. I wanted a world that he didn't know. I was evasive when he asked what I was listening to. Oh, Grandpa, why does life have to be so damned complicated, all these knots! "We need boards and we need a saw/we need paint and lively songs."

I was so happy when Dad and Palli made me an able seaman on the *St Mary*, was convinced that everything would then be fine, no more barriers between me and Dad. I felt as if he'd invited me to join his band, that now I was one of his friends. But the next day it was the same distance and the same barriers, some as high as the highest heaths, lashed by fierce, dark storms. Later I realised that the bottle of red wine that Dad had brought with him on our fishing trip, and of which he'd drunk a good portion, had played no small part in making him so wonderfully ingenuous and relaxed . . . I think, Grandpa, that over time I realised that I couldn't confide my feelings to Dad. Of course, I knew that . . . the disconnect between me and Dad saddened you and Grandma, and it made me so genuinely glad to see you so happy when Dad and I played together on Christmas Day here in the living room. The only time there was real harmony between us? Yes, probably, unfortunately, after I reached adolescence. I was so glad, if not blessed, to witness your joy. Blessed but also sad, because I knew that behind that moment, disappointment awaited us all. When everything went back to normal. But Grandpa, am I not more responsible for this situation than Dad? You know how he is, has always been. He can be a real charmer, but can't stick things out. You can't trust him. And, you know – you can't tell Grandma that! – but I was nervous about introducing Tove to Dad. I really looked forward to introducing her to you two, dreamed of it constantly, but filled with anxiety when I thought of Dad. I think I was just as afraid that I would be embarrassed by him as that she would fall under his spell. How complicated life can be, Grandpa! Oh, if only you'd met Tove! If only you and Grandma could have seen us together, because then you would have seen me happy, smiling, laughing, under no shadow. I dreamed of bringing her here, but couldn't. I couldn't betray Tove, put her and her family's world in danger. I couldn't even invite you to visit. Or else I convinced myself that I couldn't. That it would be much better next year because then everything would have come out in the open and Tove and I would have had nothing to hide, then . . . My God, how sorry I am!

But Grandpa, do you remember when we sat together for days

over Vera Rubin's book on dark matter, and discovered that this dark matter constitutes about eighty-five per cent of all the matter in the universe? That most of the substance of the universe is completely invisible, and that no-one has been able to explain its existence properly. I remember how enthusiastic you were and wondered if the dark matter wasn't the force that your dad and my great-grandma talked about. But eighty-five per cent of the world is invisible; that's precisely how my life had become! Eighty-five per cent hidden from the world. Only fifteen per cent of me lived in the everyday world, just enough to do laundry, cook simple meals, watch football matches, but not much more. I was incapable of doing things in an organised way, and it was only in music that I felt fully alive. And then of course with Tove. Grandpa, we were so happy together! But that happiness was also doing us in. It paralysed our lives. We neglected everything but love. Tove neglected her children, her husband, of course, her friends; I neglected my friends – and you. You might also say that we've neglected life, which must be considered one of the deadly sins. But that's why, Grandpa, I didn't come home during the last few years of your and Grandma's lives. That's why I failed you. That's why I pretended not to notice any changes when Grandma got sick. How her energy dwindled. I was probably just relieved when she stopped calling and settled for writing me emails. Few things are as selfish as love. It takes possession of you. It's like a drug. It can turn people into slaves. Especially the love that can't be seen. Then it turns into the dark matter that rules the world. I failed you both. I'm not sure it's forgivable. And that's why I can never come back to live here.

FATE IS STRANGER THAN KINDNESS

So many people are dead, yet life just goes on, no matter who and how many die. It goes on undisturbed, as if nothing had happened. It doesn't care about fairness or justice. Because they're all dead: Hafrún, Skúli, Aldís, Margrét, Jón, Hulda, little Agnes, and Eva, the daughter of Pétur and Halla. And more, many more; for remember:

Guðríður "steps out and everyone is dead".

Which means that she's dead. And Pétur. And Halla, who had hands of light. And Gísli, and his and Guðríður's daughters. Björgvin and Steinunn are dead. As is their son in Canada, despite having been in business with death. They're all gone. There can't be many more left. The brightest lights go out. That's how it is; you die but life goes on, undisturbed and acting as if you never existed. It never stops, not for a split second, no matter who dies, no matter how many die, but goes on unstoppably, perfectly indifferent, and we're forced to chase after it, forced to leave the fallen behind, we abandon them, we leave them behind so we can chase after life. And life is constantly on the run from death, yet is always running towards it. It's the paradox that governs everything. Which means that fate isn't just socks from Paris, a flat tyre, Guðríður's smile, and Búðardalur, but first and last this paradox.

First and last, repeats the sanctified coach driver. But yes, fate is certainly also the heel of Aldís's shoe hitting Rúna in the eye, Pétur announcing the arrest of Émile Zola, Jón rolling over on his back and choking on his own vomit, and Chet Baker falling out of a window in Amsterdam with no Eiríkur nearby to catch him. It's Svana handing Eiríkur over the kitchen table, fate is having a dead mother and inadvertently thinking of her when you masturbate for the first time, it's being unable to bond with others because . . .

. . . I hunch over the pages in the hope of escaping my intrusive and sometimes aggressive companion. I hunch over them and see me and Rúna wave to Lúna and Dísa on the front steps at Hof and Védís, Dísa's daughter, trying to teach the dog a new TikTok dance in the farmyard; but how many days, weeks, if not months will it take us to drive past Hof and finally make it to the hotel? Let alone the party that Eiríkur and Elías are holding in honour of life, Presley and Páll . . . Oh, that's right, Páll is also dead. Remember, lying under a heavy rock and Kierkegaard's words in the churchyard out at Nes. And Presley, he's dead, but everyone knows that. No-one wants to miss this party,

Sóley had told me; and no-one will be turned away. I have a suspicion, she said, that some people will travel long distances to be there.

Long distances? Very long, even?

The party is in honour of Páll, Presley and life, and they're both dead. Does that mean, in other words, that it's in honour of life and the dead? And that the guests are coming from both of those places, both of those continents? Maybe Guðríður herself is on her way with her smile, and then presumably Pétur, too, to explain to us why Émile Zola was arrested? Will Ólafur the Impassive and his wife Kristín, the frigate, come, will Hulda wipe the vomit off Jón's face, lift him to his feet and bring him with her to the party, and, oh, Eva, the apple of her father's eye, will she get to come, too, finally get to return to the sunshine, even leading little Agnes, who has longed and looked forward for eighty years to run into her brother Skúli's arms; who will surely come, too, along with Hafrún, and Aldís will bring her mother and mother-in-law with her and pour the latter a sherry – who knows, maybe Hölderlin will get to watch the party from the slope above, he who is able to console with loneliness?

So is that it, the real explanation for Death's playlist, the list we continue to inch our way along; is that list not just Eiríkur's way of consoling death but also to come to an agreement with it about opening its gate tonight in this fjord that's shaped like an embrace? Fate is the author of everything, it says somewhere, and if it's fate that has summoned the living and the dead to a dinner party here, for an evening together, then fate is probably stranger than kindness.

A wonderful song, says Rúna, when "Stranger than Kindness", by Eiríkur's half-brother, Nick Cave, sounds in the car, and we of course put the song immediately on Death's playlist.

The priest, who conceivably has his PCV licence so that he can drive Fate itself, refills his shot glass. He has finished half the whisky bottle, keeps it for himself but pushes a cup of black, hot coffee over to me. Love makes some people slaves, he says, which is fine, and likely true. But Eiríkur says to his grandfather, "I failed you both. And in doing

336

so, I failed life. I'm not sure it's forgivable. And that's why I can never come back to live here." Yet a few years later, he's still here in the fjord. Does that mean he found forgiveness, and could therefore return? Few things are as beautiful as forgiveness. It and love are the left and right arms of Christ. But if it was the forgiveness that allowed Eiríkur to return, why did he fire a shotgun at a lorry, is he on his way to prison, does he live alone, why did he seem to look like a thin, dark string of sadness when we saw him in the farmyard this morning, with the guitar on his back; is forgiveness not bigger than that?

I sigh softly. Take the cup of coffee, sigh because I thought I was on my way west to Snæfellsnes, to Guðríður in the doctor's house in Stykkishólmur. Pétur has just announced that Émile Zola is to be arrested; I want to know what happens next.

I'm not stopping you, says my companion. You can go where you want. I won't get in your way.

I look down at the pages. Skúli has been buried and life goes on as if he never existed. I see that Eiríkur returns to Marseille. That he lives there. In that city that is getting ever hotter, as if hell is approaching. He makes a living playing musical instruments, composing advertising jingles, lives alone in his small apartment and misses Tove. I see him becoming a regular at an Arab restaurant, playing chess with the owner, watching Liverpool compete in the Champions League with his sons, I see a tall woman with eyes that are as dark or dangerous as the desert night, but I don't know the nature of their relationship, if they actually have one. But then he's standing over two suitcases in the farmyard at Oddi, probably three years ago, with no-one there to welcome him but the August night and a one-eyed cat.

I'm not stopping you, said the sanctified coach driver, as he pushed the coffee towards me.

I'm not stopping you.

Obviously, this man's words are as unreliable as the paradox in which we live. Didn't I smell sulphur on his fingers?

I don't seem to have much control here.

Sometimes You Lie and Betray
Because of Love

ALMOST EVERYONE IS DEAD, YET HERE THERE ARE NO LETTERS OF THE ALPHABET THAT BARK LIKE DOGS

Eiríkur returned to the fjord one night around midnight after his long exile down south in France, summoned there by his father, Halldór. It was growing dark, the August twilights were deepening, and the stillness seemed to breathe in the darkness between the stars.

I had forgotten that such deep stillness could exist, Eiríkur thought in the farmyard outside the unpainted house, with the two suitcases at his feet and the cooling car engine making popping noises.

He'd forgotten the stillness, and also, in fact, that the night sky sometimes appears so close here that it's as if it's part of the country-side and thereby nearer to humankind than elsewhere.

Eiríkur lifted the heavy suitcases, stepped in, set them down in the vestibule, and greeted the old one-eyed cat, which came walking stiffly, mewing, from inside the house; two of the ill-tempered chickens had gouged out one of its eyes when it was a kitten. Eiríkur knelt down, petted the cat, and won its trust immediately. He'd thought of starting by going throughout the house to greet it, but was so overwhelmed with emotion in the vestibule that he didn't get further than the kitchen, where he sank into a chair at the old kitchen table, upon which was a wooden bowl full of small apples and stacks of foreign music magazines. He sat there motionless for a long time, distractedly petting the cat in his lap, his dark hair hanging down over his brown eyes. He must have dozed off, exhausted after his trip and all that had been going on in his life lately, but opened his eyes when the cat mewed softly to ask him to continue his petting. Which he did, tilting his head to read the front page of the magazine *Jazz*

Journal, which was lying on top of the stack, and saw that it had an article about the album *Chet Baker Sings*, from 1954; an album that was one of the soundtracks of Eiríkur's youth and that he knew inside out. Anything new in the article? he thought, just as he was going to reach for the magazine, gently, so as not to disturb the cat, but then he noticed an old A4-sized envelope lying under the stack. What's this, Eiríkur muttered, pulling the envelope over to him. It was unmarked and had once been taped shut, but the tape had long since dried out and hung like a withered memory from the open flap. Probably something to do with the farm, he thought, some old documents or papers that Halldór and Páll have been looking at for fun; maybe old records on the livestock, the names of the sheep, their health statuses, how many lambs they bore this or that year; or else yellowed household accounts, which could be fun to look at, because they could be like a time machine – a journey into the lands of memories and over the landscape of years gone by.

This will be fun, Eiríkur thought, sticking his hand in the envelope and pulling out a letter that Hafrún had addressed to him on the evening of October 7, 1980, when Eiríkur was only about three months old. A three-page letter, along with his birth certificate. There you sleep, she writes.

Eiríkur had to read the letter twice to let its contents sift all the way in. Until he managed to grasp the fact that his whole life had to a certain extent been based on a lie. There you sleep.

Three pages filled with Hafrún's small, staid handwriting, written at that same kitchen table, which had of course been in the old house, a few hours after Eiríkur was handed over it. She wrote the letter with her elbows propped on the table, tilting her head as she did, concentrating, weighing each word, describing the visit and his mother; her appearance and the streaks and flashes of personality she'd glimpsed in the younger woman during that short but fateful visit. Mentioned her ardent love for Halldór, and that about the glass of water.

Three pages, staidly written. No letters that barked like dogs. On the contrary, they're all mannerly – but warmth and affection stream between the lines. Flow like a great, tranquil river underneath the sentences. While the exhausted Eiríkur sleeps in Skúli's warm embrace:

There you sleep, exhausted in an unfair world, missing your mother whom you'll probably never meet. You're a beautiful child, with that strange but charming space between your eyes. Like your father, like your grandfather who is holding you now. And I understand that your great-great-grandmother, Guðríður, had it as well. Sometimes I feel as if that space harbours a third eye, and I often tell your grandfather that he hypnotised me with that damned third eye when he was brought here to this fjord by the postman. He was only seven years old then, while I was almost nine, and I couldn't forgive him for making me fall for him, two years younger than me. How silly of me. I don't know when you'll read this, my sweet boy, or what the world will look like then. I just know that the future will always be very different from what we imagine. But I beg you to forgive me, forgive us all, your grandfather, your father and uncle, for having decided not to tell you the truth. It's difficult to make a conscious decision to lie, and few things are further from my nature. But life bends us as it wills, and then that is the only right way, we have no other choice. Of this I'm certain, and I have little more to say about it.

A three-page letter in which she addresses Eiríkur both as a sleeping infant in Skúli's arms and then as a full-grown man in the future, newly returned from a long exile and everyone is dead. Or almost everyone. Eiríkur opens the envelope, he reads the letter and discovers the lie about his origin.

SOMETIMES YOU LIE BECAUSE YOU LOVE

How does a man of almost forty react upon discovering that his life has been based on a lie? That everyone around him lied to him from the start, that the people he cared for most, who protected him and enwrapped him in their warmth and love, had lied to him from birth,

343

or, in other words, the world in which he lived had in a certain sense never existed – how does he react, how does he deal with it; does this perhaps explain why he got drunk, fired at the lorries and is on his way to prison, because his life was based on a lie, never existed?

How did he react?

He placed the cat gently on the chair beside him, got up, took a bottle of Calvados from one of his suitcases, fetched a glass, poured himself a double, downed it, and closed his eyes as the strong apple liqueur flowed through his veins and all the way down to his stomach. Then he walked throughout the house that he'd never been in before. He hadn't been to the fjord since Skúli died. Why should he have come? Was there any reason for it after the old house burned down? Hadn't that fire been a message, a declaration that his youth was burned up, that there was nothing awaiting him here – but disappointment?

Yet he has come back, and is now looking over the new house for the first time. Páll's room is warm, as he expected, very neat, every-thing in its place; photographs of several philosophers on the walls, the Beatles, Bach and van Gogh, three books on the bedside table and reading glasses on top; selected poetry of Cavafy in Norwegian, *Siden jeg ikke kan tale om min kjærlighet* (*Since I Can't Talk about My Love*). Halldór's room is more chaotic – also to be expected. A pile of books on the bedside table, photographs of Eiríkur, Skúli and Hafrún, black and white photos of life in the countryside half a century ago, a painting by Georg Guðni. One of the house's four bedrooms is obviously his. The brothers had bought a double bed but his old desk was there, photos of his grandmother and grandfather, of himself with the sisters at Nes – they'd even hung up his hammock: "So you can dream in mid-air." They'd furnished the room as if Eiríkur lived there and had just stepped out. He ran his hand over his old desk, looked at the photos, the books that they'd arranged neatly on three shelves; he felt like lying in the hammock, letting it rock him, comfort him – most of all, he wanted to lie there and cry. But he hurried out of the room, fearing that he wouldn't have the strength to get out of the hammock if he lay down in it; he wanted to keep

344

looking around. Find something that could help him understand. Letters, papers, photos, or just something that could knock a hole into the world that for some reason had been kept from him. Something that would . . . yes, why not, bring him his mother who hadn't died, then, but lived, and was possibly still alive.

He ended up in front of the big, old living-room cabinet, built with driftwood by Skúli in the first year of his and Hafrún's marriage, and there found a stack of his father's diaries; the first entry in November, a month after Eiríkur came to the fjord. He was astonished. That his father had had the patience to keep a diary, and, yes, had dared to do so. Eight diaries in two stacks. But when Eiríkur took them from the cabinet, he discovered some letters addressed to him from Halldór, letters that had never been sent. The first had been written the same evening as the first letter that Halldór sent to his son in Marseille.

Oh, there's so much I need and long to tell you!

Eiríkur sat down at the kitchen table, poured himself another Calvados, arranged the diaries and letters in front of him in chrono logical order, and began to read. He only skimmed many of the diary entries, though, feeling as if he hardly had any right to read them while still searching for what might possibly help him understand; he read to find explanations. Read all the entries he found that had to do with his mother, read about the recent journey of the brothers out west to Snæfellsnes, where they visited their grandfather and grandmother's graves before going up to Uppsalir and standing for a long time over the ruins of the farm. He read, and little by little, his father's world opened up to him. Sat at the kitchen table over which he'd been handed just over forty years ago, read, felt his father's heartbeat, his regret, his sadness, self-pity, self-incrimination, but also read descriptions of everyday life and happy times. Finished his reading in the early morning, leaned forward, and fell asleep on the table around the time that the household at Skarð fetched the cows for their milking. Through his sleep, he heard the cows' mooing; it carried easily across the nearly two kilometres to the farm in the morning calm.

But the first letter he read that night, and also the oldest . . . yes, we can probably call it *The Letter Under the Baler*.

THE LETTER UNDER THE BALER.

OR: EXPLANATIONS FOR CHICKENS' ILL TEMPERS

I didn't want to bother you at sea, Hafrún had said to her older son when he came home after spending the herring season on a trawler based in Siglufjörður, about three weeks after Eiríkur was handed over the kitchen table and said goodbye to in a few words about a glass of water in the future. I didn't want to bother you at sea, it wouldn't have changed anything. Fate had spoken and we can't change its pronouncements. But it may be in our power to adapt to them.

She showed him the birth certificate and the letter she'd written to Eiríkur, addressed to the future. Afterwards, she'd sealed the envelope with the tape that had turned yellow and dried by the time Eiríkur opened it almost four decades later.

I don't know, and will of course never know, Halldór wrote in *The Letter under the Baler*, if we reacted in the right way, made the right decision, or just accepted Mum's decision – sometimes I feel as if the choice paralysed me in some way. Disconnected something. Which is an ugly thing to say, because you came into our lives and were our constant happiness. On the other hand, I understand your mother and respect her difficult decision. She's the most beautiful, best and most charming person I've ever known. I fear that my life ever since has been little but longing for her and for the world in which I never got to live. In which we never got to live together. I think, fear, that the main reason why I haven't yet been able to settle down with a woman is that I was always trying to find your mother in other women. Which could hardly have ended well . . . nor did it. You saw her once. Do you remember it? She came to the farm when you were seven or eight years old, asked for a glass of water, as she had promised to do. She had called from Hólmavík, so we knew that she was on her way, and it was arranged that you and no-one but you brought her the glass of water. I was going to keep – and should have kept! – my distance because nothing should spoil the moment for her. Do you remember it? We two were in the recording studio. I was working on editing my interviews with the elderly brother and sister who lived alone at Reykjanes; I recall that their farm was abandoned one or two years later. They were so old that it was hard to imagine how they managed to keep the farm running; they had around fifty sheep, two cows and twenty chickens. Ágúst was worn down and completely toothless, and Árelía so round-shouldered that she was beginning to resemble an upside-down "u" and had those two big warts on her face, riddled with coarse, black hairs. You went there with me once but were so scared of Árelía that you refused to go in the house! But I was working on editing the interviews with them, which was a lot of material, you hanging over me, when your grandmother came to get you.

I was going to keep away, of course, not jeopardise anything, but as it turned out I wasn't strong enough; it wasn't long before I slunk out and crawled under the baler, which was about fifty metres away from the house. I lay there unseen, watching everything through binoculars. Those were my best moments in my life. Rarely have I been so sad.

But I could do nothing. I was bound by the arrangement. Bound by punishment for the recklessness of my youth. To have dealt with love so carelessly. Even before I met your mother, I had hurt too many people in my selfishness, my egocentrism, acting as if I thought one could live without responsibility. That one should always and unhesitatingly follow what my father once called the magnetic needle of the heart. I don't know where he got that, or if that blessed needle even exists. But in those years I was just so in love with life that I found it completely obvious that I should follow that magnetic needle – anything else would be sheer betrayal of myself and my existence. Anything else would be cowardice, capitulation. I still have a certain sympathy for that opinion, or vision, but there's so much more. The heart is perhaps wise in its own way, and it can probably only tell the truth. It's beautiful, but I've learned that life can't always bear that truth.

It's evening here in the fjord. You know, I'm enjoying sitting here at the kitchen table, writing to you and playing my music – right now it's Bill Evans. I'm enjoying it because I almost feel as if we two are sitting here together, as if you're with me and we're just chatting, as people do, as families do, as fathers and sons should do. But it can be difficult, looking up and seeing the empty chair facing me. Then reality slaps me. Bro and I miss you. You should see how much we did to decorate your room, especially Palli. I know he lies in the hammock sometimes, takes naps there. He doesn't talk about it, but yes, he misses you a lot. Our greatest grief is to have lost you. Or that's how we feel sometimes. Years have passed since we saw you. Your emails are sporadic, and don't ever actually tell us much about your life. We don't know how you feel, how your heart beats. We do know, however, thanks to the sisters at Nes, that you live quite comfortably, and that there are people around you who care about you. But you must know that we don't blame you. We failed you, it's no more complicated than that. Or, I failed you. Not Palli. He has never failed anyone. He's incapable of it.

But where was I?

Yes, under the baler. And I couldn't do anything. Strictly speaking, I wasn't supposed to watch, either. But I can tell you that even if the punishment had amounted to a thousand years in the worst place in hell, I couldn't have resisted the temptation to watch, unseen. Watch that first and unfortunately only meeting of yours with your mother. Watch your mother's face as you approached her with that glass and your long, black hair. You forbade your grandmother to cut it after you saw a photo of the members of Led Zeppelin in *Rolling Stone* – to which I had a subscription. You'd heard Haraldur and Aldís say great things about that group, and that was all it took – you've been a fan of them ever since. But do you remember, Eiríkur, the moment when brought out the glass and the stranger was waiting for you by her car – do you remember the woman? Do you remember how I then tried, awkwardly, I'm afraid, naturally having trouble hiding the quiver in my voice, to find out whether you'd felt anything? Didn't you notice that she never took her eyes off you? Not even as she drank from the glass. I never suspected it was possible to take a drink from a glass of water so gracefully. I didn't know that just seeing a person drink from a glass of water could make me cry. Did you notice how she held the glass, with both hands, tightly?

I remember how cold the ground was underneath the baler. I remember wishing that your mother would lose her self-control. I mean, that she would fail to hold back her feelings, which I knew were simmering, roiling beneath her quiet, calm exterior. I wished she would take you in her arms and hug you. That she would hold tightly to what she must have missed every single moment since life forced her to leave you in your grandmother's arms. I wished, and thought that then I could come out from under the baler! Then I would dash over to you and everything would be good and beautiful and we would always be together. But fate is apparently little given to writing such scenes, because your mother, of course, kept her composure, her quiet poise. She finished drinking the water, held the empty glass between her hands for a moment. I imagine that she'd wanted to let all of her love and longing for you flow from her palms into the glass before handing it back to you. I saw her looking at you. I saw her smile and then hand you the glass, which you took. She looked at you once more, said something, then turned around, got in the car, started it, drove off and out of our lives. Only then could I come out from under the baler. With my binoculars. And whether you believe it or not, I haven't dared to look through those binoculars ever since – I simply bought myself a new pair. I like to imagine that the old ones preserve that one moment in which we were all together, in a certain sense.

I don't know if there's life after death. Frankly, I know nothing about death. And maybe I don't know much more about life. But when the time comes, I want to be buried in the churchyard out here at Nes, alongside my mum and dad. And all I ask is that the binoculars be put with me in the coffin. I know it's completely illogic-al, but the thought gives me some comfort. Completely illogical. It's true. But that's just fine, because I think that both love and happiness are fundamentally illogical. I imagine they're like music that one doesn't try to understand, but just enjoys and experiences. And I would like to add, by the way, that when I'm dead, though after many years, hopefully, many good years with you always within earshot and surrounded by a lively group of grandchildren, that when I'm dead and in my place in the soil out at Nes, I would really like it if you would, preferably on my birthday, though all depending on the weather, which has ruled everything in this country ever since it was settled – I would really like it if you would play ten or fifteen songs over my grave. Make sure the equipment is good and turn up the volume loud enough for the music to carry for sure over the border. Half of the songs can be ones that I know. I'll include a list at the end of this letter; I'll put together a list of about two hundred songs, so you'll have enough to work with. Then you can choose the other half yourself, though I'd much prefer if they were written after my day. That's what I'm most dissatisfied with, or fear the most, that death won't just cut us off from life, but also from music, and that you miss out on all the songs that'll be written after your life is over. Can you imagine a blacker injustice?

Eiríkur, the contents of my bottle have diminished alarmingly and it's time to stop, before I become embarrassingly sentimental. I also need to start writing the song list for myself and death – which will be fun! And it's been wonderful to sit here at the kitchen table and write this letter, along with the other one, which I'll post tomorrow. The tone of that letter might give you a start. Namely, I decided not to hold back any longer and wrote freely, unhindered. I think it's the best way for me to reach you. By following the magnetic needle of the heart? Maybe. I've decided, at least, to follow it in my life, and it's about time. But you know, I suspect that that rascal cat, the one-eyed pirate, got into the bottle, because it looks to me as if he's busy composing a love poem for the chickens and is going to recite it to them tomorrow. Even if it costs him his other eye. I actually think that chickens have something against literature, which is why they're so ill-tempered.

Interlude: the Big Picture, Responsibility and a Burning House

My love, now everything will be fine, Jón muttered, because he'd just discovered that life will always be bigger than death, and tossed aside the bottle because he who knows this and seeks eternity has no need to drink anymore. My love, he muttered, and rolled over onto his back to see the sky better. You should always, his mother Guðríður had said, raise your eyes to the sky where life and beauty reign. Set your sights by the sky rather than man, and then you'll be big. I'm big now, Mum, he thought, rolling over onto his back and choking on his own vomit. That's why the postman brought Skúli to the fjord. That's why Svana handed Eiríkur over the kitchen table to Hafrún. But now she is dead. I can't live without her. Her name is Hafrún, and that will be her name for ever; death can't change that. I don't know how it will go.

Can fish swim if they're deprived of water? Is it worth it for the Earth to keep turning if the sun goes out? Those of you who are still alive must answer this for me. For that moment, my love, I will live. You should write about that smile, Pétur had said in a letter to Hölderlin, who replied, I have long since done so: You smiled, and now I no longer know if I dare to exist.

Is that a poem?

Yes, unless it's a life, which sometimes amounts to the same thing. And written by the blind poet of the soil.

Life or the poem?

Same thing.

So you have learned something, says the sanctified coach driver, turning on the radio, which has suddenly become so big that it was nearly the size of a solar system and, because of it, plays for the entire universe. Plays "Blue in Green" by Miles Davis and Bill Evans.

If I dared, I would call the earthworm the thought of God. Please try to judge my effort rather than the result. Excuse my presumption. I know that every person should know his place. But who decides that place?

Can you hear it? Pétur mutters to Hölderlin when he reads the letter from her, in which certain letters of the alphabet, particularly the F, the R, and probably the Þ can start barking like dogs; which is why Skúli was brought to the fjord by the postman, why his coffin was lowered into the open wound of the churchyard out at Nes. We closed it with our bereavement. They're going to arrest Émile Zola, which is why Halldór carried the furnishings out of the old house before he set it on fire. Oh, the old house burned down, Halldór wrote to Eiríkur. Palli and I, however, managed to save most if not all of what was left in it.

Managed to save everything from a burning wooden house – it must have burned slowly, Eiríkur thought; he had his suspicions but asked nothing. Unfortunately, he was perhaps most deeply grateful to his father for ensuring that he no longer had any reason for returning to the fjord. His youth had gone up in smoke, and is lying in the churchyard at Nes.

Apparently, Kierkegaard means "churchyard".

Eiríkur: Like the churchyard out at Nes?

Exactly, like the churchyard out at Nes. The poor man was called "churchyard" – what a heavy burden to bear! A name full of death, crosses and dead people. No wonder the man was a little down sometimes.

And no wonder we're a little down right now – so many people have died here, it's your fault.

Mine? I exclaim, looking up into the blue eyes of the sanctified coach driver, the only eye colour that's allowed in hell, which is why he can drive his coach through it; is it my fault that people have died? Am I responsible for the deaths of Hafrún and Skúli, Eva and Agnes, am I responsible . . .

Isn't this your writing? he asks, pointing a long finger at the scrawled-over pages in front of me, the messy handwriting.

Yes, unfortunately. But that doesn't mean I'm responsible for their deaths.

You're writing, you're responsible, who else should be?

So who are you?

Strange question from someone who has no idea who he himself is. Remember the old saying: Find yourself before you go looking for others! But you're right, Guðríður sends a letter and an article to the journal, Pétur comes to visit on his horse Ljúf. I know your name, says Gísli when Pétur introduces himself. I've heard about you. To what do we owe the honour of this visit? Might he then have been able to answer: To make it possible to bury Skúli next to his Hafrún in a hundred and ten years?

That answer would have been absurd.

For those who are confined to the details, yes, certainly. But perfectly logical for those who know the big picture. But Halldór burns down the old house where happiness had dwelt, its attic was a smile over the countryside, and life always smiled back when it passed through the fjord. I'm not sure it's forgivable, to burn down a house, why did he do that? Nor is failing others forgivable. As they both did, Halldór and Eiríkur, and consequently, are cursed.

Cursed, that's a pretty harsh word. Let's not forget that until the age of forty, Eiríkur believed that his mother died because of him, and that he was to a certain extent responsible for Halldór's sadness, and therefore his drinking, too; and that it was therefore his fault that they had such trouble being close – especially after he orgasmed over the cover photo of his mother. The only time they connected afterwards was in the living room at home at Oddi, when Hafrún got them to play a few songs together. They felt good, then. Halldór was so happy that he had a hard time refraining from smiling all the time. "Ashes to Ashes" became their song, they played it the last three Christmases, you should have heard their voices, I´m happy, hope you're happy too . . . They're not cursed, but unhappy. And Eiríkur . . .

Watched his grandfather's coffin being lowered into the grave.

Halldór set the house on fire. How will they be able to talk to each other now that Hafrún and Skúli are gone? Eiríkur returned to Marseille after his grandfather's funeral, but came to the fjord three or four years later, with two heavy suitcases; a one-eyed cat and an empty house welcomed him, why was that, what has happened? Elías and the others are going to hold a party for the living and the dead, and then Eiríkur might go to prison, the punishment can be up to twelve years. The dogs will all be dead when he gets out. It isn't enough for you to kill people, you've also started on the dogs. This can't go well. Unless you manage to change something.

Worlds Merge

A RUSTY TRACTOR SENDS A LETTER. WHAT MIGHT THAT MEAN?
". . . it's been wonderful to sit here at the kitchen table and write this letter, along with the other one, which I'll post tomorrow," wrote Halldór to his son in the *Letter under the Baler*. "The tone of that letter might give you a start. Namely, I decided not to hold back any longer and wrote freely, unhindered. I think it's the best way for me to reach you."

It's the best way for me to reach you – which has clearly been the case, because Eiríkur returns with two suitcases, a one-eyed cat greets him with its mewing and hopeless love for chickens. A cat, an empty house, the absence of the brothers and Eiríkur discovers, at nearly forty years of age, that his greatest grief, actually the tragedy of his life, was based on . . . a misunderstanding. If not a downright lie? Unless, on the contrary, it was the courage needed to make a painful but necessary decision?

The letter, the first one, which Halldór sent to Eiríkur in Marseille, is waiting for him in the mailbox when he's on his way out. He is startled when he sees who it's from, but then sticks it hurriedly in his backpack, he's already quite late, his band is booked into a studio to record a few advertising jingles that he'd been asked to compose for a radio station in the city. A project that should have been finished by midday, but Eiríkur is so distracted because of the letter that they only finish at dinner time, and instead of reading it at home in his small apartment, he chooses to go to the Arab–Italian restaurant that he's been frequenting in recent months, run by a husband and wife, their three children and daughters-in-law. The host, Ekram, is a short, slender Jordanian, with small, dark eyes that shine with enthusiasm, while his wife, Melania, is Italian, more than a head taller than her husband, reminding Eiríkur of the tall Sophia Loren; she wears colourful, beautiful dresses, imposing, loud, and warm. And although the food is always good, it was in fact the cheerful and homely atmosphere that Eiríkur fell for; so homely that it evoked memories of the kitchen at home at Oddi. About half of the customers are regulars whom the family treats as friends, even sitting down with them to chat over a glass of wine – the couple's sons, twins, short, like Ekram, with the same gleam of enthusiasm in their eyes, have taken Eiríkur with them several times to the bar next door to the restaurant to watch Liverpool, their team, compete in the Champions League.

A warm evening, his usual table on the square outside the restaurant empty and Ekram seems to understand that Eiríkur wants to be left alone, waves his grandchildren off the square, wordlessly brings him a big, ice-cold, dark Leffe, pats him on the shoulder and slips away. Eiríkur drinks the beer, regards the envelope with the neatly written address – although in some of the letters, there is a tremor, a bit as if they're stuttering; Halldór has wrestled with trembling hands in recent years. Probably because, thinks Eiríkur, lighting a cigarette, they never manage to sober up entirely.

He smokes, drinks his beer, looks at the envelope.

Their exchanges have been sporadic ever since Halldór drove his sixteen-year-old son south for junior college, and Morrissey desperately asked to be touched. Months can pass without Eiríkur hearing from his father, and he feels no need to break that silence. But almost a year ago, emails suddenly began to stream from Halldór. Admittedly, they were only about everyday events and occurrences in the fjord and the lives of the brothers, but Eiríkur sensed that something unspoken lay just below the surface, and suspected that the emails were Halldór's attempt at rapprochement with him; that his father was waiting for some sort of signal permitting him to open up and write . . . freely. But Eiríkur remained closed. He wasn't convinced of Halldór's sincerity. Fortunately, he thought as the emails began growing longer, became more confused, often written at night when Halldór was obviously drunk, causing the sincerity to combine with sentimentality, the sentimentality to turn into self-pity, soon leading to all sorts of accusations being made, and everything was shaken together into a cocktail that Eiríkur couldn't stand, that disgusted him, in fact. And one morning after reading eight such night-time emails, he'd had enough. He answered the last one tersely and sharply: "In the future, spare me any more of your intolerable, drunken, sentimental and rambling emails! I simply can't stand them! They're humiliating to both of us!"

He immediately regretted sending this email and had difficulty concentrating all that day. He felt as if he'd committed an unforgivable act, but refused to apologise. He waited worriedly, nervously, fearfully, for an answer, expecting everything from remorseful emails to anger and accusations. But there was no answer. Not that day, not the day after. Weeks passed, months, and the silence spread out between them like an ocean – but then came the letter.

Eiríkur sighs, empties his beer glass, opens the envelope. Oddi, July 29, 2017, dear Eiríkur, a letter from the old, rusty tractor at home in Iceland, you're probably thinking, and not liking the look of it – what must it mean!?

WE'LL HAVE TO WAIT FOR YESTERDAY

Oddi, July 29, 2017. Dear Eiríkur! A letter from the old, rusty tractor at home in Iceland, you're probably thinking, and not liking the look of it – what must it mean!? Naturally, you don't like the look of it after all the emails I sent you this summer, and especially if you have the last ones in mind. Full of the blather of a drunken man. Blather, miserable sentimentality and self-pity. And now a letter! What must it mean, what brought it about?

The explanation, so to speak, lies in my dreams. Over the past five to ten years, I've repeatedly dreamed the same difficult dream, in which I come face to face with myself as a seventeen- to eighteen-year-old. It's obvious that the young man is ashamed of me and blames me bitterly for having failed him. Even having betrayed him. But when I try to defend myself and explain to the young me that life is much harder than one realises at his age, that it can easily bend the strongest individuals, I'm incapable of uttering a single word – and then he starts cutting the ties that connect us. I fill with despair, can't imagine losing him, try to say something, try to reach him but can't move a muscle, and feel my soul tearing itself from me towards the young man. I finally manage to let out a piercing cry – and usually wake up to my own commotion. The dream last night was unusually painful and I reacted so badly that Palli woke to my noise and was sitting worriedly over me when I woke up breathless and sweaty. Said he tried to wake me up, was very worried because I was moaning terribly, curled up as if I was in agony. I woke up, saw Palli and said: Now I'm writing Eiríkur a letter.

And here it is!

But first, before I started writing it, I forced myself to read over the last emails that I sent you. Ugh, what a gauntlet that was! It's so shocking to see how short the distance can be from sincerity to humiliating sentimentality and self-pity, and how painfully blind a person can be to those things in himself. And also how short a distance it can be from self-pity to the ridiculous accusations it engenders. A poison cocktail!

In any case, I made the decision last night to write you a letter. I promised both myself and Palli that I wouldn't write it under the influence of anything stronger than coffee! It's my hope, Eiríkur, that with this letter, and those that follow, if I'm allowed to send you more, that I'll be able to bridge the difficult gap and the painful silence that has been between us for so long, to my great sorrow. Few things have grieved Palli more, either. I know that he has sometimes written to you in the hope of breaching your defences somehow. Yet I want you to know that I understand and respect the fact that you have often had to resort to shutting me out. Yet it's as Palli says: We only have each other and life is far too short and strewn with thorns to push aside loved ones. I know that I haven't made the best of my life. I know that people pity me. I see and feel how they look at me, and it hurts. I know that many have practically given up on me and barely tolerate me, like some hopeless case. Some people have told me that the only solution is for me to enter treatment. But I say that each person's strength is measured by whether he can help himself or not. After all, it's not really the alcohol that's my enemy, but myself. The most important battle any person fights is the one against himself. I need to get my own house in order. I need to find the courage to face myself, both here and now, for only then can I make peace with the young man who haunts me in my dreams. Writing you a letter, Eiríkur, is supposed to be an important step in that process. I would be happy if you answered, even just in a few words, even just in message style – but I'm not asking for anything. All I hope is that you read this letter and . . . the others I would like to write to you, if you'll allow it. If you care to let me. And that you see, entirely at your own pace, reason to forgive me even slightly for how much I've failed you and all those whom I love. I'm going to try my best not to fall into the trap of apologising, but just chat with you as . . . an ordinary person about everything and nothing.

Do you remember the Tom Waits song "Yesterday is Here" off the album *Franks Wild Years*? A wonderful song, a pearl, which I've even used as a slow-dance song at countryside dances. The song has been with me since I first heard it, and maybe because I feel as if Tom Waits has summed up my life in that sad and beautiful song. As if he's describing how my life has come to a standstill.

You'll have to wait until yesterday is here: I think that could be the title of my life, unfortunately. At least for the last few years or so. Or, as bro says: You don't make a decision and are paralysed!

But enough is enough!

Eiríkur, my dearest Eiríkur, my dear son, my pride and happiness! This letter shall mark that beginning! Now I shall begin to exist again for real. Now I will become a real participant again. And do you know what I have dreamed of for many, many years? That we two sit down in peace and happiness at having each other and play the song "I'll Follow the Sun" together. That's my dream. And I suspect, no, I know, that it's entirely up to me to make that dream come true!

ONE SHOULD NEVER CONFIDE HIS LIFE TO OTHERS

Eiríkur is reading the letter for the third time when Ekram comes out to him with dinner and a carafe of red wine, even though he hasn't ordered anything. This dish, says Ekram, almost solemnly, is called mansaf. You haven't had it here before, as we prefer to keep it off the menu. Mansaf is actually the dish that is served to reconcile enemies, to win someone's heart, to delight friends, comfort those who need comforting. So it isn't something that's brought out every day. I told my Batool that you looked unusually melancholy and that she had to prepare a very special dish for you. So I'll prepare mansaf, she said. Some say that it's a dish for kings – I say that when prepared by Batool, it's a dish for gods. Perhaps my daughter means to make you a god tonight, Icelander!

Eiríkur is too distracted and upset after reading the letter that he doesn't even think to thank him, and his head doesn't clear until Ekram has served the food, poured a glass of red wine, patted him on the shoulder, and disappeared back into the restaurant.

Maybe she means to make you a god.

Ekram is an energetic man; he's talkative and lively and sometimes makes such grand statements that Eiríkur isn't always sure how much his host expects to be taken seriously. But Eiríkur is grateful for the meal; he hasn't eaten since that morning, realises that he's famished and the mansaf dish is so delicious that it manages to settle the intense emotions swirling inside him after reading the letter. Such confused, messy emotions that he simply doesn't know how he's supposed to feel.

His first reaction, however, is anger. Eiríkur thinks that Halldór is making unfair demands on him. Nor does he want to end up stuck with him.

Then he reads the letter again and his anger subsides, only to be replaced by uncertainty.

Eiríkur knows, of course, that the letter would have gladdened Hafrún and Skúli. He knows that he should – if only for them – acknowledge it. And give Halldór a chance.

But can I trust him? he thinks. If I give him my little finger, won't he tear off my whole arm? Couldn't I then expect him to start calling me at all hours, completely drunk, and make me listen to his sentimental ramblings, his self-pity, his alcoholic accusations? But don't I owe it to my grandparents to give Halldór a chance . . . or does the problem, the knot, lie maybe no less with me than with him? Might I be the young man in his dream?

He starts reading the letter for the fourth time and is just under halfway through it when he senses a change in the air. He looks up and sees Batool, the daughter of Ekram and Melania, coming out of the restaurant with a bottle of raki and two shot glasses. Three or four men at other tables instinctively straighten up and follow her with their eyes as she makes her way between the tables, tall and long-legged, like an Arabian horse, careless of her own beauty. She stops at Eiríkur's table, puts the bottle and the shot glasses on it, lays her hand on the back of the chair opposite him; may I, she asks.

He leans back, surprised.

Batool is tall, like her mother, but more delicate, and is the family member who mixes least with the customers. She occasionally comes out of the kitchen to check on her son, a cheerful five-year-old boy who often plays there near the restaurant with other children his age; it's clear that he and his mother are very close. Eiríkur has sometimes chatted with him, but has never seen any father around. Batool is always amicable if one of the customers talks to her, but there's something in her demeanour, something in her big, dark eyes, that keeps her interlocutors at a distance. Not coldness; more like haughtiness, and Eiríkur has never seen her sit down uninvited at one of the customers' tables, let alone with a bottle of strong liquor.

May I, she asks again, and Eiríkur nods. She smiles slightly, perhaps at his silence, sits down, fills the shot glasses, pushes one over to him, raises the other, tilts her head gently back, and lets the strong alcohol run slowly into her mouth. Her long, black hair is tied in a bun, revealing her long, soft neck to Eiríkur.

She refills the glass, then looks at the pack of cigarettes on the table in front of Eiríkur. Oh, she says, and I quit smoking. She reaches for the pack, pulls out a cigarette, lights it, crosses her arms and leans back in her chair to smoke it in silence as Eiríkur finishes his meal.

He knows almost nothing about her. They've only spoken to each other twice before. She'd come out to check on her son and stopped at Eiríkur's table to ask him about Iceland, the country and its language. She only stopped briefly, but there was something about her that had piqued his curiosity. Something other than the beauty and charm that her careless attire couldn't hide. He finishes the dish, tries to appreciate its flavour, but is so flustered that he feels it would be best just to go home. Before he says anything foolish . . .

A wonderful dish, he says. Mansaf – to reconcile combatants or to comfort; I'll sign to that. You're a magician in the kitchen. Thank you for making it for me! And yes; all the dishes that I've eaten here!

Batool smiles. She has a beautiful smile that reaches out into her sharp facial features, though it manages only just to ripple her deep, dark eyes.

Dad said you seemed quite upset about that letter, she says with the cigarette burning between her long fingers, and he was worried about you. That's why I prepared this dish for you. I hope no-one has died.

She refills their shot glasses and he immediately drains his, in the hope that the alcohol will still the uncertainty and turmoil within him. Which are due to the letter, but perhaps also due to her presence. I need to get home, he thinks again. But I can't just leave. Not after she brought this bottle and sat down with me. I owe her an explanation, at least.

Again she refills his glass, and once again he drains it immediately. Not a good idea, shoots through Eiríkur's mind when he senses his concentration starting to slip. Stay focused, he orders himself. And it's forbidden to look into those eyes. They're so dark and deep that

366

you could easily get lost in them. I'll just tell her that the letter is from my father, then say goodbye and go.

The letter is from my father, he says, smiling and adding, I've never got a letter from him before; this is the first.

The first, he repeats.

The first letter.

I'm not asking for anything.

That's my dream.

A rusty tractor.

I've become a man that the young man inside me is ashamed of. Despises, in fact.

But it's late, and it's been nice talking with you. Very nice. Thanks again for all the meals you've made for me. You could probably change the world with your cooking. I like coming here, I feel good here. And it's fun to talk to your son. I've never seen his father – maybe he has no father?

Damn, what the hell am I on about?

Forgive me, he says, that was both stupid and inconsiderate of me!

She looks down at the tabletop. I've enjoyed cooking for you, she says, speaking slowly, as if weighing her words carefully. I've seen you and your band play in the club. You might say I was checking you out. And am beginning to believe that you are beautiful inside. But I've thought the same about other people and been wrong. You know that some people are so small and petty that they can be cruel, given the chance. But unfortunately, my little Jojo isn't the fruit of an immaculate conception. God would never look at me. Yet he has no father.

He has clearly hurt her. I've got to get home, he thinks for the third time. But because of my stupid remarks, I owe her an explanation – and after she prepared this wonderful dish for me! I owe her and her family for welcoming me so kindly night after night; they've actually provided me with a refuge. I'll tell her that I'm upset because of the letter, confused, a little drunk, and that it's best for everyone that I be alone. I can rightfully say that my relationship with Halldór is complicated, without of course going into it any further. I have no right to do so, neither regarding Halldór nor her. As Javier Marías puts it; one should never confide his life to others, because it would be unforgivable.

Eiríkur looks at her, and she looks up. Those eyes, he thinks, and suddenly feels such a deep desire to unburden himself that he starts speaking before he knows it, and can't stop. He practically starts mid-sentence. Or mid-thought. As if this woman knows the story, the context.

I've failed those I love. I'm sorry, I have no right to tell you this. But I failed my grandmother, I failed my grandfather. They raised me. They were my parents, and I wasn't with them when they died, which is painful, it hurts, yet what's worse is that I was far from them while they were alive. I've loved. But it's over now. Yet it's not over, not inside me. Now I belong to loss, and that will always be the case. This all has to do with dark matter. And with living just fifteen per cent, which is just enough to wash socks, drink beer and fail those you love. And now only Dad and I are left, and Uncle Palli. Palli is a giant. I would say he's as big as the moon. A bright and beautiful soul, but sometimes I think fate uses him as a harp to play the blues. God Lord, how I miss him! I've also failed him. You become paralysed and you fail those you love. Palli is a fisherman and holds a doctorate in Kierkegaard. The name means churchyard. You're faced with two choices, Kierkegaard said, both of which will fill you with regret, choose neither and you change into fifteen-per-cent life. I think Palli is the most beautiful human being I know. He stutters, sometimes so much that it's as if life is trying to silence him.

Your mum? he hears Batool ask. And he answers immediately, she's dead because I was born. That was the deal, life for death, and I'm still paying that bill. We're both paying it, Dad and I.

Who has now written you a letter?

Yes, who could have expected that? But when I was a child, Eiríkur hears himself say, I dreamed of becoming my dad's best friend. Being the one he wanted to have with him in a band, yet I always felt uneasy and anxious when he tried to be sincere or wanted to hug me.

I stiffened up when he put his arms round me. That's hardly good. I'm thirty-six years old and I think we haven't hugged in thirty years. Something in him died when I was born. He drinks too much. I grew up in a fjord in the world's north, with my grandmother and grandfather who gave me all their love but got very little in return. Dad was like the migratory birds in Iceland; he came in the spring, left in the autumn. Apart from that, was seen sporadically. I don't really know what his life was like. But I think or fear that I never realised which feeling was stronger in me, the anxiety or the anticipation, when we were expecting him home. I always felt like I needed to prove myself to him. That I had to be fun, smart, but at the same time make sure I didn't tire him out, didn't annoy him by my presence. There was nothing I longed for more than his approval.

Dad is an accomplished guitarist, played in bands when he was younger, I think he still plays today. But every time he went away, as he always did to work in the south, east, west, at sea, in construction, many months of absence ahead, he would choose a song that I was supposed to learn on the guitar and play for him when he returned. I remember the first song was "I'll Follow the Sun" by the Beatles, a wonderful gem written by McCartney. I was only seven years old and practised as if I were possessed, knew the tune perfectly and the lyrics to a "t" by the time he returned. But as soon as I saw him step out of the car in the farmyard at home I became so stressed and anxious that I withdrew into my shell and my stomach turned into a heavy rock. Dad put me on the kitchen table, and I started playing. I did pretty well, I think, my fingers knew the song after tireless rehearsals, but I was so frightened that I nearly fainted from stress, forgot the lyrics almost completely and sang over and over again, in my thin, broken child's voice, the few words I remembered: And now the time has gone, and so, my love, I must go. I don't think anyone noticed how I felt; maybe no-one expected me to know the song properly, a seven-year-old kid. Dad, however, was overjoyed. He took me in his arms and, before I knew it, I was behind the wheel of his cool car, got to drive it all the way up to the school, which is about half a kilometre from the farm, take laps in the car park there until Dad was certain that enough people had seen us. And the other kids hardly talked about anything else over the next few days, and the boys were terribly jealous of me for having got to drive a car and for having such an awesome dad. But no-one longed more than me to have the dad they thought he was.

A FEW WORDS ABOUT THE COLUMN OF TEARS,
AND HOW HIGH IT CAN REACH

Oh, this doesn't sound good, I say, looking quickly in the direction of the sanctified coach driver. Quickly and questioningly – did he already know about it when earlier, I described how Eiríkur played "I'll Follow the Sun" up on the kitchen table at Oddi, how he'd picked the simple, poignantly beautiful melody and sung "over and over again the only lines he had managed to learn"? Did he know then of Eiríkur's angst, his non-stop practising, how he'd really felt, but still let me recount those things in such a way that they must be missing . . . their end? And kept it to himself in order to savour his superiority over me? I take a quick look at him but read nothing in his lined face, those damned blue eyes, and, once more, uncertainty grips me.

I look back down at the pages; I want to know what happens next, how Eiríkur reacts to the letter, how he deals with the effects that it has on him; and what happens between him and Batool, with her dark eyes – I look down at the pages, but then Marseille is gone and Eiríkur has just put on the song "Mosaïque solitaire" – Solitary Mosaic – by the Belgio-Congolese musician Damso, for Elías; and the mournful but aggressive composition sounds over the fjord's surface, which is so still that it resembles happiness.

Je pleure que de l'intérieur pour que mes soucis se noient.

My French is so rusty, says Elías, that I'm having trouble understanding the lyrics – what's he saying about tears?

I cry solely on the inside, says Eiríkur, because in that way I can drown my sorrows.

Elías: I thought so. Not a bad line, and it reminds me of those unforgettable lines from a poem by Werner Aspenström: "How high does the column of tears inside you reach? / Up to your navel? Chest? Up to your neck?"

Eiríkur: A good poem by an important poet.

You know, young man, says Elías, looking over the fjord, nothing of life on Earth can be seen from the moon, and most of us are such incredibly short-lived news in geological history that in a hundred years no-one will remember us, all traces of us will have vanished. Yet it can be bloody hard for a person to exist. Bloody hard. You know how much I miss him.

I know, says Eiríkur. I miss him, too.

For a long time, however, I believed, says Elías, that time would slowly deaden my most painful longing. I was convinced of it, that's how it has to be, that's the way we survive – yet my sense of loss and regret are just as painful as they were three years ago. Did you know that I talk to him every day, usually starting as soon as I wake up? Well, Palli, I say, barely out of bed myself, now it's time for coffee! Oh, Palli, would you mind maybe feeding the cats while I make it? Of course, I don't know if he hears me. I don't know how far our words carry. Some days I fear that they carry only as short a distance as life, and that I do little other with this rambling of mine than feed my bereavement. Feed and fatten it. Still, I carry on. Still, I can do nothing but carry on.

We owe it to all of them to do so, to carry on, says Eiríkur, laying his hand over the long, slender back of the old professor's, where the veins branch out like a blue river. He lays it there softly, presses firmly, presses warmly and adds: We'll help each other to do so, to carry on. Something very good will happen soon. I'm sure of it.

Then something inside Elías breaks and silent tears flow from the corners of his eyes, they stream down his thin, smooth-shaven cheeks.

How high does the column of tears inside you reach?

Je pleure que de l'intérieur . . .

. . . *pour que mes soucis se noient*. I think Eiríkur taught us all, me, dad, the sisters, Dísa and Elías, to listen to rap, says Rúna when we stop in the hotel car park, step out and Damso's song fills us like a dark, majestic bird. I look over at Oddi, where the outline of the old farmstead can still be seen. The brothers cleaned up carefully after the fire, although they wanted vestiges of the old farm to remain, and the ruins face us like a scar in the landscape.

Why did Halldór burn down the old house, I ask Rúna. Was it falling apart?

Rúna, who had been watching the cheerful Japanese tourists with a smile as they splashed, shouted and laughed in the warm pool, comes up next to me.

Falling apart, she says, built by Skúli and maintained by love, absolutely not! But Halldór gave no explanation, she adds. Mum, however, was so angry about it that she didn't say a word to him for weeks, while poor Dad squirmed anxiously in the silence between them. I was in the United States when it happened, but Dad says that Halldór tried to convince him that the memory of his parents and their happiness was so overwhelming in the old house that it paralysed him; and therefore drove him to drink more. I think he even managed to convince himself that it would help him find his balance in life and get him back on track if he built his own house and burned down the old one. Sheer irrationality, of course, and self-deception.

And it burned to the ground?

Yes, it went right up. After all, memories make excellent fuel for fires. Oh, it was difficult for everyone. Palli wanted to keep living in the old house, but in the end he gave in to his brother's nonsense. Let him decide. I think he didn't have the stamina to stand up to Halldór, all his energy went into living, waiting, and hoping, and . . . but, yes, the brothers emptied the old house, they stored the furniture for which there was no room in the new one in the barn. Some pieces of furniture are memories, said Halldór, and you can't just get rid of them. Which, of course, is absolutely true. But it can't be said that it ended well.

Maybe nothing ends well, crosses my mind as Rúna walks over to the hotel, where her sister is standing on the pavement outside the lobby, chatting with the Canadian couple. The man, tall and with such a big, protruding belly that it's as if he has swallowed a small whale, is beaming and laughing merrily at something that Sóley is saying, and his wife, thickset, with a mild, warm aura, laughs with him. The sisters look smilingly at the couple. Rúna a little shorter, darker, resembling a minor note next to her sister with her bright, infectious energy. And that smile that has such an effect on me that I turn round and close my eyes as quickly as possible, perhaps in the hope that my mysterious companion will tap the whisky bottle, yank me back inside the caravan that I can see clearly from here in front of the hotel, tell me what fate has in store for us, explain to me where words stop, and then send me back – into the past. Then I can escape. Because when she smiles, something happens that I don't understand.

You smile, and because of it, I long to live.
      You smiled, and now I no longer know if I dare to exist.

HE DOESN'T KNOW WHO ÉMILE ZOLA IS AND BECAUSE OF IT LOSES HIS TREASURE, THAT MUST BE THE PRICE

Is that a poem, Pétur asked Hölderlin as he rides towards Stykkishólmur on his mare Ljúf – a few hours later, he steps into the drawing room of the doctor's house and announces that the bastards are going to arrest Émile Zola!

Guðríður's heart beats so hard when Pétur comes in and charms everyone with his presence and enthusiasm that she fears it will carry over the high heaths all the way home to Uppsalir, home to Gísli. Which it absolutely must not do. He mustn't hear how her heart beats. She looks at Pétur and thinks, Gísli doesn't know who Émile Zola is.
      Which is true. He doesn't know who Émile Zola is. And may not even have heard of the Dreyfus affair.

373

Gísli doesn't like reading, either. It takes time away from work, and, besides, is generally boring. Oh, yes, he can be needlessly surly, but once he stole something, possibly solely to see Guðríður smile at him as she alone can smile.

Isn't that beautiful in its own way, even a kind of love poem?

Stole something to see her smile. Stole because he has always feared losing her. Possibly so much that it was one of the reasons why he wanted to move to the heath back in the day, contrary to most people's advice.

Perhaps the main reason, in fact?

So it wasn't a stubborn desire for independence that drove him up there, as everyone thought, and even gave him credit for, in a certain way, but his fear of losing Guðríður; the incessant struggle in harsh conditions up on the heath was his great love poem to Guðríður?

Good question. But now almost twenty years have passed.

And Gísli is sitting in a manger in a sheep shed while Guðríður is in Stykkishólmur, attending a fine dinner party in the company of intellectuals.

She left this morning. She sat her horse so well. It was delightful to see. There she goes, then, the housewife, Sigrún had said behind Gísli.

Diligent Sigrún. She'd come to them yesterday. Sent by his mother, Steinunn.

Of course, Gísli had suspected, in fact known, when Doctor Ólafur wrote to Guðríður this summer and invited her to the meeting of the editorial board in Stykkishólmur in September, that if she left his mother would send Sigrún to them. He immediately began looking forward to having her up there on the heath, and his anticipation eventually grew so great that sometimes he lay there awake next to Guðríður while recalling how Sigrún had slowly removed her nightgown and then turned around so that . . .

The anticipation of experiencing this again had been like a constant itch for two months, dulling or pushing aside his anxiety over Guðríður spending all that time out in Stykkishólmur – knowing that she would be there among educated men, that priest being one of them. He looked so forward to seeing Sigrún undress at night and thought again and again about how he would lie in bed and pretend to sleep as she did so, after the girls were asleep. Looked forward to seeing her expose her big, heavy breasts, then slowly bend forward so that her buttocks parted, and . . . he in bed, fondling his rock-hard penis, aroused at the thought that Sigrún would wake up and hear his suppressed moans . . .

And now she is here!

And is waiting for him inside. He knows that. That she's waiting. He saw how she looked at him over dinner. Which is why he fled here to the sheep shed and hardly dares to go back in the house!

Because the simple, obvious, stark fact faced him, when he felt Sigrún's fiery gaze upon him, that if he were to give in to his desires he would betray Guðríður. It was impossible to interpret it differently. And then he would lose her. That must be the case. The Almighty would then see to it that something terrible happened. He who betrays deserves little good. He loses his treasure, that must be the price. That must be the fee. Which is why he doesn't dare go back inside the house.

I close my eyes and see Gísli in the sheep shed, see that his shoulders are starting to quiver. I close my eyes and see Halla at Pétur's desk in his office, where every little thing reminds her of him. Reminds her of the man she still loves as passionately as when their lives intertwined a good twenty years ago. The man she can't stop loving.

I love you, Pétur, she had said when he set out that morning.

He'd been standing next to Ljúf and was clearly looking forward to the trip. He held the reins and in his eyes was that charming gleam that she could once so easily evoke, and which makes him wonderfully boyish-looking.

I love you, Pétur, she had said. Said it so softly that it was as if she wasn't allowed to say it anymore, and then hugged him tightly, held him in her arms for a long time. She wanted to say so much, yet longed even more for him to say something to her. Longed for him to say her name. And that he loved her. Because then she would no longer need to be afraid. As she has been afraid for many years. She hugged him tightly, whispered his name, and he stroked her back. Almost as if he were stroking a horse. Then she swallowed and released him. Pétur mounted Ljúf and she said his name again, unable to restrain herself. Said it imploringly, and that sensitive look came over his face. She saw his lips move.

She listens to the farmhand singing lullabies to her girls on the other side of the partition. She knows that the younger maid is lying close by with her eyes closed, enjoying listening. I need to write a letter, Halla had said before fleeing into the office to be alone. Listens to the singing and before she knows it, the tears have started to flow. They run silently down her beautiful face, hang for a moment helplessly, dejectedly from her delicate chin before plunging onto her blouse. My love, she whispers at the desk. Reaches for the jumper that Pétur has left next to the chair, holds it up to her nose, inhales its scent, breathes it in, and cries so hard that it can be heard throughout the house.

I open my eyes, look over the fjord, hear Halla's bitter crying within me and fear that it's not in my power to comfort her. Fear that life can be so unfair that sometimes no consolation is to be found. That sometimes there's no other way for a person than to cry and take the pain – in the faint hope that she or he will survive it.

. . . SCARED TO SAY I LOVE YOU – AND WORLDS MERGE

Is it quite certain that he's innocent, this Dreyfus? asks Ólafur the Impassive, looking at Pétur with a smile.

Well, says Pétur, innocent, who is completely innocent, can a person ever be perfectly innocent, or, who doesn't bear some sort of guilt? But where does that guilt begin, in thought or action, and is there any major difference between them? And then there is this: what one person considers guilt, even an unforgivable crime, another sees as the courage to do wrong in order to keep life from suffocating.

Suffocating like . . . like a blind earthworm in the soil, he concludes, raising the glass that the young maid had brought him and gathering courage to look directly at Guðríður, whom he hasn't seen since he rode away from Uppsalir on Ljúf. But then she was in her environment, an uneducated housewife in a cottage on the heath; now she is in the luxurious home of Steinunn and Ólafur. Now she'll be put in a completely different context, and it isn't at all certain that it will suit her.

It isn't at all certain, he'd told Hölderlin on the way out to Stykkishólmur, that it will be to her advantage.

Do you mean, asked Hölderlin, that it will not suit her to be taken out of her normal context – that moving her between worlds, from that of the indigent and poorly educated to that of the wealthy and learned, would demean her?

Doubtless. I expect so. I'm a bit uneasy. Quite uneasy, in fact. Be careful, I said to Halla. That's how I said goodbye to her this morning. I believe Halla is the best and most beautiful person I've ever known. I owe her everything. Once upon a time, I loved her passionately. Without her, I would hardly exist. I saw that she was fighting back tears and knew well what I should say, knew well what she longed to hear. Yet all I said was that: be careful! Careful in what? She asks for love, asks for comfort, a hug, I stroke her back like a horse and then tell her to be careful! Am I some sort of monster?

Is it courage or cowardice to love, asked Hölderlin, are you weak or strong if you manage to suffocate love, are you selfish or pure if you follow your heart?

I'm asking you for help, not questions!

I'm dead and my role is to ask. You're alive, and it's yours to seek answers.

With a smile, Pétur raises his glass, makes his remark about the earthworm and then looks at Guðríður as she sits, thin, hunched, rustic and grey, in the big Danish armchair. He's safe!

What a relief!

No, unfortunately that's not the case.

Because she isn't thin, but slender. And not at all rustic.

And sits upright, straight-backed, sits so nobly and of course has to be more beautiful than he wished to remember. More beautiful than he dared to remember. He curses Hölderlin, makes his remark about the earthworm, and raises his glass to her. Don't smile, he asks silently, you mustn't smile, I . . .

. . . I'm not sure I can bear it, I think, opening my eyes and turning around in the hotel's car park. There are still a few Japanese people laughing in the pool, but I see that others have gone to pick juicy blueberries on the slope above the hotel. The sisters, the bright and the dark, are still talking outside the hotel door, but the Canadian couple have disappeared. Then Sóley goes in. With her slender back, her bright, infectious energy. Goes in without looking at me, and I'm safe. That is, until she has to go and hesitate for a moment at the door, as if having remembered something, then she looks round, looks over her shoulder at me – and smiles. And it turns out to be her forbidden smile, the one that seems to change everything around it. She smiles and the gods impose a curfew. She smiles, and I have to rewrite everything, she smiles and Hölderlin mutters: Life becomes death, death becomes life, and worlds merge.

She smiles, goes in.

I see her slender back disappear, and at the same time a plaintive piano begins to sound from within me. Or else from Death's playlist. I no longer distinguish between the two; now worlds conjoin. Plaintive notes and then the voice is added, bright yet broken and pained: I'm scared to say I love you, afraid to let you know.

From where I'm standing in the car park, it's only a few steps to the hotel door. Why don't I just go in there, take hold of her narrow shoulders and say what has been said so many times before in this world, by so many, in all the languages of the world? The only words that never seem to wear out. If I say them, something will happen. If I say them, I'll remember everything.

*

378

I love you, Pétur. I can't stop loving you. Don't leave me, don't abandon me, my love, I'm so scared, because how can I live if you've stopped loving me?

Be careful, says Pétur, and he rides away.

Once Gísli stole, once he committed a crime, it was his love poem, and now he's sitting in the sheep shed and doesn't dare go back in the house.

And Zola is to be arrested!

Has anyone else sat so upright in the history of mankind, or wept so bitterly at her husband's desk? Pétur rides away, Gísli remains seated in the manger, Halla cries, Guðríður sits upright but Sóley disappears into the hotel, I watch her disappear as the song continues playing, as it resounds between solar systems, between universes, That simplest of words, won't come out of my mouth . . .

Yes, I know, I know, I mutter at the pages, the messy handwriting, making sure not to look up at the sanctified coach driver standing at the window facing the hotel and watching me from there. I know that I must put my love aside, even if it seems to be the only thing remaining in me from a previous life; and possibly the only thing that could lead me back. But maybe that love must be like the song "Scared", it must be hidden – it must be a *hidden track*. I stare down at the pages and see all this: Pétur rides away, Halla cries, I see that Gísli doesn't dare to stand up, and I see that Guðríður is sitting so nobly that Pétur is probably done for.

The space between universes is precisely this.

And it's also the song "Scared", the space is a *hidden track*.

The space is failing, crying over a desk a hundred and twenty years ago. The space between universes is deciding not to empty yourself into a sock, it's raising a glass to guilt, courage, blind poets, the space is drinking too much, the space is the letters that were never written, or never sent, the space is the first letter that Halldór sent to Eiríkur in Marseille.

The space is the pain of losing you.

The space is the pain of losing what will never be.

379

ON BETRAYAL, ON WHAT WE DON'T UNDERSTAND AND
THE DIFFICULTY OF CHOOSING THE RIGHT MUSIC
It's fine to miss someone, but you also have to live.

Eiríkur had said all of this to Batool, things that he would never have confessed to any living person; and now the time has come, and so, my love, I must go. Yet no-one wanted more than me to have the dad they thought he was.

He said everything he couldn't say. Batool sat there quietly for a moment after he finally fell silent and stared straight ahead, pensively. Then she stubbed out her cigarette, got up, and went back into the restaurant. Without saying goodbye. Left him there with the bottle and himself. Of course, he thought, I went way too far! I should have paid better attention to Marías, who has translated Shakespeare and written such thick, excellent novels that he must know a thing or two.

Eiríkur sticks the letter in his backpack, takes out a collection of poems by Jorge Luis Borges, and reads three poems, trying in that way, to compose himself before going in to pay, but he is so dissatisfied with himself, his mind in such an uproar, that he's unable to focus. He empties his glass of wine, gets up. Knows that he'll never come here again. That he has lost this refuge. He who opens himself to strangers no longer has any place of refuge, he's vulnerable and the world strikes out at him.

He gets up to go in and pay, but smiles with deep-felt happiness when he sees Batool walk out of the restaurant towards him – and then they are at his place. It just happened.

Thank you for telling me all of this, she said when she came out again. It touched me, it was beautiful. You were generous, because I don't think you're used to opening up in this way. Don't worry, it won't go any further. Everyone needs to open up at some point. Tell about his life. Otherwise, you turn to stone. I'll walk you home, she added. Or announced it, rather. As if he needed protection. Or that they needed each other. And he thought, for some reason having become perfectly serene; whatever happens, happens.

And it happened.

They go to his place.

To the small apartment that no woman had entered before. Except Tove, and the apartment seems embarrassed, seems not to know how it should be. Tove had last come just over a year ago, and had spent the night. Which was their last night together. I will always love you, she had said. But I can no longer live like this. I can't leave my husband. I can't, I mustn't destroy his life and therefore do damage to the lives of my children. I've got to choose, and I choose the option that will hurt only the two of us. Forgive me. I see no other way. But I will always miss you. You will always be in my heart.

Always in my heart. Locked there. Permanently.

And now Batool is standing next to the couch, in the same place where Tove stood when she said those things and locked him in her heart. Stands there, tall, long-legged, with her long black hair tied in a bun, filling the apartment with her presence. He's so happy to have her there, but also afraid. Afraid of falling for her. And in doing so, betraying Tove. Betraying . . . his pain at losing her. In another universe, he thinks, in another life, I would have longed to sleep with her. But in this one, I can't. I mustn't. How can I convey that?

He opens a bottle of red wine, which is good because then his hands have something to do. She looks around the small living room, takes its measure, takes the measure of his life, the three bookshelves, the high quality audio equipment, the wall of records and CDs. But for the longest time, she looks at the big aerial photograph of the fjord hanging over the couch. Are you from there? she asks. He nods. It's very beautiful, and shaped like an embrace, she says. Does it hug you or hold you captive?

I'm not sure I know the difference, he says, pouring two glasses of wine and handing her one, then reaching for the remote control. He has neither the quietude nor the focus to choose an album or CD, so he lets Spotify take care of it. Of course he'd forgotten what song he'd been listening to that morning, and it starts playing now at the point where he'd switched off the system: "Love Sick". The song that seems to have been written about his pain at losing Tove.

Sorry, but would you mind if I change songs?

She shrugs, almost imperceptibly, this is your home, she says.

I'm sick of love, I wish I'd never met you, sings Dylan.

I've probably listened to it too many times, he hears himself say, apologetically, and adds, because he's already told her practically everything: Sometimes I feel as if Dylan wrote this song about me.

What's her name? Batool asks.

Whose?

The one you keep thinking about so much that it's impossible to reach you.

He smiles apologetically: is it so obvious? Is it written on me? Well, I can tell you her name, that's innocent enough, you hardly know her. Her name is Tove. All Danish women are named Tove. Sorry, he adds, unsure of whether he's asking Batool, Tove or Dylan for forgiveness; he raises the remote to change tracks, but the song ends and of course it's Billie Holiday, queen of the blues, who has to be next up. Her voice is so raspy that in it, both Eiríkur and Batool sense the end, the dark, final end. I'm a fool to want you, ... to seek a kiss not mine alone.

Eiríkur is standing in the middle of the room with the remote in one hand, the glass of wine in the other; a dark lock of hair has come loose and is hanging down his temple like a dark string. He raises his arms, drunk from all the shots, vulnerable after opening up as he did, and says, as if in surrender: I'm sorry, but here you'll probably find nothing but heartache.

Then Batool puts down her glass, goes over to him, and says: I have nothing against heartache, it's beautiful. And it's fine to miss someone, but you also have to live.

MAY I BIND YOU?

She stands right up against him, barely five inches shorter than him. He feels the warmth of her body, breathes in her scent, sweet, warm, spicy. It's been too long since he has stood so close to a woman. He fights the urge to lean forward to nibble at her beautiful neck, and feels his cock harden. It happens so fast that he can't stop it. She feels it and something changes in her gaze, something he doesn't understand. I'm sorry, he says, it just happened, I can't help it. That wasn't my intention. Sorry.

Do you mean, she asks, that you didn't want it to happen?

I don't know, he says frankly, looking into her dark eyes, dark and dizzyingly deep, and blurts out: Whom did you kiss, God or the devil, to get such eyes?

I'm a fool to want you, Billie sings, pity me, I need you, I know it's wrong.

You asked, she says, seemingly unperturbed by his stupid question, whether my son had a father. He's the most beautiful and best thing I have ever had. What I have loved most, most intensely and deeply. He is my purpose in life, yet came to me through hatred. No, he has no father. He was conceived in hatred, contempt, violence. Maybe it was the devil, because he doesn't make the same demands as God. Maybe that's why I have these eyes now. I didn't know it was so hard to live.

She runs her long fingers hesitantly down his arm, then moves her own arm up, strokes Eiríkur's cheek with the back of her hand, his ears and the nape of his neck with her fingers, as if examining him, taking his measure. I've been thinking about you, she says, since you first came to the restaurant and we didn't know whether you were a poet or a rock star on the run from life. I asked my brothers to find out who you were, and I've come four times to listen to you play. I wanted to know how you were on the inside. Still, there are many things that I don't understand yet. I've prepared thirty-eight meals for you, maybe trying to seduce you with every single dish. I think I want you because you're sad. I want to fuck you because I believe that you're not dangerous, certainly not evil, because I believe that you're good, sad and lost. I want you because I believe that you love another woman and therefore cannot love me. I want you because I'm almost certain that you would never hurt me.

She strokes his face, strokes his lips, leans forward, lays her soft, broad lips loosely against his and whispers, may I bind you?

And did he let her bind him? Did he have ropes or cords long enough, or did he have to go and borrow some from his neighbours: sorry, my name is Eric, I live here on the fourth floor, we've met sometimes here in the stairwell, do you have any ropes I could use? I have a woman visiting, she's as tall as an Arabian horse, with eyes as dark and deep as the desert night itself. To share a kiss that the devil has known – I suspect she's had the devil himself as a lover and now it's my turn, which is intense, if not incredible. I suspect that her spine has a curve more beautiful than Salvador Dalí could have drawn, suspect that her breasts could start a war, and that Christ himself couldn't have stopped looking at them and entertaining thoughts that could never have been included in the Sermon on the Mount. And she wants to bind me. I haven't tried that, have hardly ever considered it, but I admit that it's an exciting thought, to let myself be taken in that way, let her fuck me like that. God, hopefully you have ropes! I haven't been so excited since I masturbated over the autobiography of a prostitute a quarter of a century ago. I'm so eager for her to take me that I . . .

Are you finished, I ask, upon putting down my pencil and looking in surprise at the coach driver. Surprised at this . . . eruption of his, half-expecting him to have transformed into the Evil One himself, or at least to have put back on the silly shorts and music-idol T-shirt that befit his sex-laden monologue; maybe a picture of the Stones before they turned into smoked mummies, of Rihanna singing "Sex With Me". But he's still in his dark outfit, and his lined face with its reddish beard and eyes that open the gates of hell and have therefore seen everything, contrast drastically with what he's been saying.

Are you finished? I ask. He doesn't seem to be listening and just looks out the window, as if he'd never said anything. Looks up at the hotel, watches Rúna and me as we wait on a bench next to the sun-baked wall. She has just told me that Sóley has made arrangements for the Japanese group to have a beautiful dinner buffet to which they can help themselves, which will allow all three of them, she and the

Syrian sisters, to attend the party in honour of life, Elvis and Páll. Rúna only mentions the three of them, she and the sisters, and not Ómar, almost as if he's evaporated, as if I'd managed to write him out of this universe, and why not? – much the same has happened in the history of mankind, in which one contradiction propels the next. So what if a character disappears without a trace from a story? He who seeks reality, finds fiction. He who seeks fiction finds himself. He who seeks himself can move between universes.

I look down at the pages, read:

I CHOSE YOU BECAUSE YOU ARE LEAVING
Eiríkur let her bind him.

May I bind you? she asked, and he hesitated but then nodded and said, yes, because I trust you.

Using power cords, she tied his hands and feet to the kitchen chair. Cut his clothes off, removed her own and he thought, now I've seen beauty. Then she stood over him and looked down at his penis. At that erect, hard organ that has done so many unspeakably ugly and cruel things in history but that now quivered defencelessly, pleadingly, on its docile beast of burden, and such a peculiar look came over her face that for a moment Eiríkur feared that she was going to go and get the knife that she'd used to cut off his clothes and slice off his penis. But then she grabbed him tightly by the hair, yanked his head back, looked deep into his eyes as she lowered herself onto his penis, and said, I forbid you to close your eyes. And then she began to fuck him. Fucked him slowly but determinedly, almost angrily, almost harshly, her long fingers gripping his hair so tightly that he couldn't move his head.

Then she untied his hands and left.

So did the days pass. He wasn't allowed to come to the restaurant, but she brought him meals late in the evenings, watched him eat, then tied him to the chair or bed and took him. Fucked him hard, even violently. Three nights passed in this way. He let her decide, let her control. He sensed something terribly fragile inside this proud woman and didn't want to ruin anything, longed to get closer to her, to be allowed to hold her in his arms, and, for this reason, he let her take charge. But in his bliss, he whispered her name, and on the fourth night he was allowed to kiss her; on the fifth she said his name when she orgasmed, on the sixth she stopped binding him, and after that they always made love on the couch, under the big photo she was so fond of. She said that she was fascinated by its blend of naked beauty, gentleness and harshness. I'll make you something to eat, she said, and, in return, you can tell me about your fjord. Tell me how it's possible to live in a place where, as you claim, the temperature doesn't go above seventeen degrees in midsummer, and the winters are so long and dark that it's as if the world is dead.

And for the first time in many years, Eiríkur wanted to talk about the fjord. He was filled with a burning desire to convince her, and perhaps himself at the same time, that it was his fjord, that it was a place worth living in.

He began by describing what he had never stopped missing: the stillness, the birdsong, the fresh smell of the sea, dark winter nights, such starry winter skies over the fjord that they seemed closer to the ground than anywhere else on Earth. And then he told her about the people. At first it was stories from the distant past, stories he knew well through Halldór's research and interviews and reading the *Strandir Courier* as a child at home at Oddi.

Your eyes shine so beautifully when you talk about your fjord, said Batool, that the sadness disappears from them. Keep going, don't stop!

And he kept going, told it all, moving slowly but surely closer to his own time, closer to himself. Felt that he wanted to, longed to. Told about Kári and Margrét, about Aldís and Haraldur who discovered that fate is blown tyres, that it's Dylan and Cohen in a red Zetor. Batool enjoyed both of those stories so much that she wanted to hear them every night.

And he told about his grandmother and grandfather.

Grandpa came like a parcel, brought by the postman.

He told about his eighth birthday, if you're sour, be sweet. He even recounted how he masturbated over the book *When Hope Alone Remains* while thinking of his mother. And finally he read her the letter from Halldór, first in Icelandic, and then translated into French.

Have you answered it? she asked.

No, he hadn't been able to. I don't know how to write a letter to Halldór.

Why do you call him Halldór and not Dad?

Because he's much more "Halldór" than my father. I sent him an email, thanked him for the letter; surely that's enough.

What did you say in the email?

Thanks for the letter. It came as a surprise. But it made me happy.

Nothing else?

Nothing else? It took me an hour to write that!

Read the letter again, she asked. Which he did, and she said, you'll get another letter because you sent him that email.

Which is what happened. Another letter came. Halldór was obviously extremely happy to have received a response to his letter, so much so that Eiríkur was moved, it brought tears to his eyes; and then, before he knew it, he'd written a long letter in reply.

The next night, he read both letters to Batool. She lay silently beside him for a long time after they made love, and he read her the letters. She seemed sad, ran her fingers through his hair, ran her long ring finger along his slender body. These are beautiful letters, she finally said. They're so beautiful that now we can let each other go. I want you to know that I chose you because you're kind, fragile and sensitive, because I wanted to hold you and because you were kind to my boy. Because when you play music, something inside me cries, and because I knew you were leaving. Now you've saved yourself by writing to your father, and that is why you must go home to your fjord. Until then, you won't be able to start living again. Go home, Icelander. Go before you lose what you have but have neglected. Go home before it's too late. Go home before something ties you down.

Marseille, August 24, 2017. What's this? I thought when I saw an envelope in my postbox a good three weeks ago. I was late for a recording session, the band and I had booked studio time to record three jingles that I'd conjured up for a local radio station, grabbed the letter, stuck it in my backpack but couldn't read it until the evening . . . and it moved me so much that I haven't actually been able to answer it, except with this brief email. It rooted in the thick sediment of my life, stirred it up so thoroughly that I couldn't see through it.

One should never confide his life to others – this is perhaps one of the darkest phrases I know, one of the saddest, yet it has been my mantra. It has been my dark sun, my dark moon, my beacon. But he who never confides his life to others turns slowly but surely into a kind of mollusc. He moves slowly through life, curled up within his shell, wraps himself around his own core – and all the important things you never talk about merge with the shell, which thickens and hardens over the years, with the result that it becomes increasingly difficult for others to reach you, and for you to draw nearer to others. The shell becomes both a defence and a prison. Do we want to live that way? Do we want to die that way?

Oh, he wrote, I would love to introduce you to the family that runs the Arab–Italian restaurant that has been my second home for half a year. I know that you would get along well with the owner, Ekram. Who says he's very happy to see me in the evenings on their little square with a glass of wine, a shot of liquor, a cigarette, reading a book. Says that since I look like a combination of Nick Cave and Johnny Depp, I'm the perfect advertisement for his establishment – and because of it, gives me a thirty per cent discount! A wonderful man! He can talk all night about Elvis Presley, his singing, recordings and life, without repeating himself; or recount in detail what are in his opinion the fifty best chess games in the history of the world. According to him, the best and most momentous one was played in the Jordanian desert many thousands of years ago, when God and the devil played for dominion over mankind. It's a good thing God won, I said. What makes you think that God won, Ekram replied . . .

But ever since your first letter came I've thought so much and then talked so much about our fjord that it has visited me in my dreams. And this morning I woke from a dream in which the fjord was sitting like some person at my kitchen table, with its stillness, its low, old mountains, the smell of the sea, the chattering of the arctic terns, the summer sounds of the snipe, the bleating on the slopes, the mooing of the cows at Skarð . . . when I went to the kitchen, it was sitting there with a cup of coffee and said: Well, Eiríkur, I've come to get you. It's time for you to come home.

And then I knew it! You and Palli can start dusting things off in my room – I'm on my way home! And you know, I'm looking forward to it. I'm really looking forward to breathing in the fjord's air, and seeing you and Palli. Dear Palli, whom I haven't hugged since Grandpa's funeral. I've never been able to tell you how much of a shock it was for me to lose him and Grandma. For many years following their deaths, I couldn't imagine returning home to the fjord. It was so terribly, terribly empty and destitute without them. I thought they simply couldn't die, and that therefore it was fine though I didn't spend time with them. Though I rarely let them know what I was up to. I thought that they were too important to die, and that I had enough time. My regret about what never was, over what never happened, is heavier than anything found under heaven.

One of the songs I play over and over again these days is "One Day" by the American rap group U.G.K. Well, well, they sing and rap; well, well, well, hello baby . . . if you got kids, show 'em you love 'em 'cause God just might call 'em home, 'cause one day they're here, and baby, the next day they're gone.

You can certainly laugh now, and shake your head, because, if I know you right, you've never been able to appreciate rap, but I've decided that the three of us, me, you and Palli, will record "One Day" in the studio, in our own way, when I come home! Three farmers up north in Strandir recording American rap music; who could have foreseen that? You know, God tends to call on people in the middle of a sentence, in the middle of a party, in the middle of happiness, in the middle of a kiss, and then it's too late to say the word that needs to be said, too late for three farmers in Strandir to record American rap music in a studio in an old barn, The next day you're gone, baby – I can't even begin to say how much I'm looking forward to hearing deep-voiced Palli utter that line . . .

. . . and now I'm going to start tying up loose ends here in Marseille. It will take time; contracts need terminating, it will be a shock for the boys in the band, but they'll understand me and be happy for me. It'll take time, but, that being said, I'm not giving myself more than four weeks. I've already booked the flight home. I really can't wait! Or as it says somewhere: "Eager anticipation is what moves people between universes."

EVERYTHING ENDS SOMETIME

It was a thick letter. Eiríkur hadn't written a longer, more continuous text since he studied in Paris, which was actually in another life. But he didn't expect a reply from Halldór, that is to say, not a letter, what with barely four weeks before he went home when he sent his – but he did actually expect a phone call or an email. The email came. And it turned out to be the last one that Halldór wrote to him abroad.

It always comes down to that, for all of us. The last one. That's the way it is.

The last kiss. The last smile. The last orgasm. The last touch. The last cup of coffee. The last song. The last letter.

A long email in which Halldór begins by thanking him for the letter that Sigga the postwoman had driven out from Hólmavík with two days before, and which had made Halldór so incredibly happy that he "felt the day turn into a smile and my arms into wings!"

The letter arrived on a Wednesday, he went to Hólmavík that Friday to buy enough groceries for the next few days and was quite proud of himself when he managed to refrain from going into the liquor shop next to the Co-op. That hadn't happened for a very long time. Yet he didn't mention it in the email. Just that he'd had to go to Hólmavík to do some grocery shopping, and was surprised to see Palli's car in the farmyard at home when he returned; he'd thought that he was at sea with Elías.

The email was mostly about Páll.

The dyslexic, stuttering expert on Søren Kierkegaard, a long-time comprehensive-school teacher in Keflavík who ended up a small-boat fisherman with Elías, the old professor of history.

A professor of history and a Master of Arts in philosophy on the same fishing boat. In the depths of Húnaflói Bay, it is considered an honour to be caught by the two of them – and they catch the fish with the highest IQs. Sorry; it was considered an honour. They've stopped fishing together. Remember, everything ends sometime. The last car ride. The last race. The last book. The last meal. The last beer. The last fishing trip.

THEN ALL FALLS SILENT, THEN ALL IS LOST
That's how it happens.

Halldór brings the bags of groceries from the Co-op inside. Palli isn't in the house and Halldór assumes that he's out in the recording studio reading *Captain Nemo's Library* by Per Olov Enquist – the fortieth novel that Páll has recorded. He'd started recording it for Hafrún when she was worn down from cancer and found it so calming and rewarding that he continued it after her death. Halldór makes four copies of his recordings, sends them to friends, here in the fjord, down to Reykjavík, to Keflavík and sometimes to Eiríkur down south in Marseille. Halldór prepares dinner and then goes to find his brother. He opens the barn door to find the old coffee table – which the brothers had put in a corner of the barn – standing there damaged in front of him. One leg has broken off it and it is slumped forward like an animal that's been shot; slumped forward onto its snout with its rear end sticking up, making it resemble the stern of a sinking ship.

With Páll hanging from the rope above it.

One leg was so weak, Halldór writes in his email to Eiríkur, that it couldn't support Páll's weight, all 130 kilos, and broke under him, with the result that the table slumped forward and Páll lost his footing.

"But he must have tried desperately to slide the table back underneath him, or the part sticking up, in the hope that he could rest his weight on it. That must have been the case because his neck was badly chafed and bruised, and the table had shifted so much that it was obvious he'd fought for his life. Besides, Palli would never have wanted to die in that way. You know what my brother was like. Nothing but consideration, nothing but tact, wouldn't hurt a fly. I just know that he would never have committed suicide. He was so sad, mournful, and I think I know why. But I also know that he didn't want to die. Maybe he wanted to prove to himself that that wasn't the way to go. Maybe he meant to stand there for a while until he was sure he wanted to live. But then the leg broke. I'm so afraid that my brother died crying, though not from fear, but from anguish over the grief he would cause us all . . ."

I HAVE KISSED *HER*

Halldór spent the night making a coffin out of the driftwood that he'd planed and thought of using to enlarge the chicken coop. But he didn't work on the coffin alone.

Your father called me late that evening, Elías would later tell Eiríkur, and told me what had happened. He was the only one who knew about my relationship with Palli. That we'd been lovers. I went immediately and we built the coffin together. But I didn't dare to tell him then that it was my fault that Palli came home early and did what he did. Because when we went out fishing that morning, I gathered my courage and told him that I wasn't strong enough for our love. I was still married to Fanney and that game of hide-and-seek, which had gone on too long, was very difficult for both Palli and me. I said that I couldn't take it anymore. And said that I had to choose to continue with Fanney. That it was my duty. Yet I'd never loved anyone but Palli. And he knew that. I'm afraid he also knew that the real reason for my decision was that I lacked the courage to make the right choice. To choose our love. I feared the judgement of society. Cowardice is the most terrible of vices, it says in *The Master and Margarita*, and that's the verdict passed against me. But I helped your dad build the coffin. Then he went south to meet you.

Went to meet Eiríkur, who had got a flight back to Iceland and would land early the next morning. Halldór drove south, but arrived so early that he drove into the town of Keflavík, parked his car at the church, and went for a walk around the old neighbourhood. He wandered around there listening to Páll's recording of Hamsun's novel *Pan* on his iPod.

We don't know how it happened, not exactly.

It's possible that Halldór had been so deeply immersed in Hamsun's story and his brother's reading, lost in his voice, that he didn't pay attention as he crossed Norðfjörðsgata Street on the way back to his car. Didn't pay attention, didn't look around, Páll's voice so strong and deep that Halldór didn't hear the oncoming SUV, driving up the street at a considerable speed. The driver was on his way home from a night shift, fatigued and drowsy, and was focused on trying to find "Something in the Night" by Bruce Springsteen on Spotify to help him stay awake; it's actually one of Halldór's favourite songs by that American musician. The driver found the song, started playing it, looked up, and noticed the slim farmer too late.

The car hit so hard that it broke Halldór's hip and threw him against the front wall of a house standing at the very edge of the road; his head hit the wall and he died instantly. The driver panicked and fled the scene, but a fourteen-year-old newspaper girl discovered Halldór about half an hour later, knelt down next to him, bewilderedly picked up the headphones that had flown off Halldór, put them in her ears, and Páll's dark, beautiful voice read to her: "I have kissed *her*! I thought. I stood up and remained standing."

Eiríkur landed just over an hour later, and was met by tragedy.

Hello, Eiríkur, said tragedy, I'm tragedy, welcome to Iceland, welcome home. Your father gives you his regards.

The driver turned himself in two days later.

Devastated and full of remorse, ready to serve his sentence. Remorse is a beautiful word, and it's respectable, yet has never been capable of calling the dead back to life. Which is why Eiríkur returned alone to the north after a long absence abroad, with two suitcases, his father's body, and Páll's reading of *Pan* by Knut Hamsun. I have kissed *her*.

Sometimes It's So Difficult to Live that
It's Visible from the Moon

"There is nothing troubling me, but I long to be away, I don't know where, but somewhere far away," writes Lieutenant Glahn in *Pan*, the one who had kissed, then stood up and remained standing. Nothing troubling me; yet he shot himself and Hamsun had to go and write about it. Just as we had to go and write about Palli's suicide. And the rest of it as well, a car accident up on a heath, Aldís dead, Haraldur paralysed; had to write about when Pétur and Halla's daughter died, when Jón suffocated in his own vomit, when Hulda and Agnes died, when Margrét died, when Hafrún and Skúli died; and now about Halldór's shattered skull in Keflavík. Why do we not write more about joy, since there are so many happy people in the world? People are laughing in cafés, now someone is honking the car horn from sheer *joie de vivre*, now someone else opens a bottle of champagne just to celebrate life, and some children laugh so heartily and infectiously that it alone can prevent world war. Should be able to prevent it, were there enough sense in this world of ours. Which there is not, which is why Officer Glahn shot himself, which is why Páll hanged himself, but probably by accident because he was just measuring himself against death, muttered, would you like to dance, yes, thanks, said the dark sire, stepped up onto the table towards Páll and the weak leg couldn't take the weight and broke, because everything is awry and there's no getting around writing about it. Someone kisses someone, and shoots himself.

Páll hangs himself, Halldór and Elías construct his coffin, then Elías goes home and confesses to everything. The betrayals, the love, the cowardice that turned into a noose, which then became a broken table leg, and Halldór drives south. A day later Eiríkur comes home to the fjord, and almost everyone is dead; comes home to the fjord nearly forty years after Svana handed him over the kitchen table, into Hafrún's arms.

This has all been told.

And it all happened because Pétur and Guðríður rode to Stykkishólmur around one hundred and twenty years ago. Each on their own mare, both of which were named Ljúf.

She arrives at midday, he in the evening and informs them that Émile Zola is to be arrested – why so?

Because she sits so upright in her seat and is willing to betray everything?

Because he has that gleam in his eyes, boyish, full of melancholy, and, when he looks at me, I'm willing to do what is unforgivable, what must not be done?

And this is why Émile Zola is to be arrested?

Yes, but also because she wrote an article about the earthworm, the blind poet in the soil, and because of her article he made a day-long journey on horseback to a small farm on a heath, carrying three books, one of which had been owned by the devil's brother. That could hardly have gone well – nor did it.

But what do we really know about whether something will go well or not, sometimes it's a matter of definition, with a variable result, depending on our point of view.

I know your name, says Gísli, I've heard about you, to what do we owe the honour of this visit?

To what do we owe – does it have something to do with the arrest of Émile Zola?

Maybe so. Maybe so. And simply because both of them, Émile Zola and Pétur, and Guðríður, too, in fact, followed the magnetic needle of the heart. That was how it all started. She writes an article about the earthworm, says that it's a blind poet, the thought of God, and the magnetic needle of the heart began to quiver. Unless it was the magnetic needle of fate – few are capable of making the distinction.

But who doesn't bear some guilt; shouldn't we discuss that? Shouldn't we try to determine what cowardice is, what courage is, determine when it is that we're betraying, and when we're following our heart? Without forgetting that what one person considers an unforgivable crime, the next sees as the courage to do wrong so that life doesn't suffocate. That is why grief is the attendant of love, and betrayal its bosom friend. And that's why it can be so difficult to live that it's visible from the moon. So difficult that you have to bind the one you love with a power cord before you fuck him – and you fuck him because you don't dare to make love with him, you're too scared, because once you were raped by someone you thought you loved and could entrust with your heart; you were raped by him and his three friends and, because of it, don't dare to love again.

Then she dies. Then he dies. Then Páll dies. Then Halldór dies. So many people have died that there's really no-one left but Eiríkur.

Might it then be said that Eiríkur Halldórsson is a sorrowful full stop at the end of a terribly long sentence that fate began writing when Guðríður sat down on her and Gísli's bed, and, using her knees for a desk, started working on the article about the earthworm? Half a year later, Pétur raises a glass of wine to her in the drawing room of the doctor's house in Stykkishólmur, and thinks, you mustn't smile! But she did so, of course; looked at him and smiled.

And betrayal and grief took over?

These were the questions, now they're all here, where are the answers?

I'm dead and my role is to ask questions.

You're alive and your role is to . . .

. . . tell it correctly, says the sanctified coach driver, my companion; his voice sounds more authoritative, his expression is dark. He is clearly unamused, if not offended.

I look up, and find it difficult to hide how pleased I am to see him upset, to sense that he isn't as composed as before. A kind of joy or feeling of freedom passes through me, so intense, in fact, that

I have a very hard time keeping from smiling triumphantly. I feel as if I'm free, somehow. From what, I'm not exactly sure – maybe from him. Or from what he stands for.

What do you mean? I ask innocently.

Not everyone has to die, it's never that way, he says, stretching. He grows so large that his presence seems suddenly to fill the caravan. And you had no right to make Halldór die. Too many people have died by your hand over the years, more than you suspect – because you remember almost nothing. The only thing left of your old life is the memory of Sóley's smile. There's nothing but that, yet it's too much. You shouldn't remember anything. Your old life, its memories and feelings, should have lain so deep that your mind wouldn't have been aware of them. That's the way it was supposed to be. We can say that that was the deal. You stepped into the light that cleaves the darkness, and were supposed to wake up completely amnesiac here in the church, so that you, your memories, your life, wouldn't get in the way and colour what you would go on to recount. You were supposed to be perception, not consciousness. It didn't work. Instead of your memories being erased, they lay in your depths like painful loss. It didn't work. Almost nothing has worked. Which is good, because no life can prosper without mistakes. One may even go so far as to say that mistakes are a necessary magnetic deviation of fate. I expect you know that God and the devil created man in collaboration? The last thing that God gave man was consciousness – and then declared that his creation was perfect. But then the devil added the subconscious. Why did you do this, God asked, do you not see that you have given man what even we don't fully understand? You have turned him into a mystery.

And what did the devil say?

Nothing, he didn't need to, God realised the answer just by asking the question.

And the answer is?

Pretending not to have heard my question, the sanctified coach driver looks out the window, looks over at the hotel where I'm talking to the Canadian family, but Rúna has gone in. They're all smiling, and

400

I'm taken aback when I see the daughter's smile. I've seen that smile before. We've all done so. I look uncertainly at my companion, who pushes new pages across the table to me, and there Halldór . . .

. . . crosses the street in Keflavík, so immersed in his brother's dead voice that he doesn't notice the jeep approaching at unnecessarily high speed, the driver sleepy after his night shift – and it crashes into Halldór. But this time, the driver manages to swerve slightly at the last moment, so that he hits Halldór from the side rather than head-on. That being said, the impact is still so powerful and the driver is so startled that he loses control of the car, drives straight into the back of a lorry, and is knocked unconscious. A fourteen-year-old newspaper girl witnesses the accident, runs first to Halldór, kneels down next to him, asks if he can hear her. His headphones have been knocked off, his iPod has popped out of his pocket, skipped over the reading of Hamsun, and has started playing *Gymnopédie* by Erik Satie.

A work that Pétur played on the piano at the doctor's house in Stykkishólmur one hundred and twenty years ago.

"Gymnopedia" is a Greek word, and means naked young men, dancing.

I look at the sanctified coach driver.

There's not much left, he says.

What We Don't Understand
Enlarges the World

AND THEN IT'S FINISHED

Gymnopédie has been with us ever since Pétur played it for Grandma Guðríður in Stykkishólmur just under one hundred and twenty years ago, says Eiríkur as he puts down his guitar, having just played the work of the French composer for Elías.

They're in the house at Vík, which Elías has completely renovated over the last two years. The house's ground floor, which was previously divided into smaller units, has become an adjoining living room and kitchen. The large living-room windows, with a view of the bay, the fjord, Nes, and the church beyond it, reach down to the floor in many places, and can be slid open directly to the garden.

That was incredibly beautiful, says Elías; it's rare to hear this piece performed on guitar. Feel free to record it for me if you have the chance. But your grandmother, you say? – it's a bit further back to Guðríður than that. Wouldn't she be your great-great-grandmother?

I just don't think that fits, Eiríkur answers, reaching for the photo lying on top of the pile of papers on the long dining table, material on Guðríður and Pétur that he and Elías have gathered in recent months. I don't think that fits, it seems too far back to her. I've felt her presence so strongly since I stood over the ruins at Uppsalir this spring.

You know that some would be tempted to call your experience transcendental?

Oh, transcendental, I'm tired of that word! But something happened there. I stood over the ruins, closed my eyes to breathe in the surroundings, but then smelled warm pancakes, up there on the heath, far from any other human habitation. Strange, I thought – and then she walked through me. Or I felt as if someone were walking through me, and, at the same time, I knew it was her. I called Dad on the way home and told him about what had happened, what I'd experienced. He and Sævar were still in Canada, stuck there because of Covid but being taken good care of by our relatives. And then another strange thing happened, because that morning, Dad had got this photo here from our relatives – and had just emailed it to me!

Elías puts down his knife, wipes his hands, sits down next to Eiríkur on the other side of the table, and looks at the photo.

They're beautiful together, he says.

Yes, Eiríkur agrees, smiling. I imagine it all started there. That soon afterwards, Pétur gets up to sit at the piano, plays *Gymnopédie*, and it all begins. I know that that wasn't the case. Still . . . but look how beautiful they are together! And how well-suited they are for each other. Literally beaming with happiness. They could be happy there, they were allowed to be – for that brief moment.

Because then it was over.

I EXIST BECAUSE WORLDS WENT OFF COURSE

Because then it was over, the coach driver repeats, and again I think I catch a whiff of sulphur from his fingers.

He has a new bottle of whisky, Talisker. He's got good taste, I must admit. The shot glass in front of him is half full and the smell of smoke wafts from it. He's finished a whole bottle, started on another, but the whisky doesn't seem to have any obvious effect on him. He twists the shot glass, timeless as the air. I look down at the pages, at where Rúna comes out of the hotel wearing a green blouse she got from her sister, and which goes strikingly well with her dark hair. She's smiling. Simply can't stop smiling, because the journalist from Paris is on his way here. Landed just after three thirty in Keflavík. He's arrived, he wrote in his text message, "with my love like a sundial. Prepared to live at the end of the world as long as you're there. As long as you wish to look at me. When I think, I think of you. It's been like that since I first saw you. You know it. Your presence makes me so happy and joyful that the angels envy me. And with you, I'll fire at fenceposts with a shotgun for the next hundred years if you love me."

It's such a wonderful declaration of love, Sóley had said, that he must be worthy of you. You say he's a good and gentle lover; it's just a question of whether he can actually help you with the lambing.

But Rúna had answered the Frenchman: "The party will start when you arrive. So come straight to Vík. Everyone who's anyone will be there. If I'm wearing a green blouse, it means that I love you."

You know that the Frenchman isn't alone in the car, says the coach driver, without taking his eyes off the photo of Pétur and Guðríður.

But don't you have to tell soon when it all started, when everything was set in motion?

I have no idea how it all started, so I couldn't answer that question.

No idea? Who would know it, then? Don't you bear full responsibility here?

Yes, probably. But then I'm both God and the devil, because I've managed to create something that I don't understand. Which is good, I think, because what we don't understand enlarges the world.

There you go, says the coach driver, smiling his rare smile, there you go!

I hastily look back down at the pages so he doesn't see how happy I am with his encouragement. And read:

She wrote the article about the blind poet of the soil, Pétur played *Gymnopédie* on the doctor's piano. The photographer had arrived earlier in the evening at Kristín's request and taken four photographs. In the first three, Ólafur and Kristín are sitting together on the sofa, with the other four standing behind. But when everyone thought that the last photograph had been taken, Kristín said, oh, one more, and now with you young people together on the sofa. So I'm still young? Pétur asked with a smile, and then he sat down with Guðríður on the sofa, looked quickly at her, then at the photographer. And the photo was taken. A moment frozen in time.

One hundred and twenty years later, we regard the photo.

They're sitting impermissibly close together. Pétur has laid his hand over the back of hers, as if apologetically, as if he'd said, oh, forgive me, but I had to put my hand somewhere. He's smiling. They're both smiling. And Guðríður's eyes shine so brightly that everything becomes beautiful, even the betrayals.

Because sometimes something has to crack, says Eiríkur, looking at the photo. Sometimes someone has to sink into unhappiness and grief. It's so unfair, but there's very little we can do about it. All this had to happen. I exist because worlds went off course.

THEY HARDLY SLEPT AT ALL

Because then what must not have happened, happens. Pétur plays *Gymnopédie*.

An acquaintance of mine in Copenhagen, he says, sitting at the piano, keeps up to date with the newest in music and sent me the score to this unusual but captivating work this winter. I'll do my best, but don't judge me too harshly, I've only ever played it on my church's tired old harmonium, which can be so out of tune that it agitates the dead!

He closes his eyes, takes a deep breath, opens his eyes, looks at Guðríður, and begins to play. She gasps, her eyes fill with tears, and then she weeps.

She weeps because she hasn't heard a piano being played for a quarter of a century, ever since the French ship's captain, her father's friend, played Chopin's nocturnes for them at the merchant's house. She weeps because the music is so beautiful. She weeps because she misses her father so sorely. She weeps because Pétur is so handsome. She weeps because it dawns on her that as long as she lives on the heath, with her Gísli, she is missing out on the beauty of the world. Pétur plays and sees her weeping.

Two hours later, he crawls in through the window of the large bedroom in which she sleeps.

The window is on the ground floor, but is so high up that Pétur has to stretch to tap the pane lightly with his fingertips. Almost immediately, she looks out, as if she'd been waiting for him. They look into each other's eyes for a few seconds, and then she opens the window, steps back, and waits. But it takes Pétur some effort to get in. He has to heave himself up and hardly has the strength to do so, but he tries to make it easier for himself by kicking and waving his legs. Ridiculous, he thinks, what if someone were to see me now! He then falls headlong into the room, entangling himself in the window curtains. When he manages to scramble to his feet, she steps up to him and slaps him.

They hardly slept at all that night. Or the next night. They couldn't. They were simply unwilling to. And it was intimate, it was beautiful, it was completely unforgivable, it was the deepest betrayal.

Nevertheless, there is a fifty–fifty chance that the jury with authority over Earth and heaven, always comprising equal numbers of inhabitants of heaven and hell, has acquitted them. Existence is truly incomprehensible. Or, as it is written, all it takes is a simple whim of fate and you're unexpectedly faced with two difficult choices.

Neither of which is right.

Yet they're both right.

THE SERVANTS OF BACCHUS

I exist because worlds went off course, said Eiríkur, and he could have added: Because so many died.

And that's right; there are far too many deaths here. Yet there is life.

Because Halldór didn't die.

He is certainly hit by an SUV, as its driver, Sævar, is returning home from his night shift. Tired, sleepy, searching for Springsteen's song

409

on Spotify, looking forward to singing along loudly to the American musician who has been an important companion of his for decades. He finds the song, looks up, and hits Halldór. That's true. But at almost the last moment, he manages to swerve a bit to the side, so that only the SUV's side glances Halldór. However, the SUV is so bulky and is travelling so fast that Halldór is thrown to the side, seriously injured, while Sævar drives straight into a parked lorry, the bed of which crashes through the SUV's windscreen on the passenger side.

When Eiríkur lands at Keflavík Airport almost an hour later, the ambulance carrying Halldór has nearly reached Reykjavík.

A broken pelvis.

But it could have been much worse, the doctor says to Eiríkur. Possibly far, far worse if your father hadn't been drunk, piss-drunk, to tell the truth. Because his body was softer and more relaxed when the blow came.

In the end, it was the drinking that saved my life, Halldór says with a wide smile to his son when he regains consciousness following his operation. But he immediately regrets his words, the stupid smile, his attempt at humour, which fall completely flat, because Eiríkur stiffens up – and countless fragments of memories of similar reactions in his son rush like dark comets through Halldór's mind. I disgust him, he despises me, thinks Halldór. But instead of apologising, he starts talking about needing someone to feed and look after his poor cat, Bowie, and the blessed chickens. I can hardly do it from here, he says.

Eiríkur refrains from mentioning the obvious, that all they had to do was call Dísa or Lúna at Hof and ask them to drop by Oddi to feed the animals. Instead, he says, I'll be in touch regarding Palli's funeral. He drives home, ashamed of feeling gratitude towards Sævar, who was lying in the room next door to Halldór's and called Eiríkur over, devastated about the accident.

Unforgivable carelessness, he said. A criminal lack of concentration on my part, he said. Springsteen, he said. "Something in the Night".

A pretty good song, off a good album, Eiríkur said involuntarily, but then he had to bite his lip to keep from thanking the man for having saved him from being met at the airport by his piss-drunk father. It wasn't your fault, he then said. My father was so drunk that he had the presence of mind neither to look around him nor to get out of the way. Strictly speaking, it wasn't you who hit him, but his drinking.

Then Sævar looked down.

Of course, I didn't know it then, says Eiríkur to Elías, moving the stack of papers to another table to free up space for their dinner preparations, that Sævar, like Dad, had long been a servant of Bacchus. But I was so angry with Dad that I wished I would never have to see him again. He felt he'd betrayed me, deceived me, lured me here with the two letters in which he tried to come across as someone who could be trusted. We hadn't seen each other for three years, Palli had just died, and he was going to pick me up at the airport completely drunk. I was angry at him, angry at myself for having trusted him. I came home to Oddi around midnight, went straight out to the barn to see Palli, and stood there for a long time over his coffin.

Then I sit down at the kitchen table, open the envelope holding my grandmother's letter, and realise that the world I lived in had, in a certain sense, never existed.

MAYBE I DON'T EXIST

A few days later, Elías drives south to get Halldór.

Like Hulda around eighty years ago at the tip of the Snæfellsnes peninsula, Eiríkur and Elías had traversed the shore in search of the right rock for Páll's gravestone, found it, brought it by tractor home to Oddi, put it in the barn, and built a low platform for it so that Halldór could sit comfortably and chisel his brother's name and Kierkegaard's words onto it.

Which he sat there working hard on doing for fifteen hours a day. He worked so eagerly, was so focused, that it was as if his life's work was to be gathered into his brother's epitaph. How empty and hopeless life would be if you forgot me!

But the hand that held the chisel trembled with a craving for alcohol, it trembled with sorrow, regret, self-reproach.

And it trembled with self-pity.

*

Don't be so cruel to him, Elías pleaded.

He and Eiríkur dug the grave with shovels; anything else was out of the question. Dug down into the darkness, down into time, met the blind poets there. But at home at Oddi, Halldór's hand trembled.

Don't be so cruel, Elías pleaded. Anger and vindictiveness distort our thinking, skew everything, deprive us of oxygen. Forgiveness, on the other hand, opens doors and enlarges life.

I know that, said Eiríkur, I just can't help it. I feel as if I'm stuck in a crevice. As if I no longer know who I am. I feel as if all my life, I've been someone other than myself. An unexpected letter from my grandmother was waiting for me when I came back. Written almost forty years ago. And because of that letter, I feel as if until now, my life has been a kind of Truman Show.

My mother's death, he said, has always been a mountain by which my life has involuntarily taken its bearings. In other words, it made me the person that I am. But now that I'm nearly forty, I realise that that mountain was never there, and therefore that I've been shaped by what didn't exist – might that mean that the person I am is an illusion, my life a misunderstanding? And that those who have connected with me over the years, cared about me and even loved me, have connected with a person who never existed? I loved a woman for four years, and she me. Then she left and I think that for a long time, I was trapped in the pain of losing her. Or in my love for her. You can actually be in love with your loss. But did she love me, or the man we both thought I was? I'm a guitarist, not a bad one, either, good enough to be a sought-after session musician, especially on jazz and blues records. I have a recognisable tone, both clear and sad. That tone was naturally interwoven with the person I am – which was based on a misunderstanding . . . My life was paralysed by loss until another woman bound me to my kitchen chair. She said she heard me play, and, through it, saw my inner person. I think I love her, and I think that she loves me. But now it doesn't matter, because she loved a man who didn't exist. I'm sorry, I'm gibbering and whining, it's shameful, I know. But worst of all, I'm so angry at everyone I cared for the most. So angry and riven that it nearly suffocates my sadness and longing for Palli. I'm even angry at Grandma and Grandpa and catch myself cursing them. Which I have no right to do. I despise myself for it.

Sometimes, said Elías, it's hardest to forgive yourself. And sometimes it's most important, the start of everything.

Maybe, said Eiríkur, maybe that's right. But don't you need to know who you are in order to forgive yourself?

HELLO DAD, HELLO SUNSHINE

Elías and Eiríkur dug Palli's grave; it was a deep gash in the ground.

The rock was placed over it. A rock with Kierkegaard's words and Palli's name chiselled so deeply upon it that time has its work cut out for it in erasing it.

Halldór's life's work?

That's how he thought of it. When he began the work, and the hand that held the chisel trembled with sorrow, regret, a craving for alcohol, and self-pity. Eiríkur looked at his father and thought, I can never trust him, while Bacchus laid a blanket softly over Halldór's shoulders and said, you know that I am the only one who will never judge you. I am the only one who really understands you. In my dwelling are many rooms. And this is truly your life's work, he added when Halldór put down his hammer and chisel, leaned back to regard the inscription. You can be proud of it, and from now on no-one can demand anything from you. Eiríkur will take over the farm, you don't owe him anything. You saw how he looked at you. With cold contempt, I would say! He doesn't know the meaning of the word gratitude. And he has never understood you. You know that no-one understands you but I. Halldór lifted the hammer, weighed it thoughtfully, and then threw it at Bacchus, saying: I hereby quit!

Then Bacchus laughed. Countless were the times he'd heard something similar, said by so many, in so many eras. He laughed and polished his hook called Self-Pity. That's fine, he said. You'll come crawling back, but that's fine, too, because as far as I'm concerned, even humiliation is beautiful. I forgive everything. That's why I'm loved.

Eat shit, said Halldór.

And he went south. After the funeral. As had been the plan. Rehabilitation following the accident and operation. He would be staying with friends, and expected to return in a few weeks. That's what they both thought, the father and son. And both dreaded it. But his days in the south proved difficult, and his craving for alcohol soon became overwhelming. Elías, who called Halldór every day, could hear in his voice how he was feeling and went south in the hope of convincing Halldór to admit himself to the Vogur Detox Clinic for treatment.

Give it a try for a week, he suggested. You owe it to Palli, you owe it to Eiríkur, and you owe it to yourself.

Halldór finally agreed. He was too scared to do anything else. He'd never been so scared in his life. Had never felt so vulnerable, even. He was admitted to Vogur ten days later, and whom should he meet there but Sævar, who had also newly arrived.

Springsteen and I are both here, said Sævar, surprised but happy, and now you! It must be fate. Maybe we two should just start a band, along with fate and Springsteen!

They stuck together through the six-week treatment, always with Springsteen between them. I drank away everything, said Sævar, my job, wife, family, got a job as a nightwatchman through friends, and have been holed up there the past three years. Work at night, come home in the morning, drink and listen to music until noon, wander around my little terrace house with Bruce, Billie Holiday, Bacchus, self-pity and loneliness. You fall in love with lonely, you end up that way. I thought it would always be that way and was starting to accept it. Or pretended to be happy, but of course was just numb, because King Bacchus is like the spiders that numb their victims and then feed on them. Eat them alive, suck out all their insides and leave the casing behind so that the victims believe they're still alive. But then I hit you, which I'm convinced will turn out to be the best thing that ever happened to me. I think we're both such failures that we need each other.

Following treatment, Halldór moved south to Keflavík and, without a word or objection, Eiríkur took over the farm. Two hundred sheep, fourteen chickens, a cat on its eighth life, and then he added three Border collie puppies when their owner, an old loner who lived a little north of here but had always kept in contact with the folk at Oddi, was diagnosed with incurable cancer and sailed out to sea on his small fishing boat before the disease stripped him of his dignity. While the coast was still visible, he sent Eiríkur a text message asking him to take in the puppies. Eiríkur went and got the puppies, put them in a cardboard box lined with soft hay and an old fleece jumper, and stuck his hand in it every time they started whimpering on the way back to Oddi. The three of them cuddled up against his hand and licked his fingers – and Eiríkur smiled.

Halldór and Sævar soon founded the company *Hello Sunshine – Construction and Repairs!*, which did so well that they decided to take their dream trip to the United States. They visited Elvis in Memphis, Billie Holiday in Baltimore, Jim Morrison in Florida, and ended at Bruce's place in New Jersey, where they had their photo taken. The photo that was waiting for Eiríkur on his phone the next morning.

The father and son hadn't spoken much since Halldór moved south. Eiríkur was glad that Halldór had stopped drinking, but couldn't bring himself to trust him. So he kept him at a distance. Their only communication had to do with the farm and its operation. Mainly emails and the odd phone call, all short and difficult for both of them. But then comes this photo of Halldór and Sævar, both with huge grins, outside Springsteen's childhood home. They have their arms over each other's shoulders and Halldór's eyes are full of light and pure happiness. Under the photo were the words: To my son, Eiríkur: Hello sunshine, won't you stay?

Eiríkur looked at the photo for a long time, zoomed in on Halldór, widened his eyes and stared. Then he opened his computer and wrote an email to Batool, his first in two years: My dearest Batool! Are you alive, happy, still with legs so long that cathedrals burn at the sight of them? I'm coming to Marseille on a business trip in ten days, staying for two weeks; beer?

He sent the email, then reached for the phone, looked up Halldór's number and called. Hello, Dad, he said.

Hello, Dad, hello sunshine.

BEER, CHAMPAGNE, OR FIREARMS?

Halldór was so touched to get a call from his son, and hear how open and warm Eiríkur's voice was, that he began weeping. The column of tears rose quickly and unstoppably up his neck, dampened his voice, made Halldór so unclear or inarticulate that Eiríkur stiffened up. He's drunk, he thought, goddamn it, I'm hanging up, this was a mistake, he's fooled me yet again! Halldór could feel the sudden, cold silence at the other end of the line and clutched the phone perplexedly, unable to say a word. Then Sævar put his arm around his friend's shoulders and held him tightly, and it helped. I'm sorry, Halldór managed to say, my voice just broke and I almost started to cry. I was so happy to hear from you. How sentimental I've become! You mustn't tell Kári about this!

Then Eiríkur laughed.

And he meets Batool two weeks later in Marseille.

She'd answered the email the same day and suggested meeting at a café. Eiríkur arrives in good time, his heart beating fast, while constantly trying to remind himself that it's over between them. He'd seen to that with his silence. Besides the fact that he'd heard she now had a lover. He thinks, I just need to see her one more time. After that, I'll be free. She makes him wait, arrives a good twenty minutes late, and laughs when she sees how he looks at her.

You're laughing at me? he says, uncertain, half-happy, half-hurt.

Yes, she says with a smile, without sitting down. Because now I understand why you have shunned me.

I'm sorry, he says. Forgive me. I disappeared, I know that, and didn't contact you. But can I explain why? Won't you sit down and give me a chance?

She looks at him with those big, dark eyes. I've been waiting for you since you left, she then says. I wanted to contact you but knew that the initiative had to come from you. You're one of those people who could love out of pity, and I don't care for that sort of love. I said goodbye to you just over two years ago. And encouraged you to leave because a person who loves is vulnerable. It's so easy to hurt that person, abuse her, mistreat her. To love is to entrust your heart to another. I didn't dare it. And was so glad when you left. I've never been so sad. Mum said I would have to wait. If he's worthy, she said, he'll come back. This would be the test. I would have to arm myself with patience. But it must be admitted that I was starting to worry.

I heard you had a lover. Is that right?

The waiter who had been standing near their table, watching them, a respectable middle-aged man, moves closer, pulls back the empty chair to offer it to Batool, and asks with a smile: What may I offer you; champagne or beer, or perhaps firearms?

Let's start with beer, says Batool, and she sits down and waits until the waiter is gone, but then says, yes, that's right, I found a lover. Are you jealous?

Me? Why? I have no right to be.

Do you have to apply for a permit for jealousy? Did you think it was okay, did that news have no effect on you?

Yes. I actually didn't sleep for a few weeks.

Oh, how happy that makes me! Mum also said that if you were upright, you would lose sleep over it. But there was only one. And it didn't last long. I hoped he would quench my longing for you, fill the emptiness I felt at your absence. But that only made things worse. You won hands down, in comparison. I've missed you so much that I was close to seeing a doctor. My dad and my brothers talked about going to Iceland to teach you a lesson, they found it so hard seeing me that way, half-devastated with heartache. You have to suffer, my mother then said, and miss someone so much that you feel as if you're about to lose your mind. Until then, you don't know if you really love that person. But now you're here. I saw how you looked at me when I arrived. Does that mean you're mine?

Eiríkur opens his mouth, starts to speak, but at the same time a car drives slowly past, the driver's-side window is rolled down and Kanye West is at such high volume that Batool doesn't hear what Eiríkur says, his voice drowns in the music: Hey hey hey hey hey, please say you will, for real … I pray you will!

The waiter brings them the beer but turns around when he sees how they look at each other – he takes the beer back inside and brings the champagne.

TO FORGIVE IS SOMETIMES THE SAME AS RECOGNISING YOURSELF

You're so wonderfully naïve, says Batool when the champagne bottle is almost empty and Eiríkur has told her about everything, the suicide that wasn't supposed to be a suicide, his father hit by Springsteen and Sævar, piss-drunk on his way to the airport to pick up Eiríkur; Eiríkur who went home to Oddi and discovered that his whole life was an illusion, there you sleep, exhausted in an unfair world. Since then, I've felt as if I no longer know who I am. That's why you heard nothing from me. I felt as if I had no right to . . . you. That I first needed to find out who I really was before I started living. I just got so confused. Sometimes I wish I had never met you. But I dream constantly of you. Of life with you. And your son. Here, or at home. But first I had to get rid of the anger in my blood. I had to overcome that anger in order to forgive those I love. I had to find myself first, before I came to you.

You're so wonderfully naïve, says Batool. You don't know who you are, and have never been the person we thought you were? Do you think I haven't always known who you are? I've looked into your eyes at those moments when you're completely defenceless, completely sincere. You give all of yourself when you make love with me. You come entirely to me. I miss it so much. Everyone's core is innate. The events in a person's life affect him, of course, but if he is solid, they do not change his nature. You are who you are, and have always been so. But you have to forgive. Forgiving is sometimes the same as recognising oneself. He who forgives finds himself. And he who finds himself is free.

WHICH IS WHY WE CAN CARRY ON

Happiness and unhappiness come from the same source, which is why it's sometimes so difficult to live that it's visible from the moon.

The moon that Eiríkur fired his shotgun at as the two lorries rushed by – and one of the drivers took a photo of him, waving the shotgun around.

So Eiríkur wasn't, the coach driver says to me, shooting at the lorries, angry and grief-stricken because of the puppies, but, on the contrary, went out with his shotgun to celebrate life. And was absolutely not "so inebriated after half a bottle of Calvados that he was obviously more likely to hit the moon or himself than the lorries", because Elías, Rúna and Sóley stood there smiling in front of the farmhouse, he with a beer, they with glasses of red wine.

I know, I say, raising my hands apologetically. But I just didn't know any better then, nor did I know that Páll was lying in his coffin in the barn when Eiríkur returned home. That's alright, too. We describe the world as we see it at any given time.

And no-one has ever described it so well that it's impossible to do so better.

Which is why we can carry on.

HÖLDERLIN LOST HIS MIND AND CAN THEREFORE CONFIRM EVERYTHING I'M SAYING

I'm so confused, Guðríður wrote to Pétur, having returned from her stay in Stykkishólmur, with his voice, fingertips and kisses like the lingering heat of a burn on her body, so confused, because I had never suspected that happiness and unhappiness were one and the same thing. Never suspected that it could be a betrayal to love. I wish I had never met you, I count the days, the hours, the seconds until I meet you again. Do you think that love is the same as losing your mind? My love, write to me! You must never write to me! Come and visit! You absolutely must not come and visit!

This was a good meeting, Ólafur the Impassive had said when he and Kristín said goodbye to Guðríður and Pétur. You have a positive effect on us geezers; the journal will be better with you on board.

And you'll be travelling together, that's good, said Kristín, hugging them both in parting.

I think she knows, said Guðríður, as they rode away.

Do you think she . . . heard us?

No, says Pétur, or, I hope not! But I think she's known this ever since she heard me say your name for the first time.

Sometimes I think she sees through the mountains.

But she won't judge us?

She loves us both with her big heart. I think she feels sorry for us.

They accompanied each other most of the way back to Uppsalir, and then he turned around and headed home.

And she rides home to Uppsalir.

With some books that Kristín and Ólafur had given her, sweets and toys for the girls – and payment for attending the meeting. She who had never before been paid in cash.

She comes home, the girls dash out of the farmhouse and shout as they run to meet her, the dogs hopping happily around them. Gísli is waiting for her in front of the house, glad to have her back yet standing up against the house wall, almost as if he's shy. My love, she says, with a lump in her throat, leading Ljúf behind her with the two happy girls on the mare's back.

Two days later she writes to Pétur, I'm so confused, come, don't come!

Then the winter passes.

The month of April returns with its light, and there is another meeting of the editorial board. Guðríður's eagerness hardly allows her any sleep during the nights leading up to it. And her sadness. Because she has made a decision. Pétur had written her six long letters that winter, sent them hidden among material related to the journal. I think only of you, he writes, always, ceaselessly. It's as if I'm losing my mind, yet I've never been so happy!

Will she be there again, the woman from the heath? Halla had asked when Pétur was getting ready for the April meeting. Her name is Guðríður, he replied, yes, she's on the editorial board, you know that.

And then Halla's heart stopped beating. She had asked the question the way she did because she wanted to hear Pétur say Guðríður's name. And his voice gave him away. His voice and the gleam in his eyes. He left, four nights have passed, she could hardly sleep, and now he's probably on his way home. Evening falls, she combs her younger daughter's hair, tries to smile at her chatter. She'd just read a letter from her sister in Reykjavík, who says she has heard that the benefices at Lágafell and Kjalarnes would soon need filling. She combs her hair, tries to smile, thinks of the gleam in Pétur's eyes.

Ow, Mama, not so hard, said her girl. Isn't Papa coming home today?

Yes, he's coming. The latter meeting behind him.

The latter, because two would be all that Guðríður would attend. Two meetings, and then it was over.

She sits her horse so well, so nobly.

She dismounts. They have come up onto the heath, Uppsalir in this direction, the rectory in the other.

That's the way it is.

And she is leaving.

There has to be an ocean between us, she had told him the night before. That alone can stop me. Otherwise I'll throw everything away, come to you, and destroy so much that it will never be repaired.

She dismounts. Hold me, she asks. Don't let go, she asks. You must never let me go. My love. I must go. I'm nothing without you. My heart will always be with you, be gentle with it.

I was born to hold you, he says. Born only to see you smile. Hear you speak. I won't be able to live if you leave. You mustn't go. If you do, my life will be darkness.

This life is not meant for us, says Guðríður, kissing him.

I'll kiss you and we'll always be together.

Just ask Hölderlin, he lost his mind and can therefore confirm everything I'm saying.

AND WE WILL ALWAYS BE TOGETHER

We drive the winding side road down to Vík. A road that is often buried in snow in winter, forcing Elías to park his car up on it, where there's less snow. Sometimes, however, the entire fjord is buried in snow, and then Elías grabs his skis or starts the snowmobile. But there is no snow now, of course not, it's summer, it's August, the verdant earth glows with sunshine, the trees above and beside the house are fragrant, they resound with birdsong. We drive down the winding road and Eiríkur and Elías have come out to meet us. Elías taller, a bit stooping, having just spoken to Batool, who had reached Þröskuldur Road along with her son, parents and the French journalist, whom they met on the plane and found out was coming to us as well. She called to confirm that Elías was preparing mansaf, as she had instructed him.

Rúna stops the car. I'm sitting in the back, between Wislawa and Oleana, my heart pounding so hard that they feel the shock waves. Eiríkur is kneeling next to his bitch, scratching her lovingly behind her ears, watching us approach. The party is about to begin.

I'm sitting in the back seat and at the same time here in the caravan, where I see Ási coming out of the house at Nes with Haraldur in his arms, Gummi right behind holding the wheelchair like a folded wing. They all have their song lists with them, the ten best songs in history starting with "Please Please Me", looking forward to submitting their lists to Eiríkur, trusting him best to decide which of them is worthiest. Haraldur's phone rings, while he's still in Ási's arms. It's Halldór, who wants to know if they're at the party. Sævar and I just passed Hólmavík, he says, where are you? In Ási's arms, Haraldur answers. Then Halldór laughs and McCartney fills his and Sævar's car with the song "Do It Now", the song that Halldór and Eiríkur are going to perform together at the party. The ode to life, they call the song.

Do it now, because tomorrow maybe everything will be gone. And then we'll be left with regret.

Goodness, I think everyone's on their way here, says Sóley, turning in her seat to look at me.

I'll kiss you and we'll always be together.

But that life wasn't intended for us.

The working title of Pétur's autobiography is *Loss*. Around three hundred handwritten pages, stored in the depths of the National Library.

"That life wasn't intended for us." – The first sentence of the autobiography.

Written in the vicinity of Reykjavík, where Halla and her two daughters moved to early in the last century. Photocopied about eighty years later by Elías.

The autobiography is dedicated to "the women in my life, Halla Magnúsdóttir and Guðríður Eiríksdóttir". But it's unclear whether it was written with Halla's knowledge. Stored in a box, along with a rather large collection of letters, and Elías was the first to open it. Hundreds of letters, many of them to Hölderlin, and around thirty from Guðríður. The majority sent from Canada, where she moved to early in September, almost five months after she and Pétur said their farewells on the heath. Where they held each other for so long that the mares began to grow restless.

She left Iceland with Gísli and his parents. The father and son both went to work for Gísli's brother, went to work for death, and Gísli never wrote his autobiography. Of course not. But that autobiography could probably have had the same title as Pétur's, because Gísli never stopped missing Iceland. He missed his sheep, missed the light on the heath, missed the fragrance of the hay, missed being able to go fishing at sea, missed being able to call the dogs. They left, and his life became homesickness. In exchange, he got to continue living with Guðríður by his side, he got to wake up next to her thousands of mornings more.

Or until she died in her sleep, thirty years later.

I'm coming to you when I die, she wrote in her first letter to Pétur from abroad. And he thought that, too, when they sailed away from Iceland. When she and Gísli stood together on the deck and saw Iceland sink. And Gísli wept. That tough man. Wept and groped blindly for Guðríður's hand. Wept because he knew he would never again see his country rise from the sea. Wept because that was the price he had to pay to have Guðríður with him. It was his third love poem to her. To sacrifice his country in order to live by her side. To be able to hold in his arms the woman whom he knew deep down that he'd lost. And had maybe never had.

The mountains sank, the sheep sank, the dogs and the mare that changes her name, everything sank and he groped for Guðríður so as not to drown. She stood beside him, saw everything sink and thought, there sinks my heart. Yet despite that, she couldn't help but feel a slight eagerness. She looked forward to being able to put the girls in school, and to get to keep them with her longer. Looked forward to settling down among people and having opportunities there to hear musical performances, see stage plays, have access to more books. I'm starting to be able to read books in English, she wrote to Pétur proudly, about a year later.

Everything sank, she stood on deck with her legs spread wide in order to keep her balance, five months pregnant.

The first word he said was Mama, not Mom, she wrote to Pétur, which made me happy. But this is what we look like now, the mother and son, she added, and enclosed a recent photo of her and Jón.

I've stared for so long at the photo that I'm going blind, he wrote back.

I'll kiss you and we'll always be together.

My love, so you're here, Pétur said happily when Guðríður came to him one night, many years later. Almost thirty years later.

Yes, don't you remember what I promised, that I would come to you when I die. And now I'll always be with you.

I'll kiss you and we'll always be together.

And it goes as it goes, says the coach driver.

He has stood up, and suddenly seems as big as everything beyond my comprehension. Are you leaving? I ask; there's still so much that's unclear, so many questions unanswered. So much left. What about Svana, Eiríkur's mother, and what about . . .

Of course much is unclear, and of course many questions are unanswered. That's how it must be. You know that as well as I do. Otherwise, we have no reason to continue.

Rúna stops the car, shuts off the engine, looks at her sister with a smile.

Eiríkur gets to his feet, our eyes meet, and then it can begin. The party that everyone who's anyone is attending, living as well as dead. The beer has got very cold in the creek. Death's playlist is ready. So there is nothing left to do but live.

And we will always be together.

Death's Playlist (excerpt)

It's All Over Now, Baby Blue	Bob Dylan
Vegir liggja til allra átta	Ellý Vilhjálms
(Roads Lie in All Directions)	
Fyrir átta árum (Eight Years Ago)	Haukur Morthens
One of Us Cannot Be Wrong	Leonard Cohen
No Introduction	Nas
It Takes a Lot to Know a Man	Damien Rice
The Train Song	Nick Cave
Þarf þig (Need You)	GDRN
I Don't Want to Spoil the Party	The Beatles
Summer in the City	Regina Spektor
Broken Bicycles	Tom Waits
Í hjarta mér (In My Heart)	Bubbi Morthens
Where is My Mind	Pixies
SOSA	AZ
Suppose	Elvis Presley
Can't Help Falling in Love	Elvis Presley
In a Sentimental Mood	John Coltrane, Duke Ellington
Accordion	Madvillain
Vaknaðu (Wake Up)	XXX Rottweiler hundar
I Love Paris	Ella Fitzgerald
Afgan (Afghan)	Bubbi Morthens
Good News	Mac Miller
Pastorale in F Major	Bach (Pablo Casals)
I'll Follow the Sun	The Beatles
Bell Bottom Blues	Derek & the Dominos
Rock 'n' Roll Suicide	David Bowie
Your Possible Pasts	Pink Floyd
I'd Rather Go Blind	Etta James

Eniga meniga	Olga Guðrún
My Love	Paul McCartney
All the Lazy Dykes	Morrissey
Real Love	The Beatles
Back to Black	Amy Winehouse
The Same Deep Water as You	The Cure
Ashes to Ashes	David Bowie
Non, je ne regrette rien	Edith Piaf
(No, I Don't Regret Anything)	
Lonesome Town	Paul McCartney, David Gilmour
Just Say I Love Him	Nina Simone
My Funny Valentine	Chet Baker
You Really Got Me	The Kinks
Stranger than Kindness	Nick Cave
Blue in Green	Miles Davis, Bill Evans
Yesterday is Here	Tom Waits
Mosaïque solitaire	Damso
(Solitary Mosaic)	
Scared (hidden track)	Paul McCartney
Love Sick	Bob Dylan
I'm a Fool to Want You	Billie Holiday
One Day	U.G.K.
Something in the Night	Bruce Springsteen
Gymnopédie (Gymnopedia)	Erik Satie
Hello Sunshine	Bruce Springsteen
Say You Will	Kanye West
Do it Now	Paul McCartney

Bob Dylan, "It's All Over Now, Baby Blue". © Sony/ATV Music Publishing LLC

Ellý Vilhjálms, "Vegir liggja til allra átta". Lyrics: Sigfús Halldórsson. © Sena

Haukur Morthens, "Fyrir átta árum". © Íslenskir Tónar

Leonard Cohen, "One of Us Cannot Be Wrong". Copyright © Sony/ATV Music Publishing LLC

Nas, "No Introduction". Lyrics: Erik Ortiz, Kevin Crowe, Kenny Bartolomei, Nasir Jones. © Warner Chappell Music, Inc., Universal Music Publishing Group

Damien Rice, "It Takes a Lot to Know a Man". Lyrics: Brian Kelley, Chase Rice, Jesse Rice. © Warner Chappell Music, Inc.

Nick Cave, "The Train Song". Lyrics: John Samuel Carter, James Clay Fuller, Russell Black III Jones, Charles Clarence Pruet, Michael Ashok Sain. © Universal Music Publishing Group

GDRN, "Þarf þig". © Alda Music

The Beatles, "I Don't Want to Spoil the Party". Lyrics: John Lennon, Paul McCartney. © Sony/ATV Music Publishing LLC

Regina Spektor, "Summer in the City". © Sony/ATV Music Publishing LLC

Tom Waits, "Broken Bicycles". © Zoetrope Music Co., Fifth Floor Music, Inc.

Bubbi Morthens, "Í hjarta mér". Lyrics: Bubbi Morthens. © Steinar

Pixies, "Where Is My Mind". Lyrics : Charles Thompson. © Universal Music Publishing Group

AZ, "Sosa". Lyrics: Samuel Barnes, Jean-Claude Olivier, Anthony S Cruz. © Trackmasters

Elvis Presley, "Suppose". Lyrics: George Goehring, Sylvia Dee. © Kobalt Music Publishing Ltd, Raleigh Music Publishing

Elvis Presley, "Can't Help Falling in Love". Lyrics : George Weiss, Hugo Peretti, Luigi Creatore. © Kobalt Music Publishing Ltd

Madvillainy, "Accordion". Lyrics: Thompson Daniel Dumile, Jackson Otis Lee. © Madlib Invazion Music, Lord Dihoo Music

John Coltrane & Duke Ellington, "In a Sentimental Mood". Lyrics : Irving Mills et Manny Kurtz. © Impulse!

XXX Rottweiler hundar, "Vaknaðu" © Dennis

Ella Fitzgerald, "I Love Paris". Lyrics: Cole Porter. © Warner Chappell Music, Inc.

Bubbi Morthens, "Afghan". Lyrics: Bubbi Morthens. © Steinar

Mac Miller, "Good News". Lyrics: Jon Brion / Malcolm McCormick. © Kobalt Music Publishing Ltd, Universal Music Publishing Group

Bach, *Pastorale en Fa majeur*

The Beatles, "I'll Follow the Sun". Lyrics: Lennon John Winston, McCartney Paul James. © Mpl Communications Inc.

Derek & The Dominos, "Bell Bottom Blues". Lyrics: Eric Patrick Clapton, Bobby Whitlock. © Warner Chappell Music, Inc.

David Bowie, "Rock'n Roll Suicide". Lyrics: David Bowie, Jorge Seu. © Tintoretto Music, Chrysalis Music Ltd

Pink Floyd, "Your Possible Past". Lyrics: George Roger Waters. © BMG Rights Management

Etta James, "I'd Rather Go Blind". Lyrics: Ellington Jordan, Billy Foster. © Arc Music, Arc Music Corp

Olga Guðrún, "Eniga meniga". © Spor

Paul McCartney, "My Love". Lyrics: Paul McCartney, Linda Louise McCartney. © Sony/ATV Songs LLC, Warner Chappell Music Canada Ltd., Sparko Phone Music, Sony/ATV

Ballad, Bulbyyork Music, Songs Of Hear The Art, Nyankingmusic, MPL Communications Inc, 23rd Precinct Music Ltd

429

The **narrator**, anonymous, suffers from amnesia.

The **mysterious companion**, the coach driver, the priest, the devil.

Guðríður, a farmer's wife who lives on a peat farm called Uppsalir up on the plateau and is married to **Gísli**, a sheep farmer and fisherman; they have three daughters together. Guðríður is inquisitive and reads a lot. She writes an article about earthworms, whom she calls the blind poets of the soil. She submits her article to the journal *Nature and World*, where the priest Pétur is on the editorial board.

Pétur is a priest in Snæfellsnes and his wife Halla has "hands of light", as he refers to them. They have three children, a son and two daughters. When the youngest daughter Eva dies, Pétur loses his zest for life and starts writing thoughtful letters to the late German poet Hölderlin. One day he receives an article about earthworms submitted to the journal *Nature and World*, meets Guðríður and his life changes radically.

Jón is a fisherman, a drunk and well read. He is known as Jón the Learned, is the son of Guðríður and Pétur, and is married to **Hulda**. Jón and Hulda have two children, Skúli and little Agnes. When Jón, Hulda and little Agnes die, Skúli is sent to a foster family in which there's a son named Kári.

Kári is married to **Margrét**, whom he meets as a young man when he goes to another farm to borrow a bull to breed with his cows. Margrét is the only one who can control the breeding bull and must therefore accompany Kári and the bull back to Kári's home. On the tractor ride home, the two become close. They marry and have four children.

Skúli is a farmer in Oddi and married to Hafrún. Together they have two sons, Páll and Halldór, and later take on Halldór's son Eiríkur as a much-loved latecomer.

Páll is a giant, a bright and cheerful soul, at the same time it seems as though fate uses him as a harmonica to play the blues on. He studied Søren Kierkegaard at university. Kierkegaard is my guitar, says Páll, and there's a quote from Kierkegaard engraved on his tombstone.

Halldór has a short-lived relationship with Svana, who is married and has two children. The love affair results in a son, Eiríkur, whom Svana secretly gives birth to and later gives to Halldór's parents, Skúli and Hafrun, with whom Eiríkur grows up.

Eiríkur gets his hands on a guitar at a young age and learns to play with his father. He later goes to France and joins a band, becomes romantically involved with **Tove** from Denmark, who is married and has two children, and later meets **Batool**, the daughter of a Jordanian and an Italian.

Aldís is nineteen when she heads up north with her boyfriend. When their car breaks down, she meets a farmer named Harald, who gets off his tractor with Bob Dylan's Greatest Hits playing full blast. Afterwards, she can't forget him, breaks up with her boyfriend and takes the bus north to meet him again. They have two girls: **Runa**, who lives alone on Nes with her father and falls in love with a French journalist wearing different-coloured socks. And **Sóley**, who has had a relationship with the unnamed narrator and is the manager of the hotel the narrator finds himself in.

Married couple **Einar** and **Loa** live on a farm called Framnes. Einar is the brother of Ásmundur (Ási), and Loa is the sister of Margrét.

Ásmundur (Ási) lives on the farm Samsstadir and is married to Gunna. **Gudmund** (Mundi) has a summer house located on Samsstadir.

The beautiful **Dísa** lives on the Hof farm with elderly **Lúna**, a representative to the Alting for the Progress Party. Lúna is Margrét's friend and Margrét appears to Lúna in a dream and asks her to take care of Kári who has gone to the dogs after Margrét's death.

Sævar gets into a traffic accident with Halldór, then they become friends, playing music together and travelling to the USA. Visiting Elvis in Memphis, Billie Holiday in Baltimore, Jim Morrison in Florida and ending up with Bruce Springsteen in New Jersey where they have their picture taken.

Ólafur Ágústsson, doctor and editor-in-chief of the journal for which Guðríður writes, and which hosts the editorial meeting. Married to **Kristín**.

Wislawa and **Oleana** – the two Syrian sisters, one of whom Ási rescued from trafficking and the other subsequently moved to Iceland. The sisters work at the hotel and cook indescribably good food.